IN THE

DARK

OTHER MONTLAKE TITLES BY
LORETH ANNE WHITE

The Dark Bones
A Dark Lure
In the Barren Ground
In the Waning Light
The Slow Burn of Silence

Angie Pallorino Novels

The Drowned Girls
The Lullaby Girl
The Girl in the Moss

PRAISE FOR LORETH ANNE WHITE

"A masterfully written, gritty, suspenseful thriller with a tough, resourceful protagonist that hooked me and kept me guessing until the very end. Think CJ Box and Craig Johnson. Loreth Anne White's *The Dark Bones* is that good."

—Robert Dugoni, *New York Times* bestselling author of
The Eighth Sister

"Secrets, lies, and betrayal converge in this heart-pounding thriller that features a love story as fascinating as the mystery itself."

—Iris Johansen, *New York Times* bestselling author of *Smokescreen*

"A riveting, atmospheric suspense novel about the cost of betrayal and the power of redemption, *The Dark Bones* grips the reader from the first page to the pulse-pounding conclusion."

—Kylie Brant, Amazon bestselling author of *Pretty Girls Dancing*

"Loreth Anne White has set the gold standard for the genre."

—Debra Webb, *USA Today* bestselling author of *The Secrets We Bury*

"Loreth Anne White has a talent for setting and mood. *The Dark Bones* hooked me from the start. A chilling and emotional read."

—T.R. Ragan, *New York Times* bestselling author of *Her Last Day*

"A must read, *A Dark Lure* is gritty, dark romantic suspense at its best. A damaged yet resilient heroine, a deeply conflicted cop, and a truly terrifying villain collide in a stunning conclusion that will leave you breathless."

—Melinda Leigh, *Wall Street Journal* bestselling author of *Secrets
Never Die*

LORETH ANNE WHITE

IN THE

DARK

Montlake
Romance

Text copyright © 2019 by Cheakamus House Publishing

Published by Montlake Romance, Seattle

www.apub.com

Amazon, the Amazon logo, and Montlake Romance are trademarks of Amazon.com, Inc., or its affiliates.

ISBN-13: 9781542003834
ISBN-10: 1542003830

Cover design by Caroline Teagle Johnson

Printed in the United States of America

For my Mom and my Man, and all the doctors and nurses who cared for them over the time it took to start, write, and finish this book. And for my dear siblings and daughters from near and far who helped keep the home fires burning. I love you all. More than words can ever say.

NOW

Sometimes the only thing to fear . . . is yourself.

Sunday, November 8.

Before the waitress delivers my breakfast, I take the sugar packets out of the container on the diner table and quickly sneak them into my pocket. I wolf down the "Kluhane Bay loggers' three-egg special" she brings, then call her back to ask for more toast. I break the toast into bits, use them to mop up bacon fat and yellow smears of egg residue on my plate. I gulp down the rest of my coffee, then shoot a glance around the diner.

It's empty.

The server has gone into the back.

I drink the contents of the cream pitcher. My belly is now bursting. Even so, I take a white napkin and wrap it carefully around a leftover piece of crust that I simply can't fit in. I slip the crust into the pocket of my loaned down jacket where the sugar packets are hidden.

The diner is warm, yet I keep the jacket on because a deep-seated cold still lingers at the very marrow of my bones. The doctors said I'm fine. They said I was lucky. They all said the same thing—the cops and paramedics, the search and rescue people. I believe it. I am incredibly lucky, and I thank the stars that aligned in order for me to survive.

And here I am, with only a bandage around my skull plus a headache and a few cuts and bruises. I'm the one who made it.

For in the end, there can only be one.

And to make it to the end is to reach a beginning, is it not? Wasn't it T. S. Eliot who wrote words in that vein? That the end is where one starts, and only those who have risked going out too far can possibly learn just how far one can actually go?

Perhaps I will feel warm again tomorrow. Perhaps then my feral need to eat will subside.

A movement outside the window attracts my eye. It's the female police officer, Constable Birken Hubble, coming up the sidewalk from the lake. Hubb, the others call her. Hers was the first face I saw when I came round at the tiny facility that serves as a hospital in this remote northern town. She's one of the three cops stationed in Kluhane Bay, this place I found myself in after being plucked by helicopter from the raw jaws of the wilderness.

I watch her walk. Hubb is short, blonde, and substantial, with a gun-belt swagger more akin to a waddle. She has a pink-cheeked, happy resting face that peeps out from under a muskrat hat with furry earflaps. Behind that deceptively congenial countenance, she's still all cop, though. I know something about wearing a Janus mask. Perhaps that's why they've sent her to fetch me—they think I might slip and tell her something. They believe I am hiding something.

The Kluhane Bay Mounties want to interview me again, formally, they said, at the tiny clapboard Royal Canadian Mounted Police detachment down the road from the lake. They already asked me countless questions at the hospital after I was evacuated, and after I'd been stabilized by the doctor and nurses. I've told them everything I can.

The diner door swings open. Hubb enters with a blast of cold air. She wipes her nose with the back of her big black glove and nods at me. I'm the sole patron in the establishment—hard to miss. The diner occupies the ground floor of the only motel in town. I've been put up here by the cops.

I rise from my chair, pull on the gloves I've been loaned, and ask the waitress to put my meal on the hotel tab. I follow Constable Hubble out into a biting wind that blows from the lake.

As I walk alongside Hubb, hunched into my borrowed jacket, the wind makes my eyes water and my nose run. With my gloved hand I dig into my pocket for a tissue I put there earlier. As I pull out the tissue, the wrapped toast crust comes out with it and tumbles to the frozen sidewalk. I stop in a flare of panic, then quickly snatch it up from the ground. I tuck it safely back into my pocket, and joy suddenly fills my soul. I laugh. I have saved the toast. I will not go hungry later. And it's beautiful out—the misty swirls and tatters of clouds, the soaring, snowcapped peaks all around, the lovely quietness and isolation of this remote northern British Columbian town.

I am struck by the poignant, incredibly sharp, almost unabsorbable exquisiteness of the world, of just being. It's a feeling incommensurate with the direness of my situation. But fifteen days ago I was dropped into a fathomless pit, right into the black wilderness of my very own soul. And down there I saw the Monster, and the Monster looked back into my eyes, and I saw that the Monster was me.

But I turned away from those accusing eyes. I climbed and clawed my way back out. And I left the Monster down there. Far, far away.

I have been saved.

Reporters will come. Cameras, questions, judgment. It's a gauntlet I must yet run. But right now, on this crisp, snow-blown morning on the shores of Lake Kluhane, it's just Hubb and me. I have a pocketful of sugar and a toast crust, just in case.

Once inside the police station, Hubb ushers me into a tiny windowless room with dirty-white padded tiles. In the center is a bolted-down table, plastic chairs, one on either side. I glance up at the ceiling and spy a small camera in the upper corner.

"Sergeant Deniaud will be with you in a moment," Hubb says, and closes the door. Almost immediately the suffocation starts. My hands clench and unclench. I met Sergeant Mason Deniaud at the hospital. He was with the search party who helped bring me out of the woods.

The clinic nurse told me that Mason Deniaud is new in Kluhane Bay. He's a veteran big-city homicide detective who—for some reason yet to be ascertained by the members of this small community—has opted to relocate to this northern policing backwater.

I eye the camera again. And a bead of unease lodged deep in my chest begins to swell and pulse.

The door opens.

Deniaud enters holding a file of papers and a notebook and pen. His dark hair is shot through with silver at the temples. He wears an RCMP uniform and a bullet-suppression vest. I imagine as a homicide investigator in the city, he'd have dressed in nice suits with a tie. His eyes are gray, his gaze equal parts shrewd and assessing, and wounded. This man has been damaged. His is a quiet demeanor that belies some dangerously dark and crackling undercurrent beneath his skin.

What are your secrets, Mason Deniaud?

What lies do you tell?

Because we all lie.

Every one of us, and whoever claims they don't is the biggest liar of all.

A flash blinds me—a memory. Blood. Terror in the eyes of another. My heart beats faster.

"How are you feeling this morning?" Mason says as he goes to the opposite end of the table. He sets his file and notebook down on the table before shucking off his RCMP jacket. He drapes it over the back of a chair. "How's the head injury doing?"

I touch the dressing on my brow, almost expecting my fingers to come away bloody again. I feel only the rough, comforting fabric of the bandage.

"I . . . Much better, thank you. Just a small headache."

"Sleeping okay at the motel?"

4

"Yes," I say. "And you—did you sleep well?"

His gaze ticks to mine.

He studies me.

He's assessing whether my question is born of innocent politeness or whether I'm mounting a subtle challenge to his authority—trying to make him human, less law enforcement official, put him more on my level.

"Yes. Thank you," he says calmly.

But the lines at the corners of Mason Deniaud's eyes tell a different story. I suspect he's not slept well, and perhaps insomnia is some kind of new normal for this ex–homicide cop. I'm not a bad profiler of people. I know all about new normals.

"Thank you for coming in." He holds a hand out to the chair closest to me. "Please, take a seat."

I glance again at the camera and cautiously seat myself. I place my palms flat on the table, but the urge to escape continues to mount. I feel it as a pulsing, mushrooming pressure beneath the bandage around my skull. Can feel it in the throb of my toes. This claustrophobia, too, is some kind of new normal after my existing in mountains and forests for so many nights and days. In that feat alone, I tell myself, lies real power. I'm powerful now. I've done things others could not, and did not.

I survived.

"Coffee? Tea, juice, water?" he says.

I shake my head.

Mason opens his notebook, scans a few lines of scribbled text, tells me that our interview is being recorded, and asks me to state my name for the record. He then looks me directly in the eyes and says, "Would you like to have anyone present?"

I shake my head.

"Are you certain? We can provide you with a victim service worker, or you can ask for counsel—"

"No."

He studies me for a beat. "Okay. Feel free to ask for a break at any time."

"Who's watching?" I ask with a tilt of my chin toward the camera.

"Two RCMP officers."

"Detectives?"

"Yes."

I worry my lip with my teeth and nod. My palms are going sweaty on the tabletop, despite the chill inside my bones.

"I'd like to go over again, in detail, what happened after the group left the lodge."

Another memory flash. The sound of gunshots. A body swinging by the neck. Screams—such terrible screams . . .

"Take it slow," he says. Friendly. Gentle. Encouraging. "And again, let me know if at any time you decide that you'd like someone present."

Nine Little Liars thought they'd be late.
One missed the plane, and then there were eight . . .

"Let's start with the morning of Sunday, October 25—the rendez-vous at the Thunderbird Lodge floatplane dock when everyone met."

I stare into his probing, gray eyes. How can this Mountie ever begin to understand? How can anyone?

We became a group with feral instincts, each of our weaknesses exaggerated and sharpened by guilt and fear and hunger and exhaustion. By the very need to survive. To live. That kind of struggle amplifies aspects of a personality in disturbing ways, ones you might never anticipate. It changed our reality. Perhaps I never understood Reality until now.

Now I know Reality is a fluid and ephemeral thing, and it's contingent on those around you. And out of context, what you experience might never be grasped by one who was not there. How do you explain that you were taken, within a matter of hours, from the heart of civilization into the dark of the woods, into the black heart of a Grimms' fairy tale?

I clear my throat. "There were eight of us on the dock that morning," I say carefully. "Eight including the tour guide."

THE SEARCH

MASON

Friday, October 30.

Darkness came early in Kluhane Bay at the end of October, especially in the long shadows of the granite mountains. And when it arrived, it was complete. No soft, anthropogenic light haze over the town. Kluhane Bay was barely even a town. It was unincorporated in that it had no municipal status, no mayor, and no town council. Policing fell to a small three-officer satellite detachment of the Royal Canadian Mounted Police's North District of BC, which was headquartered in Prince George.

Kluhane was home to maybe six hundred year-round residents who lived in wooden houses that hunkered along the few windblown streets on the shores of Lake Kluhane, one of the largest natural lakes in northern British Columbia. Summers were beautiful, and drew outdoor enthusiasts. But in winter the lake would freeze, and the wind would howl fiercely from the north. There was a small airstrip, a new waterfront promenade, a tiny post office, and some other essential stores and services, including a bakery, a gas station, and a motel with a diner downstairs. Beyond the last streets of town, only logging roads and ATV tracks punched thin access threads into dense, endless forests and craggy mountains. Kluhane Bay was the definition of isolation, and Sergeant Mason Deniaud felt it now as he fisted the wheel of his 4x4 police truck and negotiated a steep and rutted logging road up into a twilight that seemed to close in concert with the trees and clouds behind him.

The call had come a half hour ago.

Two hunters had stumbled upon the crash site of a floatplane. The aircraft had gone down in trees along the side of a ravine that funneled the white waters of the Taheese River down from Taheese Lake. The hunters had managed to radio a friend, who'd called the Kluhane Bay police via landline. No cell service in Kluhane. Nothing for miles and miles. Mason was technically the cop in charge of the detachment, but this was no desk job. One of his two officers, Constable Birken Hubble, was already on scene taking statements from the hunters. His other officer, Jake Podgorsky, was on his day off.

Mason's headlights lit upon another water bar. The logging road had been deactivated—deep ditches cut diagonally across it at intervals to mitigate erosion. Engaging his four-wheel drive, he approached the ditch at a thirty-degree angle. It lost him traction on the incline. As his leading tire hit the bottom of the trough, he spun his wheel in the opposite direction, then came carefully up and out the other end. But the rear of his truck had insufficient clearance. His exhaust pipe and bumper clunked and scraped against stones. He cursed.

The trees closed in as he climbed higher. Branches and twigs scored the sides of his vehicle like fingernails on a chalkboard. It reminded him of school, and of Jenny and Luke. A vivid image flashed into his mind: Luke with his little dinosaur backpack on his first day of school. Mason's gloved hands tightened on the wheel as his pulse quickened. He tamped the memory down and checked his GPS reading. He should be near the river. The evergreens around him were bigger now. Fat trunks covered in moss. Mist rolled down the mountain and sifted in ghostly fingers through the branches. It made his headlights look like hazy tunnels through the gloom. Perhaps he'd made the wrong move in taking this post.

Usually an isolated northern posting like this was the preserve of rookies fresh out of Depot Division in Regina. But for Mason—a veteran major crimes cop with twelve years of law enforcement under his gun belt—it had been a Hobson's choice, and an uncommon one. He'd put in the request himself.

It was either this or digging himself into deeper shit on a road toward disciplinary action. Or worse: dismissal.

Maybe he should've just resigned, quit while barely ahead. But something deep down inside Mason urged him to hold on, just for a while longer, to try to buy time to think in a place that was quiet, safe, under the radar. Maybe he'd pull himself right. Maybe after two years or so in these backwoods, he'd be ready to return to a major urban environment and serious crime work. Maybe he'd want to keep living by then.

But the other part of Mason—the destructive part—whispered in his ear that he was deluding himself. He was washed up. Soiled goods. No one was going to want to work with him or trust him again.

This is your last option.

He rounded a steep bend and saw Hubb's marked SUV ahead, parked beneath the sagging boughs of a Douglas fir, the engine puffing clouds of white into the dusk. The windows were fogged, but Mason could discern the silhouettes of three occupants inside. In front of the SUV was a mud-caked all-terrain vehicle painted in camouflage greens. A blaze hunting vest lay on the seat. Mason pulled in behind the SUV. As he put his vehicle into park, Hubb got out of the SUV and swaggered over to his truck, her arms held out in an unnatural position to accommodate her duty belt. Hubb was short—maybe five two in her steel-toed boots, and the heavy gun belt and bullet-suppression vest under her jacket bulked up an already padded frame. Hubb liked her doughnuts from the bakery across the street from the station. Her nose and cheeks were ruddy with cold, her eyes watery bright.

"Hey, boss," she said as Mason got out.

He zipped his uniform jacket to his neck. The damp weather at this elevation had a way of fingering under one's clothes. He heard the sound of rushing water.

"Crash site is that way." She pointed toward dense trees and berry scrub brown with autumn leaves. "It went down the gulley screened by that vegetation over there. I couldn't really see the wreck from up top, but the hunters said the tail of the floatplane is hanging right in the river, the rest is stuck up on a ledge of slippery rock."

"Those the guys who found it?" Mason nodded toward the two men hunkered inside the marked 4x4.

"Yeah. I got their statements. I asked them to hang around so you could speak to them, if you want. Left them inside the vehicle where it's warm."

"Any signs the wreck has been there long?" Mason asked as he made his way toward the screen of trees that hid the ravine. Hubb followed behind him, boots crunching on stones. The rushing sound of water grew louder. Moisture boiled up in clouds behind the evergreens.

"They said it wasn't all rusted up and stuff. They figure the crash could be fairly recent. Who knows. I saw in the news the other day that a search party found a wreck that was thirty years old. Near Clearwater—found it while they were looking for some other missing plane from Alberta."

It was Hubb's failing. Talking too much. She didn't stop, and it drove Mason nuts.

He parted a section of foliage that Hubb had flagged with strips of fluorescent-orange tape. He stepped through scrub. Holding on to a hemlock branch, he tried to peer down through the bushes into the gorge. His stomach swooped—the ground dropped clean away just ahead of his boot tips. Water rumbled and thundered about forty feet below, throwing up a cast of tiny droplets that clung to everything. To say he was afraid of heights would be an understatement. It was a flaw

Mason had managed to hide. Until maybe now, just when he needed to prove himself capable to this new team, and to the townsfolk who were already wary of his ability to handle this remote wilderness post.

"I've already put in a call to Cal," Hubb said cheerily from behind him.

He glanced over his shoulder. "Cal?"

"Kluhane Search and Rescue. Cal Sutton is the manager. We're going to need SAR techs with ropes and swift-water experience if we want to haul that wreck up that bank. I also put a call in to the Transportation Safety Board."

He stared at her.

Her cheeks flushed a deeper red. "I . . . uh, Ray—Sergeant Ted Newman, who was here before you—he usually left the SAR tasking to me, so I, uh—"

"So you took the initiative."

"Correct, but if you'd rather—"

"It's fine. We'll stick with the routine. For now."

Until I've been here long enough to figure out how the hell things function up here.

She swallowed, and her eyes lost their smile. "Yes, sir."

Mason clearly had big shoes to fill. He'd arrived only two weeks earlier, and it was obvious his predecessor had been both well loved and respected. So much so that the Kluhane Bay residents, in an unusual move, had campaigned to have Sergeant Ted Newman's tenure extended. But now they had Mason. Who was not in the mood for making friends.

"Did the TSB say if there were any reports about aircraft going down or missing in this area?" he asked.

"Negative, sir. No reports of overdue or missing planes in this region over the last two years. TSB investigators are standing by and will dispatch a team as soon as we have more information."

Holding tightly to the branch, Mason gingerly tested the matted ground underfoot.

"Careful, sir. It drops right off beneath that moss."

It felt solid. Slowly, carefully, he transferred weight onto his front foot, edging slightly forward. He leaned over a little farther. He could see part of the fuselage down below, and a pontoon. Upside down. Bright yellow with blue detail. The floatplane lay wrong side up on a ledge of rock. He could just make out part of the registration painted in bold black letters on the fuselage. He inched forward a little more. The left wing was crushed into the side of the ravine, the tail in the river, causing white froth to foam around it. He swore softly and called back to Hubb, "How did they even find it down there?"

"Wounded a bear," she yelled back over the crashing of the water. "Placed a bad shot on a black male last night. Been tracking the animal since first light. It climbed down into the gorge and they followed it."

"Down *there?*"

"Guess the bear wanted to live real bad."

And the hunters must have wanted to kill him real bad if they tried to climb down these rocks.

"Did they see anyone inside the wreck?" he called, leaning a tiny bit farther over the edge to see if he could make out the cockpit. His arm began to shake. His stomach heaved.

"Negative, sir."

The branch in his hand cracked with the report of a rifle. Before Mason even registered, it broke free of the tree. He fell fast, bouncing down against rocks. He smashed into a bush growing out of a crevice. It broke his tumble. He grabbed at a handful of twigs, but they sliced out of his grasp. He slid and bumped down rocks and over slick moss, grabbing wildly, blindly at scrub and saplings nestled in the crevices. But he failed to find purchase. He slammed hard onto the ledge that jutted out over the roaring river. He rolled and landed with a thump against the upside-down plane fuselage. He stilled, heart racing, head spinning.

The section of the ledge upon which he'd come to rest tilted precariously toward the foaming water, the surface as slippery as wet soap.

The wreck gave a metallic creak, then a groan. He felt it move against his leg. Mason held dead still.

"Sir! You okay, sir? *Sergeant?*"

"Fine," he barked up, adrenaline pumping. Slowly—very slowly— he turned his head toward the cockpit window. His heart stopped. Directly in front of his face—close enough for him to touch if he dared move his hands—was a corpse hanging upside down in the pilot seat, held fast by a harness. The face was fish-belly white, bloated. The mouth hung open. Milky eyes stared back at Mason. The corpse's hair was white blonde, cut very short. He noticed an earring, and it struck him—the dead pilot was female. From his position he could see no one else inside the plane, but it was a bad vantage point. Mason sucked in a deep breath, counted to three, then inched carefully backward up the sloping ledge, away from the fuselage and the water's edge. The aircraft creaked. Metal grated against rock as it slid a little deeper into the churning water. The current tugged harder at the tail.

He keyed the radio near his shoulder. "Hubb? You read me, Hubb?"

He released the key and swore to himself. The plane moved again. Time elongated. His vision narrowed. A buzz started in his ears. Vertigo. He closed his eyes, trying to tamp down the panic surging into his chest, the dizziness. Sweat broke out over his face.

"Sir?"

He keyed the radio again. "Got someone inside the cockpit. Pilot. Looks female. Deceased. Get on the sat phone. Call the coroner and activate a full SAR response." He paused and refocused, trying to bring his adrenaline and panic under control.

Silence.

He keyed his radio again. "Hubb?" No response. "Can you hear me, Hubble?" Carefully, he looked skyward. But his movement redistributed his body weight and gave power to gravity. It shot him over the slick moss and back down the rock. His body hit the plane fuselage again with a bump. The plane groaned. Water boiled higher around the tail, tugging more forcibly at the plane.

Fuck.

"Hoi!" came a yell from above. "Sergeant Deniaud! Sit tight. Do not move! I'm coming down. Don't move!"

He didn't dare. If he slid any farther, he was going right into the churning white water along with the mangled wreck.

A rope's end hit the rock ledge near his face. He heard movement above. Small stones and debris skittered over him. He shut his eyes to avoid the dirt raining down.

A few moments later the climber landed on the flat and drier part of the ledge. Mason opened his eyes, saw boots. A gloved hand reached down for him.

"Can you take hold of my hand?" The voice was female.

He swallowed and reached up toward the voice. The climber grasped hold of his wrist. Relief shot through him.

"Hold tight around my wrist—can you do that? It forms a more solid lock, like a chain."

He grasped firmly so they were clasped wrist to wrist.

"Good job. Now I'm going to pull you toward me. Try to use your feet to assist. Got it? Dig your toes into the rock to get a grip."

He nodded. As his rescuer pulled, he found traction with his boots. Carefully he edged himself free of the wreck and closer to the climber, but as he did, the floatplane gave a massive groan and slid into the water. It made a loud sucking and crunching sound as the boiling foam embraced it. Then it was gone, swallowed by the raging and frothing water.

He froze.

Fuck.

He'd just sent a crashed floatplane and dead pilot, and a whole barrel of evidence, downriver.

"Don't look. Keep your focus on me. Just focus on coming toward me."

Mason inched up the slippery incline with his rescuer's assistance. Finally, after several slips and starts, he made it back onto the flatter, drier section of the ledge. The woman helped him up onto his knees. He was breathing hard, drenched with sweat and river mist. It had started to rain, too. Immediately she secured a rope and harness around his torso.

"Are you hurt?" she asked once he was securely fastened.

"Negative," he said.

"You sure?"

He looked up from his position on his knees. She wore a helmet and headlamp. It was getting darker, and her headlight blinded him, so he couldn't really see her features under the helmet.

"I'm Cal," she said. "Callie Sutton. Kluhane Bay Search and Rescue. I'm sorry we couldn't meet under more favorable circumstances, Sergeant Deniaud." She smiled—he could see that much below the glare of her headlamp. A big, wide grin full of white teeth.

Irritation punched through Mason. Callie Sutton's apparent conviviality in the face of his having sent a planeload of evidence into a raging river was the last fucking thing he needed.

"Did you see any sign of survivors?" she asked.

"Negative. But I can't be sure. The pilot looked like she'd been dead awhile."

"She?"

"Could have been male, but the earring made me think female."

"Right. We can start a search downriver at first light. Sending my guys out in the dark will risk lives, especially in these conditions. There's a storm moving in. And this section of the Taheese is dangerous in high water. Come, let's get you hauled back up. I've got someone to belay us from the top."

Callie hooked him up with more ropes and carabiners. "You ever done this before?" she asked.

"Nope." He was certain she could feel him shaking.

She gave him instructions. Mason struggled against vertigo and the blood thumping in his eardrums to focus on her instructions.

"Ready?" she asked.

He blinked against the light from her headlamp. "As I'll ever be."

She stilled for a moment, reading his fear, hearing it in his voice. "It'll be fine," she said gently. "Just relax and follow my lead." She raised her gloved hand and made a big winding motion to whoever was handling the ropes from above. "Okay, bring us up!" she yelled.

He was swung out into the void.

Way to prove yourself to the new guys, Deniaud. Just don't piss your pants now.

He'd managed to hide his acrophobia from his colleagues for twelve years. Mason figured it was all about to go downhill from here. To calm himself he called up a mental image of the bottle of whiskey waiting for him at the isolated waterfront cabin that was now his home. He told himself he could always just drink it all and walk into that goddamn lake if it all got to be too much.

THE LODGE PARTY

DAN

Saturday, October 24.

Dan Whitlock sat at the rear of the Executive Transit shuttle bus. His tour group had been on the road for two hours since leaving the Gateway Hotel at Vancouver International Airport. He checked his watch for the umpteenth time.

He needed a smoke. A drink. Or four. He glanced out the tinted window. Endless forests and mountains blurred past as the shuttle began to climb the twisting Sea to Sky Highway into the mountains. There were eight on the bus, including him, a tour guide, and the driver. They were headed for Thunderbird Ridge, a brand-new ski and golf destination resort north of Squamish due to open to skiers for the first time this year. But it was still autumn. Too late for golf, too early for skiing. A fresh dusting of snow coated the peaks, and it was cold out. Dan hated cold. He'd tolerated it once, but no longer. At age fifty-nine it hurt his joints. His gout played up.

He checked his watch yet again. Not too long now. He'd hit the hotel bar first or, at the very least, crack open something from the minibar in his room. Booze—everything on this junket—was on the house. Courtesy of the RAKAM Group, which was hosting the jaunt. The plan was for their group to overnight at the spanking-new luxury hotel in Thunderbird Ridge; then tomorrow at 10:00 a.m. they would board a chartered West Air floatplane and fly to a high-end wilderness lodge and spa located at a secret destination in the BC interior. There they would be wined and fine-dined, be given treatments like Swedish and hot stone massage, and enjoy outdoor saunas by the lake. Or they could "luxuriate" in front of wood fires in "architecturally designed" waterfront cabins for ten days, surrounded by nothing but "nature" plus room service and open bars. Dan had won the trip at a casino function in July.

From having spoken to the other tour participants over a buffet breakfast at the Gateway Hotel this morning, he'd learned that the Forest Shadow Wilderness Resort & Spa had yet to officially open to guests, but the new managers were seeking to "partner" with businesses that offered services like housekeeping, catering, security, and expertise in advertising to niche markets. To this end, several professionals were being flown out to undergo the "lodge experience" and decide whether they in turn wanted to put in tenders for long-term contracts.

Dan didn't much care either way who was there for what reason. He'd accepted the prize because he never turned his back on a free-bie. Ever. Especially when it came with booze and high-end cuisine, and words like *luxuriating*. He was a run-down old private investiga-tor who'd catered for most of his life to clients who generally crawled out of some gutter, so it wasn't like he was going to be able to afford anything like this out of his own pocket. Besides, he might get lucky. He'd be rubbing shoulders and schmoozing with some rich folk—real influencers. And that could lead to business opportunities. Even rich folk did dirty shit. And dirty-shitters needed PIs like him to clean up their crap—good old gumshoes who operated beneath the radar and around the legal fringes. Even PIs from top law firms sometimes passed the shady stuff under the table to him.

The woman in the seat in front of him turned around and smiled. "I so love a secret, don't you?"

Her name was Monica McNeill. A breathy brunette in her early fifties with perfect makeup. She was married to the balding dude sitting beside her, Dr. Nathan McNeill, a professor of mycology at the University of Toronto. Monica was a grocery-chain heiress who'd moved her family empire into the whole foods/organic era and made a killing out of her Holistic Foods chain. Her company now owned "green" supermarkets in pretty much every city across the country. Holistic Foods also boasted a catering arm. Which was why she'd been invited on this junket.

Dan cleared his throat, uncomfortable under her sudden scrutiny. Attractive women did that to him.

"Yeah, sure," he said. "I mean, who doesn't?" He sure loved secrets. The deeper and darker the better. He made a living unearthing other people's secrets. Secrets were collateral, their power directly proportional to that of whoever had the most to lose—or gain—by their revelation.

"I can't wait to see where we land tomorrow." Monica deepened her smile.

He nodded, wondering if she might be coming on to him. He'd be better able to tolerate this group once he got more alcohol into him— the nip he'd taken from the minibar this morning had long worn off. Monica's smile faded. She turned to face the front and resumed quietly talking to her mushroom-professor husband.

Who in their right mind would choose to specialize in fungi?

Dan turned his attention to observing the others. A talent of his.

Bart Kundera was driving. He owned a couple of these buses, along with a fleet of town cars. Bart was after the Forest Shadow transport contract, which would entail shuttling guests between Vancouver International and the floatplane dock at Thunderbird Ridge. Dark-haired, swarthy-complexioned, he was medium height. Strong build.

A gym rat, Dan figured. He possessed an easy confidence and was good with people. Nice guy. Upbeat outlook on life.

Amanda Gunn, their tour guide, sat directly behind the driver's seat, glossy black hair piled atop her head in a complicated bun. She was checking something on her tablet, moving images with long, manicured fingers. Runway-model thin—too skinny for Dan's taste. Give him boobs any day. He liked her mouth, though. It was wide and painted bloodred and full of whitened teeth. Her eyes were dark and liquid. She wore designer sunglasses pushed up onto her head, more for fashion than function, he reckoned.

Across the aisle from Amanda, Katie Colbourne—a travel-documentary maker—filmed out the window with a fancy little digital camera she'd told Dan was waterproof. Katie was super attractive. A bottle blonde. Mid- to late thirties. Katie had told everyone over her plate of low-carb breakfast that she'd moved into travel documentaries after quitting her career as a television news reporter. She now had her own YouTube channel. Becoming a mother, she'd proclaimed, had prompted her career switch. Dan recognized her from her TV days—they all did. Over a decade ago Katie Colbourne had been a nightly fixture on the city news channel. He couldn't quite recall what it was, but there'd been some controversy surrounding her.

Behind Katie, a woman named Deborah Strong gazed out the window. A quiet brunette. There was a quality about Deborah Strong that made Dan think, *Still waters run deep*. She owned a company called Boutique Housekeeping, and she was gunning for the spa housekeeping contract.

Across from Deborah sat a sturdy woman with eyes so intense and dark they looked black. Jackie Blunt. Late forties. Something unsettling about that woman, the way she regarded Dan when she thought he wasn't looking. He'd swear on his life that he knew her from somewhere. And he'd put money on her being an ex-cop. Took one to know one. Maybe that was what accounted for the disquieting sense of familiarity. From the way Jackie Blunt was observing him, Dan figured she recognized him, too. Then again, Jackie Blunt seemed to be scrutinizing everyone with the same unnerving intensity—like she was sucking up micro-signs and tells and banking them all for some future payoff. She ran a company out of Burlington, Ontario, called Security Solutions, and she was obviously a candidate for the spa security contract.

There was one more guest due to meet them at Thunderbird Ridge—Dr. Steven Bodine, a cosmetic surgeon and the medical director of the Oak Street Surgical Clinic. Tomorrow they would also meet their pilot, Stella Daguerre.

Amanda turned in her seat and flashed her hundred-watt smile at the passengers. "Almost there!" she proclaimed.

The words from Amanda's overly cheery breakfast presentation echoed through Dan's brain.

The location is amazing. Simply stunning. Sumptuous luxury right on the shores of a sparkling lake located in utter pristine wilderness. Absolutely nothing—nothing—around in any direction for miles and miles and miles. It's perfect for guests of means seeking seclusion, privacy. The Forest Shadow Wilderness Resort & Spa will meet all the needs of our primary target markets, which includes a cosmetic and wellness tourism component. The RAKAM Group in Malaysia is currently in negotiations with two private surgery clinics in the Lower Mainland. The idea is that guests who are seeking a new look—brand-new breasts, slimmer tummies, more youthful faces—or other nonessential medical procedures—can fly into YVR, where they will be picked up by a company like Bart's Executive Transit. They will be discreetly transported to one of the clinics, where they will undergo their procedure, after which they will travel by shuttle for an overnight at the five-diamond Thunderbird Lodge, from where they will be flown by floatplane to the remote and private wilderness facility to recuperate and relax in peace with a full suite of spa treatments including pools, steam room, and lakeside saunas fired by wood in the old Scandinavian tradition. Plus gourmet West Coast–inspired cuisine created from the freshest natural ingredients . . .

Dan thought this was nuts. What kind of business plan called for two days of travel after surgery before patients could recuperate in nature? But who was he to judge? Rich folk did all kinds of shit that made zero sense to him, and he didn't really care either way, as long as they paid his bills and picked up his bar tab. The bus slowed. The indicator ticked. Bart turned the shuttle bus off the highway and onto a newly paved road. A large wooden sign carved with an eagle pointed the way: Thunderbird Ridge.

Through his window Bart saw a bank of dark clouds amassing in the northeast. The wind blew through the trees. An odd little feeling of anxiety pinged through him. He needed a drink—that was all it was. Alcoholic withdrawal jitters.

But as the shuttle bus started twisting up the section of new road, the dark evergreens hemmed in closer, and Dan's anxiety deepened to a sense of unspecified dread.

He never did like the wilderness.

THE LODGE PARTY

STELLA

Sunday, October 25.

Stella Daguerre ran through her preflight checklist. Everything was in order. She shaded her eyes and surveyed the surrounding mountains, visualizing her takeoff and landing on the other end, etching emergency protocols and egress points into her mind, so once she got into that pilot's seat, everything would be second nature should unexpected problems occur on the flight.

For the most part the weather was gorgeous. Bluebird sky. A white dusting of snow on the amphitheater of surrounding peaks, veins of deciduous orange and gold shooting through evergreen forests on the flanks. Thunderbird Lake glimmered with sunlight, and Stella's de Havilland Canada DHC-2 Beaver Mk 1 bobbed gently alongside the floatplane dock. But the wind sock had begun to fill and creak on its stand, switching direction as the breeze began to shift and blow more insistently from the north.

It was a cold wind.

It would bring closer that big bank of black weather hulking in the distance. Stella needed to get her chunky plane up into the air and over that spine of mountains sooner rather than later. Crosswinds in this terrain could be tricky. And deadly. She checked her watch. Irritation flickered through her.

The RAKAM Group contact person, Amanda Gunn—the one who'd hired Stella's West Air charter—had informed Stella that her passengers would be on the dock and ready to board before 10:00 a.m. The Beaver's doors were open and waiting. Stella was prepped to load baggage, warm up her bird, and give a quick safety briefing. But it was now 10:23 a.m. and still no sign of the tour group. Tension tightened her stomach. She glanced at the wind sock again. It puffed and flicked and snapped as the breeze gathered force. She reached for her cell. But as she was about to call Amanda, a gleaming black minibus with the Thunderbird Lodge logo pulled into a drop-off bay on the bank above the floatplane dock.

Relief washed through her. Stella pocketed her phone as the bus door opened and a very slender woman disembarked, black hair ruffling in the wind. She was dressed in black jeans topped with a black leather jacket. A white, diaphanous scarf wound voluminously around her neck. Under her arm she carried a clipboard. A man in a hotel uniform alighted behind her. He scurried to the rear of the bus. The woman directed him to offload the bags as the rest of the passengers started to disembark. She then hastened down the stairs toward the floatplane dock and picked her way carefully over the gangway in her high heels.

"Amanda Gunn," the woman said breathily as she reached Stella. She proffered a delicate hand and monstrous smile. "We met on the phone."

Stella couldn't read her eyes. They hid behind big, black designer sunglasses. She shook Amanda's hand. The tour guide's palm was cool and as smooth as a baby's bum in contrast to Stella's chapped, working hands. The wind swirled and gusted, sending a waft of Amanda's scent toward Stella along with a scattering of dry autumn leaves at her feet. The woman smelled of perfume and menthol cigarettes. Stella disliked her on the spot.

"I'm *so* sorry we're late," Amanda said. "One of our guests woke up sick, and—" She glanced over her shoulder to check that the hotel porter was helping the guests carry their bags down. "I thought he was just hungover." She spoke quickly, as if to get it all explained before the others arrived on the dock. "We had an open bar last night, and there's always one or two who hit these things too hard. I thought he'd get himself into shape after a hot shower and some strong coffee this morning, so we waited, but he really is quite ill. He claims there's no way he can fly today, so you're one passenger down, I'm afraid." She tried to force another smile but came off flustered.

Stella fetched her passenger manifest. "Who are we down?" she asked.

"Dan Whitlock," Amanda said. "I have a rental waiting. I'll take him back to the city with me, drop him off at a doctor on my way. The shuttle bus will remain here for the return trip when you bring the guests back."

Stella scanned the list in search of Dan Whitlock's name. As she did, the hotel porter approached, carrying two bags.

"Where shall we put the luggage, ma'am?"

She motioned to a spot near the rear of the plane where the loading door had been lifted upward.

"Shall I load it right in?" he asked.

"Not yet. Just stack it in front of the loading door." She wanted to cross-check each bag against the passenger list. In her experience, guests did not take seriously the weight restrictions required of small-aircraft travel and often tried to sneak on extra belongings. Loading a plane badly could result in a deadly accident, especially during takeoff or landing, when weight radically affected aircraft performance. She found Dan Whitlock's name, crossed it off her list. "Have you weighed the bags?" she asked Amanda.

"Before we left the hotel at YVR yesterday, and again this morning. Everything's on target." The guide looked increasingly edgy. "I made it clear that everything they required would be provided by the spa, from eco-toiletries to top-of-the-line alcohol and food."

As she spoke, the guests gathered around them.

Introductions were made, and Stella checked each passenger off her manifest: Bart Kundera—transit-company guy. Monica McNeill— catering woman. Nathan McNeill, Monica's husband and her plus-one for the junket. Deborah Strong—housekeeping woman. Katie Colbourne—travel journalist and ex–TV news personality. And Jackie Blunt—security woman. Jackie held Stella's gaze for a moment too long, and Stella saw a questioning look in the woman's intense and close-set eyes. It sent a frisson through Stella, and a tiny bead of concern formed down deep in her gut.

"Have we met?" Stella asked.

Jackie's eyes narrowed. "I don't think so."

But the way she said it made Stella believe Jackie might think otherwise. While they spoke, Katie panned her small camcorder across the group, causing Jackie to step back slightly, and her facial expression turned benign.

"This place is freaking Swiss-chocolate-box gorgeous," Katie said, turning in a slow circle to capture the amphitheater of snowcapped peaks.

"Swiss chocolate boxes have nothing on this," Monica said, her voice lounge-singer husky. "This is a real slice of heaven. And right in our own backyards."

"Right? What did I *tell* you guys?" Amanda offered them all a big white smile, working to keep her clients in a good frame of mind.

Stella gave the porter the go-ahead to load the bags.

"What kind of plane is this?" Katie asked from behind her camera.

"De Havilland Beaver Mk 1," Stella said, conscious of a need to address potential viewers. "The iconic Canadian bush plane, a post–World War Two workhorse. The first Beaver was rolled off a Toronto production line in the forties. It was called the aerial dogsled of the north."

Katie panned her lens over the bright yellow-and-blue floatplane as Stella spoke.

"Okay, everyone," Stella called out, "gather round and listen up. Number one rule, do not cross that red line painted on the dock." She pointed. "Because we're pressed for time, I'm going to start warming the aircraft, then I'll give a quick safety briefing. But you need to score that no-cross line into your minds. A meeting with that propeller will change—or end—your life."

Glances were exchanged and the mood shifted slightly. Stella was glad to assert her authority, making it clear she was boss as long as they were in that plane. She made for her cockpit door.

"Oh, wait," Amanda called from behind Stella. "We're still waiting for one more guest."

Stella stilled. She did a quick head count.

"We have six passengers."

"Yes. But we're still expecting Dr. Steven Bodine. He'll make it seven, then." Amanda consulted her designer watch. "He phoned from Squamish about twenty minutes ago, so he really should be here any second now."

Stella eyed Amanda steadily, then reached again for her list. She checked it carefully. "There's no Steven Bodine on my list."

"There must be." Amanda came closer and looked.

"I don't see a Bodine," Stella said.

"He's the cosmetic surgeon from the Oak Street Surgical Clinic. He's key on this trip."

Stella drew the woman aside and lowered her voice. "Look, I had seven passengers on my list including Dan Whitlock. My plane, as it's configured, takes a maximum of eight including me, the pilot. Your boss was made aware of this when I was contracted. I made it clear. So how can there be an extra passenger if the RAKAM Group didn't know

Dan Whitlock was going to get sick and bail? We wouldn't have gotten them all on board if he didn't."

Amanda blanched. Her brow furrowed. Quietly, urgently, she said, "I *sent* you the list. I'm sure Dr. Steven Bodine was on it. Wait . . ." She riffled through the pages attached to her clipboard. "Here—here is my list."

Stella's and Amanda's lists did not match up.

In Stella's peripheral vision she saw Jackie Blunt watching them intently, clearly trying to eavesdrop on their discussion. Amanda flicked a glance toward Jackie, then angled her body to block her line of sight. She drew Stella closer. The wind snapped at a flag up near the hotel shuttle van, and the halyard began to clunk against the pole. The wind sock stiffened. Urgency crackled through Stella. She glanced toward the bank of dark weather moving closer over the mountains from the north.

"There must have been some misunderstanding," Amanda whispered. "Look, I'm really sorry. This is my first PR gig with this company via the temp agency I'm signed with. I . . . I'm a little nervous. To get it all right, you know? It's potentially a great contract if they decide to take me on longer term." She swallowed. Gusts of wind loosened strands from her hair spray–stiffened topknot.

Stella's feelings toward the woman softened slightly. "It's just as well Dan Whitlock is not coming," she said. "We can work with this. But if Dr. Bodine is not here within the next five minutes for the security briefing, he doesn't fly. Okay? My charter. My plane. My rules. Safety first. Like you, I also want a long-term contract out of this, and for all I know, this is a test of both your and my professionalism. Part of the audition."

"Right. Right, of course. I'll phone him again." A tremor of nerves hitched Amanda's voice as she reached into her jacket pocket for her cell. Clearly she badly wanted her contract with the RAKAM Group.

Stella returned to her cockpit. Jackie's dark and penetrating gaze followed her, deepening Stella's sense that the woman recognized her from somewhere.

Stella loosened the primer knob near the base of the door and climbed up into the seat. Ahead, beyond the single prop blade, the lake stretched in a narrowing V between the mountains. She checked the oil cap—locked. Fuel gauge, wobble pump gauge—all looked good.

She pumped the primer knob, set it in the locked position, and turned on the master switch. She then worked a lever on the console gently up and down before flicking a small starter switch. The engine made a sound like a whining car struggling to start. She hit the mags, and the Beaver engine coughed into noisy, uncertain life. She adjusted the mixture until the engine settled into a more rhythmic, throaty, and comforting growl and the single prop whirled into a blur. She felt adrenaline rise like a nice buzz in her veins. This was her element, where she felt safe. Her plane. Flying.

Her preference was to wait for five to six hundred rpm before she considered her plane nicely warmed up.

Stella got out, but as she was about to commence her briefing, a convertible roared into the parking bay. Everyone swiveled to stare up toward the road as a low, silver Jaguar screeched to a halt behind the hotel van.

A man alighted from the Jaguar. Tall. Healthy head of sandy-brown hair ruffling in the wind that was picking up far too fast for Stella's comfort. Irritation snapped at her. She checked her watch again and glanced at the wind sock. Dry autumn leaves skittered in a wave across the dock. The man reached into the back seat of his convertible, yanked out a backpack, hoisted it over one shoulder, and came striding heavily down the gangway, his hiking boots thumping against the planks, his gait long and confident, a boyish smile across his tanned, middle-aged face. *A Peter Pan,* she thought. *With a surgeon's God complex.*

"Oh, thank heavens," Amanda muttered as the surgeon loped toward her.

"Amanda? You *must* be Amanda," he said loudly.

Amanda reached forward to shake his hand. "So *good* to finally meet you in person, Steven." Relief was palpable in the woman's voice. But out of the corner of her eye, Stella saw Monica McNeill stiffen sharply at the surgeon's arrival.

Intrigued, Stella turned to look. Monica's face had paled. The woman glanced at her husband, who was opening his mouth to say something. But he shut it and frowned fiercely at Monica. Katie filmed the whole interaction while Jackie and Bart fiddled with their cell phones. Deborah seemed to shrink away from the bright, bold light cast by Dr. Steven Bodine's shining presence. The plane engine growled. Stella wanted to get moving.

"Everyone!" Amanda raised her voice. "This is the last member to round out our party. Dr. Steven Bodine, who heads up the Oak Street Surgical Clinic, and who is looking to expand the clinic's cosmetic travel business."

"Stella Daguerre." She held her hand out for his bag. "I'm your captain on this trip."

The doctor's eyes met hers. Stella felt a momentary challenge from the alpha male. His smile faded ever so slightly as he relinquished his hold on his brand-new backpack.

As she loaded his bag, she heard Dr. Steven Bodine say, "*Monica?* My God, what a surprise. It . . . it's been an age."

"Steven," Monica said tonelessly. "This is my husband, Nathan."

"We've met," Nathan said brusquely as he gripped Steven's hand. "At that fund-raiser, wasn't it? The one your clinic organized for the children's foundation. The minister of health was there."

"I guess it was." A glance at Monica. "Gosh. Spaced that event. It was a long time ago." Steven thrust his hands into his pockets, shifted his weight. "What brings you guys to this junket? Food?"

"Potential catering contract," Nathan said swiftly. Monica cleared her throat and looked away.

"And we still don't know exactly where we're going, do we?" Steven turned to Stella as she was securing the baggage door. "Stella?" He raised his voice over the engine as he addressed her. "Can you tell us where you are taking us all now—where this secret destination is?"

Oh, the Shining Gladiator, saving the group—leading the way. Beating his chest in the face of Mr. McNeill and his wife.

She dusted her hands on her pants. "That remains a surprise the RAKAM Group has asked me to keep." Stella raised her own voice. "Okay, everyone, listen up."

The group gathered close. "The cabin is climate controlled to ensure your comfort. Each seat is equipped with a harness." She held one up to demonstrate. "There are advanced noise-canceling headsets hanging near each seat with which to enjoy music, as well as two-way communications with me." She ran through the rest of the safety briefing.

"In the unlikely event the aircraft goes down in water, the most confusing challenge can be to orient yourselves underwater, and to find the exit while upside down. So when you take your seats, do take a moment to locate the exit in relation to your right knee." She tapped her right thigh.

"If the exit is on your right while you're upright, it will still be on your right even if the aircraft comes to rest in another position."

She briefly covered underwater egress procedures.

"Remember to take a deep breath before being submersed underwater. Open your eyes. Orient yourself in relation to your remembered emergency exit. Get a firm grip on a reference point—you can't do that with eyes closed underwater. If you're seated beside an exit, wait until the water has filled three-quarters of the cabin before fully opening any exit. Release your safety harness only then. Using your hands, grip and pull yourself underwater to the exit, then pull yourself free from the cabin. Only after exiting, inflate the life preserver." She explained where to find the life preservers and showed how to inflate one.

She waited as looks of concern crossed faces. Good, she needed them to absorb this and take it seriously. Deborah glanced nervously at the plane. Her hands were balled into fists. She was the one most afraid of flying, Stella guessed.

She quickly explained where to find the emergency locator transmitter, survival kits, first aid kit, fire extinguisher, and other safety equipment. She then demonstrated how to safely board and deplane.

"And remember, most important in *any* emergency or survival situation is to try to remain calm. Panic is *always* the biggest killer."

As they began to board, she said, "No smoking. And please put your phones on airplane mode." She smiled. "And welcome to West Air."

"Oh, wait!" Jackie said, hurrying toward Amanda. She held her cell phone out to the guide. "Could you quickly take a photo of us all in front of the Beaver?"

The group gathered in front of the yellow-and-blue plane.

"Smile, everyone!" called Amanda. She shot a few images. "Deborah, move in a bit closer." Amanda waved her hand. They shuffled into position closer to one another. "Say cheese, everyone!"

Everyone grinned. "Cheese."

Amanda handed the phone back to Jackie, who fiddled with it as others commenced boarding.

"Instagramming?" Steven said to Jackie. "Posting your hashtag-mystery-tour, hashtag-flying-into-the-wild-wild-woods photo?"

She glanced up. Unsmiling, she said, "Facebook. And yeah, something like that. Before we lose cell service." She pocketed her phone.

Once they were all aboard and the doors were secured and the moorings freed, Stella strapped herself into her harness. She taxied her plane out into the lake.

As they left the protected bay, wind ruffled the surface, and the plane began to rock on small swells. She opened the throttle, thinking again about the passenger list and about missing Dan Whitlock.

It was 11:45 a.m. by the time she lifted her bird into the air and felt the strength of the first crosswind. Via radio she reported in to West Air dispatch.

THE LODGE PARTY

AMANDA

Amanda Gunn hurried out of the Thunderbird hotel elevator onto the fourth floor. The hotel manager's urgent call had come right after she'd seen off the tour group at the dock. She ran down the corridor, rounded the corner at speed, and was stopped dead by the tall frame of the manager. He placed his hand on her shoulder, his eyes watery, his cheeks red. He smelled of sweat.

"He's gone, Amanda. I'm so sorry—he . . . he's dead."

Blood drained from her head. Her world spun. She reached for the wall to steady herself and stared, disbelieving, at the manager, who'd stopped her before she could reach Dan Whitlock's room. She could see the door just beyond him. It had been propped open.

"What?" she said slowly.

"Dan Whitlock has passed. The paramedics tried everything, but he was gone before they got here."

"How? What . . . I mean, what *happened* to him?" She'd been convinced her tour guest was just severely hungover, and she'd been frustrated—angry—with him. Worry crashed through her as she tried to see around the manager and in through the open door to Dan's room.

It's a terrible mistake. That's all it is, just all a terrible mistake, has to be.

Around the side of the manager, she could see two EMTs bending over the prone shape of her charge on the hotel floor. Panic spiked through her. She pushed past the manager and entered the room. Amanda stalled. They were still working on him, still doing CPR, trying to bring him back. His skin was a pale blue. Like he'd been deprived of oxygen. Her heart began to beat up inside her throat.

"What happened?" she asked the manager again as he came up behind her. She swung around, glared up at him. "He wasn't like this when I left him! He was just nauseous, throwing up. I . . . I just went down to the floatplane dock to see everyone off—how could this have happened so fast?"

"I don't know," said the manager, looking ashen himself save for two hot spots riding high on his cheekbones. "The guest went into medical distress and called down to reception about forty minutes ago. The desk staff on duty said no one spoke on the other end of the line. Just a weird breathing sound. They sent someone up to check on him. There was no answer when we knocked on his door, but our staffer heard choking and coughing, and a banging sound. He used a master key card to access the room." The manager paused and regarded the heavyset man lying on the floor. He rubbed his brow. "The guest—Dan Whitlock—was found clutching both hands to his throat, choking, couldn't breathe, going blue. Our staffer called 911 right away, from that phone next to the bed." He pointed. "And then he tried CPR. The paramedics . . . they just got here, but they haven't been able to do anything."

"But . . . he had a hangover, he just had a headache." She clamped her hand hard over her brow.

A prank. That's what this is.

The bizarre thought took hold in Amanda's brain. Denial. Anything but this. She latched on to it.

This is a test—like the pilot suggested. Part of the job interview. To see how I might handle a potentially stressful situation with very high-end, secretive clients who value their privacy. To see if I'm able to keep it quiet and treat it all respectfully and with elegance if they overdose on drugs or something.

She moved slowly toward Dan Whitlock's body on the floor to ascertain for herself whether he was maybe alive and messing with her.

But one of the paramedics held her back, his hand firm on her arm.

"Let go of me!" she snapped, shaking him loose.

"Ma'am, we need you to step back. Please."

Tears pricked into her eyes. "Can . . . can you tell me what happened?" she asked, quietly now.

"It looks like he went into anaphylactic shock."

She stared at him. "Like, an allergic reaction?"

"We found a used EpiPen on the floor near his hand."

"He's deathly allergic to shellfish—he even told everyone at the buffet last night," Amanda all but whispered. "It was on the form I sent them all to fill in. I was careful." She spun to face the hotel manager. "You made it clear to your kitchen staff, didn't you, that he was allergic?"

"Of course. It was also underscored to the buffet and serving staff. The seafood was kept well away from the rest of the food."

Her gaze shot to a half-eaten plate of scrambled eggs on a table beneath the window. "He got room service. He called for room service—did everyone know, did the morning staff know of—"

"Ma'am," said the paramedic. "You need to step out of the room. The coroner is on his way. You need to leave everything as it is."

"Coroner?"

"It's protocol in an unexpected death."

"Will there be an investigation? Will the coroner inform next of kin?"

"When we know who they are, and there's always a death investigation in cases like this."

Her knees buckled slightly. She couldn't swallow. Absurdly, she wondered how this was going to look on her résumé. Would the RAKAM Group still consider her services in the future? What if it was *her* fault that he'd ingested shellfish? Or eaten food that had come into even the briefest contact with allergens?

The manager took her arm, but she shrugged him off. "I need to call my boss."

Amanda marched out of the room and walked a short way down the corridor. She stopped and dialed the number she'd been given for her contact at the RAKAM Group.

It rang and rang. Then it clicked over to a recorded message.

"This number is no longer in service."

She frowned, checked her phone. Had she pressed the wrong button? She tried to call again.

It rang four times, then came the same message. "This number is no longer in service."

Dumbstruck, she slowly lowered her phone. The voice of Stella Daguerre, the pilot, echoed through her ear.

It's just as well Dan Whitlock is not coming . . . My plane, as it's configured, takes a maximum of eight including me, the pilot. Your boss was made aware of this when I was contracted. I made it clear. So how can there be an extra passenger if the RAKAM Group didn't know Dan Whitlock was going to get sick and bail?

Amanda tried the number one more time.

"This number is no longer in service."

THE LODGE PARTY

DEBORAH

Deborah Strong peered out the plane window. Beyond the yellow wingtip, ragged mountains speared up from shimmering lakes, and rivers cascaded and sparkled. Pristine snow lay thick upon the taller peaks. Brutal, brown avalanche scars were scored down the steeper flanks. The forests were dark green and endless. She saw no sign of human life anywhere. It was beautiful. Distant. Hostile. The plane banked sharply. Her stomach swooped and she turned away, feeling slightly nauseous, wishing she hadn't downed that breakfast muffin so fast, because it was about to come up.

Deborah was seated at the very rear of the plane, right in front of a canvas curtain that divided the passengers from the luggage. Beside her, at the opposite window, sat the security woman, Jackie Blunt. Jackie had a really dark aura. Deborah found her intimidating. Every now and then she'd catch Jackie staring at her.

Katie Colbourne was seated in front of Deborah. Katie filmed out the window. Bart Kundera sat to Katie's right. Deborah liked his looks. Handsome in a bold sort of way that could almost be ugly with a few genetic tweaks in another direction. Such was the lottery of life. Bart had won. And he had a good vibe. Easy smile. He appeared capable.

Nice. Nice enough that Deborah had glanced at his ring finger. He wore a wedding ring. Of course he did. Not that she was looking, just that in her experience all the good ones were taken, and many of the not-so-good ones as well. She knew all about the not-so-goods.

The older married couple, Nathan and Monica McNeill, sat directly behind pilot Stella Daguerre.

Stella was all confidence and authority. Definitely the kind of attributes Deborah wanted of a pilot who took a heavy chunk of yellow-and-blue metal up into the sky, and who consequently held passengers' lives in her hands. It amazed Deborah that this thing could even get into the air, and now that they were in the sky, it all actually felt quite graceful, especially with the high-end headphones canceling the raw, throaty growl and shuddering metal parts of the plane. There was something magnetic about Stella. She wasn't pretty. Kind of hardened and gaunt, really. Perhaps it was her clear gray eyes, her cool silver hair cut pixie short, her slender, athletic physique that all combined to make her compelling. Perhaps it was her centeredness. Her self-assuredness. Her ease with being a strong and capable woman. Deborah admired that.

Stella was the kind of woman she'd want as a friend. But also the kind of woman Deborah felt was above her, and who might never deign to see Deborah as an equal should she even begin to make overtures. The cosmetic surgeon, Dr. Steven Bodine, sat in the copilot seat beside Stella. He'd made a beeline for that seat, not bothering to even feign a gesture of offering it to anyone else.

Deborah's phone vibrated in her hands. She glanced down at the device. As soon as they had taken off and were safely in the air, she'd posted to her social media account one of the photos she'd shot at the floatplane dock. Already three little hearts showed under her post. She smiled at the sight of them.

"I thought the pilot said to put phones in airplane mode."

Deborah's head shot up at the sudden sound of the voice inside her headphones.

Jackie Blunt.

The woman was staring at her. There was a strange look on her rough face. A prickle of unease crawled up the back of Deborah's neck.

"Still got reception, then?" Jackie asked, her voice once again coming in through Deborah's headset. It felt too intimate, as if the woman were right inside her brain. Deborah nodded, heat flaring into her cheeks. She was both embarrassed and angry that Jackie had called her out via a system through which everyone on the plane could listen in.

"I forgot," Deborah said quietly, coolly, and she turned off her phone.

Jackie's gaze dropped to the phone in Deborah's hands. Deborah realized Jackie Blunt was studying not the phone, but the small tattoo of a swallow on the inside of Deborah's wrist. Deborah quickly turned her wrist over and looked away. Her heart thudded. She felt as though this security woman had seen right into her, knew exactly who she was, where she'd been. What she'd done. Her therapist's words filled her mind.

You do not need to be defined by the darkness of your past. You deserve a good life, just like everyone deserves a good life. You have atoned. You have a right to feel worthy.

Deborah sucked in the meaning of the words. She had no reason to fear Jackie Blunt. Zero reason to feel inferior to Stella Daguerre, or anybody. She had as much right and status on this junket as anyone else here. She was being considered for a high-end boutique housekeeping contract, and she'd worked her freaking butt off to get to this point. Harder than most would ever have to work, because she'd started in a shittier place than most. And she'd discovered she was good at the housekeeping business, good at managing staff, good at finding the right people to build her team. Good at making contacts in the industry. And through it all she'd met a wonderful man with whom she planned to spend the rest of her life. And she had a secret. She was carrying his baby. And when he returned home, she would tell him, and they would marry.

"You remind me of someone," Jackie said quietly in her ear.

Deborah started. Slowly her attention returned to Jackie. The woman's dark eyes narrowed as she studied Deborah. "Kat . . . Kata . . . Katarina, I think her name was."

Deborah's heart clean stopped. Her mouth went dry. *Blink. Breathe. Be normal.* She gave a dismissive shrug.

"Have you ever gone by that name?" Jackie asked.

Breathe.

"No."

But the woman continued to study her. Her attention dropped back to Deborah's wrist with the tattoo.

Fuck. I should've had it removed. I knew I should have. How can this be? How could this woman know Katarina?

Deborah broke eye contact and looked out the window. But her eyes watered. Her pulse beat in her carotid. She could *feel* Jackie watching the back of her head. Everything had changed with that one word.

Katarina.

The plane banked again, affording a sudden view of a tiny town far below—a scattering of colored buildings along the shore of a lake that stretched into the distance like an ocean. Stella's voice came through the headphones as she called in a GPS location to her dispatch. Deborah heard her say they were flying over the town of Kluhane Bay.

I am Deborah. I am Deborah Strong. I am strong. I'm a fiancée. A mother-to-be. I've never heard of Katarina. I run a successful business. I don't know any Katarina—

"Do you mind if I film you?" Katie Colbourne asked as she peered around her seat.

Deborah's pulse beat even faster, her face going hot. "No, sure. Go ahead," she said as calmly as she could. They'd all signed forms agreeing to being photographed and filmed. They'd also agreed that any shots or footage could be used for spa promotional materials.

"Can I ask you some questions?" Katie asked, leaning farther around her seat and focusing her camera on Deborah's face. A fall of flaxen hair tumbled across Katie's cheek. She had a real TV-host look. Pretty.

Deborah fiddled with her engagement ring. "Sure."

"You seemed lost in thought while looking out of the window a moment ago. What were you thinking?"

I am Deborah. I am Deborah Strong. I am strong . . .

"Beautiful." She smiled. "I was thinking that it's so stunningly beautiful down there, and exactly like the provincial car registration plates say: 'Beautiful British Columbia.'"

"You're Deborah Strong," Katie said for her future viewers, or for her own record. "You own your own business?"

"Housekeeping. A boutique-style service, usually for smaller, luxury establishments." She glanced at the others. She knew they could all hear in their headphones what she was saying. But they showed no apparent interest.

"You're BC born and bred?"

"Excuse me?"

"Were you born in BC?"

Alarm bells started clanging. Fear rushed into her chest. *No, no, it's okay. Deborah Strong has nothing to hide, stay close to the truth . . .* "Alberta, actually, near Edmonton. I moved out to BC when I was . . . a lot younger."

A pause, Katie waiting for Deborah to say more. Deborah offered nothing extra. She felt the security woman watching, listening.

"Do you think you might be happy to relocate to a remote setting for periods?"

For a brief, outlandish moment, Deborah wondered if perhaps Katie Colbourne worked for the RAKAM Group, and her recordings and questions were all part of the greater job interview, and she'd show her footage to her bosses.

"If it works out," Deborah said carefully. "For periods of time."

"Do you have children?"

She cleared her throat. "Not yet."

"But you do have a fiancé?" Katie smiled, lowered her camera, and turned it off. Her eyes were kind. "I saw the ring."

The thought of Ewan—coupled with the fact that Katie's apparent interrogation was over—eased her mind. "He's in the military—air force. Stationed at CFB Comox," she said. She was proud of Ewan. She *liked* to talk about him. "He's away for extended tours, so this contract would work well for us. How about you?" Deborah asked, steering attention away from herself. "You got kids?"

Katie beamed. And this polished TV woman looked suddenly incredibly human and relatable. Her smile struck Deborah as startlingly honest. And it made her instantly like Katie.

"A daughter," Katie said proudly. "She's just turned six."

"What's her name?"

"Gabby." Katie pulled up a photo on her phone. Reaching around the seat, she held it out for Deborah to see.

"Oh, she's beautiful," Deborah said, taking the phone for a closer study. "She looks just like you."

"I think she looks like her dad."

A memory flared hot into Deborah's mind. Her own father. Chasing her through green summer grass spiked with wildflowers. *You bad little girl! Get over here, Katarina, you little shit. Now.* She shook the image.

"She's going to miss you while you're away these ten days," Deborah said, handing the phone back.

"One day down, nine more to go." Another grin. "And it's more a case of me missing her." Katie pushed the fall of hair back from her startlingly blue eyes. "I used to travel a lot for work, but I cut back after Gabby was born. It's why I left the cable news station to go into travel documentaries. Best change I've ever made. Far more flexibility being my own boss, and I can spend more time with my daughter."

She'd already told them all over breakfast.

"So Gabby's with your husband now?"

"Her dad. We divorced a year after she was born."

"Oh." A feeling of cold washed through Deborah's gut, and her image of the happy Katie Colbourne tilted slightly. It was disheartening to think of all the excitement and work and emotion that went into falling in love, and into committing to a life together, and into the decisions around having a child, becoming a parental unit, only for it all to be smashed apart later. Her hand went instinctively to her belly, where her own little secret grew.

Stella Daguerre's voice came through the headset. "We're nearing the lodge. If you look carefully, you can glimpse it between the trees at the end of the lake below."

Excitement shimmered. Everyone leaned forward to look out their windows as Stella banked her plane into a slow curve, affording them all a view. Below, the long, narrow body of water sparkled. It was nestled into a valley between two mountain ranges that rose sharply up on either side. Densely forested slopes scored by the gray scars of avalanche chutes plunged down to the water. The lake looked deep, and very dark—a blue that seemed almost black as it reflected gold dollars of sunlight.

No roads were visible anywhere, not even a trail around the lake. Again, Deborah was struck by the utter absence of human presence. The plane lowered, flying toward the head of the lake.

"The lodge lies at the far northern end." Stella pointed.

Steven Bodine's deep voice came through the headsets. "Can you reveal the name of the lake now?"

"Taheese Lake," Stella said. "Just over thirty-two kilometers long, or twenty miles. But while long, it's narrow, only two kilometers wide at the widest part. At the southwest end it flows into what becomes the Taheese River, which feeds all the way down to Lake Kluhane."

"So that small town back there was Kluhane Bay?" Nathan asked.

"Correct," Stella said into their headsets. "Very small town, but it gets busier over the summer months." She dipped the nose of her de Havilland Beaver. Their altitude dropped sharply. Deborah felt her stomach rise to her throat. She held her belly tighter to stop the feeling of airsickness as the waters of Taheese Lake came up to meet their little yellow bird. She caught sight of the bank of dark clouds looming in the north. Crosswinds slammed suddenly into the plane. The aircraft rocked violently. Deborah held her breath. Everyone in the plane exchanged looks of worry.

Silence thickened inside the de Havilland as Stella battled to steady the craft. She banked again and began another downward sweep in a long, lazy spiral, the wings rocking on currents of wind.

Mountains and wilderness spun around and rose to meet them. Deborah was gut-punched with awe, fear. She moved her hands to clutch her knees tightly. Her teeth clenched. The wind whomped them again, and the plane teetered violently.

"I don't know about anyone else, but I'm sure looking forward to that welcome drink described in the email brochure," Bart Kundera said loudly into their headsets, breaking some of the tension.

Others laughed. Uneasily.

Deborah saw small white-water caps on a stretch of the lake that was unprotected from the crosswinds.

"Oh, look!" came Monica's voice. "I think I see it, the lodge—is that it, at the end there?" The plane turned.

Down below, at the foot of a tombstone mountain of black granite, the dark shape of a building emerged between trees that grew dense. Deborah heard Stella calling in their GPS coordinates again and telling West Air dispatch that she was coming in for an approach. She also reported the strength of the wind, and mentioned that the storm front was closing in fast.

As they neared their destination, the lodge building took more distinct shape, and a feeling of foreboding rose inside Deborah. It looked nothing at all like she'd imagined. Nothing like any of the images she'd seen in the brochure, or on the spa website.

"It . . . looks different," Monica said, voicing what they all had to be thinking.

"That's not the lodge," Steven said. He turned to Stella. "That's not the place, right?"

Stella remained silent, her hands tight on the de Havilland's controls as she battled the crosswinds.

Deborah's pulse raced. She closed her eyes as the water rushed up to meet them while the plane was still wobbling, and she bid a silent prayer to whatever gods might listen.

They hit with a hard thump. Deborah's eyes flared open and she gasped.

The plane lifted, rocked, whomped, and bounced back onto the lake surface a few more times. The sound of the engine changed. They'd made it. They were down. Stella taxied slowly toward a dock that listed into the water among reeds and rushes.

Along a path that led up from the dock, a monstrous totem pole rose like a sentinel between the lodge building and the water. It had a raven's head on top. The raven had been carved with a long beak full of wooden teeth and massive, outstretched wings. The raven caricature had in turn been fashioned atop the head of a stylized bear. The bear also had humanlike teeth, and a tongue that stuck out in an aggressive, warrior-like fashion. Another totem, slightly smaller, had been erected a short way behind the first. Paint peeled off both, and they were grayed by the weather. They stood like ancient warnings to foreigners who might dare to come upon on this shore. *Not welcome.* The words seemed to rise from the pit of Deborah's stomach and whisper deep inside her brain. *Not welcome.*

Everyone was quiet.

Stella appeared tense. She leaned forward, studying the place as she taxied up to the listing dock.

The front of the lodge came into view. Rain began to spit. The sky turned suddenly dark. They'd entered the shadow of clouds that poured over the granite mountain behind the lodge. The wind lashed suddenly at them.

The building was constructed of logs. Double story. All the logs had been worn so dark that the building looked silvery black in this light. Rows of windows watched them from upstairs, dark-green shutters like eyelids placed at their sides. Above the front door hung a rack of bleached antlers.

The area around the lodge was overgrown with brambles and covered with mosses and lichens.

Bart said, "This cannot be right."

"Looks like the Overlook," Monica whispered.

"The what?" Nathan asked.

"That spooky hotel in that Stephen King novel."

"No, it does not," said Bart. "This place looks nothing like the one in the movie. And it's smaller."

"That's how the hotel looked in my imagination," Monica said quietly. "I never saw the movie."

"Stella, what *is* this place?" Steven demanded, his voice strident in their headsets. Deborah watched Steven as he glared at their pilot. His neck was tight, his shoulders stiff. The bold and shining surgeon who could cut people open on his operating table and sew them back up in prettier shape looked as though he might be scared.

"These are the coordinates I was given," Stella said quietly. She brought them up alongside the dock. The rain rapped harder. It ticked on the roof and against the windows and danced upon the water, making a billion pocks and bubbles on the surface. The wind gusted as the storm began to hunker down.

"Radio someone," Jackie ordered suddenly from her seat in the back.

Deborah glanced over her shoulder at Jackie. The woman had powered on her cell phone and was checking for cell service. She came up empty. Her black, inscrutable eyes narrowed to slits. Her jaw tightened. Katie started filming out the window, silent. Deborah swallowed as a pontoon nudged up against the moss-covered dock. It looked like it hadn't been used in years.

"Radio someone," Jackie demanded again, louder. "Find out what's going on. Check if this is the right place."

"I did radio the coordinates in."

"What did they say?" Jackie demanded.

Stella turned to face them all. The expression on her slender, angled face made Deborah's heart sink.

"This is the place. These are the coordinates to which West Air was contracted to fly you all."

"No, no way," Steven said. "I did not sign up for . . . for *this*." Steven waved his hand in the direction of the hulking building. "You have got to take us out of here. Fly us back. Now."

As if on cue, the rain began to pour harder, and the wind bore down, sending waves lapping over the edges of the dock and the plane rocking.

"Let's just take a look, shall we?" Stella said, powering down the engine. "Whatever this is, there is no way I can fly us out of here until this weather blows through. I fly visual flight rules. And with VFR you need daylight. You need to see, or we will crash in these mountains."

"Yeah," Bart said. "She's right. Let's just check it out." He unbuckled his harness. "The actual spa could be through the trees or something, or around in the next bay. Maybe this is just a joke, or something." He didn't sound convinced.

"Maybe we've been duped," Steven said darkly.

"But why?" Monica asked.

Stella opened the pilot-side door. The wind blew in cold and wet.

One by one they alighted from the Beaver, stepping gingerly from the pontoon onto the slippery green slime that covered the dock's planks. Deborah was the last to deplane. Steven held out his hand to assist her.

Her foot touched a plank. But as she transferred weight, it slid out from under her so fast that she was flat on the dock and tumbling into the water before she could even register what happened. The cold lake stole her breath. Shock blinded her. She thrashed wildly at the brackish water, at the reeds, going under, gulping for air. A hand groped for her jacket. By her collar, she was hauled dripping out of the reeds and dragged up onto the dock. She sat on her butt, coughing and choking, terrified, her eyes filling with tears, her hair plastered to her face.

Stella bent down. "Are you okay?"

"I . . . I can't swim. I can't swim. I—"

"It's all right, Deborah." Stella reached for her arm. "You're out—you're safe now." She helped Deborah up to her feet with Bart's assistance.

Deborah shook like a leaf. Water poured from her clothes and squelched in her shoes. She could barely breathe from the shock and cold. She tried to take a step and gasped in pain, her left leg buckling under. "My ankle. I . . . I think I've hurt my ankle."

They all stared at her. All shaken. White-faced. It made Deborah feel even more frightened. The wind gusted and the rain lashed at them.

"Monica and Nathan," Stella said, taking command of the situation. "Can you guys help Deborah up to the lodge? I need to secure the aircraft to the dock. Bart, maybe you could check to see if there is actually a real spa around the bay, or another building somewhere?" She reached for a rope. "Jackie, can you give me a hand and hold fast on to this strut here while I moor the Beaver to the dock?"

Jackie acquiesced. Nathan and Monica put their arms around Deborah and helped her limp carefully along the canting dock, keeping the bulk of her weight off her ankle. Deborah was petrified of going into the brackish shallows again—utterly terrified—and great big palsied shudders took hold of her body. Steven just stood there glowering at them all, as if refusing to accept his lot, as if blaming them all for bringing him here. Katie quietly filmed the whole thing. Thunder rumbled.

With the assistance of Monica and Nathan, Deborah reached solid ground. As they began up the narrow and overgrown path toward the lodge, she heard Jackie's and Stella's voices rising in argument down on the dock. Jackie said something about calling for help on the radio again, and Stella cut her off angrily, then lowered her voice. Deborah glanced back over her shoulder.

Through the pelting rain she witnessed Stella pulling Jackie close, and they conversed in what appeared to be urgent tones. Jackie suddenly stilled and glanced at the plane.

"Easy, there's a step coming up here," Nathan said.

Deborah returned her focus to the ground as they limped through the rain up toward the looming lodge.

THE SEARCH

CALLIE

Saturday, October 31.

"You promised!" Benjamin whined in the passenger seat as Callie navigated her 4x4 along a rutted track toward the command post her SAR team was setting up near the river to search for the downed plane. She was late. It was past 9:00 a.m., but the sun had not yet risen above the mountains, and would not do so for at least another twenty minutes at this time of year. Not that a sunrise would change much on a bleak day like today. Clouds rolled low over the mountains, and sleety rain pelted the forest. Her wipers scraped muddy arcs across her windshield. She felt a bite of irritation toward the new cop who'd sent the aircraft into the water.

"I know, Ben, I *know*. I'm sorry." She slowed down to steer through a pothole thick with mud. "I'll make it up to you, I promise." She flashed him a smile she couldn't manage to feel in her heart. "And we'll get a special dessert when we go visit your dad for dinner tonight, okay?"

Tears made Ben's black eye makeup run, streaking gray tracks through the white pancake stuff smeared over his face as he was bounced around in his seat. The black trails leaked into the bloodred lipstick he'd used to paint a ghoulish smile around his mouth. His head bobbed under a spiky, psychedelic green wig that matched the green waistcoat beneath his purple coat. Her little eight-year-old Joker. And she'd let him down. Again.

Callie's support system had failed her this morning. Just as she'd been ready to go out the door, Rachel—who always took care of Benjamin when Callie was on a SAR mission—had phoned to say her whole family was down with a terrible bout of flu. Callie had tried in vain to rustle up another caregiver on short notice, someone who'd be able to drive Ben to the Halloween party he'd been so excited about for weeks, but after a few calls Callie had been forced as a last resort to bundle Benjamin up into her truck along with his iPad and headphones and books. She'd had no choice but to bring him along.

"Everyone from my class is going, except me. I'm the loser *again*. There won't be another Halloween party until next year," he wailed. "You *promised*!" Anger showed in his little gloved fists. Guilt punched through Callie.

"I bet you won't even find the plane in time! And we won't even get to see Dad tonight. And we won't get to see the movie. We won't have the fried chicken or the dessert you promised. Because you don't keep promises."

Callie sucked in a deep breath. She felt torn. She reminded herself to stop using phrases like *I promise*. "Hopefully we will find the plane before it gets dark, Ben, and we'll still go visit Dad."

"Who's on the stupid plane anyway? Why did it have to crash?"

"A woman pilot." She took another sharp bend along the twisting track through the forest. Her tires slipped and spun in deep mud. She felt the four-wheel drive engage. "We don't know who she is yet, or how or why her plane went down. But we have a good idea where it might have gotten hung up downriver."

As the local SAR manager, Callie had officially initiated a group callout the night before, and she'd given her team of fourteen volunteers the coordinates for a rendezvous point not far from the Taheese River. It was as close as they could get with trucks. From that point the teams would need to go farther on foot, or use quads. An air search was not possible in this weather, and neither was using a drone. One of her team leaders was Oskar Johansson. She'd tasked Oskar with setting up the SAR command vehicle at the designated parking area. Callie would manage the search from the command van in concert with an RCMP member. As a group of civilian SAR volunteers, they worked under the direction of law enforcement. Always.

Legally, only the cops could task a SAR group for an operation, and it was Callie's job once she got that call from the police to set the ball rolling by contacting the provincial Emergency Coordination Centre to receive an operational task number. Without the number there would be no insurance coverage for the volunteers, and no workers' compensation for injuries incurred.

Callie had taken over the manager job from her husband, Peter. She'd agreed to do it temporarily—to keep his seat warm, so to speak. And she enjoyed it. She felt she was a good fit. She got on well with people in general, had decent leadership skills and a positive outlook, and had put in countless hours of training; plus she'd logged enough callouts to be considered a veteran of this rescue business. She'd also won the respect of her team. Yet on another level, they—including her—were all still waiting for Peter's return to the helm. There was always this sense of a ticking clock, of time slipping away.

She pulled into the clearing. Several vehicles were already parked under the trees, including a muddy RCMP truck with stripes down the sides and a light bar on top. Oskar had positioned the KSAR command van toward the rear of the clearing, leaving room for the others to park. An awning had been extended from the van, with a pop-up canopy erected over a table alongside it. On the table were two industrial-size urns, mugs, and donated cookies. Sergeant Mason Deniaud stood beside the table, under the canopy, talking to Oskar, who held a steaming mug in his hand. Oskar was a tall Norwegian with white-blond hair, an avid mountaineer and kayaker who'd made Canada his home for the past eight years. Oskar was the KSAR expert in swift-water rescue. Good at rope skills, too. Callie relied heavily on his talent, and on his sheer strength and stamina. His dry wit was a bonus.

As she backed her truck in between two trees, wet branches scraping her roof, her thoughts turned to the new sergeant. If Mason Deniaud had just waited a few more minutes until she'd arrived the day before, they could have all been spared this exercise in what was turning out to be terrible weather. Benjamin might have made his Halloween party.

Instead, she was now sending teams to search along a section of the Taheese River that was dangerous in rain, and potentially deadly if someone slipped into the frigid rapids. Her irritation mounted as she put her truck in gear, turned the engine off, and reached into the back for her SAR cap and the box of muffins she'd baked last night. Baking was Callie's way of dealing with insomnia, which had become a discomfiting companion of late.

"Come, Ben." She tugged on her cap and threaded her ponytail out the back. "You can hang out inside the van. The generator will keep it warm inside, and you can play your game on your iPad, or read a book. You could even help run the search if you like." Callie worked to keep her voice upbeat.

Ben scowled and folded his arms tightly across his chest. He hunkered lower into the passenger seat, a bizarre and angry little creature under his clown head of acid-green hair. Disquiet threaded through Callie.

"Benny?"

"I want him to move back home."

The words punched her out of left field. Her mind reeled. She swallowed. "He . . . he will, Ben."

"When?"

"Soon." She cleared her throat. "Very soon, I hope."

Her son glanced up at her with his blackened eyes and smeared Joker face. "You *promise?*"

Pain mushroomed in her chest at the irony in her little boy's tone. With it came resentment. Anger. All of it boiled up inside her in a horrible, hot, toxic cocktail. How could she even begin to think of promising her son things that were not in her control? She inhaled deeply, struggling to find the calm needed to focus on this mission.

"Why don't you ask him yourself tonight, Ben?" she asked quietly.

His red-lipsticked mouth dropped open and hung slack as he stared incredulously at her. "You're stupid!" he snapped. "He won't tell me—you *know* he won't."

She blinked at the vitriol blazing in her son's eyes. Gently she said, "You do need to ask him these things, Benny. We both do. I think it will be good. It could make him commit to doing it, to making it happen."

"You're lying."

A knock sounded on her fogged-up window. It was Oskar, gesticulating and pointing toward his watch, then at the command vehicle where Mason Deniaud waited. Callie made a motion that she was coming.

"Come on, Benny," she said again.

"I don't want to."

"Your daddy would want us to find that plane, Benjamin. Your dad would want that, okay? He'll be so proud of you when you tell him that you helped us."

"I won't be helping. I'll be sitting in the stupid van!"

"You *are* helping, Benny, by helping me. You're helping simply by hanging out. Otherwise I would not even be able to be here." She opened her door.

"I'm *Ben*. Not Benny." His lip quivered.

"I'm sorry, Ben."

Why can't I call my baby boy Benny any longer? He's only eight. Can I not just put his growth on pause until Peter comes home? How can I allow

Peter to miss out on all the little milestones of Benny's life—all the days, weeks, months?

Would it be years until Peter came through the door of their house again? How much longer until Callie might see the light and love in her husband's eyes again, hear his laughter, feel his touch, make love just one more time?

Ben turned his back on her and folded his arms tighter. His shoulders began to heave. He was crying.

"Ben?"

"Not coming. Staying in the truck."

Callie took another deep breath. "Okay. But I can't leave the engine running. When you get cold, come over to the command vehicle, all right?"

Silence. His green head remained turned away.

Her heart ached. She got out, shut the door, and ducked through the pelting sleet, making her way toward the awning, where Oskar waited with Mason Deniaud. In his hands Oskar held a clipboard with the KSAR incident sign-up sheet.

"Oh, you brought muffins," he said.

"Morning, Sergeant Deniaud. Oskar. Sorry I'm late. Ben's sitter bailed." Callie set her muffin container on the table. She opened the lid. "Help yourselves. Sunflower and pumpkin seed on this end." She pointed. "Blueberry-banana on that end. No sugar added, just Medjool dates and the bananas for sweetness."

"Call me Mason," said the sergeant. "And thanks again for yesterday."

She glanced up and met his gaze. His eyes were gray. A very light gray. Deep creases at the corners. Something about the look in those eyes gave her pause and suddenly made her want to downplay this man's error in judgment yesterday.

"Well, let's hope we find that de Havilland soon," she said crisply as she grabbed a mug and poured herself a coffee from the urn. "Shall we get started?" As she spoke, one more vehicle trundled into the clearing, wipers smearing mud across the windscreen.

"That's Julia," Oskar said. "I asked her to bring Zipper. I figured this incident would be a good first try for them as an official K9 cadaver team. I'll go get her signature for the sign-in, and we can get rolling."

Callie and Mason watched Oskar run through the mud and sleet toward Julia's vehicle. Julia exited and opened the back of her SUV to access her chocolate lab in his travel cage.

Mason selected a muffin and bit into it. "So that's Zipper?" he said with a nod toward the Labrador, now tugging excitedly at the end of his lead.

"Yeah." Callie sipped her coffee, watching as Zipper leaped about at the end of his lead. Steam rose against her face. She turned her attention to the other members, who'd already arrived and were either checking their gear, organizing their packs, or chatting in small groups beneath the cover of the trees. They knew to leave her and Oskar alone while they planned the search.

Sleet drummed steadily down. It dripped from the bills of KSAR caps and from the heavy wet branches of the surrounding woods. It would likely turn to snow by evening. And visibility would be shit. Callie was thankful this wasn't a live search. Victims didn't last long in wet cold like this. Maybe a day or two. Sometimes as little as four hours, depending on the psyche of the victim. She'd become an expert in profiling the missing, predicting who would travel where, and why, and what their chances of survival would be on any given mission. She'd gotten so good she was often called out to assist other SAR groups on particularly challenging searches throughout the province.

"Who's Ben?" Mason asked.

She turned to look at him. He'd stopped chewing. He held a wad of paper napkin in his hand, folded around what Callie guessed had been his bite of her muffin. She nodded toward the object in his hand. "That bad, huh?"

He pulled a face. "Pretty terrible."

She snorted. "That's what I get for trying to serve healthy stuff to cops who like doughnuts."

"Who said I liked doughnuts?"

"You're a cop, aren't you?"

He smiled. It put dimples into his gaunt cheeks, and it made something go quiet inside her. She shook the sensation aside, but on some deep level it had set her off-kilter.

"Ben is my son," she said. "He's eight going on eighteen, and he's pissed to be missing his Halloween party."

Mason's smile faded. "Eight?"

"Well, just. He turned eight last month."

Mason's gaze ticked briefly to her ring finger, then to her truck, where the dark shape of Benny's little wigged head could be seen as a shadow behind the foggy window.

"It's a good age," he said softly, still staring at the truck. "Enjoy the moments. Don't let them slip by."

She frowned. "Do you have kids?"

"No." The word came out sharp. His face was blank. All cop. As if armor had suddenly gone up around him. It piqued Callie's curiosity.

Oskar ducked back in under the awning with his sign-up sheet. "Okay, everyone is here," he said in his deep voice and singsong Norwegian accent. "Let's get this show on the road."

Once inside the command vehicle, Callie spread out a topographical map over the table. The curved contour lines showed challenging terrain with steep peaks and deep troughs through which the Taheese River thundered.

Callie placed her finger on the map. "The de Havilland Beaver Mk 1 was last seen here, at the Taheese Narrows. The pilot was strapped inside, deceased, and possibly female. For this first operational period, our search objective is body and plane recovery."

"And we're certain she was deceased when first seen?" Oskar asked.

"I'm certain," Mason said.

Oskar rubbed his square jaw as he studied the map. "And no sign of any passengers?"

"I didn't see any, but my vantage point was poor," said Mason.

"A de Havilland Beaver Mk 1 can accommodate six to eight occupants," said Oskar. "Depending on how it's been configured inside. The aircraft is commonly used for glacier sightseeing around here. But so far no one has reported any planes missing, or any pilot overdue."

Callie said, "We'll brief the team to keep an eye out for indications there were more occupants. The Beaver went into the rapids at the narrows here"—she moved her finger down the twisting line of the Taheese River—"and given the high water levels and power of the river right now, after the rains and warmer-than-usual temperatures at higher elevations, I believe the wreck could have washed over this first waterfall in the series of the multistep falls here, and our highest POD—maybe a sixty percent POD—is right there." She tapped the map. "That big pool below the first waterfall."

"POD?" Mason said.

Callie met his eyes. Again she felt an odd frisson. She cleared her throat. "Probability of detection. We work in probabilities, maximizing search efforts in the highest areas first. If we find nothing, we expand from there."

"Too windy and foggy to deploy the drone," Oskar said, almost to himself, as he continued to pore over the map.

"The drone's infrared wouldn't help with a deceased body," Callie said.

"*Ja*, but in good conditions the camera could pick out shapes deep under the water." He pointed to the pool below the first waterfall. "We can put the K9 cadaver team in there. Julia can work Zipper along this bank. Prevailing wind is from the northwest right now, so this area will be downwind of the pool and the best location to pick up any scent coming off the water."

"So the dog would pick up the plane, underwater, in the river?" Mason asked.

They both regarded the sergeant. He might have been a big-city homicide cop, but this was clearly his first SAR command as an RCMP officer. His lack of experience could prove a problem.

"The scent from the body inside the wreck," Callie said simply. "Julia Smith has been working over the past two years to certify Zipper for cadaver work, pestering the local dentist for pulled human teeth so she could train her dog on human scent. These dogs can work from boats, too, but the handler has to understand the movement of any scent that comes up in bubbles through the water, or in other ways, in order to interpret alerts properly."

"If Julie and Zipper work out, it'll save a helluva lot of time and resources in the future," Oskar said.

"Okay, so we put the K9 team in at the big pool," Callie said. "A second team goes in via ATV farther downriver, along this old access track here." She pointed. "We'll deploy a third team to the top tier of the falls here, in case the wreck got hung up in the rocks and never made it over the first waterfall. We'll take breaks in stages and redeploy or ramp up depending on what we find, but we stop before we lose light." She looked up. "This is not rated as a time-critical mission. Survivors are unlikely, and my primary role is not to further endanger life." She said this for Mason's benefit.

Mason said, "From our end, Nav Canada also has no overdue flights or missing aircraft being reported from any of its flight information centers. No emergency transponder signals have been received. And Transport Canada has zero record of any aircraft with the registration C-FABC on the Canadian Civil Aircraft Register."

"And you're sure it's the correct registration?" Oskar asked.

"I remembered it correctly," Mason said coolly.

Callie and Oskar exchanged a look. Oskar crooked up an eyebrow.

"The CAR did have a de Havilland Beaver with that mark on file," Mason said. "But it was removed from the register ten years ago."

"What does that mean?" Oskar asked.

"The CAR allows for the removal of an aircraft from the register in cases where the aircraft has been destroyed, permanently withdrawn from service, is missing and the search is terminated," Mason said. "Or if the aircraft has been missing for sixty days or more."

"So this Beaver was withdrawn from service?" Callie asked. "It wasn't actually licensed to fly?"

"The CAR does reuse registration marks for other aircraft once a plane has been decommissioned, but there is nothing on record to indicate this has been done."

"*Faen.*" Oskar swore softly in his native tongue as he dragged his hand over his cropped hair. "So we're looking for an illegal plane?"

"Possible," Mason said.

Adrenaline hummed into Callie's veins as she regarded Mason. She pushed suddenly to her feet and reached for her jacket, which she'd removed inside the warm van. "I wonder what the cargo was—contraband?"

"Probably drugs," Oskar offered as he shrugged into his own jacket. They followed her out into the wind, where Callie called her team together for the briefing.

THE SEARCH

MASON

Mason watched Callie as she efficiently and expeditiously answered a few questions from the group after her briefing. This woman was sure of herself, and comfortable in her role as a leader. Callie Sutton had a command presence any cop would envy. Mason's attention shifted to the group of volunteers standing in the rain. The oldest person on the team looked to be in his late fifties, maybe even early sixties. The youngest was a woman around nineteen. Rugged mountain people. Mason had worked all his life with tough, gritty sorts, but this was a different kind of tough. These were folk you'd want on your side if you got lost, or if you needed assistance far away from any trappings of civilization. People who relied on themselves, and not technology.

"Keep an eye out for any signs of oil or gas slicks on water," Callie told her team as they stood with water rolling down their jackets and dripping from the bills of their caps. "And look for other signs along the riverbanks that seem out of the ordinary. Remain suspicious." She paused, meeting the eyes of each and every person on her team. "There is no such thing as coincidence on a search, and nothing should be considered too small or too inconsequential to collect, report, and record. There's always a chance that something seemingly unconnected could later become key evidence as the overall picture emerges." Her gaze touched Mason's. "So far, it appears this aircraft was flying without proper authorization, and we have no indication yet what the cargo might have been, or if there was in fact any. Evidence should be collected with a view that this could become a criminal investigation." She paused. "Any more questions?"

Heads shook.

"Okay, let's do this," Callie said. "And everyone—be safe out there."

As the SAR volunteers grouped into teams and began to deploy, the passenger door of Callie's truck swung open. Mason's attention was attracted by movement. A small, humanoid, green-haired creature in a long purple coat jumped down from the truck into the mud. Every molecule in Mason's body froze.

He watched the young boy run through the sleet toward the KSAR command vehicle. Part of his brain was saying, *It's Callie's son.*

Another part of his mind was seeing straight down a tunnel into a Halloween past. A Halloween two years back. Luke. Wearing the same Joker suit. Jenny had bought it for him at a Walmart sale one Halloween when it seemed like every second kid in their neighborhood had gotten the same off-the-rack outfit. Blood drained from his head. Sound around him turned into a buzz.

He felt a hand on his shoulder and swung around to look directly into Callie's eyes.

"Sergeant? You okay?"

He shook himself back to the present. "Fine. I . . . I'll be in my vehicle if you need me. I need to . . . brief Hubble."

He strode rapidly back to his truck, feeling Callie's gaze boring into his back. His heart raced. It had been a brutal shock. Something completely unexpected. But little Ben Sutton was almost the same age his Luke had been. Same size, coloring. Mason sure as hell hadn't thought his ghosts would follow him out here, not like this.

Mason climbed into his truck and started the engine to warm the interior. He called Hubble on his sat phone.

"Sir?" Hubb said. "You find something?"

"Search is just getting underway. I need you to contact the serious crime unit at the RCMP North District headquarters in Prince George, brief them on the status to date, and stand by for additional details as they come in."

"You think it was carrying contraband?"

"It's a possibility until we rule it out." Drugs moving up north through vast wilderness areas was an issue, and a challenge for northern cops. "Keep them apprised—it could end up intersecting with one of their files."

"Affirm. I'll call back if they offer any new information from their end."

He signed off. He hadn't really needed to call Hubb. But he had needed to feel he was being more than a spare part out here. Through his window he watched Callie talking to Ben outside the SAR van. Ben appeared to be arguing with his mom. Mason's window fogged up as his car warmed and water evaporated from his gear. He wiped away the fog to keep watching. Callie crouched down into the mud and drew Ben close, hugging him tightly. The little green-wigged head rested briefly against his mom's shoulder, and she covered it with her gloved hand. Rain beat down over them. The poignancy of the vignette stabbed sharply through Mason's heart.

It made him feel suddenly close to Jenny.

He could almost feel her presence beside him in his truck—so much so that it was painful. Another memory surfaced in faded color like an old photograph—the three of them at Christmas. Their last Christmas as a family. An ache washed through him. Visceral. It came from low in his gut and ballooned painfully into his chest. Who knew grief could be so goddamned physical, a dark and sly trickster that blindsided you when you weren't even thinking about loss, and suddenly you couldn't get it out of your mind again. A thump sounded on his roof, and a wad of slush slid down his windshield. The forest outside seemed to darken, fingers of mist curling around his truck. It was eerie. Haunting. Unfriendly. He inhaled deeply and checked his watch. There wasn't going to be much for him to do out here in the woods but wait now. And he was reluctant to go sit inside the command vehicle with Callie and Ben.

He wondered again if it had been a weirdly bad decision to take this post and stick himself out here in the wild mountains, far from everything familiar. A cold prison of sorts, one from which he couldn't escape for two years minimum, not if he wanted to keep working as a cop. Sometimes he wasn't sure that he did. Sometimes he wasn't even certain he wanted to live.

Callie took Ben inside the van. Mist sneaked back over Mason's windows. He sat in his fogged-up cocoon and forced himself to call to mind the deceased pilot's upside-down face, the milky dead eyes staring sightlessly back at him. The registration markings in bold black on the fuselage. He had recalled them correctly, hadn't he? They'd been upside down, but he'd always possessed an uncanny ability to remember sequences of numbers and letters. Was he losing his mind?

Time ticked by. He checked his watch again.

A sat call came in from Hubb. She told him Prince George had nothing in connection with the downed plane on its files.

Again, he pictured the upside-down wreck. The pontoons in the air, the wings crushed. The pilot hanging in her seat harness, mouth gaping open.

He decided to go back to the SAR van and check progress with Callie. But as he opened his truck door, Callie came barreling out of the back of the van, carrying a helmet in one hand and pulling her jacket hood up over her cap with the other. She hurried over to Mason's vehicle.

"They found it!" she called as he got out of his truck. "The K9 team. They found the wreck in the shallow end of the large pool in our highest-POD area." Her cheeks were flushed and her eyes were bright with excitement. "Oskar and the rope guys have managed to hook on to it. They're winching it out right now. Come." She thrust the helmet at him. "I can get us into the pools via ATV. You'll need to drive your own—I've got no one to leave Benny with. He has to come."

Ben exited the van dwarfed in a borrowed and oversize KSAR jacket. His wig had been exchanged for a helmet, and his arms looked overly long with adult gloves dangling on the ends. *Comical* was the word that slammed into Mason. And touching. Ben scurried after his mother, who was making for two quads parked in mud behind the SAR van. Mason followed, trying to recall when he'd last driven a four-wheeler. Mostly relief pulsed hot in his veins. They'd found the wreck. And fast. Thank God. It absolved him of his stupidity. Somewhat.

"You do know how to drive one, right?" Callie asked as she helped Ben up onto one of the quads.

"Yeah." He straddled the seat and started the engine. It coughed to life under him in a nice throaty growl. He pulled on the helmet.

Callie donned her own helmet and climbed onto her seat. Ben, sitting behind his mom, wrapped his arms tightly around her. She started her engine, made a call on her radio, and was off into the woods.

Mason followed along the twisting trail. It snaked and climbed through the trees. Callie set a fast clip. It took all of Mason's focus to just keep pace and remain upright. But twenty minutes into the ride, he got the feel, and Mason felt a punch of exhilaration, something akin to freedom. This focus on the trail, this speed, this novelty had—just for a few moments—afforded him a means of outrunning his ghosts.

Maybe Kluhane Bay wasn't going to be such a bad decision after all.

They crested a ridge, and Callie slowed. He followed suit. Going at a moderate pace now, Callie started down a steep and slippery incline.

She paused once to check over her shoulder to see how Mason was doing. He gave her a gloved thumbs-up. She proceeded down the trail.

Suddenly, through the gaps in the trees, through the shifting curtains of clouds, he glimpsed the river pools below, and he heard the roaring sound of the falls upriver. He stopped his quad. For a second he just took it in. It was stunning. Wild and utterly, rawly beautiful. In the mist, along the edge of the top pool, he saw the bright-red jackets of the KSAR techs working with ropes and a pulley system to drag the wreck out of the water.

He followed Callie down to join them.

They parked on the trail a short distance away. Ben remained on the ATV. Mason and Callie removed their helmets and climbed farther down the steep slope to the rocks along the water.

As they reached the rocks, the wreck broke the surface. The guys hauled it, creaking and groaning, onto a flat rock ledge. The aircraft had lost both pontoons, and the wings were more damaged than before, and the fuselage was crushed on one side.

Oskar waded into the shallow water and peered inside to look at the pilot. His body went still. Callie and Mason moved into the shallows to see more. Oskar straightened. He turned to Mason, not Callie. His face was white.

"You need to see this, Sergeant."

Mason waded out farther into the icy shallows. He removed his flashlight from his duty belt and bent to look into the dark shadows inside the crushed cockpit. The pilot was still strapped in. But her face had been gashed and torn. A feeling of sickness washed into Mason's throat. He'd done this by sending her over the falls. Her head hung at a different and awkward angle. He ran his beam over her. Then he saw it. The knife.

His heart kicked.

He leaned in closer.

"Shit," he whispered.

The knife stuck out of the pilot's neck on the right side. Stabbed in to the hilt. From how the blade was positioned, Mason guessed it would have severed her carotid instantly. Next to the blade was another entry wound, bloodless, diamond-shaped, gaping open. It appeared that whoever had done this might have taken two plunges with the blade. The first perhaps tentative, or missing its mark, the second likely fatal. This pilot would have bled out within minutes. His brain reeled. Could she have been stabbed up in the air? Was this what had brought the Beaver down? What of the assailant, then?

"It looks like a Schrade," Callie said quietly.

He hadn't noticed her come up to his side.

"A what?"

"A Schrade. An old hunting knife. People call it 'the Sharpfinger' because of the aggressive, hooked tip on the blade. It's vintage—see those leather washers in alternating browns around the handle?" She reached in and pointed. "And there's oxidization on the blade, just below the guard there. It's made of carbon steel, which develops that nice patina. Stainless steel is newer and doesn't do that."

He shot her a hard look. "*Nice* patina?"

"My father was a collector. I have his collection still."

"I need your team to stand back, Callie. This is now a homicide investigation."

THE LODGE PARTY

MONICA

Sunday, October 25.

Monica allowed Deborah to lean heavily on her and Nathan as they helped the woman limp up the path from the dock. Monica felt for her. Not only was the lake cold, the shallows into which Deborah had fallen were brackish, slimy, and full of reeds. A rank smell emanated from her sodden clothes, and her hair and face were plastered with fine mud and vegetal detritus.

They moved slowly through the drumming rain because the overgrown path that led up to the lodge was muddy and also slippery. Brambles full of dead leaves covered the cleared area around the lodge, and mushrooms and moss sprouted from everywhere—this place didn't get much sun.

An odd place to build, thought Monica, here in the dank fungi-infested shadows of the tombstone mountain.

Beyond the bramble patches, the trees closed in. From the aerial view they'd just been afforded, the surrounding forests were endless over impassable mountain ranges that stretched forever. Branches swayed in the wind, and the forest creaked and moaned. Thick fingers of mist sifted around the lodge. The building was big. Two stories. Constructed of giant logs that had weathered over the years. A row of dirty windows upstairs watched their approach like cataract-hazed eyes.

As they neared the totem poles, Monica glanced up.

Moss and lichen crept up the totems. Atop one of the raven's wooden wings, a live crow perched like a judge in black robes. She glanced at Nathan, saw that he was studying the totems, too. His face was tight. Her husband looked as scared as she felt right now. This thought sent an odd punch of resentment through Monica. She wanted Nathan to fix this. To be more capable. To save her like a knight in shining armor. On some level she knew, deep down, that she wished Nathan would impress Steven. She wanted Steven to be jealous of Nathan, not condescending toward him. The sad fact of Monica's life was that while her husband adored her, he sometimes embarrassed her just by being himself. She felt this reflected badly on her own image, that she should've been capable of attracting a more alpha male as her partner in life, that people took her less seriously because she'd married *Professor Mushroom*, who was losing his hair and going soft around his belly.

The crow suddenly spread its wings and swooped away, a dark shadow in the rain. It vanished into the thick clouds rolling down the granite mountain.

She glanced back over her shoulder to see if Stella and Jackie were still arguing. But Stella had climbed inside the plane and was now handing bags down to Jackie, who was passing them to Steven to carry to the end of the dock.

"They're fetching our bags from the plane," Monica told Deborah. "We'll have you cleaned up and into some dry clothes in no time. And Steve can take a look at your ankle. He's a doctor—I'm sure he'll be able to help."

"So it's *Steve* now?" Nathan said over Deborah's head. "Not *Steven?*"

Monica shot him a hot look of warning.

A noise sounded in the forest, a crack, then a sharp rustle. They all stopped in unison and stared into the shadows.

The forest around them stirred and whispered. Monica's heart beat faster. The woods appeared sentient, displeased with their arrival. Nathan liked to think of trees in this anthropomorphic way. He liked to remind her how they were all connected belowground by a mycelium network, an information highway whereby they could talk to each other, warn each other of pending danger, or death, or looming disease. It gave Monica the creeps. So much so that she resisted accompanying Nathan whenever he invited her on one of his mushroom forages through the woods near their house. He'd managed to make the woods feel malevolent to her.

"What was that?" Deborah whispered, eyes wide.

Monica squinted into the darkness between the trunks. She thought she saw something dark weaving through the trees, then it was gone.

"Probably just the wind," she said crisply. "Come, let's see if we can get inside that lodge."

Steven came stomping up the path behind them carrying two bags. "I'll see if it's open." He went past them.

"What if someone is in there?" Deborah called after him.

"Then they can light us a fire and make us some supper," he yelled without looking back. "But I doubt it—looks like it's been deserted for years."

He clumped up the wide stairs and onto the landing in front of the door beneath the antlers.

Nathan lowered his voice. "What in the hell *is* he doing here anyway?"

"You heard Amanda," Monica said curtly. "He was invited to assess the place for potential, like we were."

"It's weird."

"It's *not* my fault, okay? Stop acting like it's my fault, that I invited him. I had no idea."

Deborah began shivering hard against Monica's body.

"I didn't *say* it was your fault," he hissed over Deborah's head. "I said it's weird, as in, it's a strange *coincidence* that he's here."

"A coincidence that Steven runs a cosmetic surgery clinic? And I run an organic food outlet with a catering arm? Both of ours are top-of-the-line businesses, Nathan. What's so strange about the fact that we should *both* be invited to tender for a high-end contract? You're overreacting."

"You know what's fucking strange, Monica, is that clearly this is not about a high-end contract. That"—he pointed to the hulking black building—"is most definitely not the luxurious Forest Shadow Wilderness Resort & Spa. It was fucking weird to begin with—the idea that cosmetic surgery patients would want to travel this far to 'recuperate.' If you ask me, Dr. Steven should have thought so himself. Unless he's up to something."

She met her husband's eyes and began to understand his fear.

Their conversation from last night echoed in her brain.

"I know Bart Kundera from somewhere, but can't recall where," Nathan said. *"I don't have a good feeling about it."*

"Did you ask him?" Monica asked.

"He said he didn't think he'd met me before, but he couldn't be certain."

And this morning Monica had seen Bart studying Nathan intently over breakfast, possibly racking his brains trying to recollect something. Or had he remembered?

They also both knew Katie Colbourne's face from the nightly news back when they used to live in Vancouver. Images of Katie Colbourne holding the mike were indelibly scored into Monica's brain, coupled tightly with a nightmare she wished she could forget, because Katie had covered *the incident*. That was how Monica thought of it. *The incident.* Not naming it kept it removed from her conscience. It allowed Monica to consider it as something that didn't really belong to her.

But *the incident* had been newsworthy, so it was to be expected that Katie had covered it.

And Katie Colbourne knows nothing about my connection to the incident. *Nothing at all. We managed to keep it quiet. We got away with it. So there's* nothing *to worry about.*

But now there was Steven. He was inextricably tied to *the incident.* And he was here.

A dark, cold dread began to unfurl in Monica's chest. Something deep and unbidden began to knock at the walls of consciousness that she'd erected around the old and buried memories.

"If I'd known he'd be here, I wouldn't have come," Nathan whispered. "How can you expect me to spend a full ten days with—"

"We won't!" Deborah interjected forcibly. She shuddered, and her teeth chattered. "She . . . S-S-Stella w-will fly us out. We'll g-g-go home tomorrow. We *won't* s-s-spend ten days here. It's all been a big, t-t-terrible mistake."

They'd reached the stairs. Katie Colbourne appeared out of nowhere, filming them again. Irritation flared through Monica.

"Can you just fucking quit that?" Monica snapped.

Katie lowered her camera and looked Monica in the eyes. "I'm sorry," she said coolly. "But you all signed—"

"We signed up for a fucking luxury spa trip, Katie," Steven barked as he raised his fist and bashed on the lodge door. "So get off your high horse."

Katie scowled. Steven banged three times and hollered, "Anybody here? Anyone home?"

A hollow booming echoed inside the building.

Monica's heart beat faster.

Steven thumped the door again, then tried the handle.

It was unlocked. They all fell silent as he creaked open the heavy wooden door, his triathlon-honed body wire-tense, as if he were primed to dart backward should something come at him.

"Hello?" he called into the dark house.

Silence. The house seemed to breathe out of the door, releasing a dank, musty scent. Steven pushed the door open wider. He picked up the bags and entered.

Monica, Nathan, Deborah, and Katie followed.

"Hello! Anyone home?" Steven called again loudly.

Dust motes drifted down in the dark gloom. As Monica's eyes adjusted, shadows took shape. They were standing in a cavernous room with a vaulted roof that reached up to the second floor. Wooden stairs climbed to a balcony that ran in front of doors upstairs. A monstrous rock fireplace took center stage along one wall. Leather-covered sofas and chairs with ball-and-claw feet were grouped around a coffee table in front of the hearth. A long dining table stood near an archway that seemed to lead into a kitchen. On the coffee table was a leather-bound book and what appeared to be some kind of chess game with carved wooden figurines atop a stone checkerboard. Monica let go of Deborah, leaving Nathan to support her.

She stepped deeper into the room.

Turning in a slow circle, she took in the balcony that ran in a U shape above them. Native masks—horrific things with long, wiry black hair and gaping mouths—hung on the wall next to the staircase. A rifle and an old fishing creel were mounted on another wall above an antique-looking desk. Massive oil paintings in heavy frames adorned another wall. Spaced between them were mounted heads of taxidermy. A deer. A snarling cougar. A moose. It was like some kind of museum. Monica felt as though they'd stepped through a portal and back in time, or into some strange alternate universe.

"Hello!" Steven yelled again. More dust motes drifted down, floating softly on currents of air disturbed by their entrance. They all looked up for the source of the dust. Above them hung a chandelier made of antlers. It was the size of a Volkswagen Beetle.

"Anyone here?" Steven yelled, his voice catching slightly.

Sound boomed and bounded back at them. The house seemed to creak. Or was that just the wind increasing outside and blowing through the rafters?

"Jesus, Steven, quit your bellowing," Nathan snapped. "There's no one here."

A scurrying sounded in the fireplace. They spun to face the noise. It came again—tiny nails scritching against rock. Monica's pulse quickened.

They exchanged glances.

"Just a rat or something," Steven said quietly.

Monica went toward a door that led off the big room. She opened it carefully. "Oh, look," she exclaimed. "There's a huge bathroom in here. With a tub and everything." She entered and reached over the bath. She turned on the copper tap. The pipes banged, coughed. Water shot out of the faucet in a tea-colored gout, then another. It began to run clear, pipes chugging as a pump worked somewhere in the innards of the building.

"The water must come from a well," Steven said from the door. Nathan came up behind him, helping Deborah. Katie remained in the great room, filming again.

"Or it's pumped straight from the lake," Nathan countered.

Steven threw him a dark look.

"There's a gas heating mechanism above the bath," Monica said. "It looks like it heats the water as it comes up through the pipes." She turned the knob on the heating apparatus, and a small blue flame spurted to life. "We've got hot water at least."

"Just don't drink it before boiling it properly," Nathan said.

"Deborah, come on inside, honey." Monica held out her arm. "We can get you washed and warmed up in here. Nathan, can you fetch Deborah's bag? Steven, maybe you could see if there's a kitchen with some supplies, and make us some tea or coffee or something."

Monica helped Deborah limp over to a wooden stool under a framed piece of cross-stitched verse that hung on the wall.

There were even towels on a rail. She sniffed one. It smelled musty, like it had been in a closet a long time, but seemed clean. "See if one of you guys can maybe get a fire going?" she called after the men as Nathan closed the bathroom door.

Monica helped Deborah shuck off her wet jacket and take off her shoes and socks. Nathan returned with Deborah's bag.

He set it on the floor at her feet and hesitated. "I'm sorry, love," he said quietly.

Monica nodded. "It's okay."

He cupped the side of her face. Forcibly. Which startled her. He forced her to look up and directly into his eyes. "It's going to be fine," he said firmly.

She held his gaze, swallowed.

"It will," he said. "We'll get through."

With his words came unexpected emotion. She blinked it back. He loved her. He always had. He'd move heaven and earth for her, and he had. Maybe she didn't love him back enough, and it hurt him. She knew that. Maybe she'd pushed him too far, gotten too complacent. But being here, with Steven, and with Katie Colbourne bringing back memories of that awful time, she realized she needed him. She needed him, and he needed her, because they shared a secret that could destroy them both. Along with Steven. And the weight of bearing that secret alone all these years would have been impossible.

Nathan turned to go. But as he exited the bathroom and began to close the door, she called out to him.

"Leave it ajar, will you? Just . . . a little."

Their eyes met. He nodded.

Monica turned back to Deborah. That's when she registered the words of the cross-stitched verse above Deborah's head.

Cursed are those who Sin
And Lie to cover their deeds
For a Monster will rise within
And they must Repent.

She stilled and caught sight of her own face in the rust-pocked mirror above the antique basin.

"What is it?" Deborah asked, noticing the sudden change in Monica.

"I . . . uh, nothing. Nothing at all. Do you want some help getting into the bath?" she asked as she leaned over to turn off the taps.

But a disquiet had entered her heart.

THE LODGE PARTY

NATHAN

Nathan found Steven—golden-haired, triathlon-honed, moneyed, philandering, plastic-surgeon Steven—in the massive lodge kitchen, knocking about on an old gas range.

The kitchen was dark and sooty-looking. A huge island with a chopping board took up the center. Above the island hung an assortment of tarnished copper frying pans, cast-iron pots, and other cooking implements. On the stone surface of the island sat a wooden block that contained knives in varying sizes. A meat cleaver the size of a man's shoe lay atop the chopping board alongside a flesh tenderizer that reminded Nathan of medieval torture tools.

"Jesus," he whispered. "Like something out of another time, or a horror movie."

Steven glanced up. "Gas," he said, patting the range. "Looks like the pipe feeds in from a large propane tank out back." He wiped a smear of grime off a windowpane that looked out toward the rear of the lodge. "See?" He pointed.

Nathan came over and peered through the grime. Bart was outside there, poking around in the fog under the cover of an open-sided shed stacked with wood along one wall. Bart saw them. He raised an ax high above his head and brandished it with a gleeful grin. He pointed to the pile of logs. In his other hand he held a big knife with a violently hooked tip.

"What in the hell is he doing?" Nathan said.

Steven opened the window.

"Wood is dry!" Bart yelled. "Got an ax and tools and everything. We can make fire." He slid the ghastly knife into a sheath he'd attached to his belt. He shot them another triumphant-warrior grin before positioning a crudely split log on a piece of stump. He planted his feet wide, swung the ax up high above his head, and brought it down with a loud thump. The log was cleaved in two. Nathan felt a shiver.

"He's like a wretched Boy Scout on some adventure camp," Steven muttered, pulling the window closed. "Far too happy for my liking. He's weird."

Through the grime-streaked panes Nathan watched Bart chopping for a moment. The guy was in his prime. Muscular, fit. *Virile.* He appeared to approach life as though it was one big, exciting adventure and he had the cojones to relish it. When had Nathan stopped living like that? Had he ever relished life like that?

Maybe that was his problem. As he watched, he searched his memory again for where he'd seen Bart Kundera before. The more he watched, the more the sensation niggled at him.

"It works!" Steven hooted.

Nathan jumped.

Steven pointed at the gas range. Little blue flames danced around one of the burners. "The range works." The surgeon grabbed a kettle with a whistle from beside the stove and went to the sink. He turned on the tap. The plumbing clunked and the pumps sounded again. Water gushed out. He ran it until it looked clear, then rinsed and filled the kettle. He set it on the stove.

Nathan watched. He felt like he'd slipped into some alternate reality.

"Tell me, Steven, what ever made you think a wilderness spa thing would work with your clinic?" he asked.

Steven hesitated. For a moment he wouldn't look at Nathan. Then he said quietly, "I wasn't sure. Cosmetic tourism is a thing. There could have been a partnership, an opportunity for marketing. I just wanted to check it out."

"Why? Because you knew Monica was coming?"

Steven glowered at Nathan. Danger simmered into the air. Nathan became conscious of all the knives and the meat cleaver and the heavy cast-iron frying pans and cooking implements all around them.

"Find some mugs, will you?" Steven said as he turned toward a counter.

Nathan wavered. He didn't trust the guy, but decided to drop it, for now. Clearly everything about this situation was strange. He opened several cupboard doors in succession until he discovered one that contained glasses and pottery mugs. He reached for a mug.

"What in the hell?" Steven said.

Nathan turned, mug in hand.

Steven was holding a colorful box of kids' cereal that he'd taken from a paper grocery bag on the counter next to the stove. A frown creased his brow.

"Tooty-Pops?" said Steven. "Strawberry flavor?" He dug back into the bag and took out a sales receipt. "Bought just over a month ago. Someone was inside this lodge not that long ago." Steven looked more closely at the receipt, and his face suddenly lost color. "This is weird," he whispered. "This is fucking weird."

"What is?"

He held the receipt out to Nathan. "Look where the cereal was bought."

Nathan took the receipt. He read the name of the store. His heart spasmed. A buzz began in his ears. Slowly he glanced up. Steven's gaze locked with his.

"The Kits Corner Store," Steven said. "Off West Fourth."

An image sliced hot into Nathan's mind. Monica sobbing in their old bedroom. Her face red, bloated, blotchy, her words coming between ragged breaths. *I . . . I saw a cereal box, Nathan. It was squashed and the cereal was rolling out . . . little bits of color in the rain. And eggs, broken eggs.*

"What else is in the bag?" Nathan demanded. His voice came out low, hoarse.

Steven took out a carton containing a dozen organic eggs, followed by a Snickers bar.

Nathan's knees sagged. Time stretched. It hadn't been on the news. The part about the eggs and the cereal and the chocolate bar. The cops had held back that information for some reason. Only he and Monica knew. And Steven knew. He felt sick. He was going to throw up.

Steven had gone quiet. He stared at the receipt.

"We . . . used to live down that street," Nathan whispered. "Two blocks from that store."

But Dr. Steven Bodine knew that. He knew it very, very well.

Memories swelled between the two men. Memories shared but not shared. They grew into a tangible thing in this sooty kitchen. The thing that bound and divided them. The thing Nathan had thought he'd managed to bury and forget years ago. The thing that in the end had forced him and Monica to move east, to escape. To try and start over. He tried to focus on the cereal box. Tooty the pelican, eating Tooty-Pops. Steven standing there, holding the box. Links and chains of the past locking and clicking and twisting around them both.

Neither wanted to put into words this amorphous thing. Neither of them seemed to be able to even begin to grasp what was happening, let alone attempt to articulate it.

Bart burst in through the back door with an armload of wood. They both jumped.

"What is it?" He looked from one man to the other.

"Nothing." Steven cleared his throat.

"The gas stove and the gas water heaters work," Nathan said. "And there's plumbing." He turned his back on them and busied himself taking mugs out of the cupboard in an exaggerated fashion. His heart hammered in his chest. Sweat prickled across his lip.

"And there's tea, coffee, tins of tuna, and soup," Steven said as he hurriedly opened more cupboards.

Bart frowned. "Well, at least we won't go hungry." He made for the living area, paused. "I found a path. It looks like it leads around to the other bay, but it was getting too dark to follow without a flashlight."

"Do you think it might lead to the real lodge?" Steven asked.

Nathan blinked. It was like the doctor was reaching for straws by asking—as if hoping, still, that their pilot had just made some terrible screwup with the GPS coordinates.

Bart said, "We can check again in the morning to see if—"

"There *is* no real lodge." Jackie appeared in the doorway that led from the great room into the kitchen.

They all turned to look at the solid woman with intense eyes.

"This is no mistake," she said curtly. "This is a con, some sick game."

"What do you mean?" Bart asked.

"Did you guys not see the plaque outside, next to the front door? This place *is* called Forest Shadow Lodge. As in Forest Shadow Wilderness Resort & Spa. Here, look at this." She pulled a brochure from her pocket and smoothed it out on the kitchen island.

"I printed it off the website before I left home." She jabbed a photo of the luxury lodge. "It's fake. It's photoshopped, because it's using the same location. See this bay here? And the shape of this one here? This mountain? This is how the terrain looked from the air. It's *this* spot, but someone has photoshopped the spa into the location. They've erased parts of the forest, added cabins and trails, plus interior shots from some other spa and lodges." She met their gazes. "This whole thing was faked from the get-go. We were lured here. All of us. And now we're trapped."

A sinister cold seemed to enter the kitchen. A shutter banged upstairs, and the wind whistled. Mist, cloying and wet, pressed up against the windows. It grew darker inside.

"Why?" Bart asked, still holding his wood.

"God knows." Jackie dragged her hand over her hair. "But right now, we're stuck. We've been baited and lured into some weird kind of wilderness prison."

"We are not trapped." Stella entered the kitchen. "We have a plane. And you guys have a pilot—me. We have fuel. We—"

"We have no bloody radio!" Jackie snapped, whirling round to face Stella, her eyes furious.

"What?" said Steven.

"That's right," Jackie said. "Go on, tell them, Stella."

Stella's gray eyes flashed, shooting daggers at Jackie.

"Go on. Tell them. The radio is broken. Sabotaged, wires cut."

"But I heard you speaking to your dispatch on the radio," Nathan said.

"But it wasn't working, was it, Stella?" Jackie said. "Your dispatch couldn't hear you, could they? No one even knows where we are, do they?"

Stella's features went tight.

"So when were you going to tell us this, Stella?" Steven asked.

"I didn't want to say right away. Fear, worry, is not a good thing when—"

"When *what*? Jesus. Who are *you* to decide what's right and wrong for us to know?" Steven barked. "You're just the pilot, not the boss of our lives, for Chrissakes."

"There's a chance I could fix it in the morning. If I can—if it's an easy fix—you'd never have to have known about it."

"So you thought you'd play God?" Steven snapped. "Because we would all *panic*." He wagged jazz hands at the sides of his face.

"And you're not panicking?" she said.

Silence swelled in the kitchen. It felt for a bizarre moment as though the house were listening. Alive. Hostile. Nathan felt hairs rise along his arms. He was sensitive to these things. He could feel trees in the forest watching and listening to him.

Bart broke the silence. "When did you learn the radio was damaged?"

Stella inhaled deeply and palmed off her wet cap. "It was working when I flew into Thunderbird Ridge yesterday afternoon. I discovered it was malfunctioning right after we took off this morning."

They stared at her, stunned.

Bart cleared his throat. "So someone damaged it during the night at Thunderbird?"

"It looks that way," Stella said.

"So we have no way of getting word out?" Steven asked. "Nothing at all. And no one is expecting us to call, either, because we told family and friends we'd be out of cellular contact at some secret location for ten days."

Nathan said, "If we're not back within the ten days, at least West Air will know where to send people to find us."

"No, they won't," Stella said. "I only received the GPS coordinates by text last night. I called them in to my dispatch when I took off this morning, but that's when I realized the radio wasn't working."

"Yeah," Jackie said. "Didn't you guys notice that we were only hearing *her* end of the conversation in our headsets? We heard no replies from West Air dispatch. It's supposed to be two-way communication."

So that was what Jackie had confronted Stella about at the dock, Nathan thought. That was what they'd been arguing about.

"What about Amanda Gunn?" Bart asked. "Does she have the coordinates?"

"No. Like I said, I got them exclusively via direct text from the RAKAM Group."

"So the RAKAM Group knows," Nathan said. "They will send someone."

"Yeah, right," Jackie scoffed. "The RAKAM Group who apparently faked this whole fucking thing. Do you really think they're going to send someone to get us out now?"

"Fuck," said Bart. "Why would someone do this? What in the hell *is* this? What's going on?" He looked from one to another, his arms beginning to show strain under his heavy load of logs.

"We need to do some triage here," Stella said. "That storm front is socking us in. Right now it's just heavy rain, but it could turn to snow before morning. But we've got our bags, warm clothes. We've got wood. We can make fire." She nodded to the open cupboards behind Steven. "Looks like we won't go hungry immediately. So we'll eat, hunker down, stay warm until the storm blows through, then we'll fly home and report this."

"No . . . no, I am *not* accepting this situation." Anger pulsed in Steven's words. Anger that was underscored with panic. It gave Nathan a smug satisfaction to see the surgeon flustered, *frightened*.

"Listen to her, Steven," Nathan said. "It makes sense. We could potentially fix the radio in the morning and have it all sorted out by tomorrow. There's nothing more we can really do in the dark with the storm closing in. Monica is getting Deborah bathed and warmed up. You're the doctor—you can look at Deborah's ankle. We'll warm up some of the food from those tins in the cupboards and figure out what do next."

"How long was this front forecasted to last?" Jackie asked Stella.

"Several days." Stella rubbed her mouth. "Maybe a full week."

Another beat of silence filled the room. The wind scratched tree branches along the wall outside, and a strange moan came down the stone mountain.

A whistle shrieked. They all jumped. The kettle. It was boiling and the steam was causing it to shrill loudly.

They laughed out of nerves. An ugly sound. All except Jackie, who scowled silently at them.

Steven removed the kettle, his muscles rippling like a visible current under his shirt.

"Nathan," Stella said, "why don't you go help Monica get Deborah onto the sofa in front of the hearth? Bart, could you build the fire?"

Bart seemed to suddenly recall he was cradling an armful of split wood. "Yeah, yeah, sure." He exited the kitchen with his load.

"Where is Katie?" Stella asked.

"Filming outside the front entrance," Jackie said curtly as she turned and walked out of the kitchen.

Steven poured hot water over a tea bag and said to Nathan, "Who in the hell does that pilot think she is, ordering us around? Who made *her* boss? Who put her in charge of—"

"Oh, shut up, Steven. She's the one making sense," Nathan said, voice clipped. But something about Stella was now bugging him as well, something he couldn't put his finger on.

"And I'm not?" snapped Steven. "Is that what you're saying?"

A bitterness filled Nathan's mouth. He lowered his voice. "I *know* you, Steven."

Steven's eyes narrowed. They held a look of poison. At this very moment Dr. Steven Bodine looked like a man who could kill. And Nathan knew for a fact he already had.

"Oh, do you now?" Steven said.

"I do." Nathan's words came out slow, deliberate, his gaze locked on Steven's. "Monica told me a lot about you. We shared. Everything."

Steven swallowed.

"The reason Stella Daguerre rubs you the wrong way is because she doesn't prostrate herself in front of your golden surgical godliness—am I right? You feel she disrespects you and undermines you. She irritates you because she's actually more in control than you are, and she's a woman to boot. One who'd never think to open her legs for you."

"Fuck you, Nathan," Steven whispered. Heat crackled between the men. "You know *fuck*." The surgeon glanced at the door and dropped his voice to an even quieter whisper. "There's a reason your wife cheated on you."

"I could destroy you, Steven. I could destroy your clinic."

"And if you do, you go down, too, brother. *Both* of you." A pause. A slow smirk. "And you don't have the balls. You know what your problem is, Professor Fungus? The trouble with you is you actually love her."

Nathan's neck muscles corded. His hands fisted. He glanced at the array of knives in the block on the counter. For a wild moment he actually felt like grabbing one and sticking it deep into Steven Bodine's gut. He wanted to kill him. Yes, he did.

Steven's smirk deepened. He picked up the mug of tea. "She controls you, Prof. She's got you tight by your thinning short ones." He carried the mug past Nathan, bumping into him as he whispered into his ear, "The pussy-whipped professor doesn't have the cojones to take me down, do you now, Nathan?"

The words hung in the empty kitchen like a dare.

Nathan's heart thumped against his ribs. His fingers twitched at his sides.

He glanced again at the knives.

THE LODGE PARTY
KATIE

Katie Colbourne helped Stella carry bags to the rooms upstairs while the others got the fire going downstairs. Stella wore a headlamp she'd brought with her—part of her pilot emergency kit on the plane. And they'd lit one of several kerosene lanterns they'd found in a storage area off the kitchen.

On the top floor were seven bedrooms, each with a door opening onto the U-shaped balcony that looked down over the great living room. Four bedrooms overlooked the lake, and the remaining three had windows that faced the base of the mist-shrouded mountain behind the lodge. Each room hosted a double bed, a freestanding wooden closet, plus a chest of drawers. A small bathroom led off each. The decor consisted of antique pieces from a mix of periods.

"There's a room for each of us," Katie said to Stella as they placed bags outside the doors.

"As long as the married couple shares a bed," Stella said, entering one of the lake-view rooms. "Do you want this one?"

Katie entered behind Stella. She plonked her bag down beside a dark four-poster bed with white linen that was faintly yellowed. She touched the linen, then lifted a corner and sniffed it. It smelled stale. A small shiver chased down her spine.

Stella went to put her own bags in the adjacent room, then rejoined Katie.

"I found another kerosene lantern." The pilot held up an old copper lantern with a flickering flame. Shadows jumped and trembled around the room as Stella moved. A noise reached them from outside. A rhythmic chop, chop, chop. Bart splitting more logs for the fire.

Katie watched Stella go to the window and peer through the gloomy twilight. She was looking at her plane. Katie joined her.

"What do you think actually happened to the radio?" Katie asked quietly.

Stella inhaled deeply. The pilot's face was pale and angular in the lantern light. She looked even thinner, tired. Emotion glinted briefly in her eyes.

"I don't know. I can only assume someone got into the Beaver during the night, or in the very early hours of the morning, and cut the wires that lead to the antenna. The radio is an after-manufacture addition." She paused. "Someone knew what they were doing. They went in there with purpose."

"But *why*?"

"That's the million-dollar question, isn't it? Why *are* we all here? Why *us*?"

"What do you think is going on?" Katie asked.

The pilot pursed her lips, thinking. "I just don't know. Could be a terrible mistake that I was sent the wrong coordinates."

But she didn't look convinced.

Quietly, Katie said, "Talk to me, Stella. Tell me what you're thinking."

The pilot smoothed her hand over her hair. "I should have included a radio check in my preflight routine. But it was working yesterday, so I . . . *Shit*. I'm so sorry, Katie. This is my fault."

"No, it's not. You were brought on board for all the same reasons as the rest of us were—with a view to securing a contract. If we've been bamboozled, so have you."

"Apart from Nathan," Stella said.

"What?"

"Nathan. He's just here as his wife's guest. He wasn't invited as a potential tender."

Katie held the pilot's gaze. "Do you think that's significant?"

"I don't know." She fell silent a moment, a look of consternation creasing her brow. "I feel like I know Jackie Blunt from somewhere. And that she also recognizes me. But she says not. And . . . maybe I've even seen Dr. Steven Bodine before. But . . ." Stella swore again. "This whole thing is pure freaky."

Katie felt a tightening in her belly. Stella seemed familiar to her, too. But Katie couldn't place her. Something bigger and darker than she was able to grasp seemed to hover over them all, connecting them in subterranean ways they couldn't figure out yet.

"Is anyone on this trip familiar to you?" Stella asked.

Katie's pulse quickened. She turned to look out the window as she considered her reply, but it had grown fully dark out, and all she saw now were the flickering reflections of herself and of Stella holding the lamp. Cold air emanated from the windowpanes. The glass was thin. It let the outside in.

"I recognize grocery heiress and Holistic Foods CEO Monica McNeill, of course," Katie said slowly. "She was a big local name back when I covered the Vancouver news. Very involved in charities and the whole farm-to-table organic movement at the time."

"Monica's from *Vancouver*?" asked Stella.

"Yeah. They—she and her husband—used to live in Kitsilano." A memory washed through Katie at the thought of the swanky Kitsilano neighborhood in Vancouver, just over the bridge from the downtown core. She'd covered some hot-button stories in that area. But she could think of no place where she'd actually run across Monica McNeill in person. But the feeling she knew Stella began to bang louder among a jumble of forgotten memories inside Katie's head. While working for the TV station, she'd met so many people, covered so many stories, and it was all so many years ago that things ran together in a blur.

"Have you and I met before?" Katie asked Stella.

Stella angled her head. "I . . . don't think so. I mean, I know your face from the news channel, but I'm sure I'd recall having met a real live television personality."

Anxiety deepened inside Katie.

Stella reached out and placed her hand on Katie's arm. "It'll be okay. We'll work it out. Come, let's check out that last room and then go down and sit by the fire and have something to eat."

Stella carried the lantern toward the door. Katie turned to follow. Shadows pounced and scurried, and the movements on the wall made her turn her head. That's when she saw it—the big painting. It had been hidden from Katie's view by the antique closet when they'd first entered.

It was huge—took up half the wall. Done in dark oils. It depicted a life-size rendering of a little girl holding a lantern up in one hand. The girl looked to be about six years old. She wore a diaphanous white nightdress and had bare feet. Her face was turned, as if to look at the painter. Fine blonde hair blew in a soft cloud about her face. In her other hand the girl held a small golden scale with a shallow bowl on either side. Weighing down one of the bowls was what looked like a tiny human heart. The child's face showed a sly smile.

Bile rose in Katie's throat. Her heart began to hammer. She couldn't move. Couldn't breathe.

Stella reached the doorway, turned. "Katie? What's the matter?"

"I . . . I . . ." Katie reached her hand out toward the painting. "That."

Stella frowned and hurriedly reentered the room to see what Katie was pointing at.

"A painting?" Stella said.

"Who . . . who painted it? Where is it *from*?" Katie's voice was hoarse, strangled by sudden fear.

"I don't know."

"Read it—can you read that signature at the bottom?"

Stella gave her an odd look, then moved toward the painting of the little girl. She held the lantern aloft and bent closer to the signature at the bottom right.

"It says JUSTICE."

"Can you read the name?"

Stella looked at Katie. "There is no name. It just says JUSTICE."

Time elongated. As if in slow motion, Katie stumbled toward the four-poster bed and sat on it, suddenly unable to support her weight. She stared at the painting. She was going to throw up.

Stella quickly set the lamp down on the bedside table and seated herself beside Katie. She took her hand. "Katie, look at me. What's going on?"

"The painting . . ." Words died in her throat. Fear clawed her heart.

"It's beautiful," Stella said. "It looks like some antique piece."

"It's Gabby."

"What?"

"It . . . it's Gabby. My daughter." She felt stricken just saying the words.

"What do you mean?"

"I . . ." Tears filled her eyes. Confusion clouded her brain. With trembling hands she ferreted in her jacket pocket and brought out her cell phone. She powered it on and opened her photo app. "See?" She held a photo out toward Stella.

Stella took it. She fell silent, stared at the photo, then looked up at the painting. Her gaze met Katie's. Stella looked shocked. "It's the same," she whispered. "The same pose, same nightdress, same bare feet, same hair, the same smile on her face."

Katie swiped away the tears streaming down her face. "Apart from the scales of justice and the human heart in the bowl. What . . . what is that . . . thing supposed to *mean*?" Katie began to shake violently. The most precious being in her life was her little girl. Gabby. The child who'd changed her, everything about her. Made her rethink the meaning of the world, and even the worth of her marriage to an adulterous man.

"Did you . . . Who would have seen this photo?" Stella asked. "Did you post it on social media?"

"I . . . I know I shouldn't have. I knew it probably was not the smartest thing to publish pictures of my daughter where anyone could access them. Especially given that I was a media personality. But . . . it's such a gorgeous photo." She held Stella's gaze. "Do you think I've put my baby at risk? Oh God." Her hands flew to her mouth. "What if something is going to happen to Gabby while I'm trapped here? What if—"

Stella placed her hand on Katie's arm. "Katie, please, don't think like that. Try to relax. Hysteria is not going to help any one of us. We need to keep clear heads in order to work through this."

With trembling hands Katie smeared away more tears.

"Think for a minute," Stella said. "Who is with Gabby right now?"

"Her father."

"And you trust him with Gabby?"

"Oh God, yes. With Gabby. He . . . he might have cheated on me, but he utterly adores his daughter. He'd kill for Gabby."

A frown creased Stella's brow. She watched Katie's face for a moment.

"I don't mean he'd *kill* kill. Just that . . . if she was threatened . . ." Her voice faded.

"Then she will be fine." But as Stella glanced again at the painting, Katie wasn't so certain that the capable pilot believed her own words. Stella could just be saying things to appear solid.

"Do you have children, Stella?"

"No. I . . . I can't."

"I'm sorry, I—"

Stella waved the words away. "It's okay. Just a fact, that's all."

"Are you married?"

"Divorced," Stella said.

"Why?"

Stella snorted softly and sat silent for a moment. "It was over the child issue," she said finally, turning her face away and reaching for the lantern.

"Oh God. I'm sorry."

Stella came to her feet, lantern in hand. "It's how things go. Life. Come, let's go downstairs. I think we all need to put our heads together and figure this out."

THE LODGE PARTY

JACKIE

The wind pummeled the house and shutters slammed as the storm continued to gather power outside. Trees creaked and scraped against the windows, and strange noises came from the flue. Jackie felt as though the very forest had come alive and was trying to fight its way in.

The group gathered around the roaring fire Bart had built. More logs were stacked high along the stone ledge that ran in front of the hearth, ready to feed the flames and ward off the darkness through the night.

Katie had told them about the painting. The television woman had turned into a hollow husk since she'd seen it, her damn digital camera finally silent in her hands on her lap, her complexion white.

A grandfather clock ticked loudly. Bart had been idiotic enough to wind it up with a big key, and now the pendulum swung back and forth with a loud, judgmental *tock, tock, tock.*

Nathan handed a bowl of soup to each of them. He'd warmed the soup from tins he and Steven had found in the kitchen. No one seemed hungry, but all cradled their hands around the warmth of their bowls, as though the warm food offered a link to the civilized normality of the homes they'd left behind to be forsaken in this place far from humanity, deep in the forest.

The fire popped. A log tumbled. Smoke seeped into the room—the chimney had clearly not been cleaned in a while.

Jackie abruptly set her bowl down on the coffee table and lurched to her feet. She couldn't eat, couldn't sit still. She felt dogged by the troubling connections forming in her mind. She prowled the periphery of the circle gathered around the fire, pulling books off the heavy bookshelf along the wall. Tons of books. Old covers. Some crafted of leather. Some first editions, some signed. Traditional tellings of fairy tales like "Beauty and the Beast" and "Hansel and Gretel." With illustrations that looked nothing at all like the Disney versions of those tales and more like something out of Carl Jung's basement.

"What are you looking at?" asked Steven, his eyes glinting in the firelight.

"Grimms," said Jackie, opening a 1940s illustrated collection of fairy tales.

"Whoever owns this place had money to blow," said Nathan between spoonfuls of soup, watching Jackie intently. He seemed to be the only hungry one. "God alone knows why they just left all this shit out here to gather dust and mold in the shadows of that awful mountain."

Jackie opened another book. Dust puffed out. It smelled like the old bookstores in Toronto she loved to visit. It was her thing. Books. Although people would never guess it by looking at her. And she didn't bother to tell them, either. Didn't care what people thought of her. Not anymore. She valued privacy. She shared the intimacies of life, her passions, only with her partner.

It was an old Agatha Christie. *Murder on the Orient Express.* These closed-room-type mysteries were among Jackie's favorites. She'd loved them since she was a kid. Maybe it was even what had steered her into law enforcement. Puzzles.

She glanced up over the book and regarded Katie again. Someone had gone to great trouble to replicate the image of Katie's daughter in that painting. First they would've had to find the image on social media, and then they would've needed to paint it themselves, or have it commissioned. Then it would've been shipped out here somehow and hung upstairs. It was big. Heavy. Then Katie had been invited on a fake trip to a lodge where she could see it. There was no doubt in Jackie's mind that they'd all been lured here for some perverted reason. Somehow they were all connected. But by what? And why?

She'd recognized Dan Whitlock on the bus. It had taken her a while. It had been almost fourteen years, and Dan had aged. Badly. He'd gone bald. His complexion had coarsened and turned ruddy. His face had swollen and his jowls had grown slack. A double chin, heavy bags under his eyes, and an extra fifty pounds—hardly surprising it had taken her a while to place the seedy-ass PI who'd once hired her to handle some of his dirtiest jobs. She'd been down and out with a predilection for booze herself. She'd needed the money at the time. It had been a dark period in her life.

Suddenly Bart came to his feet. He couldn't remain still, either. He drew back the fire grate, fed another log into the flames. The blaze popped, crackled. He poked the logs, then sat down, got up, walked behind the sofa, went to the base of the stairs, removed one of the indigenous masks from the wall, put it in front of his face, then spun around.

"Whoo!"

"Oh, fuck off, Bart!" Katie snapped.

He lowered the mask. His eyes looked hurt. He hung it back up, reached for the rifle mounted on the wall, cracked it open. He held the barrel to the light and looked into it. Jackie watched as he hung it back on the wall hooks. Her gaze dropped to the vintage-looking knife he'd sheathed at his hip. Bart walked to the old desk, began opening and closing drawers.

"Hey, there's a box of ammo in here." He took out a box of bullets, and his gaze shot back to the gun on the wall.

"Leave it, Bart," Steven said.

Everyone looked at Steven.

"Just leave the gun, okay?"

Bart angled his head. His gaze held Steven's. Jackie could feel the challenge rising between the men. Bart replaced the box, but the air had changed.

Jackie's attention went to Stella, who was fiddling with the smoothly carved figurines on the large stone checkerboard on the table. Picking up one after the other, examining them. Each had been fashioned slightly differently from the others.

Deborah sat on the sofa with her bandaged ankle propped up. Pale, silent, she attempted to eat her soup. Steven had said her ankle appeared sprained, but not badly. He'd said the swelling should go down with elevation and compression. Deborah sensed Jackie looking at her and glanced up. Her eyes met Jackie's.

Where have I seen you and that swallow tattoo before, Deborah Strong? What associates you in my mind with the name Katarina? I know you from somewhere. You know that I know you. You are not who you say you are. What are you hiding? What made you so nervous when I mentioned your tat?

It struck her. A fucking lightning bolt out of a black past—a past that boomeranged right back into Dan Whitlock's orbit. She remembered exactly who Deborah Strong was. Katarina. *Katarina "Kitty Kat" Vasiliev.* A young hooker. Far too young at the time. It was the swallow tattoo and the process of thinking about Dan Whitlock that had unearthed it from deep in Jackie's memory. Her heart hammered. Heat prickled over her skin. Her gaze darted among the others in the group, trying to slot the rest of them into this emerging puzzle. But as with colored squares in a Rubik's Cube, the minute she moved one set of ideas around in her brain, another aspect of the pattern broke apart.

Monica and Nathan were seated beside each other on a sofa, looking strained. Jackie had determined at the floatplane dock that the couple from Toronto knew Dr. Steven from before, and it was causing friction between them. A prickle of perspiration glinted on Monica's upper lip. And Nathan—he kept looking at Bart. Jackie wondered if the married couple knew Bart from somewhere.

Jackie's attention returned to Katie. The TV journalist had covered plenty of stories. She could be indirectly connected via her news coverage to any one of the people in this room. What about Stella Daguerre? Jackie felt she was vaguely familiar, too. It was something in her eyes, in the twist of her mouth when she spoke.

Jackie shut *Murder on the Orient Express* and replaced the book on the musty shelves. That's when she noticed that the book lying on the coffee table was also an Agatha Christie novel. She frowned, reached for it, and dusted off the cover.

Ten Little Indians.

This hardback was old—from the 1930s. Had this Agatha Christie book ever been published in North America under this title? The original title Christie had given her mystery had used the *N*-word and had been rightfully deemed even less PC than *Ten Little Indians*. The book had finally been retitled *And Then There Were None*.

An odd ripple of foreboding coursed through Jackie's veins, more connections forming somewhere deep in her brain. She glanced at Stella again. The pilot was holding a carved figurine and watching Jackie in turn, a strange look on her face. Jackie opened the cover of the book. A piece of paper fluttered to the stone floor. She crouched down, retrieved it, and moved closer to the lantern light in order to read the typed words.

It was some kind of poem, a rhyme.

Nine Little Liars thought they'd escaped.
One missed a plane, and then there were eight.

Eight Little Liars flew up into the heavens.
One saw the truth, and then there were seven.

Seven Little Liars saw they were in a fix.
One lost control, and then there were six.

Six Little Liars tried hard to stay alive.
One saw the judge, and then there were five.

Five Little Liars filed out the door.
One met an ax, and then there were four.

Four Little Liars lost in the trees.
One got stabbed, and then there were three.

Three Little Liars realized what they knew,
One hanged himself, and then there were two.

Two Little Liars went on the run.
One shot a gun, and then there was one.

One Little Liar thinks he has won.
For in the end, there can only be one.
But maybe . . .
                    there shall be none.

Jackie's gaze shot to the figurines.
Fuck me.

"Give me that," Jackie demanded of Stella, holding out her hand for the carving.

Everyone stared at her. Shutters banged. Another log tumbled in the grate, sending smoke into the room. Slowly Stella placed the carved wooden piece into the palm of Jackie's hand.

Jackie examined it closely. She seated herself on the low stone ledge in front of the fire, her back to the flames. She reached forward and picked up each of the carvings in turn, studied them.

Nine pieces. *Nine Little Liars.*

"This is sick," she said loudly. "This is fucking mental."

"What is it, Jackie?" Nathan asked. "What are you seeing?"

She got up, retrieved the piece of paper with the rhyme.

She read it to them.

"Nine Little Liars thought they'd escaped. / One missed a plane, and then there were eight . . ." She reached the final verse. "For in the end, there can only be one. / But maybe . . . there shall be none."

The eyes of the group shimmered in the firelight, faces tight. Complexions waxen. Silent.

"It was in the Agatha Christie book," Jackie said. "The paper with the rhyme was stuck inside a book with a story about a group of individuals— all strangers to each other—who are invited by an anonymous host to a secluded island. Then they all proceed to die, one by one."

"Because they're being punished," said Deborah. "I saw the television series."

"Yes. Because a character in the story—the judge—felt they'd escaped retribution," Jackie said. "So the judge killed them. One by one. Until there were none." She pointed to the carvings. "Those little figurines— there are eight of them on the board." She scooped up another that had been toppled off the side of the board. Its head had been cut off. "And this one? A ninth. Nine Little Liars. This one has to be Dan Whitlock." Jackie wagged the headless carving at them.

"Why?" said Bart.

"Because his head is off, doofus," said Jackie.

Bart's face darkened. "So? What in the fuck is that supposed to mean?"

"That Dan is dead," replied Jackie.

Silence filled the room, save for the *tock, tock, tock* of the grandfather clock.

Katie surged up from her chair. "You don't know that!" Her voice was shrill. She waggled her hand at the checkerboard and the carvings. "This . . . this is ridiculous! You don't know any of this—none of this can be right."

She whirled around to face the others, her eyes manic, and she pointed back at Jackie. "Tell her. Tell her she's mad."

"Is she?" said Deborah.

Everyone fell silent and turned to her.

"How else can you explain all of this? Our invites, this lodge, the GPS coordinates, the painting upstairs, the rhyme typed up and placed inside that old Agatha Christie novel? That hardback was left on the table next to that board so we would see it."

"We're all being punished for something," Monica murmured quietly, her eyes going strange. "Each one of us has been specifically lured here, baited with potentially lucrative contracts that appeal to our individual business, to our greed. And now we are trapped for . . . for some sick-ass game that someone is masterminding. And that . . . that Agatha Christie–type rhyme, it's not the only verse in this house. There is one about sinners in the bathroom. It says those who lie to cover their deeds must repent." She pointed with an unsteady hand to the board with its bizarre carved figurines. "Whoever has done this, they have gone to huge trouble. They are sick in the mind. And they plan to kill us. Like in the story. One by one. And I bet Jackie is right. I bet that Dan Whitlock is dead."

Katie began to cry.

Steven lurched up from his seat. "Oh, come on, don't be so pathetic. This"—he waved his hand at the wooden figurines on the stone checkerboard—"is not some kind of reality murder mystery, for Pete's sake. No one is going to die. Get real. If anything, it . . . it's some kind of hoax."

"Did *you* speak to someone from the RAKAM Group, Steven?" Monica asked.

He glowered at her.

"Well, *did* you?"

"I spoke to Amanda Gunn. She was my contact."

Monica turned to the others. "How about the rest of you? Did anyone here have any contact with a person from the RAKAM Group other than Amanda Gunn?"

No one replied.

The wind slammed against the back of the lodge. The whole building creaked. Flames flickered in the fireplace and in the lanterns.

"Maybe it's Amanda who's behind this," said Bart.

"Or maybe Amanda Gunn was just hired via email by some anonymous person at the so-called RAKAM Group, and she in turn contacted each of us via email."

"They had a website," said Bart. "I checked their website."

"Right," said Jackie. "A site full of fake, photoshopped images, the same fake pictures we were sent in fake email brochures."

Steven yanked his phone out of his pocket and tried to pull up a web page.

"There's no reception out here, Steven," Monica said. "You can't fight your way out of this one. Not this time."

Steven's eyes blazed fire at Monica.

"Fuck this," he whispered. "I'm going to bed." He strode toward the stairs.

"Better lock your door, Steven," Nathan called out to the surgeon as he thumped his way up the steps.

"We better all lock our doors," Deborah said, so quietly she was almost inaudible, her gaze locked hard and fast on Jackie.

And Jackie could see by the look in the woman's pale-blue eyes that Deborah Katarina "Kitty Kat" Vasiliev had just figured out where they'd met in the past.

THE SEARCH
CALLIE

Saturday, October 31.

"We found the crashed plane, Dad. It's a yellow de Havirand." Benny took a bite of his pizza and spoke around his mouthful. Callie chose not to correct her son with the plane name. She was just happy to watch and listen to him chatting with his father. The fried chicken place had been closed when the two of them had finally made it through the snowstorm and rolled into the larger town of Silvercreek, which lay about an hour's drive through the mountains from Kluhane Bay. The snow had started flying heavily along the pass after she'd left Mason and Oskar in charge of things on the Taheese River. The drive had taken far longer than usual because of the conditions. And because of the delay, she'd failed Benny yet again, this time on her promise that they'd have fried chicken when they visited his father.

"And *I* helped, Dad. Mom let me." Ben shot a quick glance at her. Callie smiled, nodded for him to continue.

"When Oskar and the guys pulled the crashed de Havirand out of the river with ropes and stuff, it was upside down and all *smooshed*. And the ponts were missing, and almost one wing was completely gone. And the pilot inside was *dead*." Another glance at his mom. "I heard them say there was a knife in her neck."

Benny watched his dad's face, waiting for a reaction. Peter's eyes were open. He seemed to be watching—perhaps even hearing—his son, but there was no other response. Unlike a patient in a coma who is completely unconscious and appears to be in a deep sleep, Peter had sleep-and-wake cycles. He would open his eyes, breathe on his own, cough, sneeze. His fingers would twitch. And despite his traumatic brain injury, when Benny spoke to him, Callie was convinced she saw flickers of life in Peter's eyes.

He lay slightly propped up in the hospital bed. But tonight he looked thinner than usual. His skin was pale, almost translucent from lack of sunshine. He'd been so tanned, so robust. Her heart ached.

The TV in the corner, suspended from the ceiling, was screening *White Fang*. It was dark outside, and Callie could see their reflections on the window, along with flickering blue light from the television screen. A little family unit. Both the single room and the television cost extra per day. Callie wasn't sure how much longer they'd be able to fund these little perks. Her seasonal work as a guide with an outdoor adventure company ran from May through to the end of October. She took on admin work during the winter, but with no real end in sight she was probably going to have to look for more lucrative employment. Peter was a forester, and his disability pay only took them so far. She smoothed her hand over her hair, then pulled the band out from her ponytail. It was giving her a headache. She felt beyond tired. The search and rescue stuff was all volunteer. It was her passion, and Peter's, and it gave her a way to get out and be with like-minded people, even if the hours were not ideal. She was going to have to make some tough decisions.

She watched Peter's face carefully for reactions as their son chattered on about school, about his missed Halloween party, the funny new puppy his friend had adopted. She knew in her heart Peter was listening, knew it with every fiber of her being. Peter responded well when the musical therapist sang softly to him—she saw it in his eyes. He enjoyed the kiddie movies with action and adventures, too.

Which was why she'd kept paying for the television in his room.

She leaned forward and took her husband's hand. His skin was cool. His nails had been trimmed. Her heart squished in a vise of emotion. This hand had helped her climb so many mountains. It had been so calloused, so strong. With her thumb she gently stroked the back of his hand as she spoke. "Don't worry, Pete, Ben didn't actually see the deceased pilot." She glanced at her son. "Mostly Benny—Ben—helped manage things from the command base." She smiled at Ben. "And when Oskar called in the find, we drove out with the quad. We left Oskar to take over while they waited for the forensic ident team and the coroner to come in, before even considering an extrication. But Benny and me didn't want to miss our visit with you, so Oskar said to go." She paused. "He says hi. They all do. They're waiting for you to come back."

She froze. Had he squeezed her hand? Her gaze shot to Peter's eyes, her pulse quickening.

"There's a new policeman, Dad." Ben pushed his pizza box aside and reached for his juice box. "He came with us on the quads. He's bigger than Officer Ted was. And his hair's black, not yellow like Officer Ted's was."

Callie felt an odd clutch in her chest. She hadn't come right out and told Peter about the new sergeant who'd sent the wreck into the Taheese rapids. Hadn't told him how she found it amusing that the cop was an experienced veteran of major crimes, yet green in the wilderness and afraid of heights. Before Peter's accident they would have opened a bottle of wine on a night like this, after a find, after Benny had gone to bed. And they'd have sat by the fire and laughed and joked about the lighter parts of searches, not being very PC about it all. Being avid climbers who lived for the thrill of heights, they would've laughed smugly about the frightened new cop. And about how out of his depth he appeared. Like policing, SAR had its share of gallows humor and lewd jokes. It had its hierarchal struggles.

And then they would have snuggled. Maybe made love after.

But something had stopped her from mentioning Mason Deniaud.

"It's a homicide investigation now," she explained to Peter. A wisp of worry suddenly curled through her. Did he look even paler than usual? Was that sunken quality to his cheeks more marked tonight?

It's the light. I'm letting my mind run away with me again. I need to stay upbeat. For both Peter and Ben. They both need to believe we're going to be a family again, soon.

"Yeah." Benny nodded his green head eagerly—he'd replaced his wig, but most of his face paint had long been wiped off. It gave his complexion an odd cast. "A bad guy did it and the police will get him!" He clapped his hands. "Wham. Like that. And I helped."

Callie felt a rush of love at the pride in Benny's face, as if he really did have something to do with this. She made a note to herself to concentrate on giving him a sense of greater responsibility in her work. Making Ben feel that he and his mom were more of a team.

"Hopefully the coroner will be able to make an ID soon," she said, taking another bite of pizza and chewing half-heartedly. "Or the ident guys will find something."

Someone entered the room behind her—she saw the reflection on the window.

"Mrs. Sutton?"

Callie glanced around.

"Dr. Stewart?" She came rapidly to her feet and set down her slice of pizza. "I . . . didn't expect to see you tonight."

He smiled, but her stomach tightened as she read something in the doc's face. "What is it?"

"Can we have a word?" He glanced at Ben. "Down the hall. I'll get one of the nurses to keep an eye on Benjamin."

"I . . . uh, sure. Ben, I'll be right back, okay?" She hesitated. "Don't start on the cheesecake without me, you hear?" She made a mock stern face.

"Sure, Mom." He swung his feet back and forth under his chair, his attention shifting to the movie.

Callie followed the doc to a family waiting room.

"Peter's taken a turn, Callie. I just got results back from his recent blood work, and there are signs the bacterial infection in his blood is not responding to treatment. We're getting him onto some stronger IV antibiotics, but if things look to be worsening during the night, we might move him into ICU, where we can keep a closer handle on things."

She felt her skin going hot.

Not again.

They'd been down this road twice already. Infections. Being bedridden and in a vegetative state for more than a year came with all manner of risks. Each time Peter had pulled back.

"He's strong," she said.

"He is."

"Will you, or the staff, call if anything changes? I . . . I've booked a motel room in town, because of the weather, so we'll be close by."

"Absolutely."

Callie thanked the doc. He left the room. She stared after him, then went slowly up to the long window that looked out over the hospital parking lot. In the halos of the lights outside, soft flakes danced. The snow was settling over the cars, and along the road. Soft and beautiful. A peaceful snow globe, but also treacherous. She thought of the challenging hour-long drive over the mountain pass from Kluhane Bay to this town, where there was a large-enough hospital and a special facility to care for someone with Peter's condition. She rubbed her face hard.

It had been fourteen months since Peter's accident on the job. She hadn't known if he'd make it through the coma during those first days. He'd hung in for two weeks. Then he'd come out of the coma, and her excitement and hope had soared to dizzying heights. Then she'd learned that while Peter could open his eyes, and possibly had some level of awareness of things around him, he remained essentially unresponsive, and severely brain damaged. The doctors explained he was in a vegetative state. And she'd crashed back to earth, landed hard. And now . . . this could go on for years. She'd read about a cop on Vancouver Island who'd lasted more than thirty years in a similar state after a fellow officer's car T-boned his during a high-speed response. Maybe she and Ben should move out to Silvercreek to be closer permanently. It would mean Ben leaving his school and his friends, them abandoning their close-knit community, Callie's SAR group. Which was her other family. Her most fervent wish was that Peter would get better and just come home. It *was* possible—she believed it, wanted to believe it. It could happen any day, out of the blue. He could wake up properly one morning and see them all again. Speak to them. What was the point of permanently relocating if Peter suddenly got well? Maybe she could rent out here for a while to see how Ben coped.

Callie composed herself and returned to the ward.

"How's the movie?" she asked Benny.

"Good. Can we have cheesecake now?"

"Sure." She put a hand on Peter's brow. At least they'd be nearby in the motel tonight. And tomorrow was a Sunday. So Benny would not be missing out on school. If need be, they could stay the week, and Ben would just have to catch up.

"If we're gonna be in town, Mom," Benny said, opening the Styrofoam clamshell containing their cheesecake slices, "can we go bowling between visits to Dad?"

"Sure." She tried to smile, but mostly she wanted to cry. She felt beat.

Ben looked at his father. "I want Dad to come, too."

She nodded. "I know, kiddo. Me too."

◆ ◆ ◆

After Ben had taken a bath and was tucked up asleep in his motel room bed, Callie sat thinking in semidarkness on the other bed.

She felt so alone. Which was nuts, because she had Ben. She had so many good people in her life. Friends. Colleagues. They all took turns visiting Peter. So did the guys from his work. There wasn't a day that went by that Peter didn't have somebody at his side. And that was what mattered.

Her mind strayed to the dead pilot, and how she'd looked with the knife in her neck. Who was she?

How had she gotten there?

Did she also have someone who was waiting for her to come home?

Callie swung her feet off the bed and checked on Ben. He was sound asleep. She pulled his covers up higher around his chin and tip-toed out of the room. She went down the passage to where there was an alcove with a window near the stairwell. There was cell service in Silvercreek, so she used her mobile to call Oskar's home landline. Her call was picked up on the third ring.

"Hello?"

Callie's heart sank a little. It was his girlfriend, Melinda.

"Hey, Mel, it's Callie. Is Oskar back from the callout? I was really hoping to hear if the guys had learned anything more about that pilot."

"Not yet. But I ran into Hubb at the diner about an hour ago, and she said Oskar and the techs had been guiding the ident guys and the coroner out to the site at the river. They all wanted to get in tonight so they could set up tents and things before it snowed too much and they lost more evidence. Hubb said she figured the Transportation Safety Board investigators would be flying in by tomorrow morning."

"So no clue yet who the pilot is?"

"Not yet, not to my knowledge."

"Thanks, Mel. I'll call Oskar tomorrow."

"Are you and Benny overnighting in Silvercreek?"

"Yeah. Might be here a day or two."

"Is Peter okay, or is it road closures?"

"He's got another infection. And, yeah, I just got a road alert text that the highway has shut down due to an accident."

"I'm sorry, Callie."

Her words cracked something in Callie. She drew in a shaky breath and pushed a fall of hair off her face, unable to speak for a moment, at least without giving herself away.

"You okay, Cal?"

No. Not really. I haven't been okay for a long time, and I don't think I realized the extent of the toll this is taking on me.

"Yeah, yeah, I'm fine," she said, trying to sound upbeat. "Just wondering how things went with the incident after I left."

She killed the call. It was a police matter anyway now.

Callie returned to her motel room. Ben was still sleeping quietly. She studied his profile in silence and thought, not for the first time, that he was looking more and more like Peter these days. Tears burned into her eyes. She kissed her son lightly on the cheek and felt guilty for wondering what Mason was doing.

THE SEARCH

MASON

Monday, November 2.

Mason watched as pathologist Dr. Caleb Skinner moved the sheet back.

On the steel table lay the body of the decedent. Pilot Doe. A woman of average height, probably in her late forties or maybe early fifties. Well muscled. Fit. Skinner had performed the autopsy this morning. The sutured Y incision was a stark mark against the pale, dead skin.

Mason had come to the morgue—which was in the basement of the Silvercreek Hospital—to hear Skinner's preliminary findings, and to sign into evidence the murder weapon, the pilot's clothes, and anything else found on the body of the decedent. The RCMP North District's serious crime unit had assumed the lead on the case. The investigation was being run out of the North District headquarters in Prince George by a detective named Gord Fielding, with cooperation from Mason and the Kluhane Bay police, plus the RCMP's specialist forensic teams. The Transportation Safety Board was also investigating—customary for aircraft accidents. As more information came in, it was possible that help would be drawn from police in other regions.

There'd been no ID found on the decedent, no wallet. Only a water-damaged cell phone in the back pocket of her jeans. The phone was already in the hands of forensic specialists, who were attempting to recover its data. No registration or other papers, or cargo, had so far been found in the aircraft wreck. No sign of other passengers, either. It was possible things might have been washed out of the body of the aircraft in a crash, or by the wreck's tumbling downriver. SAR techs in conjunction with the police and a K9 team continued to search the riverbanks.

Mason leaned forward to better see what Dr. Skinner was pointing at.

"Two entry wounds in the neck," said the morgue doc. "The first incision here is consistent with the size and shape of the blade that was found inside the other neck wound here."

"So the first wound is shallower?" said Mason.

The pathologist nodded. "Still a downward trajectory, but from a slightly different angle." Skinner raised his arm high above his head, fisted his hand around an imaginary knife handle, and brought down his imaginary blade in a swift stabbing motion.

Mason crooked up a brow at the doc's enthusiastic role play.

"The first strike came in from an angle like that. Downward. But less forceful than the second, which came in harder, and maybe from higher, at an angle like this—" Again Skinner demonstrated with zeal, plunging his imaginary blade in harder.

"So her assailant was likely in a position above her," Mason said, studying the wound. "And either she moved, or the assailant did, before the second strike." He ran his gaze slowly down the rest of her body. His attention settled on her left arm.

"Looks like a possible defense wound here?" He pointed to a slash on the outside of the decedent's left arm.

"It was incurred antemortem, so yes, it's consistent with a defense wound. Incision is also consistent with the hooked tip of the Schrade blade."

Mason's attention went to the woman's hands. Her nails were cut very short, clean. No polish. The only jewelry had been her earrings—tiny silver hoops, one in each ear. And she'd worn a watch, a Garmin. Her silvery blonde hair was cut in one of those trendy super-short styles. The kind Mason for some reason associated with designers, architects.

He lifted her right hand, turned it over. It was cold. No injuries. He moved to her left hand. There was a slice across her palm.

"Another possible defense wound?" he said.

"Again, yes, consistent with the sharp tip of the Schrade."

Callie's words came to mind.

People call it "the Sharpfinger" because of the aggressive, hooked tip on the blade . . .

Mason tried to picture a scenario—the pilot in her seat, becoming aware she was about to be stabbed. Her arms going up, her left hand to protect her face and her right arm to block the attacker. He looked at her face again. The gash across her cheek gaped open. Bloodless.

"That one was incurred postmortem," Skinner said.

Mason nodded, feeling guilt. His gaze shifted back to her hair. "Is that a natural blonde, or gray?" he asked.

"Not a chance. Pilot Doe was a dark brunette. You can see from the roots." He pointed. "But she has some natural silver gray, so she might have colored it to hide that."

Mason chewed the inside of his cheek, considering Pilot Doe's nod to vanity. That and the small earrings. Everything else about this decedent seemed to scream efficiency, functionality. From the trimmed nails to the no-fuss haircut and lack of other jewelry.

"Any other injuries?" he asked.

"Postmortem blunt force trauma, and a fractured right tibia and fibula. Also incurred postmortem."

"So the postmortem injuries are all consistent with a dead body going over a waterfall in a floatplane wreck?"

Skinner nodded.

Mason winced internally.

"So the actual cause of her death was—"

"Exsanguination," Skinner said. "The first wound would not have been immediately fatal, but the second severed the carotid. She bled out. It would have been fast."

Mason looked into Dr. Skinner's eyes. Dark and hooded. The man had a thin face. Thick, black hair. Olive-toned skin. He was about six two, the same height as Mason. Skinner, he thought, was an unfortunate name for a morgue doc.

He turned his attention back to the decedent on the slab and walked slowly around the table, churning things over in his mind.

Who are you?

Were you up in the air, flying the floatplane when you were attacked by a knife-wielding assailant? Was your assailant a passenger? Why an unregistered aircraft? Where does it come from? Where were you flying—en route to pick up cargo? Or had you recently delivered cargo? Perhaps it's lost in the river.

Mason felt in his zone. On familiar ground. He was almost thankful to this Pilot Doe lying on this morgue slab for having rescued him from seeming ineptitude, for giving him the energy to get out of bed this morning. For handing him something to obsess over so he didn't have to think about himself, or his loss. Or too much about the ghosts that had followed him out here.

He went to the bagged evidence on the counter—the Schrade knife, her earrings, watch, clothes.

If the pilot had activated the GPS tracking function on her watch, techs might be able to glean information about where she'd been going.

The brands of clothing she'd been wearing were common outdoor wear brands, and new-looking. They showed no overt clues as to where she might have bought them. A Simms shirt, buttons down the front. A North Face jacket, waterproof. A down fleece by Patagonia. Eddie Bauer jeans. Jockey underwear. Socks by Icebreaker. With a gloved hand, Mason picked up one of her hiking boots. He turned it over. It looked brand new by the minimal wear on the sole. A women's size nine. Made by Merrell. She'd been kitted out in classic wilderness gear. These clothes, to him, felt like they might have all been acquired recently, as if for a special trip. It was a feeling and not a fact, but he'd come to trust his gut reactions. They presented possible investigative avenues, questions that should be asked.

He imagined Pilot Doe again, sitting at the de Havilland Beaver controls in these clothes. An enigmatic woman with short, bleached, silvery-white hair, wilderness flying skills. Fit, capable. He imagined the loud sound of the Beaver engine. Cell phone in her back pocket. He paused the image.

The back pocket of fairly fitted jeans was not the most common place for a female to carry a cell phone. She'd have been sitting on it while flying. Then again, it wasn't unusual to carry a phone there, either, especially for males. He pictured someone else on the aircraft, approaching from behind. Her assailant would have perhaps come up the aisle between the pilot and copilot seats. He imagined her turning. The shock on her face when she realized what was happening. Letting go of the controls to raise her hands in self-defense. The blade plunging in. Plane maybe going down. Pain. Deeper shock. Panic. The pilot trying to move farther back in the small cockpit space as her assailant ripped out the knife and came back in with the more forceful second strike. The killing strike.

It was close range. Personal. Bloody. Messy. Contrary to what was depicted in novels, or on television, unless one was trained to kill, murdering a person up close like this was hard. Unnatural for most. It went against every grain in the human body. Not even cops were trained to kill. Officers were trained instead to halt imminent danger by using potentially lethal force, but they were not trained killers, not like soldiers.

So had this attack been motivated by rage? Some hot passion that would have overridden more logical impulses? Or had the assailant been trained to kill—like an army vet or someone serving in the military? Had the assailant had an exit strategy?

He was eager to hear what the TSB would have to say about the mechanism behind the actual downing of the plane.

He picked up the bag containing the murder weapon. He examined the knife closely. Blunt-looking blade, apart from the tip. Nick marks along the edges. And there was the oxidation. This knife had been well used for a variety of tasks over time, but not recently, given the deep patina on the carbon steel blade.

It looked aggressive. Leather washers that had been shrunk and packed close formed a cover around the handle, which ranged in tone from rust brown to almost black. The washers were coming loose. *Good place to trap DNA,* he thought.

He'd learned more about these Schrade knives since he'd last seen Callie. These Sharpfingers had been manufactured in the United States for a period of fifty years. There were literally millions out there. They held little value for collectors because there were so many. A buyer could snap one up for anything from between five and twenty bucks. The older knives had a tang stamp—a mark on the back portion of the blade. The fact the assailant had left this knife—the murder weapon—in the decedent's neck suggested the attacker had departed in a hurry. And the murder had not been done with much forethought regarding escape. Which steered him back to a killing of passion—rage or fear. Acted out in the heat of the moment.

"Is there any way you might be able to tell from her body whether she'd been flying, and up in the air, when she was stabbed?"

"Negative," said Skinner. "Apart from the fact that I'm not seeing the kind of injuries I'd expect from a plane crash. Then again, I've learned to expect the unexpected in this line of work." The pathologist reached for the sheet. "You done?"

Mason nodded.

Skinner drew the sheet up over Pilot Doe's face. "I've seen people walk away from a serious floatplane crash that by all rights should have killed everyone on board. I've heard several freaky survival stories. Like that one about the female teenager flying in a commercial aircraft over the Amazon jungle when it exploded. Everyone died, but her seat was blown free, and she whirled down, strapped into that seat, from tens of thousands of feet like one of those whirling seedpods. The spinning and the shape of her seat slowing the speed of her plunge. Then she hit massive jungle trees and came down through the canopy with branches breaking her fall before she hit the ground. Seat helped protect her. She lived for weeks on her own before a tribe found her, before she eventually walked out. Depends on the mechanics of a crash." The pathologist handed Mason a clipboard with a sheet of paper to sign. "The TSB investigators should help with that."

Mason signed the page. "Yeah. I'm eager to hear their preliminary thoughts because it's going to take some time before those guys wrap up anything and issue a final report." He handed the clipboard back to Skinner. "You'll be sending the autopsy report direct to Fielding?"

Skinner nodded.

THE LODGE PARTY

BART

Sunday, October 25.

"Karma," Bart said loudly as it struck him. "It's fucking *karma*!"

Steven halted on the stairs. He turned slowly to stare.

Electricity crackled through Bart's blood. "Don't you *see*?"

"See what?" asked Steven, rejoining the circle gathered in front of the hearth.

"The RAKAM Group—RAKAM is an anagram of KARMA." Bart's heart beat slow and steady against his ribs in time with the *tock, tock, tock* of the old grandfather clock. His gaze shot to the shelves of dank and moldering books. Then back to the cedar carvings on the table, the burnished wood of the figurines gleaming in the firelight. Then to the piece of paper with the rhyme lying on the table next to the checkerboard.

He'd thought this was all kind of fun, a wild adventure, when they'd first landed. But now . . .

He took two strides forward and snatched up the headless carving that Jackie had set back on the table. He examined the decapitated wooden torso carefully. "It's been chopped off, and recently," he said.

"See these marks here? See how the wood is lighter, no aging, rough ridges." He held it out for all of them to see.

"If this carving does represent Dan Whitlock," he said, "someone knew one of us wasn't going to make it onto that plane, and they had this waiting here for the rest of us to find."

"Doesn't mean Dan Whitlock is dead," Monica said. "It could just be implied, to make us scared."

"Well, we certainly have no way of knowing whether he is dead or not, now do we?" Steven said.

"Thing is"—Stella sat forward—"Dan Whitlock was on my passenger manifest. There's only room for eight on my plane. If Dan *hadn't* bailed, there'd have been no room for Steven. Bart's right. Someone was *meant* to miss the flight. But like Monica, I . . . I just can't imagine he's dead."

"Maybe *he's* the sick psychopath who's behind all of this," Bart said. "Maybe Dan Whitlock feigned being falling-down drunk so we'd believe he was incapable of doing anything other than going upstairs to his room to sleep it off. Meanwhile, maybe he snuck out and sabotaged the plane's radio during the night, then in the morning he called Amanda to say he was too hungover to travel."

Silence fell over the group as they processed this idea.

"Stella," Deborah said, her voice soft, "how come you didn't notice there were too many passengers on your manifest when you initially received the list?"

"Because Steven *wasn't* on it. I only had seven people listed, plus myself."

"What about Amanda? Did she have both Dan Whitlock and Steven on her list?" asked Deborah.

"Yes," said Stella, "but she claimed to not know that I could only accommodate a total of eight on my aircraft."

"So you were set up," Bart said. "We all were."

"In Agatha Christie's story," Jackie said, very quietly, "the murderer was one among the group of people on the island. It was one of them who was doing the killing."

"So now you're saying it's one of *us*?" demanded Steven, his voice booming up to the vaulted ceiling. Fine bits of dust and debris suddenly rained down from the chandelier up high. Nathan scowled at him. Monica reached for her husband's hand and seemed to squeeze a silent caution. Bart watched them.

He didn't trust Nathan.

Especially not now, in the face of this grim game. Nathan stared at him funny when he thought Bart wasn't looking—Nathan, who'd asked Bart if they'd met before.

The tension thickened.

"So it was the character of the judge in the story who was the murderer?" asked Katie.

"Yeah," Jackie said. "The judge knew everyone in the group had gotten away with murder, and he staged the whole thing. When the group arrived on the isolated island, they gathered for a dinner party, expecting their hosts would show up. Instead, a recording was played which accused each one of a murder for which they had not been punished." She paused. Yellow light played over the planes of one side of her face, casting the other half in shadow. Her eyes glinted like pieces of black coal. "It was a reckoning," she said.

"Are you implying each of us has killed someone?" Stella asked, her voice going high and a strange look that Bart couldn't quite read taking over her features.

Tock, tock, tock, went the clock. A shutter banged again in the wind. They all jumped. Eyes were wide and faces white. Everyone was jittery.

"No, that's absurd," said Bart. "Because I *know* I have never killed anyone. It's . . . That idea is just nuts."

"If there is any logic to this," Jackie countered, "at the worst this rhyme is accusing all of us of being liars. *Nine Little Liars.* Invited to this lodge."

"Liars *and* sinners," whispered Monica. "If that cross-stitched verse in the downstairs bathroom means anything."

"And our mysterious KARMA-RAKAM host appears to want justice," added Nathan, "if that painting in Katie's room with the scales of justice symbolizes anything."

"What have we all done, then?" Jackie surveyed the group. "What have we all lied about? Which person out there in the world could think each of us has committed a sin? How are we eight in this room connected to this mastermind psycho? What person do we all know in common?"

"I don't see any point in asking this shit," Deborah snapped. Her crisp shift in tone startled Bart. The woman's eyes looked hot, and her skin was flushed. "You're all just accepting this as fact." She waved her hand at the checkerboard and figurines. "Maybe it's nothing like this at all! Maybe you all just have some guilt that is driving you to *think* you're being punished for your sins."

"The Monster rises within," murmured Monica.

"What?" said Jackie.

"It's nothing," Monica said.

Steven reseated himself slowly beside Deborah. The surgeon's whole body was wire-tight. Bart figured the doc was a hair away from snapping. He wouldn't risk going under that guy's knife.

"Look," Stella said, "answering those questions might help us get out of this. We *need* to know what we're up against."

Bart glanced up at the ceiling, then scanned the paneled walls with their freakish masks and paintings, wondering for a bizarre moment if there might be cameras hidden somewhere, if this might indeed be some weird-ass reality television show into which they'd been lured. Maybe someone would pop out in a few days along with a bunch of camera people and offer them a bunch of money if they agreed to allow this footage to air for a show.

Or was his brain just scrambling for a way out of this, for a way to see this as something *other* than a sick mastermind's plot to pick them off one by one? He cast his mind back, trying to recall anything he might have done that would induce someone to lure him here for this sick game. What had he lied about?

There was a time—well over a decade ago—when Bart had done jobs for shady people. His brother's people—mostly motorcycle-gang affiliates.

Bart had worked as a mechanic, and he'd accepted payment in cash under the table. And he never asked questions, no matter who brought him the job. Sometimes the vehicles were hot. Sometimes he did rush paint jobs. Or handled chop shop stuff. Sometimes the work came in bulk. Sometimes piecemeal. But he'd been able to demand a high price in return for secrecy, so it had paid incredibly well. The money had been tax-free and welcome. He and his older brother had lost their parents young, and they'd been poor kids who'd had to fight to find ways to survive. That's what the under-the-table work had been to Bart. Survival. And when he'd squirreled away enough tax-free income, he'd bought his first two shuttle buses. Then a third, followed by a town car. And he'd hired drivers. It had been the start of Executive Transit. He'd made good. And he'd put his questionable past behind him. Was that what this was? Had karma somehow caught up with him?

Bart's gaze shifted to Nathan again. The man's words over dinner curled through his mind.

Do I know you? Have we met before?

Bart had said no, he didn't think so.

But in this new context, he began to dig deeper toward that little niggle that Nathan's question had planted deep inside his brain. Could

Nathan McNeill have been associated with his brother's people? Bart couldn't see it—not a nerdy professor of mycology.

Could I have done mechanical work for Nathan in some other capacity?

Something began to nudge at the faded edges of Bart's memory, growing louder.

"Jackie's right," Bart said quietly. "We need to figure out how we might have crossed paths in the past. We need to say what we think we lied about, then see how it could all be connected."

"I'm not a liar," said Katie, blowing her nose.

"Everyone's a liar," Deborah said. "And if you claim you are not, you're lying right there."

Steven's shoulders snapped back. "How dare—"

"This isn't going to help, Steven," Monica warned.

"Okay," Bart said. "I'll start. Nathan, you felt you might know me, and the more I consider it, the more I feel you're correct, that we might have met. But I can't recall where." He hesitated, afraid of allowing these people in on his murky past. "I used to work as a mechanic in Burnaby before I started Executive Transit. I'm not proud to say I did jobs off the books, and accepted cash under the table to fix hot vehicles." He looked Nathan dead in the eyes. "Is there a chance I might have done some work for you?"

The blood drained from Nathan's head.

Monica reached for her husband's hand again, held tight. Steven went eerily still.

Bart was not the only one who noticed this ripple reaction. He could see that Deborah was watching the trio, and he saw Stella and Jackie exchange a glance.

"I never had any mechanical work done out Burnaby way," Nathan said.

"You and Monica used to live in Kitsilano, right?" Katie addressed Nathan. "I know this because while I was with CRTV, Monica was always in the news doing social events for the children's foundation charity. And so was Steven. You were on the board of that charity, weren't you, Steven?"

The surgeon cleared his throat. "It was good promo for the private surgery clinic."

Katie wiped her nose with her crumpled tissue. "Nathan, where did you teach before you guys moved out to Toronto?"

Nathan wavered, then said quietly, "Simon Fraser University."

"That's in Burnaby," Bart offered. "I worked in Burnaby."

"So do half the people in the Lower Mainland," Steven said curtly. "I don't see how this proves anything."

"Give it a chance," Stella said. "We might unearth some connections this way. What else are we going to do?"

"So, Monica and Nathan, you know Steven from before, right?" Bart said.

"Sure they know each other," Jackie said. "I heard them talking before boarding the plane. Nathan reminded Steven that they'd met at a charity function."

Steven cleared his throat again. "That's right. Like Katie said, the childcare foundation. I went to nearly all the events for a period of time. That's how I met Monica. And then Nathan the one time."

Color flushed Monica's face.

Bart perched himself on the armrest of the sofa occupied by Monica and Nathan. "Who else knew each other from before the plane trip?"

"I've seen Deborah before," Jackie offered. "I know that tattoo on her wrist. A swallow. I've seen that ink. And I've spoken to her. I know her voice."

They all turned to look at Deborah.

She sat still as stone, her gaze locked on Jackie.

"Deborah?" Stella prompted. "Where do you know Jackie from?"

"I don't." Her voice came out firm. But her hands trembled, and she was pressing down hard on her knees to hide it.

Jackie countered. "I have a memory for these things."

"Well, then, tell me where you met me," Deborah said in a challenge. "Because I believe you're mistaken."

Jackie eyed Deborah, and tension seemed to crackle between the two. Bart got an uneasy sense that those two did know each other from the past, and neither was prepared to say how. *A secret shared,* he thought. *Probably a dark one. And possibly a reason they're both here.*

"What about you, Stella?" Bart asked. "Do you recognize any of us?"

"Well, I recognize Katie. From TV."

They all murmured and agreed. They'd seen her face on television. Stella turned to Jackie. "So you also recognize Katie from television?"

"Yeah."

"CRTV is a BC news channel," Stella said. "It's not aired in Ontario, so if you're from Ontario, how do *you* know Katie's face from TV?"

Jackie regarded Stella in silence. Slowly, quietly, she said, "I used to work in West Vancouver. Law enforcement."

"You were a *cop*?" Stella asked.

"So was Dan Whitlock," Jackie said. "He's an ex-cop."

"How do you know?" Bart asked.

"Takes one to know one. It was written all over him. And I asked him after the buffet last night. He's ex-VPD turned private investigator."

"*Vancouver* PD?" Monica said. She looked rattled by this. She glanced at Katie. "Did *you* know Dan Whitlock when he was a cop, Katie? Did you ever interview him in connection with any crime incident?"

"I . . . Christ, I don't know," Katie said. "I interviewed a *lot* of VPD officers during my tenure at CRTV. Whitlock might've been one of them."

"Kitsilano, the suburb in which Nathan and Monica McNeill lived, is in VPD jurisdiction," Bart said. "There's connections here."

"Six degrees of separation and all that," Steven said. He looked drained suddenly, like he had no more energy for this day, or for this line of questioning. "It's hardly startling that those of us who lived in the Lower Mainland can find some vague crossover."

"When did you leave policing, Jackie, and why?" Stella asked.

"I'd had enough." The woman stared into the fire for a while. Bart regarded her profile. Hard features. Tough woman. Yet something vulnerable about her, too, he thought. If he were a gambling man, he'd bet something on the job had messed her up. He'd also bet she'd probably made a good cop.

"And you went straight from the West Van PD into security?" Stella pushed.

Jackie sucked in a deep breath, wavered, then said, "I had an old friend who was in the OPP—Ontario Provincial Police. She'd left and was starting a security company, and she called to offer me a job."

"So you went directly from policing into the security field?" Stella asked, rephrasing the same question.

Jackie faced Stella. Her eyes narrowed. Tension swelled. Wood cracked in the hearth and fire leaped. "There was a gap of two years," Jackie said, finally, her voice flat.

"During which you did what?"

"Jesus, Stella," Steven said, "what is *wrong* with you? Can't you see it must be personal?"

"What's wrong with *me*?" Stella surged to her feet. "This—*all* of this—is what's wrong with me. I want to know why *I* was contracted to bring you all here. People I don't know. To this fake location. What do you guys all have to do with *me*? Finding out who you all actually are might help *me* figure it out." Anger flashed in her gray eyes. "And that, Dr. Steven Bodine, is what's *wrong* with me."

Silence shimmered. The clock went *tock, tock, tock*. Then a boom exploded through the house.

Deborah gasped and Monica squealed as they all jumped in fright.

The boom sounded again. Echoing, reverberating through the dark lodge. And again. And again. Eleven times.

"Fucking clock! Why did you have to wind the damn thing up, Bart?" Jackie snapped.

"I had no idea some chime was going to go off at eleven."

They all looked at their watches. Spooked and off-kilter now, they regarded each other uneasily. The fire was dying to a cooler glow, and the darkness and cold seemed to press inward toward their little circle as the flames retreated. Bart could feel the cold creeping in from under the door, snaking around his ankles.

Jackie broke the awkward silence, as if she'd been knocked into revealing her answer by the judgmental boom of the old grandfather clock. "In the period between working for the West Van police department and leaving for Ontario, I handled cash-only work for a shitty, lowlife PI, who in turn took dirty jobs for bigger PI companies, who in turn contracted to top law firms in the city who didn't want to get their own manicured hands soiled. And that shitty little PI was Dan Whitlock. Okay, Stella? Satisfied now?" She got to her feet and set the piece of paper with the murderous verse on the table next to the figurines.

Bart's heart beat faster at this revelation. This was a very specific connection.

Jackie faced them all square. "I was asked to resign from the West Van PD. It was either that or face disciplinary action for my drinking habit, which had gotten to be a problem on the job. I hit rock bottom, okay? I sank as low as I could fucking go. I did what I could to survive. And then I got a call from a friend, and that call helped me crawl up out of my barrel, and it gave me a reason to put my life back on track. I moved east. I cleaned up." She held their shocked gazes.

"And I'm damn good at what I do now. My trouble"—she jabbed her fingers into her chest—"is I cared too much. I've learned to care a bit less. Now I'm going to bed. I've had enough." She got up, went to the nearby dining table, grabbed a flashlight that had been placed there, and thumped her way up the stairs.

Surprise, unease, rippled in Jackie's wake.

"You can't just walk away after that bombshell, Jackie," Bart called after her. "You *knew* who Dan Whitlock was!"

She stopped halfway up the stairs. "Yeah, and you can see why I wasn't exactly skipping through the daisies with glee to come tell you all how I knew him."

"But you confronted him? At the buffet?" Bart said. "I saw you two talking."

"Confronted? Christ, no. He recognized me, too. We just mutually agreed over dinner to not mention the past."

A movement sounded outside the window, followed by a hard knock. They all looked toward the door.

"It's just the wind in the trees," said Stella. "It's blowing debris loose. We should bolt the doors and go to bed." She reached for a lantern. "There are enough of these kerosene lanterns to go around. There's some more flashlights on the dining table, and there's the hunting spotlight from the plane." She hesitated. "Lock your bedroom doors. I sure as hell am locking mine."

She climbed the stairs after Jackie, her lantern light flickering against the ugly masks that seemed to come alive in the interplay of shivering shadow and light in her wake.

Bart felt for the knife he'd taken from the shed and secured to his belt. The sensation of the leather-covered hilt under his fingers comforted him. He eyed the rifle on the wall again. It had looked clean when he'd peered down the barrel earlier. He knew where the bullets were.

"I'll lock the front door," he said as he went to ram the big, tarnished bolt home. "And I'll take the first room at the top of the stairs." The room was closest to the gun.

If this was a sick game, he had every intention of winning it. And surviving.

The others moved quickly behind him. Nathan went to lock the back door that led out to the shed. Monica and Katie helped Deborah limp up the stairs. Steven waited for Nathan to finish locking up in the kitchen—no one trusting anyone to be left alone.

THE LODGE PARTY

NATHAN

Nathan exited the en suite bathroom in his pajamas to find Monica standing at the window with her arms wrapped tightly around herself.

"Turn the lantern off," she said quietly. "I want to see outside."

He turned the lantern knob, almost dousing the flame, but not completely. Then he went to stand beside her in the gloom. He put his arm around her shoulders. She was shivering. The wind outside was howling from the north, coming from the back of the lodge and blowing toward the lake. Fog swirled around the ghostly totem poles, and trees bowed and thrashed. The rain had turned to snow, and everything was going white. Whitecaps glowed silver on the black water. Through gaps in the swirling curtains of mist, Nathan caught glimpses of the little plane bobbing on the water.

An alternate reality. A nightmare dimension. A horror movie. That's what we're in.

"It's like it's emanating from *us*," she whispered. "From inside us. Like that verse said."

"What is?"

"Darkness. Blackness. 'For a Monster will rise within.'" She looked up into Nathan's eyes. His heart tightened at what he read in her expression.

"I love you, Monica," he said, tucking a strand of hair behind her ear. As he moved, he heard Steven's voice in his head.

"You know what your problem is, Professor Fungus? The trouble with you is you actually love her."

Nathan's stomach fisted into a ball as he felt another surge of rage. He really did want to kill that smug bastard.

"You don't have the balls."

He shoved the echo of the surgeon's words aside and drew his wife closer. Her curves felt warm against his body despite her shivering, and his heart did that thing—that weird squiggle thing. He'd loved Monica from the moment he'd laid eyes on her in the campus cafeteria all those years ago, when they were both freshmen. To him Monica had been a golden creature, anointed. A beautiful heiress, a special one among all the women there. It always amazed Nathan that she'd picked him in the end.

There's a reason your wife cheated on you.

Rage flashed through him. Again he quickly pressed it down. One thing Nathan could do that Steven couldn't was control his emotions. Nathan could be a closed book when he chose.

"I don't know what this is, Monica," he said gently. "I have no idea what's really going on here, but we both need to be strong, because when we *do* get home—and we will—we can't have let out what happened all those years ago with you, me, Steven." He felt her shudder at the mention. He held her tighter. "We cannot say *anything* here that will follow us back home, because it *will* destroy us, you, me, our kids, *everything* we have built—your company, my tenure."

"And Steven, what if *he* talks?"

"He won't. He stands to lose even more than us."

"He's a loose cannon, Nathan."

"He's also a top surgeon who values his lifestyle and status. He's a survivor that way."

"But someone already *knows*. That's why we're here. I'm certain of it now." She looked up at him again. "Bart was the mechanic, wasn't he? That's how you knew him. You said you went to someone out in Burnaby who took cash under the table. It was Bart Kundera, wasn't it?"

He sucked air deep into his chest, blew it out slowly. He nodded. He'd figured that much out when Bart mentioned his work. All the pieces started snapping together.

"And Dan Whitlock—he could've been the cop who investigated *the incident*. He was a VPD officer."

"I don't think so, Monica. You heard Jackie. Dan Whitlock was a seedy PI."

"He could have become a PI after *the incident*. We don't know the timing. And Katie—she covered *the incident*. You know it, I know it, and Steven has to remember her covering it, too. It's only a matter of time before Katie sees the links. Already she's recalled that we lived in Kitsilano, and now everyone also knows you taught at SFU in Burnaby, where Bart had his chop shop. Can't you *see*, Nathan? This is all about *us*, and what happened fourteen years ago."

He couldn't tell her about the groceries in the kitchen, the fact they'd been bought at the Kits Corner Store. Not now. It would crush her. But he couldn't keep it from her, could he?

"So how are the others connected, then?" he asked instead. "Stella and Jackie and Deborah?"

She put her face into her hands for a moment, still shaking like a leaf. "I don't know about Jackie and Deborah. But Stella . . . I . . . I think it's her."

"*Who?*"

She glanced up at him. "I think she was the mother of that little boy."

The blood drained from Nathan's head. "No," he whispered. "No, no way. No way in hell. That's not her."

"It's in her eyes. She looks different, so different, but not her eyes."

"No, you're wrong."

"Are you so sure?"

Nathan looked out the dark window at the blowing snow, thinking.

"The mother was a brunette," he said quietly. "Thick, long, brown hair."

"She could've dyed her hair. Stella's hair could have gone naturally silver gray, or she could have helped it chemically, and cut it."

"And plumpish. The mother had a full face. Softer."

"She's lost weight. Tons of it. She's gone gaunt. And gotten tanned, her skin lined from spending time outdoors or something. Like some sunbrowned, wiry vegetarian. But she was so much younger, Nathan. It's been *fourteen years*. That kind of tragedy can age and wreck a person so much they're barely recognizable in the end." She fell silent.

Tiny bits of ice blowing in the wind ticked against the window.

"I'm scared," Monica whispered. "Really scared."

Nathan stared out the window for a long time after his wife had climbed into bed.

He drew to mind the image he'd seen on the TV news. *The mother.* He thought of pictures he'd seen of homeless street people—befores and afters—what they'd looked like before life broke them, and before they became addicted to drugs and suffered from bad nutrition and poor hygiene. Unrecognizable, unless you knew to look for similarities. Unrecognizable, especially out of context.

But now they had context.

Maybe it was her. It was her and the survival part of his brain was refusing to see it.

A sick taste of bile rose up the back of his throat.

Are we finally going to go down for murder—manslaughter? Obstruction of justice? One way or the other?

Sweat bloomed on his skin. He felt dizzy. He dragged his hand down hard over his mouth.

It's going to be fine. The weather will clear, and we'll all fly out. We will wake from this terrible nightmare and realize it was all a fiction that was given life by our own guilt. Because who hasn't lied? Everyone tells lies. White ones, little ones, good ones, bad ones. Big ones. This could be anything—maybe Monica is wrong, and Stella is not the mother. Maybe guilt is messing with their heads, shaping people into things they are not—

Something outside caught his eye and stopped his train of thought.

Nathan killed the tiny bit of lantern light in their room and leaned closer to the windowpane. He rubbed a hole in the fog that had formed on the inside of the glass. He peered through the hole.

A tiny prick of light darted between the trees. Mist swept in suddenly and the light was gone. His heart beat faster. Had he imagined it? That someone was out there?

Cold crawled up the back of his neck.

He saw it again. A shadow. Carrying a tiny beam of a light that bobbed between tree trunks. Whoever was out there was not using the path straight down to the water. Hiding? From whom?

And then the small light was gone again in another thick swirl of fog and snowflakes.

THE LODGE PARTY

STEVEN

Steven squinted out the window in his room that looked down toward the lake. Was that someone with a flashlight going through the trees?

His heart kicked as he saw a second shape following the first. Or had he? He used his sleeve to smear away the fog and grime on his windowpane. But the shapes and light were gone, hidden by heavily falling snow and massive, swaying trees. Mist fingered back over his windowpane.

He wiped it off again, but still could see nothing more through the curtain of blowing snow in the darkness. Not even the dock, nor the glint of their plane.

Something was bugging him about that plane.

And about Bart.

And Jackie. And that pilot—the more Steven thought about it, the more he began to think he knew her. Those eyes . . .

He was beginning to see links where he didn't want to.

Could he stop this? Nip it in the bud—before it all came out?

Before he lost everything?

Hurriedly he left the window and moved carefully over the wooden floor planks so they wouldn't creak. He pulled on his black wool hat, reached for his jacket and boots and gloves.

THE LODGE PARTY

JACKIE

Jackie cast a quick glance over her shoulder to make sure she hadn't been followed out the back door. From her vantage point among the trees, she could see no one moving through the shifting mist and blowing flakes. Snow was settling over the bramble bushes, and along the outstretched wings of the totem poles, and on the head of that god-awful toothed raven caricature at the top of the biggest pole. The raven seemed to leer at her through the snow-brightened darkness. Jackie shivered as she listened carefully to the ambient sounds of the woods for a few moments longer. Just groaning branches and swishing leaves, and the sound of little waves lapping along the shore.

She resumed her movements through the big trees along the edge of the bramble patch, staying in the shadows and partially covering the bulb of her tiny flashlight with her gloved hand. The ground was soft underfoot.

A crack sounded.

She stilled. Held her breath. Listened. A rustle, then came the soft hoot of an owl and a whopping sound of wings. Then another noise, like footfalls on dry snow-covered leaves. Another crack sounded—a breaking twig. She switched off her flashlight and peered carefully into the shadows among the moving branches. But the noise stopped. She swallowed and moved, swiftly now, down to the dock.

Alongside the dock, the de Havilland Beaver rocked in small swells being kicked up by the wind. Snow was accumulating on the wings, and water chuckled around the pontoons. The dock creaked as she stepped onto it. As Jackie walked, it swayed and surged. She moved with care. She had no desire to end up in the icy lake and stinking reeds, like Deborah Strong had this afternoon.

She reached the plane and tried the handle of the cockpit door on the pilot's side. It moved easily. She drew the door open and froze as it gave a metallic groan. She waited, listening again, filled with a strange sense of being watched. She glanced up toward the house. The lanterns had all gone dark upstairs.

She stepped onto the pontoon, then placed her foot on the ladder crosspiece affixed to the front strut and climbed up into the pilot's seat. The plane tilted with her weight. She seated herself in the pilot seat, shut the door carefully, and panned her flashlight over the controls, keeping her beam low so as not to allow it to shine out the front windshield and attract attention from the lodge. She found what she was looking for—the radio.

Jackie leaned in closer. It looked basic. She knew next to nothing about avionics but wanted to see if those radio wires really had been cut, as Stella Daguerre had claimed. Jackie trusted no one, not even their pilot. There was something that was bugging her about Stella. It wasn't adding up in her mind that some anonymous mastermind could have lured them all out here and been convinced that their group would be immediately stranded by weather.

Sure, it was late October, right on the cusp of the November monsoons and early-winter snowstorms. And yes, this lodge hunkered in the freaky meteorological shadow of that monolithic mountain of black granite, but you couldn't take this to the bank and be guaranteed a storm would blow in right as they landed, and lock their group down for days. Jackie harbored a dark suspicion that Stella was lying to them about the radio, that she *could* call this in if she wanted to.

The radio looked simple enough. It appeared to have been inserted into an opening cut into the dash after manufacture. Jackie clenched her small flashlight between her teeth, took off her gloves, and tried to wiggle the radio out of its slot. To her shock, it came out easily. The screws that were supposed to hold it in place were gone. Her pulse quickened. She turned it over.

Shit.

The bundle of wires at the back had been neatly sliced clean through with a sharp blade. Stella *had* been telling the truth.

Or had Stella cut them herself?

Stella Daguerre was the one with the most control over them all. Stella was the only one with the means and the skill to have physically brought them here, and the one who had the ability to take them out. But the pilot could just as easily have been hired by the so-called RAKAM Group, like Amanda Gunn had been hired, like the rest of them appeared to have been invited and duped. Any one of those others in that lodge could be lying—she froze as she heard a change in the noise of the lapping waves along the dock.

Another noise reached her. A creak of planks.

Then she felt the plane tilt as someone put weight on the dockside pontoon. The pilot's door creaked open. Jackie spun her head around and looked up from her crouched position. Her heart stopped as the beam of the little flashlight clenched in her teeth lit upon a white face under a black woolen hat.

You?

It happened so fast, so unexpectedly. Jackie saw the glint of metal in the raised, gloved hand too late. She tried to scramble out of the pilot seat and into the passenger seat, dropping her flashlight from her mouth as she bumped up against the controls and got caught in the seat harness straps. She then lurched the other way, in an attempt to scramble toward the back of the plane, but the knife came down fast, and hard. She felt it go into her neck. Deep. Shock ripped through her body. Her hands went to the knife.

But it was yanked out. Jackie felt blood gush hot down her neck before she could even register pain. The blade went up again. She raised her arms in self-defense.

It came down again, harder.

One last thought went through her brain before she lost consciousness . . .

Eight Little Liars flew up into the heavens.
One saw the truth, and then there were seven.

THE SEARCH
MASON

Mason exited the morgue and took the elevator up to the ground floor of Silvercreek Hospital. He stepped out of the elevator and pulled out his cell phone to make a call while he was in an area with cellular coverage. He walked straight into Callie.

He started at the sight of a familiar face.

"Callie?"

She looked flustered, eyes reddened and puffy. She appeared embarrassed, and as though she wanted to flee. "I . . . uh, hi. I didn't expect to see . . . anyone. What are you doing here?"

"Pathologist," he said. "Deceased pilot. Autopsy was conducted this morning."

"Oh, right. I . . . We don't usually assist with homicides. I didn't think about the postmortem being done here." She stared at him, and he could almost see her brain returning from wherever it had been rushing. "Do you know who the victim is, or was, now?"

He stepped aside for some people to pass into the elevator, touching her elbow slightly so she'd also make way for them.

"Not yet." He spoke quietly in the public space. "Forensic techs are looking to see if they can retrieve anything from a phone we found in her pocket."

"Well, I . . . Let me know if I can help." She reached forward and pressed the elevator button.

The words he'd heard Oskar say to Callie before she'd left the search mission with Ben sifted into Mason's brain.

"Go, Callie. If you don't leave now, you won't make it. We've got things under control here. Say hi to him for us, will you?"

"Callie?"

She turned.

"Is everything okay?"

Her mouth tightened, as if straining to hold emotion in. Her eyes glimmered. She made a motion with her hand for him to just leave.

"Where's Ben?" he asked.

She took a moment. The elevator doors opened behind her and then shut without her. Someone came to stand close by.

He reached out, took her elbow gently. "Come, let's step away a moment."

"I'm fine. Really."

"Coffee? Can I at least buy you a coffee?"

Hesitation flickered over her features.

"Come on. I sure could use one."

She glanced at the elevator, then nodded. "Just a quick one."

They found a quiet corner table in the hospital cafeteria with windows that overlooked a small and wintry rock garden. People at the other tables watched him with interest as he went to the counter to buy two coffees. He'd need to grow accustomed to wearing a uniform again.

He bought two coffees and two pastries. Callie had composed herself by the time he returned to the table, and she looked more like the efficient climbing expert and SAR manager who'd saved his ass. He suspected Callie Sutton was inexperienced with being caught looking emotionally vulnerable.

"I'm sorry," she said, accepting the coffee from him. "You just got me at a bad moment. Benjamin is upstairs with his dad. Peter. My husband. I . . . We only have a few minutes, and then I need to go check out of my motel."

An odd sensation went through Mason at Callie's mention of a husband. His gaze ticked briefly to her wedding band as she lifted her cup to her lips. He reached for his own coffee.

"Is Peter ill? Or . . . forgive me, maybe he works here."

She inhaled, took a sip as she considered, perhaps, how to frame something. "Peter is a forester," she said slowly, setting down her cup. "Based out of Kluhane Bay—our house is on the big bay east of town. We . . . built it . . ."

Mason could see she was struggling, and he wanted to stop her right there, stop the pain of talking. But the selfish part of himself, the curious part, let her struggle on, because now he wanted to know more.

"He had an accident at work. A tree came down in heavy winds. It was rotted in the core. Big fir. One of the branches hit him and knocked him down a bank. He cracked his skull on a rock." She cupped her hands around her drink as if for warmth, or courage to continue in a composed fashion.

"It sent him into a coma." She paused for another while and looked out the window. Her face was pale. He liked her face. He felt for her. He let her take her moment, growing uncomfortable that he was putting her through this.

She suddenly met his gaze again, those moss-green eyes clear, sad. The way she looked at him, into him, sent a frisson through Mason. Her gaze was so direct that it felt intimate. Like she'd slid an invisible hand inside his shirt.

"He was in a coma for two weeks. They thought he wasn't going to make it." A soft snort. A tilt upward of her chin. Her voice grew more assured, a little louder. "But he's a fighter, my Peter. A climber. Survivor. He was the Kluhane SAR manager. Strong. Mentally and physically. He came out of that coma. Surprised everyone, but now . . . he's now in what they call a vegetative state."

The tension and emotion in her voice were palpable. He thought of her little boy in his Joker suit and surprised himself with the strength of the emotion he felt in response. But he knew why. It was because he knew loss. He *knew* this kind of pain. But he also didn't. Because his theoretically had an end. Death. She hung in limbo. In torture. Between hope and despair. Neither here nor there. But he didn't want to say the wrong thing.

"I hate those words," she said, a sharp bite of anger entering her eyes. "Vegetative state. He's not a vegetable. He's aware, I'm sure of it."

"How long has it been, Callie?"

"Fourteen months. And counting." She leaned forward, an energy suddenly coursing through her. "They tell me these states can last decades or, in very rare cases, the patient can improve over time. I know there's brain damage, but it's frustrating not understanding the full extent of Peter's mental capacity, not knowing if he has any level of consciousness. And . . . there are times we really feel he's with us, and that he understands everything we're saying. I believe he's able to grasp his surroundings, and his family. And there *is* science," she said. "Cognitive neuroscience that claims about one in five patients thought to be in a vegetative or unresponsive state actually have some level of awareness."

She fell silent. Then looked down. She picked at the flakes of pastry peeling off her untouched confectionery.

"I'm sorry, Callie."

She nodded. A muscle spasmed at the side of her mouth. "The brain is so complex," she said softly. "We've come so far with so many medical issues, but the brain is still a dark area with injuries like this." She swallowed. "Now he's got a bacterial infection. His immune system is weakened, and he took a turn for the worse on Saturday, which is why Benny and I stayed in town. Peter's pulling back today, though." She looked up. "The IV antibiotics are working. His blood work is coming back better. It's . . . it's just . . . You know, when there is no clue in sight as to when he might come back to me, come home to me and Ben."

"My wife was in a coma."

Her eyes snapped to his. Held. An electricity seemed to crackle through her body as she waited for him to say more.

Mason was committed now. "Car accident. Her name was Jenny. She was in a coma for three days before she passed."

"I . . . I didn't know." He could see her brain wheeling, reassessing him, recalibrating.

"It's been almost two years ago now since I lost Jenny and Luke, my little boy, in one devastating moment. Driver tried to overtake two cars, clipped Jenny's, she lost control and went straight into a cliff face." A pause. "I wanted to kill him, the driver."

"Mason—" She lifted her hand as if to touch his, but didn't. Her eyes gleamed. God, this woman had surfaced emotions in him, made him say things he'd not been able to say to just about anyone.

He gave a wry smile. "In fact, I almost did kill him. I hunted him down. Went to his house. Waited outside."

"And?"

"And let's just say I have some very, very good colleagues, law enforcement friends, who saved me from myself. I took some time off work, went on a walkabout—rode a bike across Australia. But when I returned home, I couldn't quite get back into things in the city, or my job. I couldn't quite shed the ghosts. Didn't even really want to. And I began to screw up."

He glanced down at his hands. He'd taken off his wedding band because he'd grown weary of the questions. He now wore it on a leather string around his neck under his uniform, side by side with Jenny's ring. Still together. A pair. The questions still came, only not voiced so overtly as they once had been when people saw his ring: *Where is your wife? How is she?*

"Was it a drunk driver?" Callie asked. "Was there alcohol involved?"

He shook his head. "He was just a kid. Had only just received his full license. Driver inexperience." He gave a snort. "Yet for a while back there, I would have been happy to kill the little bastard for his ineptitude, for his mistake. He went into a road safety and driving education program, as per the judge's orders. He was remorseful. And broken up himself, so were his parents."

"Is that why you came north?"

"Pretty much."

She studied him. Callie was the first person he'd told—at least told this much in such simple terms. Somehow it lifted something from him. Defogged his brain a little. And he felt bad because she was the one who needed his help. And he'd gotten benefit out of it himself.

"It's a long drive between Kluhane Bay and Silvercreek," she said, moving her cup aside. "Ben and I should get going. He needs to go back to school tomorrow—he's already missed today."

"How often do you do the drive?"

"Ben and I do it three times a week, usually. Peter has visitors all the time, though. The other SAR guys stop by whenever one of them is in town to shop for supplies, or do business, or run other errands. His extended family flies in sometimes. His work friends visit regularly. He's well loved." A sad smile crossed her mouth. "I need to think about relocating, perhaps. But Ben's school, my work—"

"And the not knowing," he offered. "Whether it could turn around tomorrow, and you might not need to give it all up. He might come home."

Surprise filled her eyes. She regarded him in silence for a moment. "Yeah," she said softly. She pushed to her feet. "Thank you, Mason."

He stood. "I didn't do anything."

"You helped. I . . . Thanks a ton." She turned to go, but hesitated. "How old was your son when you lost him?"

"Seven."

He saw her thinking. Ben. Almost the same age.

"He had a Joker suit," Mason said. "The Halloween before he died, Jenny bought it at Walmart. She felt bad about it—said there was a whole shelf full of them on sale, but she didn't have the energy to make Luke anything original."

Her nose pinked. Her hand went to her mouth.

"It's okay."

"I'm so sorry."

He nodded.

She turned to leave, and Mason watched her walk away. He liked the way she moved and hated himself instantly for the thought. At the elevator banks, she paused, glanced over her shoulder.

He gave a nod.

She went into the elevator.

Mason sat for a moment, feeling as though something seismic had just happened . . . and that nothing had just happened.

He was startled by the ring of his cell phone before recalling he was back in a cell coverage area. He checked the caller ID. It was the number of the Prince George RCMP detachment. He connected the call.

"Deniaud," he said.

"It's Gord Fielding. Looks like we have a preliminary ID on the decedent from the plane."

"From the victim's phone?"

"Affirmative. We have yet to confirm anything with DNA, or a dental records match, but the techs have started to recover some data—contacts, a partial call history, some SMS messages, emails, and a few photographs so far. From time and date stamps on the photos, it appears the two most recent images were shot in the Thunderbird Ridge area—it's a new ski and golf development just north of Squamish. The photos were taken at eleven thirty-one a.m. and eleven thirty-six a.m. on Sunday, October twenty-fifth. I'm going to forward them to you now."

A photo pinged through.

Mason opened the image. It showed a woman standing on a dock—the living image of the corpse he'd just seen on the morgue slab. Wearing the same clothes.

"Jacqueline Blunt," said Detective Fielding. "Seems from emails that she was more commonly known as Jackie Blunt. Owner of Security Solutions, a close-protection and security outfit based out of Burlington, Ontario."

Another picture pinged through. Mason opened the file. It showed a group of eight people, all similarly dressed. Five females, including Jackie Blunt. And three males. They were gathered in front of a bright yellow-and-blue de Havilland Canada DHC-2 Beaver Mk 1. On the fuselage was the same fake registration mark they'd seen on the downed wreck. A distinctive black mountain peak rose in the background of the photo. All eight people were smiling.

Mason's pulse quickened.

If those eight people all got onto that plane, where were the rest of them?

THE SEARCH

CALLIE

Tuesday, November 3.

Callie listened to the morning news on her radio as she made coffee. Her kitchen was one of her pleasures. She and Peter had built this house while living in a small trailer on the property when Ben had been two years old. It was their dream home, set back on a lot on the shores of Lake Kluhane with a view of snowcapped peaks across the fjord. There was swimming and paddleboarding and kayaking from their dock in the summer, and ice skating and cross-country skiing onto the frozen lake in the winter. On the walls in their living room hung framed photographs of their little family taken over the years—the three of them camping, horseback riding. Benny learning to swim and ski and skate. Benny with Peter on Benny's first day of school. Peter climbing a granite cliff with helmet and ropes. Peter and his new truck, which now sat quietly waiting for his return in the garage because Callie refused to drive it.

Ben sat atop a stool at the counter, chattering between slurping cereal from his bowl. A box of Tooty-Pops cereal was positioned in front of him, and he was reading about the prizes that would be in the new boxes. Callie glanced at the clock.

"Rachel will be here in ten minutes. Ben, you better finish up and brush your teeth." She slipped his packed lunch into his bright-red backpack.

"I don't wanna go to school today."

"Sure you do. You always like it once you get there, right? And you missed yesterday—"

"And I missed the Halloween party."

She ruffled his hair. "Yeah, bud, but we were able to spend some extra time with your dad, right?"

He nodded, jumped down from his stool, and ran on his socked feet toward the hall that led to the bathroom. He did a dramatic skid across the hardwood floor as he went around the corner. Callie smiled. She picked up his bowl and spoon and poured the leftover milk into the sink. It ran pink from the strawberry flavoring in the cereal. She didn't like giving Ben such sugary stuff for breakfast. She really should wean him off it, but it was one of the few things that made Benny really happy these days, and she was allowing her son to hold on to some of his "happy things" in Peter's absence. She paused for a moment as she watched the pink milk swirl down the drain. Pain and loneliness washed over her. It would come like this, out of nowhere, at the most unexpected times, prompted by some small thing. Or it would rise like a flood from her belly when she was faced with direct questions. Like Mason's yesterday. The memory of their conversation seeped into her mind. Again she saw the look of understanding and kindness in his gray eyes.

"Let's just say I have some very, very good colleagues, law enforcement friends, who saved me from myself. I took some time off work, went on a walkabout—rode a bike across Australia. But when I returned home, I couldn't quite get back into things in the city, or my job. I couldn't quite shed the ghosts. Didn't even really want to."

She sucked in a deep breath and gathered up Ben's backpack as Mason's earlier words reached back to her.

"It's a good age. Enjoy the moments. Don't let them slip by."

We all have our stories, thought Callie as she unhooked Benny's jacket from the coatrack near the door. *We all have pain.* Her landline rang. Callie checked her watch and frowned. During the off-season she took contract work for an adventure tour company. It was likely her boss calling about the budgets she'd sent in the previous week. She snagged the receiver of the wall-mounted phone near the kitchen.

"Callie here."

"Callie, it's Mason. We got an ID yesterday on the decedent from the plane. From the evidence, which is still coming in, there could be seven additional people lost out in the wilderness somewhere. We need to task SAR for a search."

Ben came scooting and sliding in his socks along the floor and bumped into her leg. She handed him his coat, made a motion for him to put his boots on. "Who's the pilot?" she asked.

"An Ontario resident named Jackie Blunt. ID yet to be confirmed with dental records or DNA." A pause as he appeared to muffle the receiver while speaking quickly and quietly with someone else on the other end. He came back on. "Treating it as a homicide case. And she's not a pilot."

Callie's brain reeled. "What do you mean?"

"The de Havilland was a West Air charter piloted by a woman named Stella Daguerre. Jackie Blunt owns a security company—she was a passenger. The aircraft departed the Thunderbird floatplane dock north of Squamish around eleven forty-five a.m. on Sunday, October twenty-fifth, ten days ago. Eight people on board total, including Blunt and the pilot. Destination unknown. North District headquarters has taken the lead on the case but has assigned me to task KSAR to undertake a search for the missing occupants, with a view to ramping up resources with possible assists from additional agencies as information continues to come in." Another pause as he spoke again to someone else. Adrenaline bloomed in Callie's blood, her interest hotly piqued, her brain scrambling facts together.

Ten days was a long time to be lost in the wilderness in this weather. Especially if injuries had been incurred in a crash. The chances of finding anyone alive were slim. Very slim. This was more likely to be a recovery mission.

"Can you come down to the detachment?" Mason asked. "I'm about to brief my officers, and we could use SAR input from the outset."

"Mom, Rachel and Ty are here!" Ben yelled as he peeked out the long window next to the front door.

Callie pointed to his gloves and mouthed the words *Put them on*.

"Can you give me a few minutes?" she said into the phone. She needed to check if Rachel could pick Ben up from school when she collected Ty this afternoon. If this callout turned into a full-blown multiday operation, she'd need Benny to stay with Rachel's family for a few days, as per her callout custom. Rachel and her husband were only too keen to help out in this capacity, and Ty and Ben got on like a house on fire, usually.

Callie also found it beneficial for Ben to see a good family unit in action, with both a mother and father figure. He usually came home in a positive frame of mind after his stays at Rachel's house.

"I should be there in twenty," she said.

Her phone went dead.

Callie stared at the receiver in her hand. *All righty, then*. She hung up and hurried into her mudroom. Outside the window, Rachel's SUV chugged clouds of condensation into the crisp morning air. The precipitation had abated, but the sky hung low and the morning had dawned ominously dark. The wind blew dry snow across their front yard—another front coming in. The odds of finding anyone alive had just gone down several more notches in Callie's mind. She grabbed her down coat, slid her feet into her Sorel boots, and opened the front door. Benny bulleted out toward the waiting SUV. Ty waved behind a fogged-up window as he approached. Callie followed Ben as Rachel rolled down her window to hear what Callie was coming out to say.

The wind cut cold against Callie's cheeks as she zipped up her coat.

How in the hell did the owner of a security company end up dead in a pilot's seat with a vintage knife plunged into her neck?

And where are the others?

THE LODGE PARTY

STELLA

Monday, October 26.

The day dawned bleak and steel gray. Outside Stella's bedroom window, snow swirled, but the wind appeared to have died. The old house creaked like an arthritic senior awakening to the cold morning as she shrugged into her down jacket and zipped it up to her neck. She rubbed a hole into the frost that had formed on the inside of the window, but all she could see was the woodshed out back. Behind the shed, the forest climbed densely up the base of the granite mountain. Clouds continued to roll down the flanks in great, tattered swaths.

She pulled on a woolen hat, found her gloves, and exited the room. Wooden floorboards squeaked beneath her boots as she crossed over the threadbare Persian rugs that led to the stairs.

Downstairs the scent of woodsmoke hung in the great room. The coals in the hearth had grown cold and black. A sense of being watched seized Stella as she moved in front of the paintings and beneath the glass eyes of the mounted animal heads.

She stopped, glanced up at the balcony. No one was there, observing her. It was still too early for the others to have woken. She hesitated, then crossed quickly to the front door. She slid back the bolt, opened the heavy door, and slipped out.

The cold stole her breath. She had not expected such low temperatures at this time of year, despite having studied the forecast before flying. She hadn't anticipated this much snow, either, or such low visibility. She couldn't even see the lake or her plane from the porch of the old lodge.

Tugging her hat lower down over her ears, she started down the unkempt and snowed-over path through the heavy fog and softly falling snow.

As she passed beneath the totem poles, she glanced up. Flakes settled wet against her face. Her pulse quickened—she could have sworn the raven head on the bigger totem pole had been facing the water when they'd arrived. But the head now faced the lodge. She swallowed, an uneasiness filling her chest. The wind gusted, and both the head and the wings creaked and moved slightly.

It's just the wind. That's all. The top part of the totem is loose. It was possibly carved and added later.

She continued down the path, but she was unable to shake the sense of malevolence the bird head had given her. Another gust blew, and the totem groaned. She glanced back over her shoulder. The raven had turned to watch her, as if following her progress. The words Monica and Nathan had exchanged on the plane crept into her mind.

Looks like the Overlook.

The what?

That spooky hotel in that Stephen King novel.

Stella shook the notion, but she couldn't quite suppress an image of topiary bushes moving closer and closer to the lodge in the snow, or stop herself from thinking that was what the totems were doing.

The fog was even thicker near the shore. The lake appeared invisible. She couldn't see the dock stretching into the water, or her plane. A noise and movement came from her left. Stella spun to see a figure in black emerge from a swirl of mist and snow.

"Who's there?" she said, heart beating fast. "Who is that?"

He came closer. It was the surgeon. Snow caked his black hat.

"Crap, you scared me," Stella said, feeling oddly shaky. "What are you doing out here, Steven?"

He looked edgy. Disheveled.

"I . . . I couldn't sleep. Figured I'd check out the path Bart told us about, before there was too much snow on the ground, see if it went around to the other bay." He wiped a clump of snow off his shoulder and dusted some clots of it off his hat. At this moment he looked a far cry from the slick plastic surgeon who'd roared his shining Jaguar convertible into the parking lot at the Thunderbird floatplane dock a day ago. It shouldn't please her, but it gave Stella a punch of satisfaction to see the obnoxious man brought down a peg or two.

"Well, *did* you find anything?" she asked.

He shook his head. "It went to the bay all right, but it's just another bay. Nothing else there. The path seemed to pick up from there and go farther into the woods. What about you? Where are *you* going at this early hour, Stella?"

"Down to the Beaver. I want to take a look at the radio again now that there is light, see if I can fix it."

He swiped more moisture off his face, his nose running and reddened. "You think you can?"

"Depends on the damage."

Worry tightened his features. "Maybe Bart can fix it," said the man who could fix human bodies but appeared powerless and fearful right now. "Bart said he worked as a mechanic."

"Sure. Maybe. He's a guy who worked with cars, and I'm just a female pilot who works with avionics. I'll ask him." She turned to leave, but the doc hesitated, as if wanting something more.

"Look, it's going to be okay, Steven," she said. "Even if we can't repair the radio, everything else on the plane is in good working order. We have spare gas. We have supplies to last us in the lodge. We have water, fire, shelter. We'll fly out as soon as this storm clears."

A look akin to gratitude crossed his face. "Can I help?"

"Coffee would be really awesome."

His face darkened. The challenge reappeared in his eyes.

"For the whole group," Stella added. "For morale. Waking up to fresh, hot coffee will really help."

He nodded. "Yeah. Yeah, I suppose you're right. I'll go put that kettle on—I saw a tin of instant in the cupboard."

She continued down to the hidden water's edge.

"And I'll see if there's something I can fix for breakfast!" he called after her.

"Coffee!" she yelled over her shoulder with a wave, and the lodge and Steven disappeared in another curtain of fog and snowflakes.

As Stella neared the water, she felt a clutch in her chest. The dock stretched crookedly out into the mist, but she couldn't see the silhouette of her plane. She hurried onto the dock, slipped in slush atop moss, almost went down, but righted herself.

She reached the spot where she'd tied her aircraft.

Nothing.

Her heart started to bam against her ribs.

The only sign her de Havilland Beaver had ever been here was the red-and-yellow ropes hanging into the water where she'd secured them to the planks. The offshore wind had been strong during the night. Could the plane have worked free, assisted by the movement of swells and the listing of the dock? No. No way in hell. She knew her knots, knew how to secure things.

Adrenaline surged through her veins. Hurriedly she removed and pocketed her gloves. She crouched down in the slush and began to pull one of the ropes out of the lake, her hands freezing with the cold water. The end of one came up. It had been sliced clean through with a sharp blade. Stella moved fast to the other rope and began hauling it out. The end came up.

Fuck.

Also cut.

She froze as she felt the dock move. Stella spun her head around and glanced up. It was Bart, coming along the dock toward her.

"Christ, you scared me."

"Where's the plane?" he asked.

Stella came to her feet. "It's gone." She held up the sliced ends of the wet rope. "The floatplane is gone. Someone cut it free, and in that wind last night, it would have blown for miles down the lake. We have no fucking way of getting out of here."

His gaze dropped to the rope ends. He looked confused. He tented his hand over his brow and peered into the thick weather, as if the mist might somehow part and reveal the plane bobbing out there on the lake. "It couldn't have gotten far."

Stella swore and dropped the rope ends back into the water. "Good one, Bart. Good one. There was a freaking offshore gale last night! Did you *see* from the air how long this lake is? That wind"—she pointed down-lake—"was blowing directly from the north and straight down the center of this fifty-kilometer-long body of water."

"Why would anyone do this?" he asked.

"Because of the rhyme in the lodge, that's why. Have you forgotten everything that was said last night? Someone wants to punish us. I woke up hoping it wasn't true, but it's for goddamn real now. We're trapped. No cell reception, no radio, no way out."

Bart looked up toward the lodge. "I mean," he said slowly, "who in our group would do this? Because unless there is someone else here, lurking in these woods, someone among us cut these ropes."

Ice trickled down Stella's neck as the reality—the implication—of Bart's words struck home. Her mind raced as she tried to think who in their group could have done this, because this changed everything. Until now, there'd been a way out, a way home. A link to normality. Now it was gone.

"Like Jackie said, a killer could be among us—one of *us* had to have done this."

Stella angrily swiped snow from her face, her hands trembling a little. "Then they don't have any goddamn endgame, do they? Because if they go and kill us off, how are they going to get out themselves? With no radio to fix, and no plane to escape with?"

"Maybe that *is* the endgame, Stella. Like the judge in Agatha Christie's story. He killed himself."

Emotion burned sudden and hot into her eyes.

Get a grip, Stella, get a goddamn grip. You're the one who's been telling everyone not to panic.

She sucked in a chestful of air and looked down the lake again, then at the ropes dangling into the water. She tried to center herself, think straight. Make a plan. But her plane, her lifeline, her comfort zone—it was gone. Really gone. And the realization speared fear into her heart. Her aircraft *was* her life. It defined her—Stella, the floatplane pilot. It was her freedom. It symbolized control. And now they were all well and truly trapped, and she couldn't see a way out. Her confidence had been cut adrift with her plane.

She glanced at Bart's face. But he was distracted, staring at something on the dock just past her.

Slowly, Stella turned to see what had snared his focus.

The snow at the far edge of the dock was pink and red.

Blood?

She moved quickly toward the red stains in the whiteness. She crouched down, touched a dark spot with her fingertips. There was more under the top layer of snow. A lot more. It felt sticky. She brought her fingers to her nose.

"Is it blood?" Bart asked.

"I . . . I think it is." She came fast to her feet. "Bart, we need to get everyone together inside. We need to see that everyone is all right."

Stella moved as fast as she dared over the slick and swaying dock, then began to run up the path toward the lodge.

THE SEARCH

CALLIE

Tuesday, November 3.

The civilian admin assistant at the Kluhane Bay RCMP detachment showed Callie to the briefing room.

"They're expecting you," said the woman as she held open the door.

Callie entered the incident room. The door shut behind her. Mason stood in front of a whiteboard mounted on the back wall. He was in uniform, an aura of command about him. At his side, on a stand, was a monitor linked to an open laptop on the desk in front of him. Hubb sat beneath the window at one of the three metal desks in the room, bulky in her bullet suppression vest. Jake Podgorsky, Mason's other officer, was seated on a chair near her, his long legs stretched out.

"Callie, thanks for coming in." Mason motioned for her to take a seat at one of the desks. She shrugged off her jacket, hung it over the back of a chair, and perched her butt on the edge of a desk, crossing her arms over her chest. A massive topographical map of the area covered the wall to her left.

Hubb shot her a grin, and Podgorsky crooked up a brow in his typical lugubrious fashion. She nodded to them.

Mason clicked his laptop keys and fed an image to the monitor. A woman's face filled the screen. Bleached, white-blonde hair cropped very short, intense dark eyes. Squarish face, solid neck. *The rough and ruddy complexion of a drinker and possibly smoker,* thought Callie. She judged the woman to be in her midfifties.

"Jacqueline—Jackie—Blunt," Mason said, nodding toward the image. "Our decedent from the downed de Havilland Beaver Mk 1. Age forty-seven. A partner in Security Solutions, a close-protection and security company based out of Burlington, Ontario. She's married to Elizabeth Krimmer, the other half of Security Solutions. Ontario Provincial Police are assisting our investigation out east. Krimmer flew in last night, and this morning she made a visual identification of the deceased. Krimmer claims Jackie Blunt is not a pilot, nor has Blunt ever learned to fly a plane."

"So how in hell did she end up dead and strapped into the pilot's harness in that Beaver?" Hubb asked.

"And you ID'd her from her phone data?" Callie asked. Anything she could learn about the subjects of a search would help her profile the missing, which in turn would offer up the highest-POD areas and help her direct SAR resources and formulate a search strategy.

"Our forensic techs have begun to retrieve some of the phone data," Mason said, "including a few photographs and emails. The emails indicated the decedent was Jackie Blunt of Security Solutions. OPP contacted both the company and next of kin. Both confirmed Blunt had flown out west for a trip to an undisclosed location."

Mason pulled up another photo. "Blunt has a Facebook account. From the phone data we've determined she posted this photo at eleven thirty-three a.m. on Sunday, October twenty-fifth. Shortly before reported takeoff from Thunderbird Lodge."

The image filled the screen. A group of eight people—five women and three men—gathered on a dock in bright jackets and smiles in front of a daffodil-yellow-and-blue floatplane with the prop whirring. The Beaver was clearly readying for takeoff. In the background was a distinctive black spire, or cinder cone peak. Callie knew it instantly as

Black Tusk, or Landing Place of the Thunderbird, in the language of the Squamish people. Her heart quickened. "And who are the others? Do we know yet?"

Mason nodded. "From Krimmer we've learned that Jackie Blunt flew into YVR on Saturday, October twenty-fourth via Air Canada flight 49. Blunt called Krimmer from the Gateway Hotel at YVR that night. At the hotel she also met up with the rest of that group, minus the pilot and one male." He pointed to the photo.

"From hotel staff we've learned the names of the other passengers, and the name of their tour guide. All expenses, including flights into YVR, were paid via a credit card linked to a company out of Malaysia—the RAKAM Group. Investigations are ongoing with assistance from the Lower Mainland RCMP, but at this point we know that everyone in the group was invited on an all-expenses-paid trip to a new luxury wilderness lodge and spa development at a 'secret' destination in the BC interior. The Forest Shadow Wilderness Resort & Spa. The group was bused to the new Thunderbird hotel, where they overnighted. The following morning they met up with the pilot and the additional passenger. They departed via that de Havilland Beaver Mk 1 for the location, which had been disclosed only to the pilot via text."

"How do we know this?" Podgorsky asked, chewing the end of a pencil as he studied the image of the group.

"From Amanda Gunn. She's listed with a temp agency that was contacted by a representative of the RAKAM Group. And she was hired to set up the junket. Each guest invited on that trip worked in a field that could potentially contract services to the RAKAM Group. Amanda Gunn told detectives in the Lower Mainland that if the guests liked what they saw, they would be invited to submit a tender. She said the RAKAM host was to meet the guests at the spa. Gunn herself was angling for full-time work with the spa."

"What is this RAKAM Group?" Hubb asked.

"It appears to be a front, a scam."

"What?" Hubb leaned forward.

"Everything so far leads back to a numbered company with offshore accounts. The investigation on that front is ongoing. Right now, our immediate focus here in Kluhane Bay is those missing people." Mason pointed to the screen. "Pilot Stella Daguerre. Forty-eight. Owner-operator of West Air, based on Galiano Island; Dr. Nathan McNeill, fifty-six, professor of mycology at Toronto University; his wife, Monica McNeill, fifty-four, grocery-chain heiress and CEO of Holistic Foods."

A whistle came from Hubb. "That one's going to hit headlines."

"So will these." Mason pointed to a blonde woman in the group. "Katie Colbourne, travel documentary maker, ex–television news personality."

Callie studied the enlarged photo on the monitor. She recognized the woman's face. Katie Colbourne had been a regular on CRTV news some years back.

Mason pointed to a tall male in the smiling group. "Dr. Steven Bodine, the cosmetic surgeon behind the famous Oak Street Surgical Clinic; Bart Kundera, thirty-nine, owner-operator of Executive Transit in Burnaby. This here is Deborah Strong, thirty-one, runs Boutique Housekeeping based out of Surrey. And Jackie Blunt." Mason met their gazes in turn.

"According to Amanda Gunn, there was one additional guest who was supposed to fly out that day. Dan Whitlock. A private investigator who ran a one-man show out of East Van. Whitlock never made it onto the charter. The morning of their departure, he suffered anaphylactic shock. Whitlock was pronounced dead by the regional coroner shortly after the aircraft took off. He was highly allergic to shellfish. Shellfish was served at the buffet the night before, although hotel staff claim they were careful not to allow other food served to come into contact with the shellfish. The coroner initially did not refer the file to the RCMP, but the RCMP are now taking the lead in Whitlock's death investigation, given the context."

"So nine people were supposed to fly?" Callie asked. "Because the downed de Havilland—the way I saw it configured—could only accommodate eight, including the pilot."

"Correct."

"So he wasn't *supposed* to make it?" Hubb asked.

Mason said nothing.

Hubb and Podgorsky exchanged a glance. "Shit," Hubb said as she clicked the back of a pen repeatedly. "And this pilot, Stella Daguerre, she flew charter planes with false registrations?"

"West Air has two floatplanes. Both aircraft have been found moored at the company's dock on Galiano," Mason said. "Both are properly registered. Either Daguerre owned an additional, unregistered aircraft, or she might have been provided use of this de Havilland Beaver by the so-called RAKAM Group. This investigation is escalating into a large and multifaceted operation, and all avenues of inquiry are ongoing. We'll be updated with information as it comes in. Our focus right now is to locate those missing passengers, if they are in this area." He turned to Callie. "Which is where SAR comes in."

She rubbed her chin absently, turning things over in her mind. "I know TSB crash investigations can take months if not years, but has any preliminary information come in from the Transportation Safety Board guys?" she asked.

Mason pulled up another image of the crashed de Havilland Beaver. The mood in the room sobered. This image of the mangled wreck with the dead pilot inside stood in stark contrast to the photo of the intact plane with the smiling group gathered in front of it.

"The TSB initial assessment is that this aircraft did not collide with land or water," Mason said.

The room fell silent. Outside, the wind picked up, loosening frozen lumps of snow from a tree and hurling them at the window. Urgency mounted in Callie. The weather window was closing on them fast.

"TSB investigators say the damage to the aircraft is more likely consistent with the de Havilland Beaver having been washed down rapids and then over the falls." Mason cleared his throat as Callie caught his eye.

Both knew who'd sent that plane over the falls.

"The pathologist has also determined that Jackie Blunt's cause of death was exsanguination. She bled out when the blade of the Schrade severed her carotid. It would have been fast. The most likely scenario is she was stabbed while the plane was on water and not in the air."

"Especially since she was not a pilot, and likely couldn't fly it," offered Hubb, clicking her pen. "Which begs the question: What was she doing in that pilot seat?"

Callie said, "And so far there's no clue as to their destination?"

Mason tapped a key on his laptop, and an aerial shot filled the screen. It showed a development on the shore of a long lake that had two small bays at the end. A big main building, many smaller cabins. Connecting pathways with lighting. A network of docks. A helipad marked with a big X. It had been taken in the fall, judging by the red-and-gold deciduous foliage scattered among the evergreens. Behind the development rose a large granite mountain. Callie's pulse quickened.

Mason said, "This is allegedly the Forest Shadow Wilderness Resort & Spa. The 'company' website has gone down, but this image was retrieved from a cached version. Location of those buildings is as yet unknown."

Callie pushed off the desk and walked slowly toward the image, her skin going hot. She examined it closely to be sure, then gave a soft snort. "It's fake." She turned to Mason. "That's the north end of Taheese Lake. That lodge does not exist."

"You're certain?"

"Of course I'm certain." She pointed. "That hunk of granite behind the development is Mount Warden. I know. I've climbed the west route with Peter. And those there are the two little bays I recognize. There is an old lodge at the north end. But it doesn't look like that. And these other buildings pictured? It's all been photoshopped in. See those trees? That's red oak—*Quercus rubra*." She glanced at Mason. "Peter is a forester. I know trees. He never stops—never stopped . . . talking trees." Callie wavered a moment. She inhaled, but when she spoke again, her voice came out less strident, less assured.

"Northern red oak, or champion oak, as it's sometimes called, is native in the eastern and central United States, and in southeast and south-central Canada. Those trees do not grow in this region."

"Fake lodge," Hubb said. "Fake company. Unregistered plane—this whole trip was some kind of ruse? *Why?*"

Mason said, "Our role is to focus on finding the missing." But Callie saw a look in his eyes that said he was more accustomed to leading a major investigation than being sidelined to a SAR commander role. This had to gut him. Even just a little.

"Saving lives," Callie said quietly, "is, to my mind, the priority here, no matter what end of the investigation anyone is coming from."

"Hard to imagine," Podgorsky said, "given the apparent homicide and the time lapsed since takeoff, plus the weather we've been having, that those remaining seven are still alive."

Outside, the wind gusted as if on cue, just to remind them who was in charge out here. Mother Nature. Not them.

Callie picked up a ruler off the desk and went to the topographical map that covered the wall. She reached up and tapped the map with the end of the ruler. "This is Taheese Lake. Fifty kilometers from the north end down to the outflow into the Taheese River at the south, where we found the Beaver." She faced the three officers in the room. "About five years ago I went camping at the far end of a lake called Mahood, in Wells Gray Provincial Park. There was a floatplane incident where the pilot couldn't start the engine of his aircraft. The wind was blowing fiercely down-lake. As he struggled, his aircraft drifted faster and faster toward the outflow, then it caught the current, went faster. He was sucked into the river and into white water. His plane overturned going down the rapids, and it was smashed. If, according to the TSB, there is no immediate indication of a land or water collision with this de Havilland Beaver, my first supposition would be that it could have come from Taheese Lake. And my first area of interest would be that old lodge building at the north end. The prevailing winds over the past two weeks have been from the north, and strong. Taheese Lake is narrow. The steep mountains on either side funnel the wind into a fierce force." She pointed to the north bay.

"This would be my highest POD. This is where I would look first. A plane in trouble could have blown all the way down this lake and into the outflow here. From this point the river gathers volume and velocity as it channels into the Taheese Narrows, here." She looked pointedly at Mason. "This is where the plane was first seen by the hunters. It could have come down the rapids in higher water and gotten hung up on the ledge as waters dropped again. And then it sustained further damage going back into the river and over the first waterfall. If that Beaver flew into that lodge, the remaining seven might have shelter. They might all still be alive."

"And one might be a killer," said Podgorsky. "Because someone stabbed Jackie Blunt in the neck."

"What is that lodge?" Mason asked.

"The land was owned by some old eccentric from the States," Hubb said. "The buzz in town is he had a ton of money. Something to do with Hollywood in his past. He used to fly himself in."

"Was owned?" Mason asked.

"No one has seen him around in a while," said Podgorsky.

"Did he fly in using his own aircraft?" Mason asked.

"I don't know," Hubb said.

Mason looked at Podgorsky. The cop shrugged.

"What's his name?" Mason asked.

"Franz somebody," said Podgorsky.

"Callie? Do you know him?"

She shook her head. "I saw him. Once. Maybe three years back, when he came into town. He must be in his eighties now, if he's still alive. He usually kept to himself out there when he did come in."

"We need to get out there. Stat," Mason said, shutting his laptop.

"Not by air," Callie said. "Not in this weather. And it's only going to get worse, especially at higher elevations. Taheese Lake is about six hundred meters higher than Kluhane Bay. We'll need four-wheel-drive vehicles and then SAR boats to reach the lodge."

Mason reached for his jacket. He turned to Hubb. "Find out who owns that land now." He shrugged into his jacket. "Podgorsky, you're in command of comms from the detachment. Pass on all leads that come in. I'll be in sat phone and radio contact." He paused and met the eyes of his officers. "This one is going to hit the press sooner rather than later. I alone serve as the Kluhane media liaison. If I'm not available, refer all inquiries to the media liaison in Prince George. Callie, same goes for SAR techs. No comments to reporters." He held her gaze.

She felt a cool wall go up between herself and Mason. When it came to SAR ops, his predecessor had always left commenting to the media up to the SAR manager. And she was good at it. She hit the right notes on camera. Then again, in Sergeant Mason Deniaud's defense, KSAR had not handled a search for a high-profile grocery-chain heiress, or a cosmetic surgeon, or a well-known television reporter. Nor had any of their previous subjects ended up strapped into a pilot's seat with a vintage knife stabbed into their necks.

"My team knows their responsibilities," she said tonelessly. She snagged her own jacket off the back of the chair and left the room to set an official KSAR callout in motion.

THE LODGE PARTY

DEBORAH

Monday, October 26.

Deborah huddled with the others in the great room beneath the reproachful eyes of the mangy-looking taxidermy trophies mounted on the paneled walls.

Their plane was gone.

And Jackie was missing.

When Stella and Bart had yelled for everyone to come downstairs, Jackie had been nowhere in the house to be found.

The woman's bags were still in her room, everything left as if she intended to return. A sleep shirt and leggings were laid out on her bed. Toothpaste and toothbrush and face lotion had been neatly placed on the counter in her en suite bathroom. But her bed had not been slept in. And her jacket and boots were gone.

Most terrifying of all: a second figurine had been toppled off the checkerboard, and it lay on the coffee table in front of them with its head freshly lopped off. Deborah stared at it.

Who'd done that? One of the people sitting with her now? Or had someone been watching from the woods and come in from the outside?

Wood cracked behind the fire grate, and Deborah jumped. She was on a knife-edge. Everyone was. Fidgety, frightened. Nathan had built a roaring fire this morning while Steven had made coffee. Both claimed to have been unable to sleep, and Nathan had gone out early to gather more wood.

Steven handed out mugs of instant coffee from a tray he carried. Bart paced irritatingly behind the sofa, looking truly skittish for the first time since Deborah had met him at the Vancouver airport. He kept rubbing the back of his left hand. It had been cut. He'd told her he'd banged it when he'd slipped in slush this morning. He, too, had claimed an inability to sleep and had gone out investigating in the early hours of dawn.

He'd run into Steven on the trail. Both had encountered Stella. It seemed like half their group had been outside in the dark, misty hours of dawn while Deborah had been throwing up in the toilet.

She shook her head, declining the coffee Steven offered her, worried she'd puke again. Either Jackie's direct statement last night that she'd seen Deborah's tattoo before, and knew Deborah from the past, had made her sick, or she was still getting morning sickness even though she was just over twelve weeks now, and through the first trimester. With her *and* Ewan's baby. She *had* to hold that in mind. A future. She *would* get through this. She would get home. She would be at that airport to welcome home her military hero when he returned from deployment. She would have balloons filled with helium, and she would tell him the wonderful news now that she was well past the three-month mark.

Deborah's mind went to Jackie's words on the plane.

You remind me of someone. Kat . . . Kata . . . Katarina, I think her name was.

Deborah was glad Jackie was gone. Really glad. Her secret was safe now.

Her gaze dropped to the piece of paper with the horrible verse. It lay on the table, faceup, next to the checkerboard with the figurines.

Eight Little Liars flew up into the heavens.
One saw the truth, and then there were seven.

Nathan said, "Okay, Stella, walk us through this. Tell us exactly what you found, blow by blow."

Stella dragged a hand over her damp hair. Deborah noticed it was trembling. Even their rock-steady pilot was scared. They were all cracking, bit by bit.

"I went down the trail to the lake," Stella said slowly. "There were no prints in the fresh snow, not leading down to the dock. I ran into Steven near the water."

"I was looking for the other bay," Steven interjected.

Nathan frowned at the surgeon. "So early?"

"I'm not the *only* one who was up," snapped Steven. "You were gathering wood from the shed, it seems. And Bart was out there, too."

"Yeah," said Bart, still rubbing the back of his hand nervously. "I . . . heard someone on the dock, saw a shape in the mist, so went to investigate."

"What were you doing out there in the first place, Bart?" Deborah asked, growing increasingly rattled by Bart's pacing and hand rubbing.

"I was going to do the same as Steven. Look again at the trail in the light. But I saw prints leading down to the dock, so followed those instead. Then I saw Stella. She was examining the ropes, and the plane was gone."

"Stella?" Nathan said.

She dragged her hand down over her mouth. "The mooring ropes had been sliced clean through. Someone did this on purpose. They knew that in the offshore wind last night, the plane would have drifted away fast. And we'd be totally stranded."

"First the radio," Katie whispered, rocking slightly where she sat on the sofa. "Now this." She met their gazes in turn. "And whoever did it—whoever cut our plane free, also did that—" Katie pointed to the newly decapitated figurine. "He's here. He's been inside this house. While we were upstairs sleeping, or outside."

"Or her," Steven said. "What makes you think a female couldn't do that? Strikes me as more of a female thing. Passive-fucking-aggressive."

Deborah's chest constricted in anger at the cosmetic surgeon's words, but she bit her tongue, bottling it up inside. She watched as Katie glared at the surgeon. The ex–television reporter looked wild, a mess. No makeup. Matted hair. Nothing at all like the polished anchorwoman she'd seemed a day earlier.

"A woman wouldn't mess with a mother's emotions and make her worry about her child," Katie retorted, referencing the eerie painting in her own room.

"Oh, wouldn't they?" said Deborah sharply, no longer able to hold her tongue.

Heads swiveled toward Deborah. Surprise registering in their faces at her acid tone.

Dial it back, Deborah. You need to stay in the background and not draw attention to yourself. Lay low. Focus. And you'll get out of this without needing to reveal your past. Ewan can't know about that. My new baby, our child, must never know about that. People deserve second chances. I deserve my second chance.

She cleared her throat, unable to shake the memory of some of the females she'd had to endure in prison. "Women are capable of worse things than men," she said quietly.

Monica swallowed, growing more pale.

"So you think Jackie took the plane?" Nathan asked Stella.

"Why would she take the plane? I mean, can she fly?" Steven asked.

"Not in this weather," Stella said. "Pilot or not. No one could take off in this visibility."

"And there was blood," Bart said, his eyes fixed on Stella. "A fair bit of it. Which means Jackie could be hurt."

"Or someone is hurt," Stella said quietly. "There remains the possibility that there's someone out there in the woods stalking us, sneaking into this house while we're unaware."

"Do you think Jackie could be hurt *and* on the plane?" Monica asked.

"If she is on board," Stella said, "she went south down that lake when the ropes were cut. I don't know how long she could last out there, even if the Beaver does connect with land somewhere. If Jackie was hurt and on that plane, she could be as good as dead."

"I don't think she's on that plane," Steven said. "When I went along that trail this morning, I saw a smaller path leading into the trees on the other side of that second bay. There were marks that had been made through the mud and snow, like something could have been dragged."

"Why didn't you say so?" Bart asked.

"I *am* saying so. I thought it could have been a wild animal, dragging a kill or something. It's only now that it's taking on significance."

"So someone *is* out there?" Katie asked.

"I saw something last night," Nathan said quietly. He rubbed his chin. "Through my window. It looked like a tiny flashlight moving through the trees."

"Christ, Nathan, why didn't *you* say so?" Katie demanded.

"I just thought it might be Stella, going down to check on her plane. But now I think it could have been Jackie."

Steven regarded Nathan, a strange look of suspicion—or perhaps disbelief, mistrust—twisting the doctor's face.

"What time was that?" Steven asked.

"I . . . I'm not sure," Nathan said. "We went upstairs not long after that big clock struck eleven. We changed for bed—Monica and I. We chatted awhile, then I saw the light out the window."

"I also saw something," Steven said. "And now I'm thinking it could have been you, Nathan." The surgeon turned to the others. "At about eleven fifty p.m., I also saw a light moving through the trees. A person who was staying in the cover of the trees rather than using the path. Then I saw a second shadow, following the first. My bet is on Nathan."

"What in the hell would I be doing going down to the plane in the dark?" Nathan asked.

"You tell me," said Steven.

Silence fell like a blanket over the room, save for the crackling fire.

Deborah watched the others. Her gaze settled on Bart. That's when she noticed.

"Bart, where's your knife?" Deborah asked.

His hand went to the sheath he'd looped onto the belt at his hips. "Oh . . . that's the other thing," he said, meeting their gazes. "When I woke up, the knife that I'd taken from the shed out back was missing from where I'd laid it with my jeans over a chair."

No one said a word.

Bart's face darkened. "What? You guys don't believe me?"

"How'd you injure your hand?" Steven pointed to the angry red cut along the back of Bart's left hand, which was now resting on the empty knife sheath.

"I slipped in the snow, tried to halt my fall, and connected with something sharp."

Silence as everyone struggled to process and weigh the veracity of Bart's words. The house creaked under the gathering weight of snow.

Bart's face turned thunderous. "Jesus, what *is* this? Are you people accusing *me* of something?"

"There was blood on the dock," Stella said, her gaze locking with Bart's. "It could have come from your bleeding hand. Were you on the dock before I arrived, Bart? While the plane was still safely moored there? Did you use that missing knife to cut it free?"

"Oh, for God's sake!" Bart said. "Can't you see what's happening here? We're scared. We're turning feral. We're turning on each other. Weren't you the one, Stella, who said the only way out of this is if we work as a team? Weren't you the one who said back during our safety briefing that panic is dangerous—panic is what kills?" He glowered at her, his eyes flashing dark and angry.

He raked his fingers through his short, dark hair. "Look, Jackie Blunt might be on that plane. And if she is, she's gone. But given those weird drag marks Steven described seeing in the woods, she might still be here, somewhere out in the forest, and hurt. And we need to look for her because she might need help. I think our first step is to organize a search party."

"Those woods are endless," said Nathan.

"But if there is someone out there, and if they did take Jackie, they're human," Bart countered hotly. "And a human can only get so far dragging a woman of Jackie's size. We'll search until it gets dark again."

Silence. They all watched. Fire crackled and roared as another log caught fire, and the eyes of animals suddenly came alive with reflected flame and darting shadows.

"We have to," Bart said quietly. "What would we be if we didn't?"

Stella came to her feet. "He's right."

"Oh no. I'm not going off into those woods," Steven said. "What if it *is* one of us? What if it's Bart, and he's leading us into an ambush?"

"Jesus, Steven," Monica said. "Are we going to let Jackie Blunt bleed to death? Is that what we've become?"

"What if it's Jackie?" Deborah said suddenly.

Again, all eyes swung to her.

Her cheeks heated under the intensified scrutiny. "Jackie could have staged this. Maybe she cut the plane free, and now she's waiting to finish us off in the woods, one by one. Maybe she planned this all along."

Silence.

Stella began to pace in front of the fire. She stopped. "Either way, are we any safer sitting here? Like rats in a barrel, waiting to be picked off? I think we should mount that search party. I think we have no choice but to look for her. Because if she is innocent and out there,

Bart's right, she needs our help. Left out there for the night, she will die."

Katie sat forward, her features setting into a firm line, her neck muscles cording. "Stop right there, Stella. Just because Jackie Blunt is gone, just because Dan Whitlock never got on the plane, it doesn't mean they've been 'picked off.' It doesn't mean they are *dead*. We could all be leaping to extreme conclusions here, imaginations running wild because of some . . . some psychological taunting with that book and that rhyme and those figurines. This might not actually be as malevolent as it seems."

"Wishful thinking, Katie," Deborah said. "What about the heads lopped off these carvings? That second head came off sometime between when we all went to bed and now."

Nathan glanced at Steven, then Monica, as if deliberating something. "I . . . I wasn't going to mention it, because . . ." Nathan shot another look at Steven. "It didn't have as huge a significance at the time. But it goes to the fact someone was inside not long before we arrived. Steven and I found a bag of groceries in the kitchen. The receipt shows the contents were purchased just over four weeks ago."

"Where were the groceries bought?" Katie said.

Another glance at Steven. "Kits Corner Store. In Kitsilano."

Stella froze. "What . . . what was in the bag?" Her voice came out soft, strange.

They all looked at her. The mood in the room shifted, thickening with a sense of mounting anxiety. Fear.

"A cardboard carton of a dozen organic eggs," Nathan said. "And a Snickers bar and a box of cereal—strawberry-flavored Tooty-Pops."

Stella's face went ashen. Her mouth opened. Closed. Slowly, she seated herself on the stone ledge in front of the fireplace. Her hands went to cover her mouth.

"What is it, Stella?" Monica sat sharply forward, her body wire-tense suddenly.

"I . . I . . . It's—" Stella sucked in a deep, shaky breath. "It's . . . just a bad memory. I'm fine. It's nothing."

She came sharply to her feet, dragged both hands over her hair. "We should search in twos. We . . . we should try to arm ourselves with something, in case—"

"Stella!" Monica said, her face pinched and white, borderline hysterical. "You *have* to tell us. What is it about those groceries?"

But Stella just stood there. Almost dazed. Time stretched. The damn clock *tock, tock, tock*ed.

Tears filled her eyes. When she spoke again, her voice was thick. "I made a mistake once," she said quietly. "I was a mother once. I lost my child because I . . . I was a bad mother. I . . . He . . ." Angrily she swiped a tear from her cheek, then another. "He used to love that cereal. Tooty-Pops. Strawberry flavor was his best." She swore suddenly. "I paid for it. God, did I pay. I was accused and punished for it in a court of public opinion. Even my husband blamed me for our child's death. I lost my marriage. I lost my job. Everyone out there thought they could be judge and jury of my life. Yet no one, not one, had walked in my shoes. No one had the right. *No one . . .*" Her voice cracked. She wavered. Then she reseated herself slowly and looked down at her hands.

"They said a woman like me had no right to have children in the first place. And I *couldn't* have more. It had been a bad birth." She was silent as the clock ticked loudly for several seconds.

"They said I killed my child," she whispered.

"*Who* said that?" demanded Katie. "What did you actually do—*what happened?*"

"They said I deserved to lose everything. I'd had my heart cut right out, and they said it was—" Stella went sheet white suddenly. She glanced up. "Karma," she said quietly. "They said it was karma." Her eyes darkened, and a look of fear braided with resignation settled over her face. "That has to be why I was lured here. I'm guilty of murder. Like the people in that book, I am to face a reckoning in these woods."

They all stared. Deborah saw raw terror twisting into Monica's features. Katie began to tap her knee and jiggle her foot, her blue eyes darting wildly about the room as though she were seeing ghosts in the shadows and dark paneling.

Deep inside Deborah's belly, she started to shake. She was going to be sick again. She was suddenly beginning to understand—a picture was emerging, and she was going to throw up.

"*What* did you *do* to your son?" Katie demanded again. "What happened?"

Stella shook her head, as if something was dawning on her. "You can't blame me anymore. No one can punish me any further for what happened. I've had to live with it, and I'm not going to talk about it. I don't owe anyone an explanation anymore."

Katie's gaze shot back to the figurines. She tapped her knee harder and her foot jiggled faster. "If . . . if that rhyme is to be believed, we're *all* guilty of some crime, some lie, some sin. And I'm beginning to think we'd be really stupid—all of us—not to take that rhyme very, very seriously right now."

Stella sucked in another shaky breath, sat up straighter, and squared her shoulders. But she looked older, thinner, the hollows beneath her high cheekbones deeper. Her gray eyes no longer so lucid, but rather exhausted and underlined with shadows. It was as though her capable-woman veneer had been thin, and it had been ripped right off, and her insides had been laid bare for them all to see.

Deborah swallowed. She felt Stella's pain as if it were her own. She couldn't begin to imagine hurting her own baby and being blamed for it. She reached over and took Stella's hand. "It's okay. It's going to be okay."

Tears glinted again into Stella's eyes as she looked at Deborah.

"We'll get through it," Deborah said.

"We will," echoed Bart. "Stella's right. We divide into teams of two—"

"We're seven, Bart," said Steven. "We can't pair off seven."

"I'll go alone," Bart said. "I'll take that rifle." He pointed to the gun on the wall.

"No, you won't," said Steven. "I don't trust you alone with that gun. Either I take the gun, or I go with you."

"Can you even shoot a rifle?" Nathan asked Steven. "Or are you just scared and hope Bart will protect you?"

"I've shot clay pigeons. And don't you fuck with me, Nathan."

Nathan glowered at Steven, his body almost vibrating. "Likewise, Steven."

Steven held the professor's glare. A hidden message seemed to crackle between the two men. Monica reached for her husband's hand, as if restraining him yet again from doing—or saying—something.

There's some secret being shared between those three. It started to reach a high pitch when Nathan mentioned the groceries. That angered Steven. And the mention messed with Monica's head, too. She seemed shocked. I think her husband had not told her. Why?

Her gaze still fixed on the threesome, Deborah said, "I'll stay here. You six can pair off. My ankle will hold me back anyway. And I can be here in case Jackie returns. I'll lock the doors, and if she bangs on them, I will check out the window before letting her in."

"I don't know if you *should* let her in," said Monica. "She could be behind this, and you'll be alone with her."

"There's an air horn on the shelf near the back door," Stella said, pulling herself together. "And yes, lock all the doors. If someone, anyone, comes, and you have reason to be alarmed, sound that horn out of one of the upstairs windows. It'll be a signal for us all to return."

"To return with caution," Bart said.

They all agreed.

While everyone started bustling around in preparation for leaving, Deborah announced she was not feeling well, and she hobbled up the stairs to her bedroom. She entered the small bathroom that led off her room and threw up into the toilet. Twice. Her throat burned with acidic bile as she hung her head over the bowl and held her hair back from her face, breathing hard. Stella's confession went around and around and around in her mind. Deborah placed her hand on her belly, emotion filling her chest. There appeared to be no turning back now—not with the plane, their lifeline, gone. Whatever this was, they were locked in it together. And no matter how fervently Deborah intended to hide her past from these people, she feared there might be no way out, and from this point, it was all just going to get worse.

THE SEARCH

MASON

Tuesday, November 3.

Mason sat in the passenger seat of the SAR truck, Callie at the wheel. Behind them they towed an eight-meter SAR jet boat designed for a crew of two plus twelve rescued passengers. Callie confidently navigated the steep, rutted, and muddy logging track with the heavy rig.

In front of them, barely visible through the low clouds, were the blurred taillights of a slightly larger rig driven by Callie's second in command, Oskar Johansson. The boat on the trailer in front of them could accommodate a crew of six. Both Callie and Oskar were trained and licensed to operate the watercraft—Kluhane Bay was on the shores of one of the biggest and northernmost lakes in the interior of British Columbia. The area drew a large volume of wilderness and backcountry recreation enthusiasts over the summer months, and the number of water-related SAR incidents showed it. Mason had read the reports—missing boaters, kayakers, hikers, and hunters, and swimmers in trouble, formed the bulk of KSAR callouts during the warmer season.

He checked his watch. By the time he'd updated the lead cop in Prince George, and by the time KSAR techs had reported to base and the equipment—including ropes, radios, carabiners, helmets, hunting spotlights, flashlights, food, water, camping gear, bear aversion spray, wilderness first aid kits, and litter baskets to carry the injured or bodies—had been loaded into the boats, trucks, and trailers, it had been 11:00 a.m. They'd been driving since, heading up into the densely forested mountains, aiming for a boat put-in area north of the Taheese Lake outflow. Callie had explained that the currents were too strong right now to put in any lower down, which would have been closer by vehicle.

He glanced at Callie. Her gloved hands held the wheel comfortably. She had a nice, strong profile. Clear skin. No makeup. Her dark-blonde, shoulder-length hair was thick and glossy and tied back neatly. Over it she wore a woolen hat with a KSAR logo.

Everything about her was capable. Efficient. Focused. She radiated an energy Mason found contagious. Callie Sutton was the kind of person you wanted on a team, because she would bring out the best in the rest of a crew. She came across as upbeat yet professional. She appeared to enjoy the very real challenges of what was a volunteer job. Mason's mind strayed back to their conversation at the hospital in Silvercreek—the long drive to visit her husband three times a week. Struggling to cope as a single mother, yet not actually *being* a single mother. Fourteen months was a long, long time to wait for a spouse to come home. Despite Callie's belief that Peter would return, Mason guessed the odds were stacked high against this little family. And even if Peter Sutton did emerge from his vegetative state, life for Callie, Peter, and their son would remain a series of monumental challenges.

As they gained elevation, snow appeared on the branches of the evergreens. Callie engaged the four-wheel drive as her tires struggled for traction and the mountain fell away sharply on one side. Mason knew his urban environment. The dark city streets. The gangs, organized crime, nightclubs, and other haunts. He knew the prosecutors, the workings of the courts, the snitches.

But this wildness was Callie's domain. He had to cede her that authority. He had to use her expertise and work with these rugged Kluhane volunteers on this different kind of policing during his tenure up here. He looked through the foggy windows at the shrouded trees. The rain was starting to spit again.

"It'll be getting dark by the time we reach the north end of Taheese Lake," she said with a quick glance at him. "Depending on what we find, we're geared to camp out. We could be out there a few days."

"Who's looking after Ben?" he asked.

Callie shot him a look, clearly surprised by his question.

"I . . . usually I have things well oiled," she said, negotiating another steep bend in the track. "He's with Rachel. My friend. Rachel and her husband, Ricardo, have a son, Ty, same age as Benny. They've been Peter's and my support team for our SAR work pretty much since Benny was born. Every team member needs a backup system in place," Callie said. "So they can engage at short notice, whether it's a supportive boss at work who'll allow for emergency callouts that could take days, or backup school and day care plans. No sense in saving lives while messing up your own families and jobs. It's one thing I drive home when training new recruits."

Mason sensed a defensiveness bristling in Callie, a twinge of motherly guilt. He was familiar with this kind of reaction. Jenny had been the same when asked about balancing her legal work and being a mom. So while Mason himself had never been confronted with questions about how he managed to be both Luke's father and a homicide detective, he understood. Well, he understood as best he could—Jenny had always driven home this gender disparity to him.

"What did your wife do?" Callie asked. "Did she work?"

A little quiver went through his chest as she turned the tables on him, and he suddenly felt uncertain about sharing more about his life with her. But he'd asked for it.

"Jenny was a lawyer. Family law."

She moistened her lips. Nodded. Eyes directly ahead. Her hands firming a little on the wheel.

"There was guilt," he offered. "As a working mom, Jenny had guilt, too. So do I." Mason's words surprised even himself. He cleared his throat. "In retrospect I wish I'd had more time with Luke. I wish we'd *both* given each other more time, and put more effort into being a family—just . . . enjoying the simple little things."

She threw him a hard glance. He read something in her eyes. Mason was a skilled interrogator, and in Callie's eyes he saw conflict.

"And if you did have a chance to do it over," she said, "would you dial back on work and spend more time at home? Would you change jobs?"

Mason snorted softly and stared out through the rain-spotted windshield. "Like they say, hindsight is twenty-twenty, right? I was passionate about work in major crimes. A big homicide can be all-consuming. Addictive. Jenny's work, too. When she was tied up with a major divorce case, or a major prenup, it could be emotionally draining. Dividing families like that, looking at the hard, technical legalities of fighting over assets in the face of raw emotions like love, or hate, or loss, or betrayal." He was quiet for a moment. "In the end, it's the children who suffer. Always the children."

She bit her lower lip. But said nothing. They drove in silence a few minutes longer.

Suddenly Mason said, "Jen was stressed."

Callie glanced at him. He felt hot. He didn't want to talk about Jenny and Luke, but he also really, suddenly, needed to. It felt safe talking to Callie. She was taken. So there were no subterranean pressures there. She also suffered, so she understood. She wouldn't judge him. He wondered if it was the same for her. If that's why she'd told him some of the things she had at the hospital. Or if she was just open with people.

He cleared his throat. "Jen was constantly in a rush, trying to do everything at once. And Luke was always going on about being hungry, tired, wanting to visit places, get treats, do more fun stuff, see friends, go to the beach." He paused. Then, quietly, he said, "Sometimes I wonder, if I had picked up on those early warning signs, if I could've stopped it all from happening. Maybe Jenny wouldn't have been on the road at that precise time, or maybe if she hadn't been in such a hurry to get Luke to karate between appointments, she'd have passed that spot on the highway earlier, or been more relaxed, more vigilant, driving more defensively. Maybe she would have spotted the erratic driver and—"

"Stop," she said firmly. "You can't think like that, Mason."

Startled by her sharp tone, Mason fell silent and regarded her intently.

"I've been through those kinds of questions a million times over in my mind about Peter. What if he *hadn't* been so tired, working so hard—" Emotion caught her voice. She took a breath. "What if we hadn't had that argument before he left for work, would he have been more focused that day . . . You *want* someone or something, *anything*, to blame, to rail at, and then when you can't find it, you try blaming yourself. You can't go down that road, Mason. You can't."

"Yeah," he said quietly.

They traveled in silence for a while, listening to the ticking of insistent rain on the roof of the cab, the tires squelching and crunching. Wipers slapping. Occasional gusts of wind whistled through the roof racks. It grew darker as they climbed into heavier, wetter clouds that pressed against the truck and sealed behind them as they pushed through. They lost sight of the lead rig.

"It's about another klick up this incline," she said after a few minutes of driving.

He checked his watch. "You mentioned that the owner of the lodge property, this Franz guy, was connected with Hollywood—do you know anything more than that?"

"All I know is from village scuttlebutt. The word is that Franz was possibly retired from the film and television industry. He used to be based in California. I had a sense he might've been the brains behind a couple of the really popular reality television shows shortly after *Survivor* first aired. But I've never thought to dwell on it, or question the information. Like I said, I figured maybe he's passed away, and maybe there was no family to inherit the old lodge property, because I haven't heard of anyone being seen out there. It's far. Isolated. Just . . . way at the end of nowhere. No one goes out there."

"Apart from climbers on Mount Warden."

"Rarely."

"So no campers, kids, no people heading across the lake for a bit of a joyride, bush parties?"

"Not from what I hear. People seem to purposefully stay away, to tell you the truth. Kind of a spooky place. And the lake is long, as is the road to access the boat put-in. So unless you have a plane, it's a challenge. Once you're out there, you're up against this granite rock of Mount Warden and pretty much hemmed in. And it's an area that catches a lot of precipitation. I have no idea why anyone would've wanted to build in that location to begin with—it's not like there's a shortage of places out here for people to lose themselves." She shot him a look. "Sometimes for good. Like those two women who went into the mountains last year and never came out. They still haven't been found. And the woman from the year before, who went up to her cabin alone and was never seen again."

He'd read some of those reports. It was not unusual for hikers to go missing in the BC wilderness and for the remains not to be found for years, sometimes decades, if ever.

"Do you recall what kind of aircraft this Franz guy had?"

"Also a de Havilland Beaver. Different colors—blue and white. But just about everyone who flies backcountry in Canada owns a Beaver. For a reason. Short wingspan, easy to operate in mountainous terrain—to land and take off on the smaller lakes. Peppy engine. Chunky body.

Reliable on water, dry ground, ice, snow. The parts are also simple, so they're easier to repair on the fly, or customize."

They reached a clearing along the lake edge. Muddy and slushy. Oskar and his team were already sliding their boat down a concrete ramp into the steel-gray water of Taheese Lake. Mist swirled, and waves kicked up by wind flecked the lake surface. He couldn't see beyond maybe fifty to a hundred meters.

An edginess tightened through Mason as Callie drew her truck up alongside Oskar's rig. So far the evidence in this case pointed to something deeply unusual. Sinister. He was anxious to reach the lodge.

THE LODGE PARTY

MONICA

Monday, October 26.

"Nathan!" Monica hissed, grabbing her husband's arm and holding him back in the kitchen while the others went out the rear door and to the shed.

She glanced over her shoulder to make sure Deborah was not there. The woman had opted to stay behind, but her limp sure had improved, in Monica's opinion. She was either faking it or milking the injury, and it irritated Monica.

"What is it?" Nathan asked.

"You didn't tell me. About the Tooty-Pops. The bag of groceries from the Kits Corner Store. You didn't bloody tell me. *Why?*"

"Because I knew how much it would upset you, Monica. I was hoping I wouldn't need to bring it up. But after Jackie going missing, after the plane vanishing—" He, too, looked over his shoulder, and then he lowered his voice further. "Steven was the one who found the bag. And I'd rather the information came from us, Monica. It shows Steven we're the ones in control here, not him. I wanted to underscore to him, in front of the others, that if he steps out of line, I can damage him. Irreparably."

"It would destroy us, too!"

"Which is why we play dumb about the fact we know anything about the symbolism of that grocery bag."

She buried her face in her hands. "Jesus almighty, what are we all coming to?" She looked up. "It's her, Nathan. I told you so. Oh, Jesus Christ, it *is* her—the mother. I knew it was."

"The mother's name was not Stella Daguerre."

"Are you in full-blown denial? The mother's name was Estelle Marshall. A *married* name—she said she lost her marriage. Estelle Marshall was a commercial airline pilot for Pacific Air. She used to fly the Vancouver–Singapore route. And when the media and public opinion took her to task for playing a role in her son's death, she cracked and went off the rails. She was found half-naked and drunk, wading in the water at Spanish Banks, remember? Screaming at the cameras while she should have been reporting for a flight, and they had to fire her. Based on that, and what the media had dug up on her past."

Nathan swallowed. His gaze darted to the kitchen window. Through the grime on the panes they could see the others gathering around a worktable in the shed outside. Monica could see that he wanted to deny it. With every molecule in his body. And so did she. But this was just going to blow up more the longer they were trapped here together. They were doomed.

Monica said, very quietly, "Stella is short for Estelle. Daguerre is either her maiden name or a fake one. You heard her, Nathan. *The incident* cost her her marriage *and* her job. She lost everything."

"She looks so different . . . She had long hair. It was dark, thick. She was plumper. Prettier."

"Oh, for God's sake, Nathan! *Listen* to yourself. Grief—tragedy—can do that to you. Scoop you hollow from the inside out. Render you a shell of a human." Tears of empathy pricked into Monica's eyes. With them came a strangling guilt. She swiped at her running nose with the base of her thumb. "And you do realize who scooped that story about her past, don't you? You do know who flogged Estelle Marshall for every ounce of emotion she could wring out of public opinion, and who plastered it all over her Facebook page and on message boards? And even on Twitter, which was just getting rolling? You do know who built her own image and popularity on the back of that story, among others?"

Monica saw reality bite into her husband's eyes.

"Katie Colbourne," he said softly. And then he swore.

"Katie ripped that poor, grieving woman apart, Nathan. Katie dug deep into Estelle Marshall's mental history—a fragile one she'd hidden until that point from her airline employer. Katie found Estelle had been hospitalized in a private institution twice before *the incident*, and Katie learned that social services had visited Estelle once, after a complaint from a neighbor that she was an unfit parent. See? We're all here because of that incident. The one Steven caused."

"And you caused—you are as much to blame."

Her face heated. "The one Katie covered. The one Bart helped you cover up—"

"For you, Monica. I did it for *you*."

"Either way, Bart's the link. Between the car and you and me. He's the one who could expose us."

"He doesn't know he's the link, Monica."

"Not yet he doesn't. It's a matter of time. He's already asked you outright if he'd ever done work for you under the table. They all know now that you taught out in Burnaby. That the university is near his workshop. They all know we lived in Kitsilano. When it comes out about the car—if Stella mentions—"

Nathan grasped her shoulders with both hands. He looked directly into her eyes. "Focus. Do *not* fall apart now. Don't. We need to keep our own counsel, keep our secret, or it will all be over."

"*We* did this to her. We did this." She turned her face away.

He reached up and gently wiped a tear from her cheek. "Monica, look at me."

She turned and gazed up into Nathan's warm eyes.

"I love you, Monica. We'll do this. Together. We've come this far. We won't give in now."

For the first time in a long, long while, Monica felt a spurt of love through her chest. It came with a measure of relief. He was taking charge. He was showing Steven his place. And he was doing it for her—it had all been about her from the start. And right at this very moment, she loved Nathan for being Nathan. Her geeky professor who cherished his mushrooms. When all the chips were down, he was the one still there. He'd always had her back. She'd been awful to him, cheated on him, and he'd forgiven her and stuck by her.

He pulled her close and wrapped his arms around her. She leaned into him.

"And listen, Monica—" He stroked her hair. "It still might just be a weird connection, and not really about that day at all. Because no one knew about us. Not even the cops found out."

Monica pulled back suddenly as it struck her. "Do you think it's her? That *she* lured us here?"

"Stella?"

"For revenge."

He hesitated, then shook his head. "You saw her face when I mentioned the groceries. She was in utter shock."

"She could have faked it? Maybe she hid her plane during the night. Maybe—"

"No. Look—no one knew about us. Not even the cops."

"Jackie Blunt said she worked for Dan Whitlock, who was a PI. Maybe those two are in on it, faked their own deaths, and are just waiting for us to confess."

"Quiet," he said. "Enough. This is why we can't mention a thing. All we can do is hold strong. Me. You. Steven. Not say a word. Because even if someone suspects, there is no proof. Can't be. Not after all these years."

"Bart. He *is* the connection, the proof. Between you and me and my damaged blue BMW that the police were hunting for." Monica cursed and pushed her hair back off her face. She was so goddamn sick of the strain of keeping this secret that she almost *wanted* to confess, for this all to come out. Finally. She *wanted* to see Steven dragged off in handcuffs. She hated that she'd ever fucked him. And that she'd let him drive away from the scene in her car. That she'd been so terrified, so horrified, that she'd frozen in the passenger seat. And even later she could have come forward, but she was too scared. Afraid Nathan and their kids would find out about their affair. Afraid Steven's wife would hear about it. Afraid of what the police would do to her. What would happen to her business, her employees, her life. Her friends. Her fancy house in Kitsilano. So she'd cowered in the shadows, and while Stella—a victim—was grilled, she and Steven had gotten away with killing an innocent and beautiful six-year-old boy whose name was Ezekiel Marshall, and who loved Tooty-Pops and Snickers bars. Whose mother had left him briefly outside a liquor store that forbade minors and dogs. She'd left her child holding a grocery bag and his puppy on a leash on a sidewalk in a safe, classy neighborhood, on a dark and wet autumn afternoon. And while his mother had been paying the cashier for a bottle of chardonnay, little Ezekiel, who was hugging the grocery bag against his chest, had allowed his grip on the pup's lead to slacken. The animal had been distracted by something down the sidewalk, and taken off. Ezekiel had run after it. The pup had ducked between two parked cars and darted across the road, where it was darker. The child followed.

The memory of the thump shuddered through Monica's body.

In her mind's eye she saw Estelle Marshall's wild, white face as she ran screaming out of the liquor store. She saw Estelle dropping her bottle of chardonnay, running into the road. She saw Estelle's face—those *eyes*, those broken eyes—as she'd pleaded on CRTV news for someone who'd seen the blue BMW that had killed her son to come forward. As she'd sobbed and begged for whoever had taken her son's little red backpack to do the right thing and approach the police.

But no one did.

No one seemed to have seen the blue BMW.

The BMW that Nathan had found damaged and parked in his garage with a missing license plate. And when Nathan saw the TV news, he knew. He asked Monica directly, and she'd been forced to tell him about Steven. That they'd been having an affair. How they'd been tipsy that afternoon. How they'd come back to the McNeill house to make love on the bed Monica shared with Nathan.

And Nathan had quietly taken the BMW in the night to a contact in Burnaby. The car never came back. It was fixed, he'd said. And it had been sold to a buyer in Alberta.

The kitchen door swung open with a whoosh of dank, icy air.

"Guys—" Steven stilled, hand on the doorknob, as he registered the looks on their faces. "What're you doing? What's going on?" he asked quietly.

Nathan and Monica exchanged a glance.

"It's her," Monica said quickly. "The mother. Stella is the mother of the dead boy you hit with my car. Bart is the one who fixed and sold my BMW. He's the link—he could expose us all. We could all still go down for this."

Steven swallowed, glanced over his shoulder and through the window toward the others in the shed. "Do Stella and Bart know each other?" he asked.

"I don't see how they could," whispered Nathan.

"Steven!" Stella's yell reached them from outside. They heard her coming over, her boots crunching through slush and stones. She appeared in the doorway, breathing hard. "Did you find Monica and—"

She glanced from Steven to Monica to Nathan, frowned. "What are you guys doing?"

"Nothing," Monica said hurriedly, flustered. "Just . . . worried."

Stella observed them for a moment too long. "We need to move," she said. "It'll be dark again before long. We've got flashlights and head-lamps, and some things we can use for weapons in the shed. You need to come and take your pick."

THE LODGE PARTY

DEBORAH

Deborah stepped farther back behind the wall that screened the kitchen from the great room. She'd come downstairs to boil some water. She was dehydrated from throwing up, and too afraid to drink what came out of the faucets without boiling it. Then she'd heard Monica and Nathan whispering. Then Steven coming in.

As the kitchen door closed behind them, her heart stuttered so fast in her chest she thought she was going to have a heart attack.

All the jagged pieces of this jigsaw puzzle were coming together, and what she saw terrified her.

She waited until she was certain everyone had cleared out of the kitchen, then entered carefully.

It was dark and spooky in here. Knives and cleaver and tenderizer all suddenly looked ominous. She moved slowly toward the window, her ankle feeling so much better. She peered outside.

She could see them all gathered around a workbench in the open-sided shed, sharing among themselves cans of bear spray, an air horn, and knives. Bart was loading the gun and putting bullets into his pockets. Steven glanced toward the house, and she stepped back quickly, out of view.

THE SEARCH

CALLIE

Callie guided her craft out into the choppy waters of Taheese Lake. As they rounded the point, the wind slammed her boat, and rain streamed over the windows screening the controls. Mason stood under the cover at the controls beside her. She idled her engine, waiting and watching for Oskar and his crew of three male SAR members and one female to exit the protected bay. As soon as they came around the point, Callie opened the throttle. As fast as the low visibility would allow, she bombed and bashed the prow of her craft into the small waves and sleety rain. In places, the clouds blew so thick over the water that she couldn't even discern the mountain flanks that rose steeply on either side of the narrow body of water.

"I see what you mean by the wind being funneled down this lake," yelled Mason, holding on to his cap with one hand and the railing with the other.

"What?"

He repeated himself, louder.

She laughed. She'd be lying if she said she didn't get off on the exhilaration of this job. She loved the wind slicing cold against her face, the slap of rain, the resistance of waves against her prow. Every now and then she could glimpse the sweeping mountains, dense forests, black rocks, the vicious avalanche shunts littered with giant upended root balls and boulders. It was God's country, in Callie's mind. She lived to breathe in and appreciate the lethal majesty of it.

Oskar followed with his bigger craft in her wake. After about forty minutes, she checked her instruments again. They'd covered a distance of about thirty kilometers from the boat launch. She slowed her craft. So did Oskar behind her. The noise of their engines changed as they chugged slowly forward into the low-visibility gloom. Callie couldn't see Mount Warden or the north end of the lake, but she could sense it, something big and hulking behind the thick curtains of weather. "Should be here now," she said to Mason.

"I see it!" He pointed as the clouds parted.

The lodge came into view suddenly, hunkering like a black creature in a clearing, hemmed in on either side with dense coniferous forest that fringed right up to the water's edge. Windows glinted like eyes. The totem poles stood like warnings.

Callie shook the sense of menace that seemed to curl in the shifting clouds around the place. She hadn't been here since that time she'd come to climb the south face of Warden with Peter and a few other climbers. That had been more than four years ago. The place had always felt spooky, but never more so.

They came up to the old dock. She nudged her craft up alongside the planks covered with moss and clots of slush. The dock creaked and sucked against the lapping waves. Oskar brought his boat up behind hers.

There was no sign of activity on land.

No smoke curled from the stone chimney. No lantern lights glowed inside. The only evidence that someone had been here was two ropes that had been tied to the dock. The ends dangled in the water.

Callie nodded toward the ropes as she turned off the engine. "They look new."

Mason nodded.

They took the hunting spotlights and flashlights from the crafts and disembarked in silence. While the SAR crew secured the boats, Mason crouched down on the wet dock and with gloved hands pulled the rope ends out of the water.

Callie noticed immediately that the ends had been cut. She watched quietly as Mason took photographs of the rope ends while Oskar and the others started up toward the lodge, flashlight beams bouncing back at them in the fog.

"Do you think that's recent?" Callie nodded at the sliced rope ends as Mason came to his feet and surveyed the scene.

"Yeah," he said quietly. "The Beaver with the dead pilot had the same kind of ropes tied to the struts. Same evidence of cuts."

"So the aircraft could have been moored here and cut free?"

"It's certainly a working theory as of now." He switched on his flashlight and panned it carefully across the wet planks. "Can you ask your guys to hold back for a minute?" he asked.

Callie cursed inwardly as she saw how Oskar and the others had tracked up the slush on the dock.

"Hoi!" she yelled into the mist. "Oskar! Guys! Hold back until RCMP gives the go!"

Oskar waved his hand.

Mason moved to the end of the tippy dock. He crouched down again. With his gloved hand he swished some of the slush aside. Callie saw what had attracted him—pink stains in the slush. Adrenaline hummed into her blood. She glanced toward the lodge. Oskar and the guys were waiting near the totem poles. Oskar was scanning the ground with his spotlight. He was an ace man-tracker. He'd probably seen something, too.

Mason shot more photos and came to his feet. "Let's go take a look. As of now, this could all be a crime scene. I'd like your techs to stay back until my order. At all times."

"Understood."

She followed Mason up the narrow and overgrown path that led to the totem poles where the others waited.

A creak sounded. Callie started and glanced up. The raven's head and wings moved as the wind shifted direction. The hairs on the back of her neck prickled. The loose top of the totem functioned like some primitive wind sock, yet Callie couldn't shake the notion it was alive, and watching them. She was getting a really weird sixth-sense kind of warning about this place. And Callie trusted her gut feelings. They'd saved her life on more than one occasion in the wilderness in the past.

What have those wooden raven's eyes seen playing out here?

When they reached the stairs that led up to the front porch, Mason held out his hand. "Stay back a minute. Wait here."

He drew his sidearm and moved carefully up the stairs. He banged on the door. "Hello! Anyone here?"

Silence lay heavy as they all listened for a response. Nothing came, apart from the steady drumming of rain and the swishing of wind through the forest. Mason tried the handle. The door opened. He made a motion for them all to move to the side, off the path, out of a direct line with the door. They acquiesced, exchanging glances and watching as Mason pushed open the door with his foot, gun ready in both hands.

"Hello! Anyone home?" he called again. He waited a second. "It's Sergeant Mason Deniaud from Kluhane RCMP. I'm coming in!"

He entered like a cop, weapon leading as he kept to one side of the door, then moved deftly to the other.

He disappeared inside.

They heard him calling out inside the lodge.

"There was blood on the dock," she whispered to Oskar.

"You sure it's blood?"

"Possibly blood," she corrected. But the victim, Jackie Blunt, had been stabbed somewhere, and Callie's bet was on the stains being human blood.

Oskar nodded as he continued to pan his spotlight through the gloomy twilight, surveying the ground around them. He pointed suddenly.

"Over there," he said quietly. "In the mud, along the berry scrub. Looks like prints."

She tented her hand over her eyes against the rain and peered into the mist. He was right. There were tracks of churned-up mud and slush near a gap in the brambles that led into the trees.

Time ticked on while they waited for Mason. The clouds lowered. Rain came down more incessantly, pearling off their jackets and dripping from the bills of their caps. The darkness grew complete.

"He's taking his time," Oskar said. "You think he's okay?"

Callie was growing worried. But then she saw a flashlight beam moving in one of the dark windows upstairs. "He's up there." She pointed.

A few moments later, Mason reappeared in the doorway. The group tensed as he came quietly down to join them.

"The place appears empty," he said, holstering his weapon. "But they were here."

"You sure?" Callie asked.

"For a couple of days, judging by tins and plates in the kitchen sink and on the dining table. They were sleeping in the rooms upstairs. Some belongings are still in the rooms, including a wallet with Jackie Blunt's ID."

THE LODGE PARTY

STEVEN

Monday, October 26.

Steven followed Monica and Nathan to the shed, but as Monica and Nathan went inside, something made Steven glance back toward the lodge.

He stilled. She was there—her shape behind the rimed kitchen windowpanes. Deborah Strong. Watching.

Deborah moved away quickly as she saw him looking.

That woman was a quiet, strange sort. She made Steven uneasy. She was a watcher. She sucked things into her aura. A taker.

Mist shifted in front of the kitchen windows, and a chill curled through him. *A watcher watches . . . witnesses . . .*

He froze.

Witness.

The word hissed through his mind. His heart beat faster. Jackie Blunt's words filled his head.

I've seen Deborah before. I know that tattoo on her wrist. A swallow. I've seen that ink. And I've spoken to her. I know her voice . . . I have a memory for these things.

Deborah's response: *You're mistaken.*

He recalled the tension that had crackled between the two. They did know each other, thought Steven. And they'd not revealed it—chosen instead to hide it. Why? His mind went back to Monica's shocking revelation that Stella was the mother of the boy he'd killed.

His body heated as he stared at the dark lodge building and opaque windows. He recalled the eyes of the mother pleading on television. He knew Monica was right. It was her. Maybe on some subterranean level he'd seen it himself earlier, but his survival brain had not listened.

Because he'd hit the child. He'd killed little Ezekiel Marshall.

The memory of the thud shuddered through him.

He'd not believed it possible when it happened. But he'd been over the limit. Distracted—Monica's head in his lap, sucking his cock. Her giggling. Then the *bam*.

Sweat prickled over his body despite the chill.

He'd reversed. He'd checked to be certain, seen the blood, the child's face . . . He'd panicked, hit the gas, squealed around the corner, sped off down a dark side street.

But someone had witnessed what he'd done. A woman. She'd been standing on the corner in the rain, farther down the sidewalk from the stores, where it was quieter, darker. High-heeled boots, short skirt. Shiny black trench coat. Rain dripping from her umbrella. The trauma of the event had scored her image into his mind. A sex worker, he'd figured, who'd looked right into the car window—right at his face—her mouth a round O of horrified shock.

The witness.

As he'd sped around the corner, she'd run toward the fallen boy.

But the witness had never come forward. No one knew what had happened to her, or whether she'd even existed. She'd had her own things to hide. She had looked at the boy, must have seen he was beyond repair, then had taken his backpack and the fallen, battered BMW front plate and fled the scene, too.

The mother had seen the witness running off with the little red backpack. The mother had told the cops and the media there'd been a witness, and that she'd taken Ezekiel's backpack. The mother had clearly not seen the woman pick up the battered license plate.

The police had hunted for her. They'd put up notices on poles and made announcements in the media, calling for the possible witness to come forward. But nothing. And no one seemed to know about the plate.

As time had passed, as Katie Colbourne had revealed the fact that Estelle Marshall had suffered bouts of "mental illness" and depression for which she'd sought private treatment, they'd all begun to think Estelle might have made up the witness. Especially under the stress of the hit-and-run incident that killed her boy.

A witness watches.

A cold, hard ball slid through his stomach into his bowels. The conversation with his lawyer—his fixer—snaked up from the depths of Steven's memory.

"I have someone, Steven. Ex-cop. Now a private investigator. He gets the job done. If anyone can retrieve that plate and silence that witness, he's our man."

"Who is it?"

"Best we don't get into that information. Better to keep things compartmentalized in case things go pear-shaped. Less you know, less we all know, the better."

"But this PI will fix it?"

"For a price."

"How?"

"Again, the less you know, the less potential for blowback."

"So you mean . . . this witness, she'll be paid off?"

"Something like that."

Steven tried to breathe. He tried to think against the wildness of panic setting in, confusing him. It was all there. All the dots and links.

Had Dan Whitlock been the PI? Had he in turn paid someone to put the screws to the witness?

Could . . . just could . . . the witness have been Deborah Strong?

No. No. Fuck no. This was all messing with his head. He was seeing links that were not there. His guilt, his fear, were making a monster in every corner.

"Steven?"

He gasped, spun around. The group—all of them—were watching him with weird looks on their faces, like he was mad or something.

"Are you okay, man?" Bart asked.

Monica's words echoed in his skull.

Bart. He is *the connection, the proof. Between you and me and my damaged blue BMW that the police were hunting for.*

"Yeah, I . . . I'm fine." He entered the dark, cobwebby shed. It looked like some kind of rural torture chamber, filled with implements and tools coated with dust and grime, and it smelled like sawdust and something he couldn't identify. A big freezer was pushed up against the wall at the back, next to it a generator. On the shelves, gasoline cans with spouts.

"Nothing in it," said Bart, noticing Steven looking at the chest freezer. Bart opened the lid to demonstrate. "I suppose if we were here for days, we could hunt and store shit in here. It hooks up to the generator, and those gas cans are full."

Steven looked into Bart's eyes. Then to the knife sheath still on his hip. Empty.

I did jobs off the books, and accepted cash under the table to fix hot vehicles.

Guys who fixed hot vehicles off the books were usually connected to people who stole vehicles. Criminals. Gangs. People like Bart sometimes kept records, photos, surveillance footage for leverage in case things went sideways. Could Bart have kept evidence that showed Nathan bringing him Monica's damaged car? Could there exist old photographs of the BMW?

The Vancouver news had been full of stories about the hit-and-run fourteen years earlier, full of calls for witnesses who might have seen a blue BMW with damage to the front. Bart had to have seen that news. He'd have known that the blue BMW he'd worked on for Nathan most likely had been involved. Surely there'd been some blood on the car, or even hair, or something else from the child?

And if Bart exposed Monica and Nathan, there was no way in hell Monica would go down without ratting on him.

Panic tightened like a noose around Steven's neck. He couldn't breathe.

Is there a way I can still stop this from coming out? Stop Bart from making connections out here, in this forced proximity?

Can I stop Bart . . . dead?

The thought—the word—hit Steven square between the eyes as he looked into Bart's swarthy face.

Dead.

To save myself.

Could I bring myself to do it?

Who would know? If it happened out there in the woods while they were all searching for Jackie Blunt?

"I found these," Katie said as she set several rolls of fluorescent-orange flagging tape onto the worktable beside the knives, hatchet, pepper spray, and air horn they'd collected. "We can tie pieces on branches as we go, so we don't lose our way back."

"Great. Like Hansel and Gretel's breadcrumbs," said Monica.

"At least the ravens and crows and woodland animals won't eat flagging tape," retorted Katie.

The women glared at each other. Steven could feel the tension crackle between them.

How much has Katie guessed? She has to have figured out the Stella-Estelle connection, surely? Judging by the manic questions she was asking Stella inside, the way she was tapping her knee and jiggling her foot. But Katie Colbourne can't possibly know how Monica, Nathan, and I are connected to Stella. Not even the police found us back then.

Bart seemed edgy, checking and rechecking that the rifle was loaded.

"Okay," said Stella. "Pick your defense weapons. And let's pair off—"

"I'm going with Bart," Steven stated.

Everyone fell silent.

"Look, I don't trust Bart with the gun," Steven said. "I don't know what happened to his knife. I don't know how he cut his hand, or why there was blood on the dock, okay?"

"I told you all. Someone took my knife."

"Yeah, like who?"

Bart glowered at him. Tension thickened to the combustion point.

"Fine," Stella said. "Go with Bart. Katie, do you want to come with—"

"I'll go with you, Stella," Monica interjected. "Nathan can pair with Katie."

Katie's eyes flashed. "Don't trust me, either?"

"I trust myself, and I trust my husband," Monica said. "I feel more comfortable if we split up, and Nathan and I each watch someone else."

The wind came suddenly down from the mountain behind the shed and whooshed in through the cracks.

"We need to move," Stella said. "Before the next storm comes in, and before it gets dark. Each group take a flashlight in case we don't make it back before we lose light."

"So what's our search strategy?" Bart asked. "Where were those drag marks, Steven?"

Steven explained. "I took the trail which led to the next bay. There was a bit of a clearing, and then the forest grew thick again. I saw the marks going into those thick trees, along a narrower track, at the end of the clearing."

"So who would've made these trails?" Monica asked.

"Probably people who came to stay in this lodge," Katie said.

"Or animals," Bart suggested. "They could be animal tracks."

"He's right," Stella said. "We might encounter wildlife. And that wildlife might be protecting prey. Two of the teams take a can of bear spray each. There are only two. The other will have to take the air horn."

"I think the guys with the rifle can take the air horn," Katie said, reaching for a can of pepper spray. "Or the rest of us will have nothing to actually fend off the wildlife."

"Air horns scare bears." Steven picked up the air horn can.

"Allegedly," said Monica, reaching for the last can of bear spray.

They helped themselves from the assortment of knives that had been brought from the kitchen. Stella took the hatchet.

Steven led the way, and they moved in single file, fast, along the trail through the trees to the second bay. Monica took up the rear. The forest through which the trail snaked was old growth. Big, towering evergreens. A dense canopy overhead, thick trunks, sparsely spaced. Lots of springy moss and pine needles on the ground. Emerald-green moss and white and orange and pale-green lichens grew over old, rotting logs. Mushrooms sprouted everywhere out of the loam, and conks bulged like cancerous growths from some of the trunks. Steven was grateful Nathan kept his mouth shut about all the fungi. Mist moved like specters through the trunks. At intervals they attached strips of tape to low-hanging branches or bushes.

"We don't need the tape on this part of the trail," Steven said, growing more agitated by the second. "It's clear that it leads to the lodge."

"Not if the mist gets very thick and it gets dark," Stella argued from behind him. "People get really turned around in conditions like that."

"And you know this?" he called over his shoulder.

"Yeah, I know this. I've flown tons of charters into remote places like this, and to Gulf Islands, and places up and down to the Inside Passage."

"How long have you been flying charters, Stella?" Monica asked from the rear of their column. And Steven could see what Monica was doing—digging for the truth about Stella Daguerre.

"About fifteen, maybe more, years," said Stella.

She's lying. If she really is Estelle Marshall, then she was flying big commercial aircraft on the Singapore route fourteen years ago.

Nine Little Liars thought they'd escaped . . .

"Here." He pointed. "The marks are here. You can see under the slush."

"I can't see any marks," Katie said, coming up to his side.

Professor Mushroom did his man-who-loves-forests thing and crouched down on his haunches. With his bare hand he tenderly moved aside slush and snow.

"Blood," said Nathan. "That looks like blood." He glanced at the trees into which the trail led. A tiny gap opened into deep, dark woods. Another path led into the trees a little lower down the flank of the mountain, closer to the lake.

A wolf howled. Everyone fell silent.

It howled again, somewhere up in the distant mountains. Katie shivered as the howl rose in crescendo, then died with a series of answering yips from another direction.

Steven swallowed. He felt fear. He didn't like it. He knew his hospital. He knew the city. He knew money and smart cars and fine wine and first-class air travel. He knew vineyards and Europe and London and New York. Fine hotels. This he had not signed up for.

Mist swirled, thickening, and a breeze rustled through the old branches.

"I think we should go back," Monica said.

"We split up here," Bart said. And Steven wondered if he was leading them into some kind of a trap. It could have been Bart who'd hurt Jackie and left blood on the dock. That's how he might have cut his hand. He thought of Jackie missing. He thought of wolves.

"I just keep thinking of those figurines," Katie said, her voice going tight. "And that rhyme. Monica is right. We should go back to the lodge."

"We have to look for her, Katie," Stella said. "That could be her blood down there. Something could have dragged her into those woods."

"I know. That's the problem," said Katie.

"We have to do this," Bart said.

"No, we don't," Monica snapped. "We really don't."

"And if it was *you* who was missing?" Bart said. "And hurt somewhere?"

"What are we if we don't at least try?" Stella asked.

Bart stepped forward, determination on his face. The wind ruffled his black hair. His cheeks were red from the cold. "Steven, you and I will take this path with the blood. We have the gun. Monica, Stella, Nathan, Katie—you all take the lower one, and split if you encounter a branch. Keep calling out every ten minutes or so. Make sure we all stay within ear contact."

"This is dumb," Katie said, still shivering, looking pale.

Bart ignored her. "We walk for an hour, max. Searching carefully for signs. Keep flagging your routes. After sixty minutes, if nothing, we turn back. Same path. Make sure you know how to trace your steps back."

Steven and Bart watched for a moment as the others started down to the lower trail.

"They do look like animal trails, don't they?" Bart said, returning his attention to the narrow, overgrown path. "As opposed to man-made."

"I wouldn't fucking know, now would I?" Steven snapped. "Go on, you're the Boy Scout. Lead our way."

Bart held Steven's gaze for a second, then turned and entered the gap that led into the dark woods.

THE SEARCH
CALLIE

"They appear to have written a message in a notebook, saying they were leaving the lodge," Mason told Callie and her team as he reholstered his sidearm outside the building. "But the note was ripped out. Just the first part of it is legible."

Callie looked up at the big, dark house.

"They had shelter here," she said. "Tools for boiling water, wood to make fire. They would presumably know they didn't stand much chance out in the forest, in these mountains. Especially in this weather."

"Which begs the question," Oskar said. "Why did they go?"

"Maybe they were desperate," offered one of the SAR techs. "Risking their lives in the wilderness seemed more attractive than staying here."

"Knowing more about the individuals will help toward answering those questions," Callie said.

"Callie," Mason said, "you come with me. I want your initial assessment based on what you see inside." He turned to the others. "This is a crime scene. No one touch anything they don't have to. Use gloves. Follow protocol of one approach route in, same approach out. Oskar, can your guys do a careful sweep around the sides of the building, and the rear, to be certain no one is still here?"

Oskar nodded.

"And take no risks," Mason ordered. "A woman has been murdered. The killer could be out here."

Oskar drew the techs aside and began to divide them into two groups.

Callie entered the lodge behind Mason while the two SAR teams went around the sides of the building.

The darkness inside felt like a physical weight. She and Mason ran their flashlights around the room. The darkness darted away from their beams, scuttling into corners, under things, watching and leaping back whenever they turned their beams another way. The house seemed to exhale cold, and old fire smoke, and a faintly foul, unidentifiable odor. *An evil breath.*

Get a grip. It's just been locked up, musty, things decaying—Callie started as her beam reflected on the glowing, yellow eyes of a deer head mounted on the paneled walls.

Get a grip.

On the walls were dark oil paintings, shelves lined with musty-looking old books, indigenous masks with wild black hair and garish grins.

Mason found and lit a kerosene lantern. Gold light shimmered into the void. Suddenly the interior looked a little less hostile. The room was huge, the stone hearth Gothic in design and dimension.

"Where was the note?" she asked Mason. Her voice seemed to bounce from wall to wall in the cavernous space before being cast up toward the vaulted roof. She glanced up and saw a massive horn chandelier hanging like a sword of Damocles above her head.

Mason pointed to a coffee table in front of the hearth, where a notebook lay next to a big checkerboard made of stone. On the board stood five carved wooden figurines. They looked to Callie like traditional First Nations art that echoed the design of the totem poles outside.

An additional three of the carvings had been toppled over. It appeared their heads had all been freshly chopped off, given the markings and the light color of the wood where the cuts had been made. Callie frowned and caught Mason's gaze.

But the sergeant's eyes were hidden in shadow beneath the bill of his cap, and the expression in them was unreadable. He handed Callie a pair of blue nitrile gloves he'd taken from his pocket. He was already wearing a pair of his own.

"Use these before touching anything."

She removed her cold-weather gloves, snapped on the crime scene gloves, and reached for the notebook on the table.

Someone had written in blue ink:

To whoever finds this note,

We have left this lodge to fi . . .

The rest of the note had been ripped diagonally from the book. The tear marks leaving only this corner with these few words. As if done in haste.

She glanced up at Mason. He was watching her intently, his face all angles and rugged planes in the quavering yellow lantern light.

"They wanted to leave rescuers a note, then changed their minds?"

"Or one of them didn't want that note left," Mason said.

A chill slid down Callie's spine. "You think whoever killed Jackie Blunt might be among the group? That the killer might have ripped out the note, not wanting anyone to follow? Or to delay possible help?"

"Someone cut those ropes on the plane," he said. "Setting it adrift with Jackie Blunt's body inside."

"And they'd have to have known the Beaver would blow away from the lodge in the prevailing wind. Or possibly they weren't thinking logically. Panic will do that—" A piece of white paper on the floor under the table snared Callie's attention. She set the notebook down, got down on her knees, and fished it out.

"It's been typed," she said, coming to her feet. "Some kind of verse, a rhyme."

Mason came close. They read it together as he held the lantern up for them both to see clearly.

Nine Little Liars thought they'd escaped.
One missed a plane, and then there were eight.

Eight Little Liars flew up into the heavens.
One saw the truth, and then there were seven.

Seven Little Liars saw they were in a fix.
One lost control, and then there were six.

Six Little Liars tried hard to stay alive.
One saw the judge, and then there were five.

Five Little Liars filed out the door.
One met an ax, and then there were four.

Four Little Liars lost in the trees.
One got stabbed, and then there were three.

Three Little Liars realized what they knew,
One hanged himself, and then there were two.

Two Little Liars went on the run.
One shot a gun, and then there was one.

One Little Liar thinks he has won.

For in the end, there can only be one.

But maybe . . .

there shall be none.

"*Nine* Little Liars?" Callie said. "And one missed the plane?" She looked at Mason. "The RAKAM Group tour started out as nine people, too."

"Before Dan Whitlock died of food poisoning."

"And then there were eight," Callie said softly. Her attention shifted back to the five carvings on the board, then the three without heads lying to the side.

The noise of a door bashing open boomed like a dull explosion into the quietness of the house. Callie's muscles tightened, and she spun round.

"Sergeant!" Oskar entered the big room with his hunting spotlight, breathing hard, face tight. "You need to come and see this."

"What is it?" Callie asked, stepping forward.

"There's . . . a freezer in the shed out back. It's hooked up to a generator that must have run out of gas a while ago." He paused. "There are bodies inside. Two."

"Show me," Mason said, hastening toward Oskar. Oskar spun on his heels to lead the way. Callie rushed after them.

Outside, nestled up against the trees that grew dense at the foot of Mount Warden, was an open-sided shed facing the house. Just under the cover was a stump with an ax that had clearly been used to chop wood. Split wood had been stacked against one wall. In the middle of the shed was a big worktable. The SAR guys stood behind the table in front of a big chest freezer, dark stains down the sides. Their faces looked blanched in the flickering lantern light. Someone was vomiting around the corner, out of sight. One of the guys held open the freezer lid.

Callie and Mason moved closer. Oskar shone his spotlight inside. The contents jumped into stark visibility. A woman's face and a hand were partially visible from a fold in the sheet in which she'd been wrapped. One eye stared sightlessly out at them. Callie's stomach clutched, and bile surged into the back of her throat. The smell was fetid, like carrion.

She covered her nose and mouth.

"Shit," Mason said quietly. He'd gone still, his gaze fixed on the macabre sight in the freezer. Time seemed to elongate. The wind shushed and whispered in the trees. Rain pattered on the tin roof of the shed.

"All of you, move back. Get well away from this shed, and away from the lodge building." He unsheathed his satellite phone. "We need to cordon off this entire area all the way down to the beach and dock. As of now it's all officially a crime scene."

He stepped out of the shed to call it in.

THE LODGE PARTY

NATHAN

Nathan walked in front of Katie. They'd parted ways with Monica and Stella a while back, where the path divided into two. His mind raced. Panic was beginning to override his usually rational, careful, considered, scientific mind. His scholarly objectivity. Ordinarily he could remove himself, distance himself from a problem, compartmentalize base human emotions—like rage or betrayal—while he examined things logically.

But now, out here, confronted with Steven again, his feelings were suddenly raw. Anxiety churned through him. Complex emotions fought in his heart for dominance—hurt, love, fury. His hands fisted and unfisted at his sides as he walked blindly into the dark of the forest.

"You okay?"

He spun around to face Katie. His eyes felt hot. His mind in the past—reliving how it had gutted him to hear Monica reveal she'd slept with Steven.

In my bed.

Katie retreated a step as his eyes locked with hers. She stumbled, steadied herself with a hand against the trunk of a young hemlock.

"Why?" he asked.

She looked down at his hands. He saw how they fisted and unfisted, as if of their own volition.

He held out his hands and splayed his fingers forcibly to stop the fisting. He laughed out loud, the sound harsh and strange to his own ears. "I'm sorry."

"It . . . it's okay," she said. Her eyes, her body posture, seemed to disagree. "It's . . . Everything is making us twitchy. I . . . I think we should go back."

She was scared. Of *him*. Wham—it struck him. Nathan liked that she was frightened of him—he actually did, really did. Dr. McNeill, professor of mushrooms, could make women tremble and stumble. It filled his blood with a sense of potency, virility. *That* was what his wife saw in Dr. Steven Bodine. Power. Alpha behavior. Control. Honed physique. Thick head of hair. Virility. Basic biological programming. It drove the attraction of the opposite sex. Drove them to juice up, engorge, send out pheromones, primed them to come together for intercourse. Sex in order to procreate. To fertilize eggs. Preserve the species.

Steven Bodine was a bull among cows. Full of testosterone and biologically programmed to fuck every cow that would allow him.

Basic science. The selfish gene. An expression of evolution. He knew all this. His wife sent out her feminine signals without being able to control it—big boobs, nice round ass that gave a guy a hard-on before he could even think about whether she was married and off-limits. It was just there. Hard dick. Desire. Do the programmed thing. We deluded ourselves, we humans, thinking about romantic notions of love and fidelity . . .

"Nathan?"

He shook himself. Looked at her—really looked. Katie sent out signals, too. But it was her immaturity that turned him off. She might be in her late thirties, but some women just stayed like that. Childish. Helpless. And she thought she was special because she could hold a mike and talk in front of a camera. She was a bleached-blonde airhead who thought *she* could judge a woman like Estelle Marshall, a commercial airline pilot. Katie Colbourne of CRTV had thought it would make her popular if she took Estelle Marshall down, if she revealed Estelle's mental illness so that aspersions would be cast on the woman's parenting ability, so that Estelle Marshall would be judged even *more* harshly for briefly leaving her six-year-old outside a liquor store on a dark and rainy afternoon. And now look at her, a scared mother herself, finally seeing what it was like.

"Nathan," she said more insistently, backing away, her hand going hesitantly to the pepper spray canister she'd secured to her hip.

"Thirty more minutes," he said, suddenly snapping back into focus and looking at his watch. "Then we can turn around."

She glanced over her shoulder. Toward a little piece of fluorescent-orange tape tied to a branch in the distance, along the trail they had come.

"I'm going back." She turned abruptly and hurried back along the trail.

"Katie!"

She raised her hand, kept going. "No . . . no. Stay away from me!" She tripped on a root, crashed down into black mud. She scrambled wildly onto all fours. She cast another look back over her shoulder. Nathan saw raw terror twisting her face. She lurched up and began to crash wildly through the forest.

"Fuck," he whispered.

He turned in a slow circle, wondering what to do.

Then he heard voices coming through the mist. Someone was nearby.

THE LODGE PARTY

MONICA

As the path twisted deeper and deeper into the woods, doubling back on itself in places, Monica felt as though the trees were in cahoots, trying to confuse, regrouping and closing in behind her and Stella as they moved branches aside and pushed forward.

They'd split up from Nathan and Katie at a branch on the trail about fifteen minutes back. And Monica was fastidiously affixing strips of luminous orange tape onto branches every few meters, terrified they were not going to find a way to return. With each step forward, the pull in her gut to race back to the comparative safety of the lodge intensified.

Stella stopped ahead.

"Helloooooo," she called into the misty forest. "Hoi. Hooooo!"

They waited.

From their left came an echoing call. "Hoi, hellooooooo!"

Another answering call came from farther up toward the stone mountain. "Helloooo! All gooood!"

Stella started forward.

A rustle sounded in the bushes. They halted, listened. Monica saw Stella's hand hover near the bear spray at her belt. A raven croaked, the sound dry and hard.

Silence.

Monica laughed nervously.

They pushed on for another nine minutes, Monica counting the seconds until they could turn around and hightail it back. The forest grew darker. It felt colder, dank. It smelled musty, mossy. Strange. She felt she was losing her mind in this space. She was grappling with the fact that they were even here and going through this. It was as though she and Stella were walking deeper and deeper into an alternate reality, and when Monica woke up, it would all be normal again, and fine.

She jumped at a shadow. Her nerves skittered. She saw the little boy again. Ezekiel Marshall. In her mind he was here with them, a ghost shadow among the mist specters, sifting after them into the heart of the woods, retreating into shadow every time she turned to see him.

Her brain raced. Memories twisted.

Going down on Steven while he was driving her car. They'd both had a few glasses of wine. Nathan out of town. Early darkness of fall. Rain, lots of rain. Slick black streets, smeared city and car lights behind streaks of rain on the windows. Giggling. It was so wonderful . . . feeling young. The heady rush of early sexual attraction, the excitement of an illicit affair. The brilliant plastic surgeon with all his money and status, so assertive, so virile against her drab and nerdy Nathan. Sex. With Nathan nights had become routine, both of them rolling to opposite sides of the bed just to avoid the rigmarole of pretending to be interested in fucking.

The squeal of brakes. The bang.

Monica stopped. She was breathing hard, sweating suddenly. Shaking.

"Are you flagging?" Stella asked, stopping to see what was holding up her partner.

"Yes." Monica held her sides, unable to look into Stella's eyes. Unable to shake the memory of the mother running out of the liquor store, screaming, dropping her bottle of wine to the sidewalk, the bottle shattering, her broken child lying on the road. The squashed box of

Tooty-Pops and broken eggs in the wet street. The stricken look on her face as she reached up her hand and yelled, *pleaded*, for them to stop.

"You want to rest a moment?" Stella asked.

Monica shook her head. They resumed. Monica watched Stella moving ahead of her. The angle of her shoulders, the slope of her neck. Her arms. As Monica watched, in her mind Stella fattened up and morphed into the younger woman of the past, and Monica saw her again, bursting out of the liquor store, screaming, dropping the bottle of wine, running over to her broken little boy bleeding in the road. The words came out of Monica's mouth before she even registered.

"What happened, Stella, when you lost your little boy? How can you think you killed him?"

Stella stopped, turned. Stared at Monica. The wind hushed through the trees—a sibilant, whispering susurration.

"Did I say my child was a boy?"

Monica's heart thudded.

Had she? Shit.

"I . . . I thought . . . I'm sure you said that *he* . . . liked cereal. The Tooty-Pops cereal. You said everyone believed you'd killed your *son*, that you were an unfit mother because you'd been institutionalized."

Stella's face changed. Her eyes narrowed. "I didn't say anything about being institutionalized."

"Kitsilano . . ." Panic whipped through Monica. "Isn't that what we were all talking about? The groceries. Kits Corner Store in Kitsilano."

Stella's face darkened.

"It was on the news, wasn't it? I . . . We saw the news. We all did. It was terrible. There was a photo of the Tooty-Pops on the road, all the little colors in the rain, the broken eggs . . ." Her voice choked. Tears blurred her vision. "I . . . I put two and two, pieced it together, Stella. It was all over the news, night after night, and we lived right near there, so I remember. It stuck out."

Stop, Monica, stop the fuck talking before you tell her everything.

226

"It was Katie Colbourne, wasn't it, who claimed you were a bad mother, that you were mentally fragile and an unfit parent, and you should never have left your young child alone on the dark street, not even for a few moments, and then Ezekiel's dog ran . . . I . . . Oh God, Stella, I am so sorry, so sorry."

"Ezekiel. You *know his name*?"

Monica swallowed. The forest pressed closer. The sky lowered over her head. She couldn't breathe. "I . . . I remembered," she whispered. "From the news. I . . . I'm so sorry, Stella."

"Sorry? You're *sorry*?"

"For what you went through. I watched the whole thing unfolding on TV, I . . . It was you, the commercial pilot. You look different, but I can see it now." Tears slid down her cheeks. "I remember your eyes." She swiped the tears away. "I remember you pleading to the camera for someone to come forward."

Stella cursed. She looked away, into the forest, as if trying to find words. "Yet no one did, did they, Monica? *No one* came forward." She faced Monica. "Instead, I was crucified. Because people—they always need someone to blame, to make into a villain. So they can feel better about what happened, and move on."

"You must have recognized Katie Colbourne as the one when you first saw her at the floatplane dock, or when you saw her name on your manifest."

Stella sniffed softly. "Of course I did."

"You didn't say anything? You didn't confront her?"

"Would you? If you wanted to forget everything about your past? If no one knew or recognized you, would you dredge it up again?"

A thin needle of fear went through Monica. A warning. She heard it being whispered by the trees.

"Why are we all here, Stella?"

Stella angrily palmed off her wet hat, shook the drops of water off the bill. She wiped her brow with the back of her hand. "I don't know," she said. "I just don't. I keep going back to that rhyme. Agatha Christie's story. A judge. Some deluded sense of justice. Crimes that some maniac mastermind feels need to be atoned for. Perceived crimes committed by each one of us. So we've been lured here for a reckoning." She looked away. Inhaled. "And there was a character—a woman in that Agatha Christie story who'd killed a little boy in her charge. A little boy like my son. The young woman had been a caregiver, and she'd failed the child. Adults, mothers, fathers, caregivers, they *need* to protect the innocent children. Maybe some sick 'judge' believes I wasn't actually punished enough, Monica."

The emotion in her eyes was raw. It sliced through Monica.

"So that's me," Stella said. "That's my sin. And you? Why are *you* here, Monica? What do you think *your* sin is? What is your lie?"

Flustered, shocked, Monica took a small step backward. Her mind raced. Her heart beat so fast she thought she was going to faint. "I . . . cheated on my husband."

Stella stared. Swallowed. Cold rain started to fall, drops finding their way down through the dense forest canopy.

"I cheated on my husband with Dr. Steven Bodine."

Stella's mouth opened, then closed. She seemed at a loss for words.

"And Nathan?" Stella asked finally. "Why is Nathan here? What has he done?"

Monica rubbed her wet face. "He loved me. That's all. Nathan loves me. And he just forgave me. And . . . maybe he wasn't supposed to. Maybe he was supposed to confront me. And Steven. See us both pay."

Instead of helping to hide our crime, the hit-and-run murder of a six-year-old boy. He should have gone to the police.

"He knows about the affair?"

Monica nodded, more tears sliding down her face.

"You stayed together."

Silence.

"Do you love him?"

"Sometimes."

"And he . . . never wanted to punish you—ever?"

And Monica suddenly realized what Stella was asking. A sickness washed into her gut. "It's not him. He didn't orchestrate this, lure us here. He . . . he wouldn't."

"And you're so sure?"

Monica suddenly wasn't. She was not sure about any goddamn thing anymore.

Could Nathan have done this? Brought me and Steven together to face Stella? With Bart? To mess with our heads? Could it be some bizarre way of absolving his own guilt? No. Not possible. Not at all. It's an insane idea. But everything about this situation is insane . . . and he has been behaving more oddly than usual lately . . .

Bile surged up into Monica's throat. She was going to be sick. She thought of Nathan's passive aggression. His brilliant brain. He loved reading complicated mysteries, true crime about mad minds. He was a loner who disappeared on long walks into hostile forests and who felt he could talk to trees. And that they were communicating with him. He detested Steven Bodine. Sometimes, even though he acted as though he loved her, she got strange little feelings that part of him buried deep down might detest her, too, for bringing Steven into their marital bed, for allowing him to be cuckolded like that. Inside his own home. For forcing him to hide her crime so he could protect himself and his family.

Could Nathan even be passively furious at Bart Kundera for having allowed him to help hide the crime?

Could Nathan have been *willing* someone to come forward fourteen years ago, so that he himself wouldn't be forced to do the difficult thing—turn in his own wife for manslaughter? For failing to remain at the scene of a hit-and-run?

Was he hoping someone *else* would destroy her and Steven so his kids would still keep loving him?

A sharp crack resounded through the forest. Then another. Birds scattered from branches.

"Gunfire!" said Stella, eyes wide.

A scream cut the air. Male. Raw. It curdled Monica's blood. Then another scream.

Stella broke into a crashing run through the forest, toward the sound.

"Stella!" Monica shrieked. *"Stella!"*

But Stella vanished into the forest.

Monica spun around and raced in the opposite direction, sheer terror driving her legs to pump, her arms to thrash. She scanned the trees, wildly charging from one piece of orange flagging tape to the next, back to the lodge.

THE LODGE PARTY

KATIE

Katie bashed her fist against the back door of the lodge.

No answer.

She wiggled the doorknob, yanking at it.

Locked.

Deborah was told to lock the doors . . .

But Katie was driven beyond rationality to just get inside. All she could think was that she had to find a way in, any way in. She yanked at the door again, sweat breaking out over her face. A noise cracked through the forest behind her. She froze. Another report split the air.

Gunshots!

She heard screams. Men. The sound of men screaming in feral terror was more than she could bear.

She spun away from the door and stumbled wildly through the slush around the side of the lodge, falling and getting up and falling again. She came around to the front. She ran up the stairs and onto the porch. She banged on the front door, mewling, sobbing, covered in mud, wet.

No answer.

She tried the handle. To her surprise, it opened. Katie hesitated, then darted inside, slammed the door shut, and pressed against it with both hands. She leaned the side of her face against the rough wood, breathing hard.

It took a few moments for her brain to reengage. It was dark inside. Quiet. Too quiet.

Deborah?

Katie left the door and moved to the base of the stairs. She placed her hand on the banister and listened.

"Deborah?" she called.

The house exhaled cold woodsmoke-tinged air. It creaked.

Katie hurried up the stairs. She stopped on the landing. Deborah's door was closed. Cautiously she moved toward it, raised her hand to knock, then hesitated.

"Deborah?" she said.

Silence. The house made a cracking noise, like ice defrosting in the timbers. A shudder ran through Katie. She knocked lightly, then reached for the handle. Carefully she eased open the door, peered inside. "Deborah?"

The room was empty.

Another noise came from outside. Air horn. Like a siren, it went on and on. Stopped. The alarm sounded again.

Deborah? She'd been left with an air horn. Had she gone outside?

What about Steven? Bart? They had an air horn between them, and the rifle.

Katie hurriedly left the room, rushed down the hall, and barreled into her own room. She slammed the door shut, locked it. Then leaned against it, breathing hard.

She was mad—she'd gone stark raving mad. Nathan wasn't evil . . . was he? She'd imagined it all. What in the hell was happening to them all? She sensed it suddenly and froze.

Someone was inside the room. She felt a presence. Katie stepped tentatively forward to see around the freestanding closet.

The painting.

It looked alive.

Gabby.

Her daughter's eyes bored directly into her. That little smile, sly, smug, said, *Bad mother. You're a bad mother. You accused a good woman of being a bad mother . . .*

Katie went up to the painting and looked more closely at the rendering of the golden scale in "Gabby's" chubby hand, the little human heart weighting down one end. Stella's words sliced through her chest.

I'd had my heart cut right out . . . and they said it was karma.

My heart cut right out . . . The human heart tipping the scales of justice, Katie being judged by the sly smile of her own child.

Guilt washed up Katie's gullet. She pressed her hand against her brow. She knew who Stella was now. The terrible awareness had begun to sink like a poison into Katie as Stella had recounted her story, even as one part of Katie's brain had tried to fight the realization. She was Estelle Marshall. Ezekiel Marshall's mother. The woman Katie had brought down with her rabid coverage of the hit-and-run. Unfairly. Katie was acutely aware of just how unfair she'd been now that she was a mother herself, and older.

And hadn't she done something awfully similar herself? Spurred by the exact same impulse—just a quick self-centered distraction that could've led to something tragic? She'd needed a few items from the grocery store. She'd thought she'd only be a second, so she'd availed herself of the free fifteen-minute parking outside the store and left Gabby in her car just for a minute. Doors locked, windows open a crack so no one could reach in and take Gabby. One minute had turned into twenty when the line of customers at the checkout got stuck behind an old woman who couldn't remember the PIN for her credit card and who had then gotten flustered and dropped her strawberries all over the place. It had been a hot summer's day. Katie had spat verbal vitriol at the old woman as she'd finally managed to pay and push past her.

By the time she'd rushed out of the store with her purchases, a young woman was bashing on Katie's vehicle window with the base of a small fire extinguisher.

Stop! Just stop it—leave my car!

You left a child in there! What kind of a mother are you? Do you realize how hot it is? Look at her cheeks. They're red. She's crying. This is criminal. I'm calling the cops.

The woman had set down her fire extinguisher and begun rummaging in her sling purse for her phone.

Katie had gotten into her car fast. She'd fired the ignition and reversed at speed, her wheels jumping right over the goddamn extinguisher, her heart thumping out of her chest. If the media got hold of this—Katie Colbourne locked her kid in the car . . . Katie Colbourne swore at a half-senile senior who could have used her help instead of her hatred.

"Mummy! Mummy!"

"It's all right, honey. It's fine. Mummy's just in a rush . . ."

Thank God Gabby had been okay. If this had gotten into the papers, or had gone viral on social media . . . She'd thought then of Estelle Marshall, and how she'd been party to the woman's destruction. And that was why Katie had really quit her job. She'd been shown firsthand how one stupid and selfish mistake—one charge, one accusation, one revelation—could destroy a life. Or lives. She'd wanted out of the limelight. She'd wanted to be a good mother.

Now she knew. Stella was Estelle.

We're all being punished . . . a reckoning.

She dragged both her hands over her hair, pulling it back from her face. She stared at the little girl. Exactly the same as Gabby.

Gabby, now the age little Ezekiel Marshall had been.

Why should she not be punished the same way Stella had? She'd just gotten away that day. Gotten lucky. It was the fucking luck of the draw that decided what path you went down, where you ended up.

Those of us who judge others . . . shall themselves be as harshly judged.

Another scream snapped Katie sharply back to reality.

She spun around in panic.

A woman's scream. It reached her again. It came from *inside*. Echoing, bouncing off the ceilings and against the walls, as if the whole house itself were screaming, as if the scream emanated from the pores of the fine grains of the old wood.

Terror slammed Katie from all sides.

Stay? Hide? Unlock the door, go help? Indecision rooted her boots to the floorboards.

But after a few moments, all seemed to go silent.

Katie waited some more, until she couldn't bear it any longer.

She opened her door, peered out. Nothing. She went carefully over the creaking floorboards, leaned over the balustrade. Down below in the great room, beneath the animal heads, far below the horned chandelier, stood Deborah.

Water drops clung to her jacket, as if she'd just come in from outside. She clutched her hands over her mouth. She was staring at the coffee table.

"Deborah?" Katie said over the balustrade.

Her gaze shot up to Katie. The woman's face was white. Her eyes black holes. She pointed a shaking hand toward the checkerboard.

"Another one," Deborah whispered. And the sound of her words sifted up to the vaulted ceiling like a hiss and curled all around. *Another one another one another one another one . . .* Katie fought the urge to clamp her hands over her ears.

Deborah picked up two pieces. A head. A body. Separated. Extending her arms, she held them both skyward, up toward Katie, as if making an offering to the gods.

"Head is off," Deborah said quietly. "It's been chopped off."

Six Little Liars tried hard to stay alive.
One saw the judge, and then there were five.

She couldn't help saying the words she said next. It was all going to come out anyway now. This house was going to get it out of them. It was going to stir the silent demon inside each one of them.

"I remember who Stella is."

Deborah stared blankly, still holding the decapitated head and torso up.

"Fourteen years ago her little boy, Ezekiel Marshall, was hit and killed by a blue BMW. Outside Kits Corner Store. Zeke—she used to call him Zeke—he'd been carrying a bag of groceries with a box of Tooty-Pops, a Snickers bar, and some eggs inside. And holding his puppy on a leash. I covered the story. I asked Estelle Marshall, the mother, why she'd bought those items. She was going to make spaghetti carbonara for dinner. Zeke liked it. Her husband loved it. And . . . and they were out of Tooty-Pops. And Zeke had wanted a treat so she'd bought him a little Snickers bar because at least the peanuts were healthy. And then she'd wanted wine to go with the pasta . . ."

Deborah slowly lowered the pieces of carving down to her side. Still she said nothing, just stared up at Katie.

Katie cleared the thickness choking into her throat. "Estelle Marshall told me she saw two people in that car. A man and a woman. What people would hit a little boy, reverse to check, see his mother come screaming into the road, and then gun the gas and squeal down a dark side street?" Her voice caught on the emotion in her throat. "What woman would annihilate another woman in the media like I did, because it was going to make me a name? I ask you, Deborah, who? Who am I?"

"Katie, you can't—"

"I never believed her that there was a witness on the street corner who'd stolen her fatally injured son's backpack while he lay bleeding in the street, do you know that?" Katie said. "Because honestly, *who* would do a thing like that? Estelle—Stella—claimed it was a woman. About five six. Short skirt. Umbrella. Very skinny. Maybe a street worker. She'd seen prostitutes on that corner before. But I still didn't believe her, because no one came forward, and what witness wouldn't come forward for something like that?" She paused, her heart beating loud in her ears.

"And you know what?" Katie said softly. "I think I know who that woman is now."

THE LODGE PARTY

MONICA

Monica stumbled along the marked trail with two thoughts in mind: Get inside the lodge. Bolt the door until the others return.

She was a coward. She'd always been a coward. Hidden from ugly things. Fled from them.

She pushed through brambles. Wet branches slapped back into her face. She was running away from the truth, from being exposed as what she was. Fleeing from herself. From the secret that had been dogging her with hot breath for fourteen long years. The secret that always managed to find her in the dark of night, in her dreams. And she'd wake in a sweat. She tripped and fell hard. The memory of the jolt and thump of her BMW shuddered through her body. With it came the never-ending loop of memory . . .

"Fuck! What in the——" Steven slammed on the brakes.

His erection rammed into the back of her throat with the force of the collision. Monica gagged.

A dog—we've hit a dog!

She jerked her head up from between Steven's legs. She couldn't bear it if they'd hit a dog . . .

He was reversing, fast. His fly open, his penis still sticking out, and still hard. She heard the tires of her BMW crackling on the wet street. Through the rain-smeared windows she saw store lights, reflections. A skinny woman in a miniskirt and high-heeled boots . . . crouching down next to a small person lying in the road.

Panic licked through Monica's belly.

Steven slowed the car. The woman looked up into the car window, her face white. She opened her mouth in shock. She grabbed something and ran away. Monica saw the grocery bag next. On the wet street. Then the crushed box of Tooty-Pops that stuck out of it—she knew instantly it was Tooty-Pops. Distinctive cartoon character. Bright red, yellow, and green. Her own kids, when they were younger, always squealed in the grocery store aisles, demanding that cereal. A cardboard egg carton lay flattened beside it. Yellow egg yolks and glistening raw egg whites seeped out of crushed eggshells. Then a little white hand came into her view.

It lay palm-up on the wet road, an open chocolate bar with a bite out of it near his fingertips. Blond hair. Blood dribbled from his mouth. His eyes . . . They stared straight up into the falling rain that splashed into the puddles around his head.

"Fucking hell!" Steven slammed the wheel.

He hesitated, then hit the gas. Tires screeched. Monica was thrown back in the passenger seat with the speed. Another woman ran out of the liquor store, dropped a bottle of wine, and screamed. She ran toward the child lying motionless on the wet road, waving at Steven to stop. Monica's BMW's tires screeched around a corner into an alley.

Steven skidded around another corner, clipping a parked van. The BMW fishtailed, almost colliding with an oncoming SUV. The driver laid on the horn, swerved.

"Steven! You have to stop. We have to go back!"

"Shut up." He kept driving, hands tight on the wheel, eyes fixed dead ahead. Her heart thudded. She couldn't breathe. He didn't say another word, just kept weaving through the quiet side streets until finally he slowed

and joined a main artery of traffic. He moved carefully into the bumper-to-bumper stream as it crawled well below the speed limit. As they drove with the traffic flow, he kept scanning the other cars as if waiting for cops, sirens. Rain came down harder. Wipers clacked faster. Finally he indicated and casually turned onto a road that led to the ocean.

"Steven, he might be alive. The child might be alive—"

"Shut up, Monica."

She was shaking, sweating.

He turned her BMW into a big, deserted parking lot at the rain-swept beach. Slowly tires crackled on wetness as he drove up behind the changing rooms and concession building that would be full and busy in the summer. He pulled carefully into a parking space behind the concrete building. Neat. Between the lines. A sulfurous glow from a nearby lamp fell over his face. It gave him an ugly cast.

He sat. Unmoving. She lunged for the door handle.

The sudden grip on her arm was like a vise.

"Get ahold of yourself, Monica."

She stared at him. "We . . . we have to go back. You hit a child."

"We."

"What?"

"We hit a child, Monica. You and me. Together. In your car."

He stuffed his limp penis back into his pants and pulled up the zipper.

The reality began to seep in, like ink into porous white paper. Monica McNeill. Heiress. Big grocery-chain CEO. Professor Nathan McNeill's wife. Going down on the locally famous Dr. Steven Bodine, who was the money and mind behind the feted Oak Street Surgical Clinic, where Vancouver's rich housewives all had their faces done. Dr. Bodine, who was married to an ex-model who owned a ritzy boutique downtown.

"We are both over the legal driving limit, Monica. We are both married. To other people. We both have children. Spouses with careers and reputations." He regarded her, a tight, dark look in his face. "We both have our own businesses and employees to think of."

He let it sink in.

"The media, cops, it'll be a nightmare," he said. "We'll go to prison."
He grabbed her face so suddenly, and held it so tightly between his hands,
she suddenly wondered if he might kill her. His eyes lasered into hers. Mad,
dark pools in the sickly light from the parking lot lamp. "We. Will. Lose.
Everything." He didn't loosen his vise grip. "Do you understand?"

She tried to nod.

He released her head and sat back. She could smell him. Acrid sweat.
Fear. Alcohol. Sex.

"Someone saw us," she said dully.

"A hooker. That's all."

"That's all?"

"I know that corner," said Steven. "I've seen sex workers there. Maybe
even that same woman before. Even if she does come forward, those women
are soaked to the gills with drugs and liquor. I know. I've seen it in the ER
when I did my residency. If she even remembers, she'd have to talk to law
enforcement, and they don't like to do that. It displeases their pimps. And
that could get them hurt. And even if they do talk, they're unreliable wit-
nesses. Their brains are fucked. They're useless for anything—it would never
stand up in court."

"She took something. From the street."

"So what? All the more reason she's unlikely to come forward."

"The mother saw us. She saw my car."

"Park it. Leave it in the garage. Keep the garage door closed."

"I can't just—"

"We can't go back there. Not now. Not after we fled."

He was shaking a little. So he was a bit human.

He turned in the seat. "Monica, listen to me. We both need to lay low.
Stop seeing each other. See what shakes out."

So he was going to leave her holding the bag if they found her car. Or
if anyone had seen the license plate. The paint from her BMW would also

be on the van they'd hit. There would be blood on her fender, she was sure. Tears pooled in her eyes.

"There could have been other witnesses, Steven. There were parked cars all down that street and the side streets. Someone could have been sitting inside one, watching out the window at that one instant. Maybe a store clerk, looking out of the window . . . There was that SUV you almost hit. It could have had a dashcam. There could be CCTV cameras outside those stores—"

"It was raining hard, Monica, and it was dark. You can't see anything in rain like that. Pedestrians are hit all the time in weather like that. The kid ran into the road, for Chrissakes. What was that kid doing in the road? Alone? Not our fault."

"Not our fault? Even if hitting the boy was unavoidable, we left an accident scene," she said very quietly. "You reversed, saw what you'd done, and only then sped away. You're a doctor, Steven. You could have helped that child and the mother. Maybe you could have saved his life." She was shaking hard now, her face wet with tears. She had a bad wine taste in her mouth. "Nathan will see the damage on my car."

"Then you will have to tell him that you hit something. And get it repaired."

"Fuck you," she said quietly. "I hate you. I hate you so much."

"I'm going to get out of the car now, Monica. I'm going to walk down the road and call a cab. You'll drive your car home."

"I swear, if they come after me, if they find my car, I'm going to tell them you were driving—I will tell them everything."

The horror of that night dogged Monica as she scrabbled, sobbing, back up onto her feet in the woods. She stumbled onward toward the lodge, following the bits of orange tape she'd affixed to branches along the narrow trail.

I can't do it, I can't outrun this any longer . . . not out here. Sinner, I'm a sinner, we're all sinners.

Nine Little Liars thought they'd escaped.
One missed a plane, and then there were eight . . .

. . . One Little Liar thinks he has won.
For in the end, there can only be one.
But maybe . . .
                there shall be none.

Cursed are those who Sin
And Lie to cover their deeds
For a Monster will rise within . . .

The Monster was Monica—it was inside her, and it had taken shape out of her guilt, and it had sunk its claws into her. And it was inside Nathan for helping hide her car. It was inside the mother running out of the liquor store into the street, because she'd been buying chardonnay instead of watching her dear little boy as he bit into his Snickers bar and his dog got away from him. The Monster was the skinny woman in the raincoat who had taken Ezekiel's backpack. And the license plate, as Monica had learned later, after she'd parked the car and seen it was gone—after no plate was found by the cops at the hit-and-run site. The Monster was Steven, holding her face in a vise grip, Steven who'd paid to silence the witness somehow and had never told Monica how. It was the garish Tooty-Pops cartoon on the sugary-cereal box . . . It was Bart for fixing and getting rid of her car—her murder weapon—when he *had* to have seen the police calling for people who'd seen it on the news . . . A wild feral madness filled Monica's head. She ran faster.

Sinners . . . All . . . Liars.

Monica burst out of the forest. She stood panting for a moment, orienting herself in the fog that hung over the clearing. She saw the shadow of the lodge. She ran for it, crossing beneath the totem poles with the horrible raven head. She reached the front door, her breasts heaving, the air cold and raw in her throat.

She tried the handle. It was unlocked.

She stilled, uneasy about entering because she suddenly remembered that Deborah had been told to lock the doors.

Blood drumming in her ears, Monica quietly opened the door a crack. She heard voices inside. Female.

Something about the tone of the voices made her pause. Cautiously she peered through the crack into the interior gloom of the great hall.

Deborah stood by the coffee table, her face turned up toward the balcony upstairs. In her hands she held parts of a figurine.

Katie Colbourne's voice reached Monica.

"I never believed her that there was a witness on the street corner who'd stolen her fatally injured son's backpack while he lay bleeding in the street, do you know that? Because honestly, *who* would do a thing like that? Estelle—Stella—claimed it was a woman . . . She'd seen prostitutes on that corner before. But I still didn't believe her, because no one came forward, and what witness wouldn't come forward for something like that?"

Sweat prickled over Monica's body. She was held rigid by Katie's words. So was Deborah.

"And you know what?" Katie called from above, from somewhere out of Monica's sight. "I think I know who that woman is now. I think we're all here. The drivers of that BMW, the mechanic who helped hide it—because that confounded the police. In a neighborhood like that? Someone had to know. They didn't hide it alone. Silence is a sin, too, you know?"

"Katie, stop," Deborah said.

Katie Colbourne laughed, the sound mad, shrill. "Why should I stop? Why should I be silent? We're all in the same boat. All of us around little Zeke Marshall's death. And do you know who *also* wanted Estelle Marshall to pay for allowing her six-year-old to run in front of that BMW? The man who told me so in an interview, the man who'd lost his son—Estelle's husband—Stuart Marshall. I wonder . . . maybe *he's* behind this all?"

Deborah suddenly noticed Monica at the front door. She spun to face her. "What are you doing there—what happened to you? Where are the others? What was the gunfire and air horns about?"

Monica could only stare at Deborah. Slowly—very slowly—she stepped inside the great hall. She looked up, saw Katie leaning over the balcony. Her gaze went back to Deborah. The carving that Deborah held in two pieces had been decapitated.

One saw the judge, and then there were five.

"Some . . . something terrible has happened," Monica whispered, her voice coming out alien to her own ears, her gaze fixed on the headless torso in Deborah's hand. "I . . . heard a man scream. I think the killer is out there. We need to lock all the doors."

She suddenly pushed past Deborah and clattered up the stairs. "Don't let anyone in. Lock yourselves in your rooms!"

"What about the others?" called Deborah.

But Monica rushed into her room and slammed the door. She turned the key, heart jackhammering in her chest.

THE LODGE PARTY

STELLA

Stella crashed through branches and into a small clearing almost simultaneously with Nathan, who burst into the clearing from the opposite side. She froze. So did he.

Steven stood in the center of the clearing over a man's body, rifle in hand. Hanging from a low branch in front of him was a deer carcass dripping with blood and loops of entrails. A fetid stench—carrion—hung thick in the air. Water dripped everywhere. Steven was shaking, his face and clothes smeared with blood and mud. He looked wild. Like a shell-shocked hunter lost for months among the enemy in the jungles of Vietnam. Both spatially and mentally confused.

Wham, wham, wham. The details registered like physical blows. Stella's eyes dropped to the body over which Steven stood. *Bart.*

Nathan made a small noise, like the sound of an animal, his knees sagging slightly. He stumbled to the side and braced his hand against a tree. He bent over and retched. Then again. Strands of spittle dangled from his mouth. He kept his face turned away. Stella came slowly forward.

Bart lay facedown in the mud and moss, arms splayed to the sides. Like a cross. A big meat cleaver stuck out of the back of his head, the skull split. Blood and gray-white brain matter oozed out along the sides of the blade. The cleaver was almost fourteen inches long. It was the one that had been on the chopping board in the kitchen.

Stella stared, numb. A whining sound began inside her head.

"What happened?" she whispered.

Silence.

She looked at Dr. Steven Bodine. He wasn't all there.

Dangerous was a word that hovered over her mind. *Mad. Feral.* Her attention went back to the rifle in his hand. She recalled the gunshots. Two. The male screams.

"Are you hurt, Steven? What happened?"

Did you do this? If so, I need to be calm, defuse the situation.

"Steven?"

He seemed unable to move, speak. His jaw hung flaccid.

"Give me that gun." She held out her hand and took a step toward him.

He tensed, raised the rifle. Both Stella and Nathan froze. Stella eased back. She held both hands in front of her, palms out.

"It's okay. Just set it down. Set it on the ground."

Steven bent his head. Stared at Bart.

"Steven. Put the gun down. We need to check on Bart."

He slowly crouched and laid the rifle carefully upon the moss.

Stella hurried forward and grabbed it. She went to the far edge of the small clearing and set the gun down on a rock.

Nathan moved forward to look at Bart. Steven grabbed him and hugged. Hard. The surgeon rested his head on Nathan's shoulder and began to sob. Nathan looked distraught, confused. He looked . . . wrong, thought Stella.

We're all wrong. All mad now. We've turned feral. A small tribe under assault. A wildness taking hold in our brains where ordinarily logic would reside.

She hurried over to Bart and dropped to her haunches beside him. She knew basic first aid. It was part of her pilot training. She kept her certification up to date. Stella felt for a pulse.

"He's dead," said the cosmetic surgeon from behind her. "He's dead. Dead. Dead." He began to sob again. Nathan awkwardly pushed him off.

Caution whispered through Stella. She scanned the shadows among the surrounding trees. It was suddenly getting darker. Rain was coming down heavily again, and the wind was starting to stir.

"Steven," she said firmly, urgency nipping at the corners of her brain, "what happened? Did . . . did *you* do this?"

He wiped a shaking hand across his brow, leaving a black-red smear of more mud and blood.

"I . . . Bart and I were following the drag marks into the woods. When we came deeper into the forest, there was more and more blood. The trail grew marked under the thick canopy, where hardly any snow had come through. Then . . . we smelled it. The . . . That thing—we came into this clearing, and saw it hanging there, from those branches."

Stella's and Nathan's attention went to the deer carcass in the tree. Possibly a bear's kill. Or maybe a cougar had done that, and dragged it up into the tree to stash it.

Steven said, "Bart went closer to look at it. A noise came from the brush. A crack of twigs. Then out it flew—" He gave a horrible sob and choked on his own phlegm. Steven wiped his hand across his mouth. "It just flew at us."

"*What* did?" Nathan asked, eyeing the bushes nervously.

"I . . . I don't know. Big."

"Animal?" Stella asked.

"I don't know. Misty. I was looking away." He cleared his throat. "I heard Bart scream and shoot. Twice."

She narrowed her eyes on him.

Nathan kept scanning the trees.

"Bear?" Stella asked. "Cougar? Protecting its kill?"

He shook his head.

"Did Bart hit the animal?"

"I . . . I didn't even look, because as I turned around, that cleaver came whopping through the air, right out of the fog and the shadows. It . . . it struck him in the back of the head. The sound, the thump and crunch of his skull . . ." He fell silent, just stood there with a haunted look in his eyes, as if the real Dr. Bodine had vacated his body. His arms hung limp and bloody at his sides.

"And then?" Stella urged, anxiety tightening inside her chest, fear prickling over her skin.

"Then he was dead. I'm a doctor. I knew. And I grabbed the gun and ran away. But then . . . I thought *it* might be out there still, waiting for me. So I . . . I came back. I felt for his pulse to be sure. There was none."

Stella turned to Nathan, suddenly registering that he was alone, and that Katie Colbourne had been with him. "Where's Katie?" she asked.

"Katie went back to the lodge."

"You weren't supposed to split up."

"Monica?" he said, suddenly noticing himself that Stella was alone. *"Where's my wife?"*

"She . . . I left her on the trail."

"What? Where?"

"I heard the screams and the gunshots, so I came running, and she didn't. I left her right there on the trail. She'll be fine, Nathan. The path back to the lodge is clearly visible, and we left flagging tape."

"You separated. How could you separate? How's she going to get back to—"

"Nathan, I just told you. Calm down. She'll be able to get back."

He glanced at Bart, then the carcass. "Not if . . . if that *thing* is out there. What if it went after Monica next? What if it found her on her way back to the lodge?"

Loreth Anne White

"Listen, focus. We can check on Monica soon, but first we need to take Bart back. We need to find a way to carry him to the lodge."

"Jesus, Stella," Nathan whispered, suddenly looking terrified. "It's getting dark. We—"

"And it's going to snow again. And whatever animal is out there—" She looked up at the carcass. A chill trickled down her spine. It indeed looked like something inhuman had done this. A monster. An *it*. She shivered. "We can't leave Bart for the animal. It'll eat him, drag him off."

"We should get back. I'm worried about Monica. What if she didn't make it back okay? It will be harder to search for her in the dark."

"Nathan, this man was *murdered*. What are we not getting here? Someone is going to come for us eventually, and the police will need to see Bart's body. We *need* to take him back."

He palmed off his hat and raked his fingers through his hair. "I'm not as sure as you are that anyone is coming for us."

Steven cleared his throat at the mention of the police. It seemed to pull him together. "She's right," he said, his voice thick. "We need to carry him back."

With darkness closing in fast, and rain beginning to pummel down again, they managed to drag Bart a short way through the forest until they found the drag marks along the game trail that had led Bart and Steven here. And Stella was certain now that it was a game trail, given the kill hanging gutted from the tree.

They pulled him a short way farther along the trail, Bart's face dragging through mud and stones. He was heavy. Heavier than Stella had thought he'd be. And the indignity, the awfulness, of dragging him facedown, was eating at her. It was going to tear his face apart. The dirt was going into his mouth and up his nostrils and under his eyelids. Yet turning him over and dragging him on his back would dislodge the cleaver. And she figured it would help law enforcement if they saw it in situ. The cleaver was a murder weapon. It could hold prints. So they tried lifting his corpse well above the ground, and carrying him between

250

the three of them along the trail that twisted through the bushes and trees, but it proved torturous. The trail was too narrow, the body too heavy, the destination too far.

Stella stumbled and almost fell. She was breathing hard, sweat drenching her body under her waterproof jacket.

"I need a break," she said.

They lowered Bart's body back to the forest floor. Her muscles ached. Hunger and thirst were beginning to get the better of her.

"This isn't working," Nathan said. "We need a tarp or something to make some kind of a stretcher."

Stella, Nathan, and Steven looked at each other in the beams of their headlamps, which they'd clicked on as the twilight thickened. The wind moved the trees again. Darkness was growing complete. The rain was turning to sleet. Despite the sweat over her body, Stella's hands were numb with cold, and her fingers were growing uncooperative. A recipe for hypothermia.

"I'll go back," she said. "I'll move fast and fetch that tarp and ropes we saw in the shed. And I'll check that Monica is there."

"Why should *you* go?"

"Well, do one of you guys want to go? Whoever goes will have to leave the gun with whoever stays with Bart's body, because the blood could attract the animal that killed the deer. And Bart has more bullets in his pockets. We all saw him stash them there. The one who goes can take my can of bear spray."

All three eyed each other warily. Each unsure of the others. None wanting to stay with a blood-soaked body while a predator lurked in the trees. And none seemed inclined to run alone along the dark forest trail with only a headlamp and no gun. A noise sounded, and they jumped.

"I think it was just slush falling," Stella said quietly, the beam of her headlamp probing the gloom and bouncing back at her in the fog.

"Okay," Steven said quietly, darkly, "you go ahead. We'll keep trying to carry him."

"I'll be as fast as I can."

Stella moved off into the dark of the forest alone. It closed in behind her. And in the whisper of the wind among the trees, she heard the rhyme.

She stopped for a moment, threw up, the rhyme going disjointedly through her head.

Six Little Liars tried hard to stay alive . . . One met an ax . . .

◆ ◆ ◆

Stella entered the lodge. It was deathly quiet inside. Her senses went on alert.

"Hello?" she called out. "Anyone here?"

Monica's bedroom door opened upstairs, and she came out onto the balcony above.

Stella shone her flashlight up to the second floor. Monica's hair looked damp, and she'd changed into clean clothes. She'd showered or bathed.

"Where is everyone?" Stella asked, looking up at Monica. "Where's Katie? Deborah?"

"In their rooms."

Monica had been crying, Stella realized. Her voice was thick and her eyes were puffy. She also appeared confused, as though she'd been sleeping.

"Where's Nathan?" Monica asked, appearing to come slowly to her senses. Her speech quickened. "And the others? Where are the others? Are—" She stopped as she appeared to register the blood and mud on Stella's arms and down her jeans. *"What happened?"*

Stella hesitated. The wind banged a shutter. It was picking up, another storm blowing in. Urgency bit. "Monica, Nathan's fine. He . . .

I . . . I needed to get a tarpaulin and some rope. Bart is . . . He's . . ."
She was having trouble saying it. "Bart is dead. We need to move him."

"What?"

"He got—someone . . . someone killed him." She fought for words
that felt unreal. "They killed him with a meat cleaver."

Monica stared. She seemed unable to process. Very quietly she said,
"You mean he's dead?"

Stella nodded. "He's dead."

Monica's knees sagged. She crumpled to her haunches, her hands
clutching and sliding down two vertical spindles of wood that helped
support the balustrade handrail. She began to moan and rock from side
to side, like a strange and distressed female mammal in a zoo cage. Or
behind prison bars.

Stella had been going to ask for Monica's help.

*But how much help would she be in her state? How much use would
any extra person be along the very narrow and twisting trail, anyway?*

"Go back to your room, Monica. Lock the door. Stay safe. I'll
return with lights and a tarpaulin. I saw a tarp in the shed, and ropes.
We'll carry him back in a sling between the three of us. And even if we
can't lift him, if we wrap Bart's body in the tarp, and secure him with
ropes, we can protect evidence if we drag him."

Monica moaned.

Stella cursed inwardly. Everyone was losing their shit, including
her. Her hands trembled and adrenaline bashed through her blood as
she headed for the rear door in the kitchen. In the distance she heard
Monica's bedroom door shut upstairs.

Focus. Focus. One task, one thing at a time.

She hurried into the cavernous dark kitchen, using her flashlight
because no lanterns had been lit. She stilled as she saw the gaps in the
knife board. They'd taken some of the knives out to the shed. But the
meat cleaver—it was gone.

253

The image of the cleaver splitting open Bart Kundera's head flashed through her brain.

Her own knees started to give. Stella braced against the counter.

You're a pilot. You've handled dire situations. You're trained for disaster scenarios. You can do this. You have the mental fortitude . . . You have to focus. You will get through this.

Then she looked down at her own terrible, bloody hands. And she wasn't so sure she would.

For in the end, there can only be one.
But maybe . . .
               there shall be none.

She had to make sure she stood a chance of being the one.
The one who survived.

THE LODGE PARTY

DEBORAH

From the kitchen window, Deborah watched Stella, Steven, and Nathan struggling to get Bart's body into the freezer in the shed. They had rolled him up in the pale-blue tarpaulin, cleaver in his head and all, and trussed him up with rope. He looked heavy, and they appeared exhausted. The work was clearly backbreaking as the trio labored by the quavering, flickering yellow light of the lanterns, faces gleaming with perspiration. Their shapes made grotesque leaping shadows on the shed walls. Like three witches toiling. Shadow puppets.

Monsters.

Deborah shuddered. She didn't want those three to come inside, to touch the rest of them with the horror of what they'd seen, done.

They finally rolled Bart's body into the freezer with a thud. She couldn't hear it, but it must have thudded, from the way it seemed to reverberate through them all. The only thing Deborah could hear through the grimy windows was the chugging of the generator. They'd fueled it with gas from the cans in the shed, and turned on the freezer to preserve Bart's body for the police as long as they could. Which meant until the gasoline was gone.

The rough engine noise felt strange in the wilderness. Deborah wondered if the freezer and gasoline had been left inside the shed expressly for this purpose.

She wondered if the fourteen-inch meat cleaver had been positioned on the chopping board alongside all the knives for a similar purpose. And the gun on the wall with the box of bullets in the desk drawer. Perhaps the intent was to scare them with the rhyme, mess with their heads by isolating them, force them to turn on each other in fear, all fueled by their own guilt. By their own Monsters, which lived inside each one of them.

And these tools had all been laid out as temptations, leaving them to choose how to use them.

The clock began to gong. Deborah jumped. It boomed seven times. The interior of the lodge was dark, lit by only one shivering lantern in the great room. No fire in the hearth. No one had come in to make it. Cold was crawling in under the doors and pressing through the thin windowpanes.

Deborah could go and build the fire. But she seemed unable to move away from the window, ensnared by the orange vignette in the blackness outside. Terror clutched at her heart.

She heard Jackie Blunt's words inside her head again.

"You remind me of someone. Kat . . . Kata . . . Katarina, I think her name was . . . I know that tattoo . . . A swallow. I've seen that ink . . . I've spoken to her. I know her voice."

She watched as Nathan found a bottle of booze on a shelf in the shed. He showed it to the other two. They seemed to be debating whether it was safe to drink. Nathan showed them the seal, then cracked it open.

They quaffed from the bottle in turns. Wiped mouths with backs of wrists. The three of them. Stella, Steven, Nathan. Bonded by something horrific, as if unclean, forever unable to go back and join the normal people of the world. They passed the bottle around again.

Deborah cast her mind back further. To the black-haired, solid woman with coarse skin and ruddy cheeks and a stench of cigars on her clothes. The woman who'd found Deborah via her pimp, who controlled the sex workers plying their trade in that area. It was a classy neighborhood on the fringe of the downtown core, a neighborhood of men with money, quite a few who also secretly liked their fucks with spanks and whips. Men who pretended they were normal fathers and sons and husbands, but who were no better than the rest. The woman's words crawled up from some dark place into Deborah's memory.

"I know it was you on that street corner that night, Katarina. Your pimp confirmed it. He told the PI who hired me where to find you. He said it was your night for that corner. Yeah, Kitty Kat, every man has his price. Even your pimp. He told me it was you who witnessed the little kid getting squished. You saw the blue BMW. You saw two people inside—a man and a woman. You took the license plate. And you took little Ezekiel Marshall's backpack, didn't you?"

She'd needed a fix. Like bad. So bad. No one knew how bad it could be unless they'd been there. They just couldn't imagine it. Deborah had been ready to kill for the fix that the rough-skinned woman had dangled in front of her that day. She'd needed it just to survive long enough to turn some trick so she could score more.

"Your pimp is going to cut you off, Katarina. But you can have this, and this envelope of cash here—it's unmarked, been cleaned, and there's plenty in here, but you need to give me that BMW license plate, and then you need to fuck off out of this town, like tonight. You take this money and go live somewhere else. You got that? You put one shitty stiletto boot toe back into the Greater Vancouver area, and you're dead, you hear me? If I find someone with that tat is in town, you die. Okay? And I will know. I will hear. Because your pimp will tell. Because there will be a shitload more money and drugs for him if he sees you, or hears about you, and he comes and tells me. It's called incentive."

"Who . . . who are you?"

"I'm here to keep you quiet, Kitty Kat."

"I . . . I won't speak. I promise. I haven't spoken to the cops yet, have I?"

"Because they haven't found you yet. You split out of town and they won't."

"Why are you doing this?"

"Because someone who was driving that BMW is paying someone to pay someone to pay me to shut you up." The woman smiled, angled her head. *"Simple, right? It's called compartmentalization. Understand?"*

Deborah had been shaking so hard, so desperate for a fix, that she'd barely been able to keep her hands steady enough to dig in her closet, find the battered vanity license plate, and hand it over. She'd taken the fat envelope and opened it. She'd been shocked. There'd been more money in that envelope than she'd seen in her life. She'd reached for the bag of drugs.

The woman had yanked it back.

"If the cops—"

"I don't speak to cops." Her pimp would have her killed if she did. She was underage. Another girl had vanished, and Deborah had been certain he'd done it.

"Where does the money come from?" Deborah asked. *"The driver?"*

"Take it or leave it."

Deborah took it.

"Now run, you little whore. Fuck off and run."

Tears pricked as Deborah recalled that day from her past when Jackie Blunt had visited her with an envelope of money and a packet of drugs. Back when Jackie Blunt's hair had been thick and shiny black. But Deborah was dry inside, well beyond crying now. She placed a hand on her stomach, where her baby slept in innocence, a child of her own, a life she'd never dreamed possible. She'd been a mess back then. A total wreck. She was surprised she even recalled what the woman looked like who'd come to her door that day.

But after Jackie Blunt had stared at her in the floatplane, and started saying things like she recognized the tattoo . . . after she'd mentioned the name Katarina, Deborah had known. Deborah had remembered.

In some bizarre trick of fate, her nemesis had been put on that floatplane with her and sent to this place. To be trapped. Like Katie Colbourne had said—with all the other people involved in Ezekiel Marshall's hit-and-run death. And as Deborah watched the trio in the shed, she figured that the driver of that BMW had to have been Steven Bodine.

He was the man she'd seen behind the wheel. And he had the kind of money and connections to hire a PI to hunt her down. A PI like Dan Whitlock, who'd in turn hired a woman like Jackie Blunt to strong-arm her into permanent silence.

The woman in the passenger seat must have been Monica. Because it hadn't been Katie Colbourne in that seat, and Stella was the mother.

Deborah hadn't seen the mother properly that day. She hadn't watched the news, either. She'd snatched the backpack and license plate because the opportunity had presented itself, and because the kid looked dead already. There could've been something of value in that backpack—something she could have sold for cash. And cash bought drugs. She'd taken the plate because that's what she did at the time. Took things. And things could be used for leverage. Blackmail. She'd been right. Someone had wanted to pay big to get that plate back.

After Jackie Blunt's visit, she'd fled to Victoria on the island. But it wasn't long before *Katarina* ran into trouble there, too. She'd stabbed another street worker who'd tried to move into her territory. She'd actually sliced her up pretty bad. It landed her in prison.

Best thing that had ever happened to her, prison.

It had been rough at first. But a mentor had taken her under her wing for "favors." After that she was left alone. Behind bars she'd managed to go sober, clean. She'd taken courses. She'd come out and joined a social program that hired ex-cons for cleaning jobs, and she'd slowly pulled herself right. When she'd found it impossible to get a job in a top hotel, because of her record, she'd changed her name and started her own company that contracted employees out. Where she was the boss and no potential employer would ever ask her again about a criminal record.

As the memories that Deborah had tried so hard to suppress, to bury, surfaced like a tsunami inside her, her body began to shake.

She pressed her hand down harder on her tummy.

Her own baby.

She *needed* to survive. Anything to survive.

They were coming inside now, walking through the slush toward the kitchen door. Panic kicked her. She spun around and hurriedly opened cupboards, found cans. Stew. Chili. She got out a pot and started the gas stove.

They'd be hungry. They'd need food. She had to keep pretending she knew nothing and she'd be safe. She had never been there. She hadn't seen the driver, or the passenger. She had not seen the little boy hit, or the mother screaming out of the store. She never watched news. She didn't know the mother was Stella.

Stella, who'd lost her baby boy. *Her child.*

A sob choked Deborah. She braced her hands on the counter, fighting to control herself.

The door opened. She wiped her nose, spun around. Swallowed.

They looked apocalyptic. Survivors of a zombie war in the wilderness. She cringed inside, almost wanting to take a step back. But the counter was behind her.

They stared at her as if she were suddenly just as alien to them as they were to her.

"I . . . I'm sorry I didn't come out to help." Her voice cracked. She cleared her throat. "I . . . Monica told me what happened, and . . . I've never seen a dead body," she lied. "So I'm making supper instead. I thought you . . . you'd be hungry."

They walked past Deborah, Stella holding the bottle. It was whiskey.

Deborah suddenly heard the thud of the BMW hitting the little boy. She hadn't heard it for more than a decade. *Thud. Thud. Thud.* Over and over. It wouldn't stop. She rammed her hands over her ears.

Stop. Stop. Stop.

Stella glanced over her shoulder. Their eyes met.

I'm sorry. I'm so sorry.

"I'll bring the stew."

"Thanks, Deborah," said Stella.

Deborah entered the living room carrying bowls of soup on a tray.

Nathan looked up from the sofa. His eyes were red. He was filthy with blood and muck and hadn't wiped any off. He sat with the open bottle of whiskey between his thighs, his hand clutching the bottle neck.

"Your ankle?" he said, his gaze lowering to her legs.

"It . . . it's much better. Fine. I bandaged it tight."

Steven was lighting the fire. Stella was coming down the stairs. She'd tried to clean up—washed some of the blood off her hands and face and put on some clean clothes. The men hadn't bothered.

Monica and Katie were not down yet.

Deborah stood with the tray. Unsure. Rattled to the core. Her life upended. Besieged by the terrible looming fear she was going to tumble all the way back to the beginning, become Katarina again. And she couldn't, just couldn't.

I'd rather die.

Steven came to her, took the heavy tray from her.

"Thank you."

He nodded. And she almost felt bad for him. *He's suffering the same thing I am. He's trying to hide his past. That kid ran into the road from between two cars, right in front of him—he'd been doomed to hit Ezekiel.*

Nine Little Liars thought they'd got away. But they hadn't, and they were all going back to hell.

Rattling bowls and spoons with shaky, tired arms, Steven set the tray down on the coffee table next to the checkerboard. As he did, he froze.

"The carvings." His voice came out hoarse. It shot a chill through Deborah.

"The carvings. Two—" He spun around. His face gaunt. He pointed.

"Two more. Not just one for Bart. *Two.*"

Nathan jerked forward as if shocked by a bolt of electrical current. "Monica?" he said. He spun his head round. "Where is Monica?" He lurched up, knocking the bottle of whiskey onto the floor. He ran for the stairs. "Monica!" he yelled as he grasped the handrail.

Nothing.

He thudded drunkenly up the steps.

"Monica!" he yelled again, louder, as he reached the landing. His voice boomed through the house. It tossed the name back at them, echoing up into the vaulted ceiling and roof trusses. Dust sifted down.

The others left their soup and hurried upstairs after Nathan. Deborah followed.

As Nathan reached his and Monica's bedroom door, it swung open.

Monica stood there with swollen, red-rimmed eyes and mussed hair, confusion in her features. "I . . . I was sleeping. What is it, Nathan? God, look at you. Are you all right?"

He made a weird noise and gathered her into his arms. "Oh, thank God, thank you, thank you. You're all right."

She pushed him away, her nostrils flaring at the stink on him. "What is it—what's going on?"

"Another figurine has been decapitated," Steven said.

Monica looked at the others. "You mean for Bart."

"No, another."

They all registered at once. Stella lunged for Katie Colbourne's door. It was locked.

"Katie!" Stella banged, rattled the handle. *"Katie!"* She turned to them. "Help me. Help me bust open this door."

The men put the weight of their shoulders into it. Whammed. Again and again. The wood of the door splintered against the lock, and it blew open. The two men tumbled inside and staggered, flailing, into the middle of the room.

Deborah and Stella rushed in behind them.

They all stopped dead in their tracks.

Katie hung from a rope hooked over a rafter. A chair had been overturned near her feet. Her camera lay on the bed.

She swayed there, facing the giant oil painting of the little girl carrying the scales of justice. The canvas had been slashed to ribbons. A kitchen knife lay on the wooden floor beneath the painting.

Deborah sagged and fainted.

THE SEARCH

MASON

Tuesday, November 3.

Everyone in the SAR team had retired into their tents, apart from Mason and Callie, who were still up. They sat close, in front of a fire the SAR guys had built in a small encampment in the old-growth forest, well away from the lodge. Orange flames crackled and shot yellow sparks up into the night. The rain had abated, but the low clouds remained dense. No sign of stars or moonlight. Every now and then they heard the soft *hooo* of an owl.

It had been almost six hours since Mason had placed a satellite call to headquarters in Prince George. Crime scene techs, a coroner, homicide detectives, and other personnel would start arriving at first light. Mason's job was to protect the integrity of the scene until the ident crews got here.

Oskar had been the last of the SAR techs to leave the campfire and crawl into his tent. Sounds of snoring had come quickly from inside his orange dome.

"He has the ability to do that," Callie said quietly as she poked a stick into the flames. "I find it tough to sleep while out on a mission. And this . . . Usually we search for people who've had an unfortunate accident, or made stupid mistakes. But this—this sense of malice, of malicious intent, murder . . ." Her words died on her lips. They felt rhetorical, so Mason left it there, allowing her to process the fact that they were camping not far from two murdered victims who'd been packed into a freezer for some reason.

The female victim wrapped in a sheet and lying atop the other victim had in Mason's preliminary judgment—from as much as he'd been able to see without disturbing the evidence—been hanged. There were ligature marks around her neck, a protruding tongue, and petechiae— red pinpoint dots in her eyeballs. There'd also been part of a rope hanging from a rafter in a bedroom that contained female belongings. He'd found no ID among the things in the room, but from the photo of the group gathered in front of the plane, he'd deduced the decedent was likely Katie Colbourne.

The body that had been placed into the freezer below the female victim, Mason had left untouched. It had been bound up in a bloody and muddied blue tarp with rope. He'd have to leave that for when the crime scene guys arrived.

Oskar had shown Mason drag marks and prints that led to a game trail in the woods. From the trace, Oskar believed the body in the tarp had been dragged to the shed from some distance in the forest. Prints showed that three people had done the dragging. They'd get a better read of the prints in daylight. They'd likely be able to trace them back to a possible murder scene. Oskar and his crew had also found additional prints heading along another trail closer to the water. There was a chance that trace could belong to the remaining survivors who'd left the lodge. Callie's plan was to follow those tracks in the morning.

After setting up camp, the group had eaten military-style, ready-to-eat rations warmed over the fire, and they'd consumed their meals mostly in silence, conscious of the vastness of the wilderness pressing in around them, the bodies in the freezer, and the gravity of it all.

"It's bizarre," Callie said. She looked at him directly, and Mason felt an odd little clutch in his gut when his gaze met hers.

"The carvings," she said. "The rhyme. The photoshopped lodge and spa development, the apparently nonexistent RAKAM Group. Two bodies in a freezer. One nonpilot in the pilot seat of a chartered float-plane with a vintage knife in her neck. Have you ever seen anything like this?"

"Not like this," Mason said.

"Why do you think someone went to the trouble of even putting those two bodies into the freezer?"

A log fell in the fire, shooting a soft shower of sparks up into the damp night.

"Well, it looks like the generator had been running," Mason said. "Presumably to chill the remains until it ran out of gas. So it would appear they—or someone—wanted to preserve the bodies. Rather than just hide them."

"And it was likely more than one person," she said. "Because it would have been a challenge for someone to get those two bodies up and into that chest solo, no? And there's the trace that shows three people possibly dragging the body in the tarpaulin."

"You're right." He smiled. "You'd have been a good detective."

She stopped poking the fire and studied his face. "You're patronizing me."

He laughed. "No. Actually, I think you'd probably have made a good cop all round."

She regarded him for a beat, weighing the sincerity and intent of his words. She turned her face back to the fire, said quietly, "SAR work *is* detective work. Wilderness-style, usually. Profiling the lost is like victimology in many ways. If you understand a person, it can help you guess what happened, and what decisions the victims might have made when faced with certain wilderness obstacles, or terrain, or weather, or injuries. Which can help you figure out the best area of probability to find them. Alive, hopefully. But dealing with homicides—I don't know how you can stomach that intent to harm, premeditated or otherwise, over and over again, and still be normal."

"Which is why most veteran homicide cops are not."

"Not what?"

"Normal."

She laughed. The sound was soft, gentle. Mason found it made her more attractive to him. Which was not a good thing. He began to feel edgy.

Callie is married. She's in a vulnerable place. And so are you. Don't even think *of going there.*

His inner voice shocked him. Mason had not felt like going "there" with anyone since Jenny's death. Callie, or time, or both, had managed to crack something in him. The idea that he *could* even begin to feel again made his heart beat just a little faster. It sent a soft warmth into his gut. And that was enough. For now. Just to feel a little bit alive again. To *want* to keep living. And he was grateful to Callie for giving him that.

He inhaled deeply and said, "I'm going to turn in, call it a night."

She nodded and pushed to her feet. "Yeah. Me too."

He stood, and for a moment they were close. She looked into his eyes and he felt it. A surge of something invisible but tangible. A thickening and an electricity in the air between them. She turned away quickly, clicked on her headlamp, and made for her tent.

He just stood watching her beam of light dance through the trees and bounce against the thick mist, his body tense.

Spending time with Callie Sutton was either going to be good for him, or it was going to be very bad. Because she was spoken for. And he'd be lying to himself if he didn't admit he was being drawn to her on a sexual level.

He exhaled and made for his own tent.

Somewhere in the trees, the owl hooted softly.

THE LODGE PARTY

STELLA

Monday, October 26.

That night, Stella lay in her bed upstairs. They'd cut Katie down from the rafter, wrapped her in a sheet from her bed, and carried her out to the shed, where they'd managed to get her body into the large chest freezer with Bart's.

Uncertain what to do next, the five of them had rewarmed the stew Deborah had prepared, eaten in sheer exhaustion, and decided to try and get some sleep so clearer heads in the morning might help them figure out a plan.

They'd watched each other going into their respective rooms and locked their doors.

Outside, the wind had died, and Stella could no longer hear rain falling. Perhaps it had turned to snow. But she could hear the distant chug of the generator. She couldn't decide if the mechanical sound was comforting or horrific, given the contents of the freezer.

For the bazillionth time she ran through the sequence of events leading to the deaths. It seemed that almost everyone had had an opportunity to take the cleaver from the kitchen and murder Bart.

The same for Jackie disappearing with the plane. And Stella was now certain that Jackie Blunt must be dead.

Katie Colbourne? The optics were clearly that Katie had taken her own life for some dark reason unbeknownst to the rest of them.

Stella tossed in her bed, punched her pillow, and lay back staring at shadows on the ceiling. An hour later, she checked her watch.

Only 1:45 a.m.

She tossed and turned for a few more minutes, then sat bolt upright. Someone was banging on a bedroom door down the hall.

She heard a woman yell. "Help, we need help here! Someone help!"

Stella swung her feet over the side of the bed, then hesitated. No one could be trusted, could they?

"Please, help. Steven is throwing up! He's sick."

Stella grabbed her fleece jacket and pulled on some pants. She unlocked her door and peered out.

Monica was wrapped in her dressing gown. She stood outside Steven's door.

She pointed into Steven's room. "Nathan is with him in the bathroom. He's throwing up all over the place and has terrible diarrhea. There's blood in his vomit."

◆ ◆ ◆

Tuesday, October 27.

By late morning the next day, Steven was finally sleeping. They'd brought him downstairs with a bucket and helped him lie down on the sofa. His vomit and diarrhea had gotten progressively bloodier during the night. And they'd all stayed up with him while Nathan had kept the fire going into the early hours of the morning. Deborah now sat at Steven's side and continued to bathe his brow with a cool cloth that had been soaked in water. Stella had found some electrolyte tabs in her medical kit and given them to him, because Steven's blood pressure had been dropping, and they feared dehydration. He'd appeared delirious for a time, too. His complexion was ashen, and the hollows beneath his eyes were deep and bruise colored.

They all kept looking at the checkerboard, half expecting another figurine to suddenly lose its head and topple over. Dead.

"It's like he ingested something toxic," Monica said yet again, standing behind the sofa. She looked like a wreck. Stella would barely recognize her as the well-made-up and manicured woman in expensive outdoor gear who'd boarded the plane only two days before.

"But we all ate the same thing," Deborah said. "I put a bit of stew and a bit of chili from each of the tins into all of our bowls."

Those bowls of stew had grown cold while they'd cut Katie down from the rafter, wrapped her in a sheet, and carried her out to the freezer. But Monica had rewarmed the contents.

"Maybe it was something else he took? Like some pills or something," Nathan offered.

"There was nothing in his room that would indicate anything like that," Stella said.

Steven groaned, and his eyelids fluttered open. His lips were dry.

"Hey," Stella said. She tried to smile. "You're alive, Doc."

He moaned and held his hand to his brow. "Need . . . something to drink. Thirsty, so thirsty."

Nathan came to his feet. "I'll go make some sweet black tea. I think that might be good. Anyone else want some? I saw tea bags and sugar in the cupboards earlier."

They all nodded.

Nathan made his way into the kitchen as Steven pushed himself into a sitting position. Stella began to think that the worst was over for Dr. Bodine. Whatever had poisoned his system had worked its way through.

Nathan yelled suddenly from the kitchen. "Guys! Oh Christ. Guys!"

Stella surged to her feet as Nathan appeared in the doorway. He held a shallow earthenware bowl in his hands, a terrible look on his face.

He held the bowl out for them to see.

Mushrooms.

"Do you know what these are?" he asked.

Stella glanced at Monica, who looked at Deborah. Steven stared, confused, at the bowl in Nathan's hands.

"Death caps," Nathan said. "*Amanita phalloides.*" He picked a mushroom out of the bowl and held it up for them to see. "Accounts for ninety percent of all fungus-related fatalities."

Monica leaped to her feet. "Put that down, Nathan! Don't touch it!"

He set what looked like a common, edible variety of mushroom back into the bowl. "It's not lethal to the touch, Monica. Only if you eat it."

"There were mushrooms in the stew last night," Steven said in a croaky, weakened voice.

"Not in mine," Deborah said.

"I didn't taste any in my bowl," Stella said quickly.

"Nor me in mine," Monica said.

"Certainly were no mushrooms in my stew last night," Nathan said. His attention settled on Steven. Worry creased his brow.

"Do you think someone could've put some death cap into only Steven's food?" Monica asked.

"I prepared the food," Deborah said. "And I didn't use mushrooms. I never even saw that bowl of mushrooms in the kitchen. And it was Monica who took the bowls and rewarmed them."

"But the bowls of stew were also sitting unattended on the table downstairs while we were all busy with Katie upstairs," Stella said. She turned to Nathan. "Where exactly did you find those?"

"They were just sitting there in this bowl, next to the chopping block in the kitchen."

Silence pressed into the room. The fire crackled. Stella cleared her throat. "Someone's been inside."

"Or one of us put them there while the rest of us were upstairs and not looking," Nathan said.

Steven narrowed his eyes onto Nathan. "And who among us would know which mushrooms could kill, and where to find them?"

"Oh no, no, this was not me," Nathan said, looking stricken. "God, I hate you, Steven, you know that, but I'm not a killer."

Electricity crackled between the men.

"Do they even grow here?" Deborah asked.

Nathan set the bowl down on the dining table. "They're being reported all over BC now. And there have been several deaths. The BC Centre for Disease Control has been putting out warnings. These look like they could have been harvested a few weeks ago. Death caps usually grow in BC from June to November. They are easily confused for edible mushrooms, depending on the stage of maturity."

"Could those have been growing outside the lodge, or along the forest trails we searched?" Stella asked. "I saw lots of different fungi out there."

"It's possible," Nathan said. "But I personally didn't see anything resembling *Amanita phalloides*."

"Well, thank heavens that Steven is okay now," Deborah said. "Whatever it was, it seems the worst is over."

But Nathan remained silent, watching Steven closely. Stella's chest tightened, and a sense of tension increased in the room. Nathan dragged his hand over his hair, as if struggling to voice something.

"What is it, Nathan?" Monica snapped. "Just spit it out, please."

"He's going to die."

His words hung on the air in the great room. The clock *tock, tock, tock*ed.

"I feel better," said Steven. "I'm getting better."

"It's the lag phase."

"Nathan—talk to us!" Monica said, her eyes going wild. *"Please."*

He seated himself carefully on the edge of one of the chairs, and he met their gazes in turn.

"If Steven has consumed *Amanita phalloides*, he's gone through what is called the gastrointestinal phase. It usually hits about six to ten hours after ingestion as the body tries to expel the toxin. Then, clinically, the victim will appear to be getting better. He will feel as though he's on the mend. It's called the lag phase. But during this lag phase, the amatoxins are busy destroying his liver."

"What does that mean?" Deborah asked.

"It means that in another thirty-six to forty-eight hours, signs of liver impairment will start to appear. They will get progressively worse. The toxins will totally damage his liver and kidneys. Organ failure will result, and then death in one to three weeks, unless he gets medical help fast, or a liver transplant in short order." He paused. "Steven is going to die if we don't get expert medical intervention. Soon. There's nothing else that will stop this."

Stella's pulse raced as her gaze went to the piece of paper with the rhyme still on the table.

Five Little Liars filed out the door.
One met an ax, and then there were four.

Four Little Liars lost in the trees.
One got stabbed, and then there were three.

"It's not prescriptive," she said quietly. "Things haven't happened exactly like the rhyme said. It doesn't mean we all will die. We can stop this. We must stop this."

Nathan said, "Either way, Steven is going to die if we don't get him to a hospital."

THE SEARCH

CALLIE

Wednesday, November 4.

The gray rain-whipped day dawned to the thud of choppers approaching in low clouds. Callie called Ben on her satellite phone as she watched the back-and-forth of helicopters disgorging crime scene crews, a coroner, officers both in and out of uniform, a police K9 team, military tents, and other equipment. Mason was inside the lodge, working with the lead detective, Gord Fielding, each updating the other on aspects of the case thus far.

"Heya, Ben, it's Mom," Callie said, blocking one ear with her hand and moving deeper into the trees to better hear her son's voice. "Did you have a good night?"

Benny told her about the movie they'd watched last night, and how his class was going to visit the fire station today. As she listened to her son, she watched two officers go by, stringing yellow crime scene tape among the trees all the way down to the water's edge. It billowed and flapped in the wind. It felt surreal. But she was relieved to hear Benny sounding so happy.

"Sounds like fun," she said. "Maybe Mason will have you guys over to the police station soon. And you can come to see the SAR base."

"I've seen the SAR base, Mom."

"Yeah, but your classmates haven't, right? You could help show them around. We could do a mock search."

"That would be cool!"

She smiled. "Okay. Be good. I might be away for a few days, but you can always get Rachel to call me on the sat phone if you need to talk to me, okay?"

"'Kay, Mom. Bye!"

And he was gone. Callie gave a wry smile as she signed off and slotted her phone into the sheath at her belt. From her pack she retrieved her clipboard, a water-resistant notebook, and a graphite pencil she could use in the rain. She made her way through the trees to join Oskar and the other SAR guys. They were working with the K9 team to assess tracks that appeared to show the remaining survivors had headed into the woods near the lake. The Survivor Five, as they were being dubbed.

The energy was buzzing everywhere, and the questions were flying as the painstaking process of collecting every tiny bit of evidence, and flagging and recording it, had begun. Callie had never personally witnessed an operation the scope of this one—certainly not one involving multiple homicides. While it was horrific, shocking, she also found aspects of it thrilling.

The coroner, who was a retired pathologist, felt both Bart Kundera and Katie Colbourne had died about a week earlier. From his cursory examination, the pathologist believed the cleaver had killed Bart Kundera, and that it appeared to have been thrown from a distance. It had sunk into Kundera's skull at considerable velocity. Callie didn't know many people who could throw an ax or cleaver with enough accuracy to hit someone neatly in the back of the head. The question was whether one among the Survivor Five had cleaver- or ax-throwing skills.

Either Katie Colbourne had hanged herself, or someone else had killed her. It would have required considerable strength to string Colbourne from the rafters, or possibly teamwork. Or Katie might have been threatened and forced up onto the seat of the chair found overturned near her feet, which could then have been kicked out from under her.

Mason had also told Callie that someone inside the lodge had been sick with bloody diarrhea and vomit. From the contents of one of the rooms, and the adjoining bathroom, it appeared the sick person had been Dr. Steven Bodine. It was also possible a rifle had been taken, judging by markings and hooks on a wall, and the bullets emptied from a box that had been left in the shed.

Clothing and other belongings found in the rooms had been examined, and more information on the Survivor Five, plus the three decedents, was coming in from detectives who were talking with the respective families. So far Callie had been given the heights, weights, and shoe sizes of the Survivor Five, along with basic personality traits.

Katie Colbourne, Callie had learned, was divorced and the mother of a six-year-old girl named Gabby. Not much younger than Benny. Callie hated to think of the child dealing with this heartbreaking news, learning her mother would never be coming home. The legacy of her mother's murder would haunt Gabby Colbourne for the rest of her life. If there was one thing that would enable Callie to endure and survive anything, it would be her fierce need to get home to Ben and Peter. To never leave them alone.

"Hey!" Oskar called out as he saw Callie approaching along the narrow trail.

He left the K9 team and SAR techs and came over to her with his tracking pole in hand. "We've located five sets of different boot prints," he said in his deep singsong voice. "Got some good trace over this way." Oskar led Callie to prints that had been made in thick mud beneath the heavy branches of a hemlock that had so far protected them. "There," Oskar said.

She got down into the mud with Oskar. He pointed his pole to one print—he used rubber bands, castration rings, that he'd threaded onto his pole to measure the average stride for each person. If he knew generally how long each subject's stride was, it showed him where to look for the next print in relation to one he'd just found.

"This print shows a distinct starburst pattern on the ball of the foot. And this one here, small rectangle ridges. That one over there has circular pieces on the heel, and damage in the lugs near the toe. These here are worn smooth at the heel. This one has interlocking triangle-shaped lugs."

Callie began to measure and sketch the five distinct patterns, impervious to the rain coming down on her shoulders and dripping from the bill of her cap. Her fingers were going numb from the cold, her breath coming in clouds as she took her tape measure to another sole imprint.

"This one with the starburst pattern looks like an Outrigger brand boot," she said. "It's a seven." She consulted her notebook. "According to next of kin, both Monica McNeill and Deborah Strong wore sizes six and a half to seven, depending on the shoe brand."

Callie moved on to sketch another pattern. She took photos of the different prints as well, but KSAR volunteers understood well the limitations of batteries and high-tech devices in the wilderness. Having waterproof maps, old-style compass-reading skills, and water-resistant notebooks and pencils was protocol for the team.

She looked up at Oskar. "Stella Daguerre's next of kin has not yet been located, but she did leave a pair of running shoes in a bag in the lodge room she occupied. Her bag contained some ID, so we're assuming it was her room. The running shoes in the room are a size eight. So these two smaller-size sets—the one with the starburst pattern, and the one with the triangles—must belong to either Deborah or Monica." Callie labeled her renderings of the starburst and triangle lug patterns *Deb-Mon*. She labeled the size 8 pattern as *Stella*. The men had larger feet—a size 10 and size 12.

The RCMP tracking dog started to bark nearby. The officer called for them to come over.

Callie shut and pocketed her notebook, snapped a last photo, then followed Oskar to where the German shepherd was lunging into her harness at the end of a tracking lead. The cop held on tight. "She's picked up their scent going that way." He pointed at a gap in the bushes—a barely there trail led deeper into the forest relatively parallel to the lake shore.

Oskar said to Callie, "Got all the sketches down?"

She nodded and tilted her chin toward the trail. "Looks like it shouldn't be too much of a challenge with the dog on their scent. As long as we don't lose it. We should move now. We've got enough. Let's gather our gear. I'll check with Mason, see if he's ready to leave."

Callie hurried back along the trail toward the lodge, adrenaline coursing through her system. She felt as edgy as that tracking K9 to get on the trail of the Survivor Five. The rain might change to snow again soon, and they could lose the small advantage they had.

She reached the crime scene boundary demarcated by the yellow tape and was stopped by a uniformed officer.

"Callie Sutton, Kluhane Bay SAR," she said, showing her ID. "I need to speak to Sergeant Mason Deniaud."

She could see Mason near the back door of the lodge, talking to one of the crime scene guys dressed in white Tyvek coveralls and booties. In nitrile-gloved hands Mason held what looked to Callie like a bowl.

She watched Mason and the forensic ident guys as the uniform went over to fetch him. The boiler-suited techs were placing little scene markers outside the shed and taking photographs. One of the huge military-style tents had been erected to cover the area between the lodge kitchen and the shed with the freezer.

She was fascinated. It was like SAR work, but different, of course. But it offered the same buzz, that urgent need to solve a big puzzle with stakes of life and death. The kind of thing that took her mind out of her everyday-life worries. She used to share this zing with Peter each time they got a callout. As her mind turned to Peter, she was slammed by a hard wave of grief. So strong and dark it stopped her breath.

She looked away and tried to inhale, then exhale, to recalibrate. The pain, the sense of loss, of fear—it would hit out of nowhere. She'd learned this. She'd also learned to accept it, and to bow under it, give in to it, because the harder she tried to shove it away, the harder it hit next time around, and it would be all the more debilitating.

She'd had plenty of well-meaning advice. But most of that advice was designed for permanent loss of a loved one.

Peter was still here.

She still believed he could come back.

"Callie?"

She spun around. Mason was coming over. He carried what looked like a bowl of mushrooms in his gloved hands.

As he neared, she saw what they were. She shot him a hard look. "Did someone ingest any of those?"

"Do you know what kind they are?" he asked, holding them out for her to examine.

"They look like death caps. Where did you find them?"

"In the kitchen."

She met his gaze. "They don't grow here. Or not that we've seen so far. Doesn't mean we wouldn't find them if we looked, only that they haven't yet been reported by someone who knows their fungi. But incidents of *Amanita phalloides* poisoning have been increasing across BC. Caused the death of a toddler near Vancouver last year, and a woman in the ski resort of Whistler ate one from her backyard and was seriously poisoned. And she thought she knew her mushrooms." As Callie spoke, it struck her.

"You said the detectives this morning informed you Dr. Nathan McNeill was a professor of mycology?"

"Yeah." As Mason spoke, an ident tech came over to take the mushrooms into evidence. He handed them over.

"Nathan McNeill would have known what those are," Callie said.

Mason looked at her with interest. "Meaning?"

"Meaning, it's a poison that could be used to kill someone. You also said there was evidence that someone had been seriously ill inside the lodge."

"Evidence suggests Dr. Steven Bodine had a gastroenteritic attack. Both diarrhea and emesis in the bathroom adjoining the room in which we found his belongings showed signs of being grossly bloody."

"If that gastroenteritis was caused by Dr. Bodine ingesting part of a death cap . . . that could be it." Energy speared into Callie.

"Could be Dr. Nathan McNeill poisoned him," Mason said. "If these don't grow around here, there remains the possibility McNeill brought them on the trip with intent."

"And," Callie said, "it could be a reason the Survivor Five might have felt compelled to leave their shelter. To get help."

Mason frowned. "How so?"

"KSAR was sent a brief last summer on the pathogenesis of death cap ingestion. The information originated from the BC Centre for Disease Control because the mushroom is potentially becoming a hazard across this province, and it was felt search and rescue should be aware of the signs. If Dr. Bodine ate a death cap, or part of one, he would've developed severe gastric problems, but after about six hours he'd appear recovered. That's the lag phase. But Dr. McNeill, a mycology expert, might well have known that the damage had been done. And that the poison would still silently be destroying Dr. Bodine's liver. If this is what happened, the only chance for Dr. Bodine's survival would be medical intervention. Or he's as good as dead right now."

"So his health would be worsening on the trail right now? If he's not deceased already, given the time frame?"

"Yes. My guess is they're probably trying to get around the northwest side of Taheese Lake," Callie said. "Stella Daguerre, as their pilot, would have gotten a good orientation from the air. She would most certainly be aiming them toward Kluhane Bay."

The wind gusted, bringing a fresh deluge of rain. Mason regarded Callie with intensity, his eyes as gray as the clouds.

"We need to move. Now," he said quietly. "We can coordinate with the RCMP command base and air support for backup as we go."

THE SEARCH

MASON

They hiked single file and moved fast, thanks to the German shepherd, Trudy, and her RCMP handler, Ray Gregson, who remained hot on the scent.

Mason took up the rear of the column, behind Callie. In front of Callie were two other SAR techs. Oskar hiked directly behind the K9 team, muttering about how the police dog and handler were messing up "his" footprints. But Callie had made the call to follow the dog's nose rather than man-track from print to print. A good chunk of time had elapsed since the Survivor Five appeared to have left the lodge, and in open terrain without tree cover, prints would be obscured by rain and snow.

The other SAR techs had remained behind on standby to provide support from the air as spotters if the weather lifted enough to enable a chopper to fly into the mountain peaks along the northwest side of the lake, where the tracks led.

The team kept the pace for several hours, breathing hard, clouds of mist forming around their faces. With each kilometer, each hour, each minute longer, Mason was increasingly cognizant that time was running out for the group, especially Dr. Steven Bodine, if the assumption that the surgeon had ingested death caps was correct. That the mushrooms had been left in a bowl on the kitchen counter was ominous in itself. A warning? A sign left behind for rescuers? Maybe the mushrooms and poisoning had been mentioned in the missing note?

Caution on the part of the SAR crew tracking the Survivor Five was also warranted. The five likely had a rifle and ammunition among them. Possibly taken to protect themselves against wildlife, or conceivably to hunt for food. But there remained the sinister fact that the message had been ripped out of the notebook on the coffee table.

One among the group could prove hostile.

Mason was armed with a sidearm and carried a rifle on his back with his pack. As did the RCMP dog handler. Oskar carried a shotgun. For protection against wildlife. There were grizzlies in this region, he'd said. Wolves and mountain lions, too.

Mason checked his watch. It was 2:34 p.m., and their column still moved at a choppy trot along the overgrown and uneven trail that led through forests and across shale slopes and scree, and through occasional meadows and marsh areas. The pack on his back, combined with his heavy boots, jacket, and regulation bullet-suppression vest, was testing the limits of his fitness and endurance, both of which had flagged since his return from his Australian "walkabout" after Jen and Luke's accident tore apart his life. Perspiration began to break out over his body, and his muscles protested. But he'd also settled into a rhythm, lungs burning as he breathed the clean, cold air in deep. And it became meditative. It gave him a quiet endorphin buzz, and it distracted him in good ways. It made him feel alive.

It was likely a game trail they were following, Callie had explained. But it was clear the survivors had come this way, not only from the scent the dog was picking up, but from the odd prints, dislodged stones, crushed vegetation, and broken twigs along the track.

Mason watched Callie in front of him, liking the way she moved, enjoying the intensity of her focus, her contagious energy, the way her job and surroundings absorbed her, the way she remained constantly alert to noises, signs, changes in the terrain and weather. The way pink color rose in her cheeks, and the cold made her eyes bright. She was adept in this environment. It was her world. Mason figured if you dropped Callie Sutton from a chopper alone into this wilderness, she'd find her way home. Alive.

But him? While he could retrace his route in a city using landmarks like any regular urbanite—a McDonald's here, a Starbucks there, a department store entrance on the corner, the tiny sushi place, a Korean restaurant near a busy intersection—out here landmarks were a big Douglas fir near a slope with a northerly aspect, a glimpse of water and a certain peak suddenly visible through clouds, a change in the flora showing increased elevation. It offered a different sense of space and orientation.

Up ahead the dog suddenly veered off the trail and went casting her nose about up a slope that led to a clearing on a plateau.

"Whoa!" Officer Gregson held Trudy back and raised his hand. He indicated the new direction. "Going to take a look!" Gregson called.

Oskar called a halt, and they watched as the K9 team left the trail, crashing up through brush.

"That's the thing about dogs," Callie said with a grin as they watched Gregson stumbling and falling after his lunging K9. "If they're air scenting as opposed to print-to-print tracking, they ignore the easy path and go as the scent blows from a distance. The subjects probably walked up to that ridge using a far easier approach."

The handler reined Trudy in again when they reached the plateau. "Sign of a camp up here!" he called down to them.

They proceeded to climb up the incline to the clearing at the plateau. Oskar asked them all to stand back while he closely examined the trace on the ground beneath a large fir. Oskar picked something out of the dirt. He held it up.

"ChapStick."

Mason moved forward and took it from Oskar. He showed it to Callie.

"Regular old lip balm," she said. He bagged it.

"Looks like the Survivor Five's first camp," Oskar said, pointing to more trace on the ground. "They sat here, and it looks like they rested awhile, maybe lay down, judging by the markings and changes in this vegetative ground cover. Also a wrapper from a granola bar." He picked it up with his gloved hand.

Mason took it from him. "Probably came from the lodge cupboards or one of their bags," he said as he bagged and recorded it.

"So you think they spent a night here, Oskar?" Callie asked, looking up at the giant fir. "Tree would have provided some shelter."

"Possible," Oskar said, continuing his careful examination of the ground while Gregson watered and rested Trudy. "If this was their camp for the first night, it would mean we're moving a lot faster than they were." The Norwegian glanced up, his blue eyes bright. "That's good because we will catch up, but not so good if it's illness or injury that was slowing them down."

There was no overt sign, however, that anyone had continued to throw up along the trail since leaving the lodge.

Mason took photos, logged the GPS location for forensics.

"We keep moving," Callie said, uncapping her water bottle and taking a sip.

Oskar ate a snack bar, and one of the other techs offered around some nuts.

As Oskar chewed, he said, "I'm still seeing signs of five different print sets. At this point they were all still on the move."

After another two hours on the track, Oskar called them all to a halt again so he could study some particularly clear prints preserved in claylike mud. Using his pole and the rubber rings to mark stride length again, he worked carefully over the clay patch.

"They were getting tired," he said. "Their strides are shortening."

"Still five sets?" Mason asked.

"Affirmative," said Oskar.

"No sign anyone else followed behind them?"

Oskar examined the ground in silence, measuring tracks that Mason could barely even see with his own eyes. This was an arcane art, he thought, this man-tracking. Finally Oskar came to his feet and pushed his cap back on his head.

"Got the starburst pattern. Got the size eight, and the other female, size seven. And the two larger male sets. No one else that I can see."

The image of the corpses in the freezer surfaced in Mason's mind. If an unidentified subject outside of this group of five had killed Bart Kundera and Katie Colbourne, the killer did not appear to be following and hunting the fleeing Survivor Five now.

Which left the possibility that one or more among the group were killers.

Or that the killer had left them alone for some reason.

Callie lifted her scopes and scanned the trail that climbed ahead.

"From here it continues up," she said. "We'll see if we can reach that ridge up there before nightfall." She pointed. "That vantage point will offer us a sweeping view, and judging from the terrain, the trail will head from that ridge back down toward the water. We'll set up camp for the night at the ridge."

Mason opened his water bottle, swallowed. Cold water had never tasted so good. As he capped his canteen, he said, "So those poor subjects had to go uphill."

"Clearly," Callie said, securing her binoculars to her pack. "From my recollection, there used to be remnants of a game trail along the lake that would have bypassed climbing the ridge, but water levels have been rising in Taheese Lake over the last few years. Lots of snow, warmer temperatures causing glacier melt. And a lot of precip over the past few days as well." She tented her gloved hand over her eyes as she studied the mountains around them. "My worry is the streams and waterfalls coming down into the lake right now might give us access issues."

"Would be same for the subjects, though. If the rivers stop us, they would also have stopped them."

She pursed her lips and nodded. "Although the creek and river volumes can change by the hour. Flash floods are also possible. And the avalanche chutes are tough to navigate—all conditions that could cause injury or worse. But you're correct. If obstacles held the subjects back, hopefully they were smart enough to wait things out or turn back."

"At Dr. Bodine's expense," Oskar added.

"Triage." Callie hefted her pack back up onto her shoulders. "But triage requires logic and hard decisions. Most lost subjects, if they're inexperienced, act on panic and push through at their own expense. The cost can be death."

As the group set off again, they kept an even faster pace. The incline grew steeper. Mason's muscles and joints started feeling the strain. The searchers fell silent. Mist blew in again, and precipitation turned thicker, wavering between rain and sleet.

THE SEARCH

CALLIE

By 4:00 p.m. the search party was navigating a tricky avalanche chute—an obstacle course littered with giant boulders, scree, shale, mud, fallen trees, and unearthed root balls of old-growth trees that were the size of a small car.

Tattered curtains of cloud raked through the valley, dragging swaths of sleet. Desolate. Cold. But for Callie it still held majestic beauty. Perhaps *because* it was powerful, inhospitable. To reach this kind of natural beauty—to see and touch and experience it in person—required a human to dig deep into physical and mental reserves. To Callie the payoff was exponential.

RCMP officer Gregson was carrying his dog in a harness over a particularly steep and unstable slope of scree that would break Trudy's leg should her paw slip into any of the many deep gaps in the moving stones. But they were still making good time, all bolstered by the fact that K9 Trudy was still on the scent. And Oskar was still finding physical trace showing that the group had passed this way. Mason had also received word via sat phone that a chopper with a forward-looking infrared—FLIR—system and instruments-flying capability was being dispatched from CFB Comox to assist from the air. It would be fully dark by the time the helicopter arrived, but Callie knew that FLIR often worked best to pick up heat trace from subjects when temperatures fell. Even so, it would require luck and expertise to pick up heat signatures if the subjects had gone into deep gullies or were sheltering beneath dense old-growth canopy. But given that her team was still seeing signs at this point, and all five appeared to be alive and on the move, it would improve the odds. Because long-dead people did not emit a heat signature.

Oskar was waiting for Callie when she and Mason reached the opposite side of the avalanche chute.

"I found some more tracks," he said. "The Survivor Five are getting tired. Shuffling. Looks like they stopped and rested again for a while on this end of the chute."

She looked up at the climb ahead that wound through the trees. Mason's gaze followed hers.

"I can hear rushing water," he said.

She nodded and took out her map. Callie clicked on her headlamp to study it because the twilight was thickening. "There's a deep gorge on the other side of that ridge we're aiming for."

"Something they could cross?" Mason asked.

Callie exchanged a glance with Oskar. He said, "By the sound of that rushing water . . . we'll have to see."

Urgency tightened in Callie. "If they couldn't cross the water in the gorge, they might have camped up on that ridge for a while. We might even find them up there. If the Survivor Five left the lodge right after the deaths of Bart Kundera and Katie Colbourne, given the coroner's estimation of time of death, they could have been out here a week already. That's a long time to endure wet cold without wilderness smarts. Plus, Dr. Bodine would likely have started showing signs of liver failure."

"If he's still alive," Oskar said.

Callie folded her map. Gregson gave Trudy some water. And the rest of the crew clicked on their headlamps before entering the last stand of forest that lay between them and the plateau at the gorge.

When they'd navigated through the forest and arrived at the ridge, breathing hard, they were met with a big stone plateau partially covered by a rock overhang. It was fully dark, but evidence showed the Survivor Five had indeed camped here. They'd managed to make a small fire from dry wood likely found under the rock overhang. A wrapper from a tin of soup lay near the ashes. In the ashes was a burned tin that had likely held the soup.

Trudy alerted on a bloodied piece of tissue under the overhang, and Gregson called Mason over.

Mason crouched down and studied the tissue under the beam of his headlamp. "Someone injured themselves," he said, photographing and bagging the tissue and securing it inside his pack along with the other evidence he'd gathered.

"Possibly someone got hurt crossing that avalanche chute back there," Callie said, shrugging out of her pack. She downed water from her canteen, wiped her mouth. "Wouldn't surprise me."

Oskar said, "Given that they're not here, they must have found a way to cross that gorge."

"We'll have to check it out in daylight," said Callie. "Maybe when they came through, there was not much flow coming down."

By the light of headlamps, hunting spotlights, and gas lanterns from their packs, they set up camp in the cover of the rock overhang. They found dry wood under the cover. Oskar and the techs built a campfire alongside the ashen remains of the one the Survivor Five had made.

They ate MREs to the sound of the thundering water, hidden from them by the blackness of night.

As the flames of their campfire began to dwindle, Callie got to her feet and went to look for more wood deeper under the overhang where the rock ceiling angled down low, and where windstorm debris had collected near the back.

As she crouched to gather up an armful of little branches and twigs, something white caught the beam of her flashlight. She stilled and bent closer. It was a crumpled ball of lined paper.

Callie set down her pile of firewood and fished the ball of paper out from where it lay under the area of the overhang too low to enter. She carefully opened it.

Her heart quickened.

"Mason!"

THE SEARCH

MASON

Anxiety speared through Mason as he heard Callie call his name. He hurried toward the sound of her voice, the beam of his flashlight bouncing off rock formations and thick fog. He found her crawling out from the back of the cave, where the overhang sloped and narrowed to a tight V.

"The note," she said quietly as she reached a spot where she could stand to her full height. With a gloved hand, she handed him a crumpled piece of paper. "I found the rest of the note. It was in the back of the cave with the other windblown detritus."

He took a pair of nitrile gloves from his pocket, snapped them on, and took the crumpled piece of paper from her.

He read the scrawled words under the light of his headlamp. The words started where the paper had been ripped out of the notebook they'd found in the lodge.

. . . nd help. Steven Bodine is sick. We believe he ingested some death cap mushrooms. We don't know how it happened. We believe someone came into the lodge and put mushroom pieces into the bowls that were left standing while we attended to

Katie Colbourne, who we found hanged upstairs. Steven is in a lag phase now. Hasn't got much time. Already signs of yellowing in his eyes.

Jackie Blunt and the de Havilland Beaver are missing.

Bart Kundera and Katie Colbourne are both dead. Murdered.

We are being hunted.

We have been lured, and trapped. In a hurry now—argued about leaving. Deborah twisted her ankle on the first day, and it's not that strong. Don't know if the killer is out there and will come after us. We have a gun. We have taken water and supplies. We can keep a watch on each other in case one among us has done this. But Steven will die without help.

He might have a week or two at most. Trying to reach Kluhane Bay is better than sitting here and doing nothing and being picked off.

We have tried to preserve bodies for police in freezer.

Please help. Please hurry. Heading west around lake. Hope to reach hospital in small town of Kluhane. Praying that rescue comes and we are found before that.

Signed:

Monica and Nathan McNeill

Stella Daguerre

Deborah Strong

Steven Bodine

Wednesday, October 28.

"Seven days ago," he said quietly. "You were right about their reasons for leaving shelter, Callie."

Mason read the note again.

"Why do you think it was ripped out?" Callie asked. "Why do you think it was left here?"

He exhaled, his breath clouding in the beam of his headlamp. "That it was found here implies one of the group ripped it from the notebook. And perhaps dropped it here in error, or tried to dispose of it. The logical assumption is that one among the Survivor Five does *not* want help to come."

Callie swore softly. "So one theory would be that one of the Survivor Five is the mastermind—the person who lured them to the lodge. The person who is playing some kind of psychological game."

"And then killing them, one by one," he said.

He read the note once more. His guess was one of the women had written this. Maybe Monica, given her name was signed first.

"Whoever wrote that appears to be unaware that Jackie Blunt was stabbed to death and on that plane," Callie said.

"Or feigning ignorance. I need to call this in," Mason said.

Callie nodded and bent to retrieve her load of small branches and twigs. "Want coffee?" she called as she gathered up her armload of fuel for the campfire. "I know it's late, but—"

"Would love some."

It had finally stopped raining for a while, so Mason walked a short way from the camp and climbed a rocky rise to where there was no rock or tree cover to mess with satellite reception. It was also slightly out of earshot from the rest of the group he'd left chattering around the campfire.

Sergeant Gord Fielding, the detective leading the "RAKAM party" investigation, answered on the second ring. He'd been on standby for a progress update from Mason's search group.

Mason informed Fielding about the note and gave him the location of their camp. The coordinates would be relayed to the helicopter that Mason could now hear thudding faintly in the dark somewhere behind the clouds. Fielding told Mason that the chopper crew had begun searching with infrared to the west side of the gorge, where Callie and her team felt the Survivor Five could be headed. The idea was for the chopper to work back in a grid pattern to where Mason and Callie were now located.

"Trace shows that subjects were moving slowly at this point," Mason said. "But signs remain that all five were still alive and on the move from this GPS location—no evidence so far to indicate otherwise."

Fielding gave Mason a radio frequency with which to communicate directly with the chopper.

"We've learned that Franz Gottman owned the Forest Shadow Lodge property through a numbered company registered in BC," Fielding said. "Gottman held dual American and Canadian citizenship. Owned several properties both in California and in BC, including the lodge on Taheese Lake, and a several-acre spread worth upward of ten million on Galiano Island."

"Owned?" Mason said. "As in past tense?"

"He's deceased," Fielding said. "Died August fifth of this year. Cancer. At the age of eighty-three."

"Are the properties going through probate? Is there a beneficiary?"

"Seems all his real estate is nonprobate assets. Rates and taxes are still being paid on all his BC holdings by the numbered company. We're securing a warrant for disclosure of the principal beneficiaries of that company, and we started searching his Galiano property late this afternoon. The Galiano estate was listed as Gottman's last primary address. I will keep you updated as information comes in."

"What else can you tell me about Gottman? He have family?" Mason asked, moving a little higher on his outcrop to improve reception. Fog dampened his skin and formed droplets on the bill of his cap.

"Billionaire. Worked in film and television. The mastermind behind two highly successful reality television shows: *Wild Among Men* and *Tribal*. He also provided financing for computer games development. Gottman went into the film business after obtaining a master's in psychology, then an MBA. Harvard. Stanford." There was a pause as Fielding appeared to consult his notes. "Never married. No children on record. A gay-rights activist when he was younger. Gottman has a record. Was arrested and charged for assaulting a police officer twenty-five years ago during a protest march. Also had a stalking charge. He apparently had a series of long-term relationships with various males. Retired at age sixty-five, after which he traveled and funded smaller television pilots, independent films. Liked hunting, sailing. Flew his own plane. De Havilland Beaver Mk 1."

"Where's Gottman's aircraft now?"

"Not on his Galiano property. The house has been standing empty for about six months. We've located his housekeeper, who says she continues to receive monthly checks from the same numbered company. She claims Gottman was admitted to a hospice in February, but he asked her to keep honoring her cleaning contract until she was instructed to do otherwise."

"Even after he died?"

"She didn't know that he'd passed. Only that she kept getting paid by direct deposit."

Mason frowned.

"Have you found any links between Gottman's numbered company and the company that funded this Forest Lodge and spa junket on behalf of the so-called RAKAM Group?"

"Investigation on that front is ongoing."

"Any links emerging between Gottman himself and the missing and murdered RAKAM guests?"

"Negative so far. Closest we've come is that Stella Daguerre's West Air charter operation is based on Galiano Island."

"That's a significant coincidence."

"West Air is basically a one-pilot show with one admin employee— a male who also lives on Galiano. We're questioning him tomorrow. So far we know that Daguerre divorced five years ago and is now going by her maiden name."

"What was her married name?"

"Marshall. We've located her ex, Stuart Marshall. An RCMP officer will be visiting him at his North Van home tomorrow."

Mason saw a beam of light coming around the rocks—Callie. Almost simultaneously he smelled coffee. And coffee had never smelled as good as it did right now.

Callie handed him a steaming travel mug as he listened to Fielding. He mouthed the words *Thank you* and motioned for her to wait. Mason wanted to update her in private before they rejoined the rest of their party. He trusted Callie with the sensitive details of this investigation. Also, some small details might help her predict the actions in the wilderness of their missing subjects.

"Any other connections emerging, any possible motives?" he asked Fielding as Callie seated herself on a rock nearby.

"Katie Colbourne was a well-known television news reporter," Fielding said. "She could have made enemies. We're delving into stories she covered during her tenure with CRTV, looking for anyone she might have upset by her coverage." A pause as Fielding spoke to someone else on his end. The thudding of the helicopter searching in the distance grew louder. Fielding came back on.

"Amanda Gunn remains a key person of interest. She was the primary point of contact with each of the victims and facilitated the trip. She also had opportunity in the death of Dan Whitlock—she was aware of his shellfish allergy. Bart Kundera . . . he had an older brother linked to organized crime. The brother is deceased. We're interviewing Kundera's wife tomorrow." Another pause as Fielding consulted his files.

"Ontario Provincial Police are talking to contacts of the McNeills in Toronto. The couple used to live in BC, in the Kitsilano neighborhood of Vancouver. Dr. Nathan McNeill taught at Simon Fraser . . ." A pause. "There's a link here between Monica McNeill and Dr. Steven Bodine—both served on the board of a children's charity foundation. They might well have known each other prior to this trip. We'll follow this up with the McNeills' adult children. The older McNeill son told an officer on the phone this morning that his mother had been hospitalized for a period of four weeks about thirteen years ago. A mental breakdown of some sort. It was after that episode that the McNeills made lifestyle changes and relocated to Toronto. Dr. Bodine is divorced. Ex-wife has remarried and lives in Paris. Jackie Blunt— there's no indication she knew or worked for the McNeills in Ontario. She's an ex–West Vancouver PD officer. Resigned from the WVPD amid rumors of alcoholism, which was allegedly impacting her performance on the job. An old WVPD colleague of Blunt's claims that before relocating to Ontario to work in security, Blunt did jobs for a private investigator—Dan Whitlock."

Mason whistled softly. "Interesting connection there."

"Yeah. Following it up. Whitlock is ex–Vancouver PD. He's known to the police. Seems he crossed lines a few times with his PI work."

"What about Deborah Strong?" Mason asked.

"In attempting to locate her next of kin, we learned she legally changed her name to Deborah Strong. She was previously known as Katarina Vasiliev. Daughter of Russian immigrants. Born in a small farming community in northern Alberta. Father, mother, and two brothers deceased. One older brother alive, who still lives on the family farm. He told RCMP in Alberta the family lost contact with Katarina when she ran away from home in her teens. But her staff at her cleaning company gave us the name of her fiancé—Ewan Redmayne. He's currently serving with the Canadian Air Force and is on an RCAF tour of duty in the Arabian Sea—maritime security and counterterrorism ops. We contacted him through CAF channels yesterday. He's on his way home."

Mason thanked Fielding and signed off. He sat in silence for a moment, processing as he listened to the sound of the helicopter moving back and forth, hidden by the dark and low clouds.

Callie came to sit beside him. "All okay?"

He sipped his coffee. Smiled. "Damn, this is good."

She grinned. A warmth filled him. Along with a sense of a bond. He updated her with the information Fielding had given him.

"Wow," she said softly. "Curiouser and curiouser. So Stella Daguerre, who used to be Marshall, might have known Franz Gottman?"

"Galiano is a small island. It would be hard to live there and *not* at least know about an old eccentric billionaire living on an over-ten-million-dollar estate."

"Plus, she's a pilot. And he had a plane." She fell silent. Water dripped from rocks and nearby trees. "I wonder who else is linked to this company that has kept paying Franz Gottman's bills," she said. "Surely Gottman's assets did not go into his estate, or probate. His numbered company, and whoever is behind it, must have had right of survivorship."

Mason nodded and finished his coffee.

"Deborah Strong, a.k.a. Katarina, is also an interesting one. It's also notable that Jackie Blunt and Dan Whitlock were connected. Both are dead, and both worked at some point in the PI business in Vancouver," Mason said.

"Well, if someone had to dream up a bizarre scenario that included luring and trapping people in a remote wilderness lodge, and then messing psychologically with their heads, my money is on the mind that created those two reality shows. Did you ever watch them?" '

"No."

"That was their premise. Like *Survivor*, or most reality shows, really—trap a bunch of people together, throw in some challenges, and see how they turn on each other. And there can only be one winner, one who outwits, outlasts, and outplays the others."

He snorted softly. "Except the rhyme at the lodge says, 'Maybe there shall be none.'"

THE SEARCH

CALLIE

Thursday, November 5.

The radio call came in the darkest hours before dawn. The military helicopter had detected infrared activity.

Callie listened—they all did, quietly creeping out of their tents as Mason took the call.

"Signs of wildlife activity," said their SAR spotter from the military craft.

Her pulse quickened. She exchanged a glance with Oskar, who was pulling on his cap against the rain that had started to fall again softly in the night.

"Could be wolves." The voice came through static. "Or maybe coyotes, but we think they're bigger. In a pack. Looks like seven of them."

"Any sign of human life?" Mason asked.

"Got shapes. Slightly different from rocks around. No signs of life."

"Shit," Callie whispered.

"GPS location?" Mason asked.

Callie recorded the coordinates as the voice came through the radio against the background noise of the chopper.

"The animals scattered when the pilot first lowered the bird, but they look like they might return. We'll go past and buzz them off a few times until you guys can get in, but we'll need to refuel and switch out crew soon. And we can't go too low because of the forest canopy."

"Roger. Keep us posted, over," Mason said.

"Affirm. Over and out," said the SAR tech.

They heard the chopper move farther into the distance.

"Start breaking camp," Callie said, lighting a gas lantern. "We'll attempt the gorge crossing as soon as there is enough light. How will Trudy handle the crossing?" she asked Gregson.

"I'll transport her across in harness."

She nodded, clicked on her headlamp, and consulted the map against the GPS coordinates by the beam of her light. Oskar came over to join her.

"Here," she said, tapping an area of the map where the contour lines ran far apart. "There's a flat area behind the ridge on the other side of this gorge. That's where the wolves or coyotes are."

And possibly the bodies that attracted them.

The thundering sound of the nearby white water charging through the gorge reached them as they fell silent. One of the techs lit a small gas stove to put on coffee for the crew. The blue-white flames sparked to life with a faint whiff of propane.

Mason leaned over Callie's shoulder and studied the map. "How long to reach that location?" he asked.

"Chopper can guide us in from the air if need be. Looking at this topography, once we reach the other side of the gorge, maybe an hour's hike uphill." She met his eyes. "*If* we can cross the gorge. This precip of late, and snowmelt above, is bringing the water down hard."

"Doesn't look good," Oskar said quietly. He paused, then voiced what they all were thinking. "It sounds like we've found them. But not before the wolves did."

"And now, there might be none," Callie said very quietly.

Their search for the Survivor Five might just have turned into a recovery mission.

THE SEARCH

MASON

A pale and silvery light washed into the valley. At the edge of a rocky incline that plunged into the gulley below, Mason stood beside Oskar, Callie, and the other SAR techs, awed by the force of white water rumbling down the narrow funnel between two mountains. Spray boiled up toward them in a wet, white cloud, throwing little rainbows everywhere. The noise of the rushing water almost drowned out the resonating *thuck, thuck, thuck* of the chopper in low clouds on the opposite side of the ridge.

Mason's heart jackhammered as, far below, Gregson worked Trudy along the gorge edge. Rain fell softly and sweat prickled over Mason's body. His breathing was shallow. He wasn't sure he could do this.

He also couldn't *not* do this.

The helicopter had fallen quiet for a time before dawn. It had returned to the helipad in Kluhane Bay to refuel and to rest the crew. Upon return to the area at first light, the SAR tech on board the chopper had reported the wolves had come back again, and the pilot was continuing to buzz them from the air, trying to keep the pack at bay. But tree cover was making the task difficult, and the wolves were growing emboldened.

Below, Gregson suddenly raised his hand high, giving the signal that Trudy had alerted to scent near a logjam that spanned the narrowest part of the gorge. The jam consisted of a tangle of fallen trees, branches, and muddy, stone-encrusted root balls that crisscrossed in a bridge over the water.

"That logjam would have been caused by an earlier flood," Callie said. "Looks like our subjects crossed over it. Amazing if they all made it without ropes. One slip, and they'd be gone."

Oskar and the others began picking their way down rocks that were wet and slippery with river mist and moss.

Mason felt frozen.

Callie touched his arm gently. "You okay to do this?"

His eyes met hers. "Yeah."

"Mason, listen to me. When you sent that de Havilland Beaver into the water—I saw that you had an issue with heights. That's nothing to be ashamed of. But if you do attempt to cross that jam, and if you tense, or freeze, you could make a mistake. We'll use ropes and carabiners, but a slip could put others in the team at risk."

He inhaled deeply. He *had* to do this. He had to conquer this fear in himself. For reasons he couldn't even begin to explain to himself. He felt suddenly as if this gorge cleaved his life between past and present. He'd come this far north, into this wilderness, to come upon this torrent. And either he dug deep enough to cross it, either he tried to make himself one of these people, this tribe he'd found—or he wouldn't move on. He'd stay stuck in his head and his grief forever. Or worse. He'd just find a way to check out.

"There is no reason you can't stay behind," Callie said. "And wait for another team to come in, or for extrication by helicopter."

"I'm fine." He determinedly tightened the straps of his pack across his chest, his focus on the gorge.

She assessed him.

"Callie," he said, looking at her, "I'm fine."

Far below, Gregson had put Trudy in a harness. Oskar and the others had just reached them and were busy securing a length of rope to rocks.

Still, she regarded him.

"Just tell me what I need to do," he said.

She moistened her lips, nodded slowly. "Okay. Oskar is securing rope to rocks on this end. He will attach himself to that rope and make his way to the other side, where he will secure the other end. It will create a line of support across the water. Then each of us will attach ourselves by a shorter rope and carabiner to that line across the water. And then we work our way across. If you slip, you will be attached to that line, and someone can help pull you back up."

It sounded simple in theory. But Mason could see that, given the sheer, rushing force of the white water beneath the logjam, even if someone was secured to a line, if they fell into that torrent, that water pressure could hold and trap them under. And even if someone did try to tug the person free via his rope, there were enough places to become trapped under the tangle of branches and roots and trunks of the logjam. And if he did fall, the impact he'd create on the support line could be enough to make them all slip.

He wiped rainwater off his face. His stomach churned.

"Ready?" she said.

He nodded.

They started down. The rocks were slick from the fine spray of mist and rain, and the slime of forest detritus.

His boot heel slid, and he skidded a short way down. Blood boomed in his ears. He could barely breathe.

Focus.

You wanted to die, remember? Now you can't take others down with you. They're relying on you. You're doing this for them.

Once they'd reached the bottom, Callie again placed a hand on his arm. Her eyes met his.

"Must you do this?"

He hesitated. "I need to do this."

She regarded him, reading something in his face. Mist formed tiny droplets on her eyelashes. In this light, her eyes were moss green and lambent.

"Help me, Callie," he said very quietly. "Show me how."

Something in her eyes changed, darkened. And he felt an energy pass between them. An understanding. A kinship.

She swallowed, turned to watch the water where Oskar was getting ready to cross, thinking.

"Okay," she said quietly. "I want you to rope up to me as well as hook onto the line across the water."

"No—"

"Yes." Her gaze locked on to his. "We're getting to the other side, together, and I'm going home to Ben, understand?"

He held her gaze.

"That's how I do the scary things," she said, her voice low as she unhooked a coil of rope from her pack. "I tell myself Benny is waiting. Peter is waiting. If you plan on stopping me from getting home to them, pull out now."

He inhaled.

"Because it's not that tough, Mason. The jam looks solid. We'll have the line. And those Survivor Five got across without ropes. At least I'm guessing some of them did before the wolves found them."

He gave a wry smile.

"Seriously, it's a slam dunk."

"Don't say dunk."

She laughed. Unexpected. And it cracked and shifted something in him. He was ready. He would do this.

They roped up and started carefully, testing each log before transferring weight. Step by step. The focus was intense for Mason. When he and Callie had reached the middle of the logjam bridge, water booming below them, Callie stopped.

Mason saw why.

The guideline that Oskar had secured from bank to bank across the river had gotten snagged behind a branch, and Callie couldn't keep sliding her carabiner along it. She tried to force the line free of the snag, but it was stuck fast. She tried to pull again, and Mason thought he felt logs suddenly moving under his boots. Fear sank a hatchet into his heart.

He felt his focus slipping. He stiffened, and his attention went to his boots and the logs and water gushing below. He couldn't move.

Focus. Look up. Focus.

But he was frozen again.

It seemed that below him the water was rising up higher under the logjam, mist boiling more furiously, the noise getting louder. He heard gigantic boulders knocking and booming as they were rolled around beneath the water.

He forced himself to slowly glance up, to look across at the bank on the other side. To get his mind back on goal. As he did, the trunk on which Callie stood rolled suddenly under her boots.

In that split second, Mason also noticed she'd unhooked her carabiner in order to resecure it to the line on the other side of the snag.

Before he could yell a warning, she slid off in a blur of color. Mason grabbed hold of a branch and flexed his knees, bracing for the impact of her weight against the rope secured to him.

As she went down, she lashed out and grabbed hold of a branch, just stopping herself from jerking hard at the end of her rope and pulling Mason in. She swayed in the void, holding by one hand, her boots swinging over churning water that plunged into a waterfall below her. His heart stopped dead.

He had seconds before she could no longer hold on. And when she did fall, her rope would tug hard at him. He had no idea how long the line across the gorge would hold both of them.

He heard Oskar screaming to hold fast, he was coming.

Callie yelled for Mason to grab her other hand. She reached it out to him. Time stretched into a viscous, distorted fluid. Noise warped in his ears. And all Mason could see was Callie's eyes boring into his—her outstretched hand. Her words echoed in his head.

"We're getting to the other side, together, and I'm going home to Ben, understand? That's how I do the scary things. I tell myself Benny is waiting. Peter is waiting. If you plan on stopping me from getting home to them, pull out now."

Rivulets of rain and mist poured over his face, his jacket.

Move, move.

He thought of Jenny and Luke. Of the others on their team. This little tribe—especially Callie, he realized—had already helped him confront the abyss of grief. These people, this place, were beginning to give him reason to want to get up in the morning.

He sucked air deep into his lungs, and holding fast to his branch with one hand, forgetting his fear, he slowly, carefully, crouched lower on his log. He reached over, down. She took his hand. Clamped. Final. Connected. Like she'd helped him back on the Taheese River. On one level he'd just won something big. But right now, he also faced losing everything. If his grip failed, if his courage waned, she was gone.

He held fast, gravity and balance rendering him unable to haul her up on his own. His muscles burned. All he could do was hold on. He felt the branch in his other hand giving.

"Hold on!" the big Norwegian yelled. And suddenly Oskar was at his side, and behind Oskar a SAR tech with more ropes.

Oskar lay flat on a nearby log and managed to get another rope and harness down over Callie. She let go of Mason's hold, and Oskar and the tech took her weight as the harness tightened around her. They began to haul her up.

Callie came up, shaking, white as a ghost. Water sheened her face.

"Keep . . . moving," she said, her voice hoarse, almost inaudible against the roar of the water. "It's coming down harder. Too much rain. Snow up top has been melting. Logjam is giving."

The tech quickly hooked Mason into a new line so he could undo his carabiner and rehook it to the guide rope on the other side of the snag.

They all moved carefully. Inching along the logjam using the guideline as the tangled bridge of roots and branches began to shift and creak beneath their boots.

The tech and Callie hit solid ground first, helped up onto the bank by Gregson and the other SAR volunteer. Then Oskar landed. He reached back, and Mason grabbed the Norwegian's hand as logs began to roll. He made it. But as he unhooked from the line, a loud boom sounded and the entire logjam imploded in a crash of spinning logs and whirling branches and dirt. It all roared down the gorge in a chocolate-brown pulverizing mass.

They all stared in silence. Wet. Breathing hard. Shivering. Disbelieving as their bridge vanished into a brown, chunky churn.

Rocks boomed below the water.

Mason turned to Callie. Her green eyes held his. Her chest rose and fell. Her hands still shook.

"Thank you," she whispered.

"Ben needs you," he said quietly. "So does Peter. I wasn't going to not let you get home."

Emotion gleamed suddenly in her eyes.

He bent down, picked up the coil of rope, and followed Oskar to where the others had laid down their packs under the cover of trees.

THE SEARCH

CALLIE

Oskar pointed to a canine print in the mud. "Wolf spoor."

The indentation was as big as the palm of his large hand. Callie felt a primal shiver run through her. The claws were widely spaced. Long.

"Big one," said Oskar. "*Canis lupus*, maybe—timber wolf. Largest of North American canines."

Trudy sniffed deeply. Her body posture shifted and her hackles rose. A growl emanated from low in her throat. The mood in the group shifted. They all sensed it—the pack was near.

They climbed for another half hour. The thudding of the searching helicopter waxed and waned. A breeze moved through the trees. It sounded like water rushing softly through the forest. Steel-gray clouds billowed and rolled down the mountains, curtains of rain in their wake. It grew colder as they gained elevation.

Oskar stopped occasionally, examined the ground. He frowned.

Callie came up behind him. "What is it?" she asked quietly.

"Looks like the wolves were tracking them."

"Hunting them?"

"Maybe waiting for a weakness. Almost from the gorge." Oskar crouched down on his haunches and pointed the tip of his tracking pole at marks in the moss and loam. "The Survivor Five appear to have stopped at regular intervals since the gorge. Might even have over-nighted here again." He looked up into the forest. "I figure they could have spent a day or two, or more, back at that plateau before finding a way to cross that logjam. And from that point . . ." His voice faded.

"What, Oskar?"

"I can't say there's specific signs to prove it, but it feels like they were struggling. Slow. Very slow. Maybe dragging something. See there?" He pointed to another flattened area of moss. "The moss had time to spring back, but—"

"You think one of them might have gotten injured?"

He worried his lip with his teeth. "*Ja.* Or Steven Bodine taking a turn for the worse."

They walked awhile more. Rain hovered to sleet, then back again.

They all stilled as a howl came from the depths of the mist and forest, rising up, up, up in a crescendo, then drawn out in a long, plaintive note. Another animal answered. Then more. The sounds died with a series of yips.

She glanced at Mason. His face looked grim.

She reached for her radio in her pouch. Keyed it. "SAR one, Callie here. SAR one for rescue chopper one."

"Come in, SAR one."

"How far are we from the wolf pack? Can you see us?"

The helicopter noise grew louder as it came toward them in the clouds. Suddenly they glimpsed it.

"We can see you guys. You're about a half klick out from the location and the wolves, as the crow flies."

"Roger that, thank you. Can you buzz the pack off again as we approach? Over."

"Affirm. Over and out."

As they neared the GPS coordinates Callie had flagged, her radio crackled again. "Rescue chopper one for SAR one. Going low to buzz the animals off. Got heat tracing for eight animals."

"Roger. Any sign of human life?" she asked.

"Negative."

She signed off and saw Mason check the position of his sidearm. The others were making sure that the holsters of bear spray at their hips were easily accessible. Oskar shrugged his shotgun off his back. Mason reached for his rifle.

The chopper descended over the trees with a deafening roar. Branches whipped and swirled and thrashed as pine cones and small twigs and other debris were hurled into the air.

The chopper rose and moved northward.

"Rescue one for SAR one. Proceed, SAR one. Should be clear for a while. Pack has retreated to maybe a half klick. Can't see through the canopy, but no additional infrared signatures."

Slowly they entered the treed plateau area. Big, old-growth hemlocks and yellow cedars provided them cover, protection from rain. Pine needles formed a soft carpet on the ground.

It was a sense more than anything—death lay near. Perhaps, thought Callie, some vestigial part of themselves could smell it on a primal level.

They saw it. Two shapes lying prone near a circle of stones around blackened embers. She tensed. Scanned the surrounding forest.

Trudy growled, hackles rising, lips peeling back from her incisors, gums and teeth shiny with saliva.

"I'm going to hold back and wait here," said the K9 cop. "She knows the wolves are there." His hand was near his sidearm.

Callie nodded. The rest of them proceeded forward in single file behind Oskar. Mist tendrils snaked like specters through the trunks.

"Helvete," Oskar said as his body went rigid in front of Callie. She knew Oskar well, had been on enough searches with him to be aware

that hearing him swear softly in his home tongue was a really bad sign. The word meant *hell*, which carried a much darker weight in his language than hers. Definitely not good.

Mason came up beside Oskar. His body also stiffened. He shot his gloved hand out, halting the rest of them. Callie scanned the mist, trees, again, watching for the yellow eyes of a timber wolf, her heart beating hard.

"Don't touch anything," Mason said, switching his gloves out for crime scene nitrile.

She came forward, slowly. Hesitant. Not wanting to see, but needing to.

Her heart kicked. Two corpses. Male. Wildlife had been at one. Not the other.

Only two men had left the Forest Shadow Lodge. So they had to be Professor Nathan McNeill and Dr. Steven Bodine.

She turned to the body lying closest.

Mason shot images with his RCMP cell phone.

This male lay on his back, arms and legs splayed. One of his legs at a strange angle. His face had been scavenged, half pulled off. No lips. But hair and scalp remained. Brown hair. Thinning.

"Nathan McNeill," she whispered.

Mason nodded. He reached into the decedent's bloody pockets, looking for ID.

She moved to the other corpse. This male lay on his side. A gaping wound in his cheek writhed with freshly hatched maggots. Bile rushed to her throat. She stifled a gag with her gloved hand.

Skin was jaundiced. Eyes wide open, the whites a dark-yellow color. Eerie, almost inhuman-looking. Signs of liver failure and organ collapse. This had to be Steven Bodine. And by the evidence of an advanced stage of liver failure, he'd ingested a significant amount of the lethal death cap fungus.

"Where are the women?" she asked, turning in a circle.

"Over here!" Oskar called. He'd been checking the periphery of the clearing. "Just inside the trees here."

Callie moved to join him.

He pointed down at the body of a woman sprawled in the loam. Callie gagged.

Brunette. Shoulder-length hair. But the rest of her body had been ripped and mutilated beyond recognition.

"*Fy faen.*" He swore quietly in his native tongue again. *What the fuck.* "Looks like the pack dragged this one out of the clearing and into the trees."

Callie crouched down and studied the sole of the woman's boot. She held her hand over her nose and mouth, repulsed by the smell. Putrid. Metallic. Small maggots wriggled in the loam beneath the corpse. A hunk of flesh lay nearby.

"Deborah or Monica. From the boot," she said, coming to her feet and stepping back, her stomach churning. "But we still don't know which one of them wore which boot. I can't tell just looking at the rest of her, can you?"

"Both Deborah and Monica were brunettes," Oskar said. "Both had similar-length hair."

"Maybe it's not past tense for both. Unless the other two are dead as well, and the animals just dragged them farther off." Callie returned to the clearing to inform Mason, while Oskar scouted in an outward spiral from the clearing, shotgun ready, looking for signs of the other two women.

Mason was bent over Nathan's body.

"We found—" She froze.

He'd rolled Nathan over onto his stomach.

"He was shot," Mason said. "Through the neck." He pointed to a ragged and bloody area between the base of Nathan's skull and his shoulders. "Exit wound here." He glanced at the other body. "Steven

Bodine, too. In the face. And chest. But the animals haven't touched him. It's like they sense the toxin in him, the foulness in his flesh."

Callie felt an urge mount within her to get out of this place. Away from this violence. And whatever it meant.

"No sign of the rifle from the lodge," Mason said as he visually scanned the clearing.

He saw something that glinted among the pine needles a short distance away from the bodies. He went to it, squatted down, photographed it. Then, using gloved hands, he reached for it. "Shell casing," he said. He picked it up, bagged it, then found another nearby in some pale-green lichen. He took more photos, then bagged and recorded that one, too.

Callie's mind raced as she watched Mason. One shot had been fired into Nathan McNeill's neck. And two shots into the ailing Dr. Steven Bodine. One in the chest. One right in the face. The men had seen it coming. They'd looked into the eyes of their executioner.

Mason came to his feet. "Where are the others?"

The question sounded rhetorical, but Callie said, "We just found one more, so far." She led the way back into the trees.

"Shit," he said quietly. He photographed the female decedent, then turned her onto her back. Her face was unrecognizable. As with Nathan's body, the wolves had savaged this one so badly it was impossible to guess whether she was Monica or Deborah, or even the age. All they could tell was that she was not Stella.

"Looks like it could be an exit wound there," Mason said, pointing to a dark and saturated bloom of blood on the woman's chest.

"Are you sure?"

"No. But it's possible."

"She was shot in the back?" Callie asked quietly as she glanced back toward the firepit where the men's bodies lay. "Running away? From who? From one of the men? Someone else?"

"Perhaps whoever still has the rifle," he said.

Oskar appeared out of the misty trees, carrying his shotgun. He shook his head. "Can't see any sign of the other two heading in that direction. Only signs of the wolves."

"Ask the pilot if he can do another sweep, see if the chopper can pick up any infrared trace from the other two women," Mason said. "They must have left this area of their own volition. There's only one backpack left behind in the clearing. I imagine the five would have brought more than one bag from the lodge to carry water and other supplies."

Callie reached for her radio and made the request.

"Roger that, SAR one. The pack is closing in toward your location again. Becoming more resistant to our attempts to scare them."

"Roger. Thank you. Over and out."

Mason had moved back into the clearing, trying to find better reception for his sat phone. She went to join him.

"I'm calling this in," he said. "Going to need a forensic ident team in. Body removal. Coroner."

"Wolves are closing back in. Might not be much left by the time they get here."

He got through as a yell came from Gregson. "Got trace back here! Trudy's picked up scent again. Looks like two sets of tracks heading west, along some kind of game trail."

Mason made his request and killed his call. He and Callie hurried over to join the K9 team. Trudy was champing at the bit, lunging on her tracking line.

"Did you say two sets?" Mason asked.

"Affirmative," Gregson said. "Size seven, and another set, slightly bigger."

"Stella and either Deborah or Monica," Callie said.

"Signs of blood, too." Gregson pointed to some small dark dots on leaves.

Urgency bit. Conflict chased through Callie. She was programmed to go after possible survivors. Triage. But these bodies in the grove would be finished off by the wolves as soon as they left.

"We can't leave these remains here," she said. "The wolves will destroy what evidence there is."

"We've got an RCMP team coming in stat," Mason said. "They're coming via helo. We can ask this military chopper to hang in and keep trying to buzz off the wolves while we go after the other two," Mason said. "They could still be alive. And they're witnesses."

Callie's gaze held his. And she heard the unspoken words.

Or worse. One is the killer.

THE SEARCH

CALLIE

Callie jogged with the team single file behind Gregson and Trudy. His dog lunged and muscled into her harness, hot on the scent of something fresh that had fueled her. Possibly the blood.

As they ran, Callie felt dogged by a cold breath of malevolence that seemed to exhale from the forest grove behind them, as if reaching out and grasping to pull them back to the murder site with the mutilated bodies. Her pack bounced on her back, growing heavy. Her thighs burned, and air rasped in her lungs. She heard the steady *thump*, *thump* of Mason's boots behind her. It was growing dark already. Clouds thickening and rain turning to soft blowing flakes that bit into their sense of urgency.

"More blood," Oskar called over his shoulder, pointing to leaves that had been stained with dark red. But they didn't stop. Time was critical. Someone was not too far ahead of them, injured, but still alive, judging by the trace.

Callie clicked her headlight on. So did the others. They labored like this for almost two hours, moving at a much higher elevation from the lake, but parallel with it. She knew it was out there, down there, but the water lay hidden from view by the clouds and softly blowing snowflakes.

They came upon a wide river, and they all stopped along the bank, breathing hard. Gregson allowed Trudy to cast about with her nose, up and down the edge of the swiftly flowing water.

Callie used the break to open her canteen and swallow cold water. She handed her bottle to Mason. He nodded thanks and took a sip.

She watched him. He looked good. Color in his cheeks. His eyes bright. Energy high.

He caught her looking and she glanced away quickly, her heart beating faster.

"Doesn't look too deep," he said as he handed back her canteen.

She recapped the bottle. "Maybe thigh deep at the deepest point, near those rocks there, I reckon." She tilted her chin toward the crystal clear waters.

But to their left they could hear the rushing water of rapids and what sounded like a waterfall as the terrain dropped toward Taheese Lake.

"Over here!" Gregson called. "Looks like they went in here. Waded across."

"We go over," said Mason. "We keep going."

Gregson put Trudy into a sling, and they waded into the icy water. It stole Callie's breath. It went into her boots. They wouldn't last long wet like this. The rapids tugged hard at them, but the river was shallower than she'd guessed. They made it through to the other side.

Trudy picked up scent again immediately.

They began to jog again, water squelching uncomfortably in boots, wet fabric chafing against legs.

Oskar stopped suddenly and crouched to study the ground. Callie drew up alongside him.

"What is it?"

He frowned, looked up, moved a few paces forward, and crouched once more. He studied the ground again. Snow was beginning to settle.

Oskar said, "Hard to be sure with the weather we've had, and the conditions, but . . . I think we've lost a set of tracks."

"What do you mean?" Mason asked as he joined them. Trudy and Gregson were still moving ahead. Fast.

"I'm seeing only one set of tracks. I think. Since the river." He pointed to a vague bit of an indentation in the mud, then another, both of which Callie would have missed had Oskar not drawn her attention to them.

"Which set are you still seeing, what size boot?" Callie asked.

"Can't tell. Not in these conditions. Prints have been compromised."

Trudy suddenly started to bark wildly up ahead. Gregson yelled, "Got an alert. She's alerting! Over here!"

Callie and the rest of the group caught up to the dog and handler. Trudy was leaping and yanking against her tracking harness and line.

"Down there!" Gregson yelled. "Someone down the cliff."

Shit. They had a find!

Callie hurriedly shrugged off her pack. She got down on her belly to peer over the rocky precipice.

"Hello! Anyone hear me? Anyone down there?"

Mist as thick as pea soup swirled. She couldn't see what was at the bottom. Her headlight beam danced off the mist.

"Hello!" yelled Oskar.

They all fell silent, listening. Gregson tried to quiet Trudy by taking a tug toy out of his pack and offering it to his K9 partner as a reward game. Trudy's snuffling and tugging made it hard to hear any response. In the distance they could still hear the chopper, and another one coming in.

"Hello!" Oskar cried again in his big foghorn of a voice. It echoed and bounced off the mountains around them.

Silence. Just Trudy panting.

"Someone is definitely down there," Oskar said, examining the bushes and tracks. "More blood. And prints. And the broken twigs here. If it was dark, or foggy like now, they might not have seen this drop at all, and gone straight over."

"We need to get someone down there." Callie took a coil of rope from her pack. "I'll do it. See how far I can get. You help lower me from the top."

Gregson gave Trudy water, and Mason called in their status, asking for air rescue to stand by as Callie and Oskar and the other techs set up their ropes.

Callie secured her harness and climbing helmet and started down the cliff into the mist. Working carefully, she felt her way along the rock face while Oskar directed the rope handling above.

She got about ten meters down before her feet hit a rock shelf. The wind started to gust, clearing visibility. She got a better look at her surroundings. She was on a ledge about three meters wide and several meters long. A woman lay still a few feet away.

She keyed her radio. "SAR one, come in Oskar, come in SAR two."

"SAR two, go ahead, Callie, I can see you."

She looked up. Oskar's headlamp glowed at the top of the rock face among the snowflakes. She could see the others in the gloom, too. The wind was picking up, which was good, as it would help clear visibility and assist with the rescue.

She keyed her radio. "One female. On a rock plateau about ten meters down. Can't see anyone else. She's not moving. Going to check."

Callie moved carefully along the ledge. It felt solid. She reached the woman. A brunette—definitely not Stella, then. Stella had short-cropped silver-blonde hair. She lay on her side. A small amount of blood trickled down the side of her face. Callie felt for a pulse. Her heart kicked. Hurriedly she keyed her radio.

"SAR one to SAR two. We've got a live one. Repeat, we've got a live one. We're going to need a backboard, litter basket, air extraction. Over."

She moved the woman's hair off her face to better assess the extent of her head injury. "Hey, hon, hey, can you hear me? My name is Callie Sutton. Kluhane Search and Rescue. We're going to look after you. We're going to get you help, okay?"

The woman's eyelids fluttered, and she moaned.

Callie keyed her radio. "It's Deborah Strong. Repeat, we've found Deborah Strong. No sign of Stella Daguerre."

She returned her attention to the subject. "Hang in. We're going to get you home, Deborah. Help is coming." As she spoke, she heard the second chopper. It grew louder. It must have diverted from the crime scene.

"Help is coming, Deborah. Hang in."

She groaned. Moved her legs, then her arm. Relief whammed through Callie. Not paralyzed. The sound of the chopper grew louder.

"Deborah, can you—"

"M . . . mm . . . my bay . . . baby. Is m . . . my baby okay? Pregnant."

Shit!

She glanced at the woman's legs. No blood. No overt rounding of the belly, either. Callie leaned closer, holding her hand. "Paramedics are coming. Just hold on."

White light from the helicopter washed over them. Callie signaled. "Baby?"

"Looks like no bleeding, Deborah. How pregnant are you?"

"Twelve weeks. I . . . haven't . . ." She moaned. "Told . . . Ewan." She faded out. Her eyelids fluttered. Pulse was going thready.

She radioed in. "Deborah Strong is pregnant. Twelve weeks."

"Roger that. Medical personnel standing by in Kluhane."

A SAR tech was being lowered on a long line from the helicopter above. Callie squinted against the downdraft pummeling her as she protected Deborah's face and eyes from the whirling sand and debris coming off the cliff face.

"He's almost here, Deborah." Callie was using her name repeatedly to keep the subject present. "Paramedics are almost here. They'll stabilize you. Get you onto a backboard and covered with a survival blanket. They'll make you warm and strap you into the litter basket and lift you into the helicopter. You'll be in the Kluhane clinic in no time. They'll check your baby."

Another moan.

"Can you tell me where Stella is? Did she go farther on the path? Is she still out there? Is she hurt?"

Deborah moved her head, winced.

"Don't move. Just talk, if you can. She might need our help, Deborah."

"She . . . Sst . . . Stella . . . Gone."

Callie leaned in closer, the noise deafening. The tech was coming lower, swinging on a line from the hovering bird.

"Gone? Where is she gone?"

"Fell into river . . . slipped. Ste . . . Stella . . . washed down. D . . . drowned. Dead." The woman was chattering with cold. The tech's boots hit the ledge. He made a sign to the chopper.

Callie stepped back. She pressed her back against the rock face, giving room to the paramedic on the small ledge and making way for the litter basket being lowered from the chopper. She began to shake, coming off her adrenaline rush. The news that Stella had drowned—the blow to her gut felt physical. Callie hadn't realized just how high her hopes had soared after she'd seen Deborah alive that they would still find Stella alive, too.

She struggled to keep composed against the rush of emotion, against the tears that burned sudden and sharp. She knew it was fatigue. And once again, she didn't know how people like Mason could deal so consistently with facing death. She lived to find subjects alive.

"Okay?" said the paramedic.

"Yeah, yeah, just . . . taking a break."

Her radio crackled. "Mason here for Callie," he yelled over the noise.

She sucked in a breath. "Go ahead, Mason."

"Any sign of the weapon down there—the rifle?"

She looked. The white light from the helicopter washing over the ledge was bright.

"Negative, Mason. No sign of weapon." Then it struck her. If Deborah Strong was the last one standing, where *was* the gun?

NOW

DEBORAH

Sunday, November 8.

Mason Deniaud watches my eyes as I tell him how—when the float-plane came in for a landing—we all became gradually aware that something was not what it seemed, that the lodge did not look from the air like the aerial photos we'd been sent in the brochure, or the images that populated the Forest Shadow Wilderness Resort & Spa website.

He jots another note in his book. I can't read it from this angle. I force myself to not look up at the camera, but tension crackles around the edges of my brain as I'm forced into revisiting the nightmare, the trap, the sick game we were all lured into.

I shift in the plastic chair and place my hand on my belly. Relief washes through me again that my baby is fine. I almost can't believe it. With the relief comes new tension. I need to get the story right.

For you. Everyone deserves a chance . . . a clean, wonderful start in life. A chance I never had . . .

"So it was on Monday, October twenty-sixth . . . that was the morning you all woke up and found Jackie Blunt missing?"

I try to moisten my lips. "Yes."

He flips back a few pages and rereads his notes carefully, checking what I said last time.

"Run me through it again. Please."

"But I told—"

"We just need to get some sequences sorted out, and it's for the recording."

I inhale deeply and nod. "We woke up when Steven Bodine called up the stairs that he had coffee ready for everyone."

"We?"

I reach up to touch the bandage around my head. It's itching. "Me, Monica, and Nathan—we were upstairs in our rooms at that point."

"And Steven was downstairs?"

"Yes. I told you. He called upstairs that he'd made coffee—"

"You said he'd been outside before that, in the early hours of the dawn?"

"Yes. With Bart and Stella. Bart said he wanted to explore farther down a trail he'd found the day before, and Stella said she'd gone to see if she could fix the sabotaged radio on her plane. She discovered her de Havilland Beaver was missing. The ropes had been cut."

"Why would someone do that?"

I stare at him like he's mad. "*Why?* You tell *me* why. That's the question that started to freak us all out. That's when it all started."

"It all started?"

"The head games. The second-guessing. The not trusting. Everything was set up in that lodge to mess with our minds—the checkerboard with the little pieces, like Agatha Christie's ten little soldier boys. The old crime novel specifically left beside the checkerboard. The sinister rhyme inside the book suggesting our stay at the lodge was to echo the story in the book."

"Which is?"

My eyes narrow. He knows. But he's making me say it, and I hate him for it. I hate him so hard right now. My head begins to pound where it was hit. "The guests in the story had been invited to an island for a reckoning. They were killed off one by one. I already told you about the book."

"Tell me about the other props."

"There was the bowl of mushrooms, the knives and the cleaver in the kitchen, a grocery bag with kids' cereal and a box of eggs in it, a painting of a little girl with the scales in Katie's room, the rifle on the wall, bullets in the drawer . . ." My hands are trembling. I'm breathing hard. Blood pressure rising. Not good, not good for my baby. Nor for me. I need to stop this before it all makes me unwell. Why is Mason Deniaud doing this to me? Putting me in this position when *I* am the victim. When it could hurt my baby. When *I'm* the one who needs sympathy.

"And when exactly did you become aware Jackie Blunt was gone?"

"When Jackie didn't appear that morning at the hearth for coffee along with the rest of us. When Stella called us together to tell us about the missing plane, the cut mooring lines."

He's watching me closely. I glance again at the camera again, can't help it. He sees me doing it, and it seems to interest him. He's making me nervous. I really need to get out. This room is closing in on me. After being out there in the forest and mountains . . . it feels like a cell, a prison. With a roof on top—like a lid on a box.

I don't want to think of cells, prison.

I start humming a little tune in my mind, the way the therapist suggested, to block out negative things.

Hush, little baby, don't say a word. Papa's going to buy you a mockingbird . . . I will sing that to you, my baby. We'll get one of those lovely old cradles that rock. We'll have all the nice things my family never—

"So what actually happened to Jackie Blunt?" he says.

"I don't know."

His eyes narrow slightly. He holds my gaze. *He doesn't trust you . . . Hush, little baby, don't say a word . . .*

"There was blood on the dock. It looked like blood." I find myself filling the silence in spite of myself. "We were worried she'd been hurt. We mounted a search party. But my ankle was still hurting from when I slipped on the dock, and I felt nauseous from my pregnancy, so I stayed behind in the lodge."

"Where?"

"In my room upstairs. The other six divided into pairs. Stella with Monica. Steven with Bart. Nathan with Katie."

"Then?"

"I fell asleep. At some point I heard someone come back into the lodge."

"When?"

"I'm unsure of the timing. I was dozing in and out."

"Who was it?"

"Two people came back. Monica and Katie. I . . . I think it was Katie first. Everyone was scared. They'd heard gunshots. Air horns in the woods. I heard the horns and shots, too, from inside the house. I don't remember the sequence—who came back first, or if the gunfire came before the air horns."

"How many gunshots?"

"Two. I was terrified. We all were. We went to lock ourselves in our rooms."

"Separately?"

"Yes."

"As opposed to helping?"

"You have to understand, we were scared of *each other*. We didn't know if someone was out there, leaving things inside the lodge, taking the heads off the carvings, or if it was one of us. Then Stella came back in a state. She was covered in blood and mud. She told me Bart had been killed."

"Where were Monica and Katie at this point?"

"Still in their rooms."

"Did Stella say how Bart Kundera had been killed?"

"No. Only that she and Steven and Nathan were going to bring him back. She'd come looking for a tarp and ropes to drag him."

"Why bring him back?"

"I don't know." The memory of the view I had from the kitchen window floats into my mind—the three of them working in the flickering yellow glow of the shed like wild creatures, witches. Bart's body thudding into the freezer. I clear my throat. "I saw them put him into the freezer and start the generator. Then they shared some of a bottle of whiskey."

"Why did they do that?"

"I don't know. I guess they needed to calm their nerves, and one of them found the bottle."

"No, I mean, why put Bart's remains into a freezer and start the generator?"

I regard him. Is he kidding? What is he looking for in me?

Slowly, I say, "To keep it cold. To preserve it."

"Preserve it."

"I . . . I think Steven said to preserve it for the police. Because it was a murder, and they wanted to keep the evidence for the police."

"So they were hoping help would come? They didn't want to hide anything?"

"Everyone there had something to hide. Everyone there was a liar."

"And you?"

"Everyone lies. We all lie. Even you."

His finger twitches. He knows I'm right.

"What did you lie about, Deborah? What secret do you have to hide?"

I look away, getting tenser, tighter. I see what he's doing. Misdirection. Sleight of hand. He's trying to trip me up. Me, an innocent victim. I feel walls going up. "I'm thirsty."

"Water, juice, coffee, tea?"

"Water."

"Okay." He gets up, opens the door. He asks Hubb, who is waiting right outside, to bring two glasses of water.

She brings them, hands them to him. He returns to the table, puts one glass in front of me, and goes around to the opposite side with his own. He retakes his seat, sips. He sets his glass down.

"Katie Colbourne?" he says.

"What about Katie?" I sip my own water.

"When did you find her?"

One more sip, and I set my glass down. He sees my hand is trembling. I hate him. I hate the detectives watching from another room. But I understand, they need to know what happened. It's their job. And I have to tell them. As best I can. The others have loved ones who will need this closure. And if I tell them enough, then maybe they will leave me alone. Then I will be free.

"After Nathan, Stella, and Steven came back inside," I say, "I warmed tinned stew, and brought it on a tray to the coffee table in front of the hearth. That's when we saw another carving had been toppled, and was missing its head."

"Did you see any mushrooms in the kitchen when you prepared the food?"

"No. There was nothing like that."

He recorded something in his notebook.

"What happened when you saw the carving had been decapitated?"

"Nathan immediately thought something had happened to Monica—she wasn't there. We all rushed upstairs after him."

"Your ankle was all right at that point?"

"I . . . I guess it was okay. It was getting better. Monica came out of their bedroom door, disheveled and confused-looking. And it struck everyone at once. Katie Colbourne. She wasn't with us." I reach for my glass and take another sip of water. "The guys bashed her door open, and . . . and we found her."

"Describe."

"She was hanging by a rope from the rafter. A rope around her neck. She was dead."

"What happened to her camcorder? She'd been filming the whole trip—you mentioned it at the hospital, that she was always filming. She was brought on board allegedly to document the tour."

A frisson of cold chases through me. "I . . . I don't know what happened to her camera."

"Waterproof? Small?"

"The camera? I don't know if it was waterproof. It was small."

He made another note, then glanced up. "Let's go back to when you all decided to leave the lodge. You said last time, when we first spoke to you at the clinic, that you all argued about going, or staying in the shelter."

"Steven was going to die. He appeared to have eaten poisonous mushrooms. They'd been left there as a clue, a warning." I rub my mouth. "A cruel act of psychological terror. Nathan, of course, knew what they were. He said he understood the mechanisms of the toxin, or the pathogenesis, I think he called it. He said Steven would die within two weeks if he did not get medical intervention, and most likely a liver transplant."

"A note was written in a notebook before you all left," he says. "It explained where you were going?"

"Monica wrote it. We all signed it."

"It was ripped out—someone took that note." He holds my gaze.

"I . . . I didn't know that."

"Who could have done that?"

"I . . . Stella was the only one who went back inside the house after we'd all exited. She said she'd forgotten something. She must have taken it. She wanted us all to die. She didn't want help to come."

He eyes me for a moment.

"So when Stella went back inside the lodge, she could have taken Katie Colbourne's camera, too?"

I feel nauseous. I need air. I don't know why he's gone off on another tangent. The cops *must* have already gotten proof about who Stella really was—that she was Estelle Marshall. They must know now what happened to her little boy. I'm scared. He's coming closer to Stella's motivation—the reason we were all lured there. What we did fourteen years ago.

Careful. It's coming. Remember, you are not guilty like they are. You didn't kill Ezekiel Marshall. You were a victim of circumstances at the time. Afraid. Young. You need to tell him as much as you can now. You need to stay as close to the truth as you dare, or Ewan will learn you are an ex-con. Your baby, your child, will have to grow up under that shadow. Ewan might not marry you . . .

"I suppose she could have taken the camera then."

"Why would she do that?"

I frown. "Because, like you said, Katie had filmed the whole trip. It could be evidence."

He nods slowly. He's watching my mouth, my body language. The words whisper inside me again.

He doesn't trust you. He's looking for a tell. Be careful.

"Who gave Steven the mushrooms?"

"Stella."

"Did she confess this?"

I swallow, and nod. "Yes, she . . . she had opportunity. The bowls had been left standing on the table downstairs. Then one of us warmed them up again. It . . . Yes, it was Stella who rewarmed the food. I remember now."

He sits back and regards me steadily. He clicks the back of his pen. *Click, click, clickety-click, click.*

My heart pounds against my ribs. I'm sure he can hear it.

"So when did you find out who Stella Daguerre really was, Deborah?"

He knows things. He's asking me questions where he already knows parts of the answers. Careful now.

Perspiration prickles across my lip.

"By the time the remaining five of us left that lodge, we all five knew Stella Daguerre was Estelle Marshall—the mother of the little boy killed in a hit-and-run fourteen years ago. Monica was the first, I think, to recognize her, even though Stella looks nothing like she used to. Monica said it was her eyes—she remembered her eyes from television, from pleading for someone to come forward with information on the blue BMW that had killed her son." I hesitate.

Do it. You have to tell him. As much as you dare.

"It was Monica's BMW."

He doesn't blink at this information. He knows. Of course he knows. But how? Or maybe he didn't know. He's messing with me.

Sweat pearls and dribbles between my breasts. I can smell the anxiety on myself now.

"And I . . ." My voice goes hoarse. I reach for my glass, take two hungry gulps. I set the glass down. It wobbles. I clear my throat. "The pieces all started coming together from that point. That Steven was the driver. That Monica was the passenger. That they were having an affair."

"They were?"

My gaze meets his. "Yes. Nathan McNeill helped Monica cover it all up—the accident. He took the damaged BMW to Bart Kundera, who fixed it under the table, and Bart said nothing to the authorities, even though news outlets everywhere were calling for information on a BMW with a damaged front."

"So Stella set this all up? It was her who lured you, sent out the fake invitations?"

"She admitted it. On the trail."

"Who helped her, Deborah? She had to have had help."

"I don't know."

"How did Stella come to reveal this to you all?"

I inhale deeply, my mind darting back down the dark warrens of my memory to the terrible series of events before my fall down the cliff.

"Monica freaked out along the trail," I say carefully. "We were all hungry, tired, Steven getting sicker and sicker. Nathan hurt. The rain and cold just kept coming. We'd heard wolves following us. Their howls were coming closer at night. We were all going to die. We all knew it. We were not getting out of there alive. And Monica just said it—she said it to Stella around the campfire, that she was sorry. She was so sorry Steven had hit and killed her boy, and that they had never come forward. And she didn't want to die without saying sorry. Everyone started fighting—Steven yelling at Monica to shut the hell up, Nathan yelling at both Monica and Steven for talking, and it came out. All of it. Stella had the rifle. She was aiming it at us, said she was going to kill us all right there if we didn't look her in the eyes right then and *all* say we were sorry."

"This happened after you crossed the gorge?"

Confusion chases through me. I try to remember which bits come first. Which come last. Feeling the terror all over again. And I realize he's gone on another tack. Because he hasn't yet asked me how *I* am connected to the hit-and-run. Why Stella wanted *me* to say sorry. Or how Jackie Blunt, Bart Kundera, Katie Colbourne, and Dan Whitlock were involved.

He knows, goddammit, he does.

Those detectives in the other room know.

You are not *guilty. Stay close to the truth, and you can still walk away. Think of Ewan . . . going home . . .*

Yet panic crackles around the edges of my brain. I'm skating on dangerous ice. My mouth is dry. My pulse races. *Focus. Just focus.*

"Yes. It was after we crossed the gorge." I think for a moment more. "Nathan hurt his leg while we were navigating the logjam. His foot slipped between two trunks, and he twisted his leg and cut it. Steven said he thought it could be fractured. Steven bandaged and splinted it on the other end of the gorge, and we helped Nathan up the trail into the forest on the other side. We moved very slowly, stopped several times. Nathan developed a fever. And Steven was worsening. His eyes and skin had turned dark yellow. He was growing weak fast. Shivering, shaking, hot, cold." I reach for my glass and finish the last of the water.

"And then?" Sergeant Deniaud prompts. His eyes are kind, but he's a cop. He's playing good cop right now. While the others watching via the camera are assessing me.

"And then we heard wolves. We believed they were following us and closing in because they were sensing our weakness. We were scared. No more food. Temperatures dropping. We'd gotten wet from crossing the gorge. We finally came to a grove in old-growth forest. It was a flattish area. And under the dense canopy of old trees it was drier, a little warmer, more protected from the wind and rain. We managed to make a fire. We were there for two days. Everyone went mad under those trees. We became a feral group. Turning on each other. That's when Monica snapped. And then Stella went sort of wild, crazy, aiming that rifle at us, saying we all had to pay, we all had to say sorry. She said she'd brought us all out there to die. She confessed to everything."

"Everything?"

I blink. I'm unsure what he wants.

"She . . . Yes, she confessed to killing Jackie Blunt—"

"So you know that Jackie Blunt is dead?"

Panic whips. "I . . . Well, that's what Stella told us."

"How did she kill Jackie?"

"With a knife she took from Bart Kundera's room. She stuck it in Jackie's neck." I pause. "Twice. She said she stabbed twice."

His gaze holds mine.

I place my hand on my tummy.

"What else did Stella confess to?"

"Cutting the plane free. Killing Bart Kundera with the meat cleaver. Bringing the mushrooms with her from the island where she lived. Leaving them on the kitchen counter for Nathan and everyone to see. So Nathan could use his knowledge to terrify everyone. She put the checkerboard there, and she cut the heads off the carvings. The painting in Katie's room. The rhyme—she wrote it. She put the book there." I fall silent. My blood booms in my ears.

"What about Katie Colbourne?"

I nod. "Yes. She hung Katie—she said she hung Katie."

"Must have been difficult."

I'm beginning to shake. Deep inside. "She . . . she said she forced Katie up onto a chair by threatening her. With a knife. She threatened Katie by saying she'd hurt her daughter."

"How—what threats exactly?"

"She didn't tell us."

He angles his head slightly. "So Stella told everyone she'd done these things."

I nod.

"And then?"

"And then Steven lunged at her, for the gun."

"What happened then?"

"She shot him."

"Where?"

I inhale, memories slicing through my brain. I wince as I hear the gunshots again. Tears fill my eyes.

"I'm sorry, Deborah. I need to ask."

I nod, moisten my lips. "In the face—she shot him right in the face. Again in the chest. Nathan tried to scramble backward, away from her. He was sitting near the fire. She shot him, too. Through the neck." I clear my throat. "Monica fled into the trees. As she was running, stumbling, screaming, Stella fired. Into her back. She went down and—" My voice chokes. With a shaking hand I push hair back from my eyes.

"Monica McNeill crawled, crying, into the forest. I . . . I didn't even think. I picked up a rock from near the fire, and screamed and hit Stella in the back of the head." I swallow. "Hard."

He watches me. I feel the others behind the camera watching, too. I feel time ticking slowly. I'm hot, my skin is hot. So hot.

"Then?"

"Then I ran. Away. I left her lying there, and just ran."

"Where's the rifle?"

I blink.

"Stella fell down on top of the rifle. I thought I had killed her. I was terrified, I just ran, but she wasn't dead. She got up and came after me with the gun. She chased me. I heard her coming after I'd gone quite a distance. She was moving faster than me. She was gaining on me. We got to the river."

"Did she fire at you while you were running?"

"I . . . I don't know."

Think. Think very clearly, Deborah. Bolt-action rifle. Holds four rounds, plus one in the chamber for a total of five. Four shots were fired in the grove. Two into Steven, one into Nathan, one into Monica. There would be casings there. Four of them. One bullet left in the gun that Stella was chasing you with . . .

"No. I don't think so. Maybe she did, but I was in a blind panic, and I didn't hear a shot that I can recall."

"And when you reached the river?"

"She'd gained on me. She came wading fast into the river after me."

"Was she bleeding?"

I nod. "From where I hit her head with the rock. Blood pouring down her face, and into her eye sockets, mixing with the rain. She looked like a mad animal. She grabbed me, and I went down into the water. We grappled and fought, and I got the gun. I . . . I shot her."

He doesn't blink.

"Where?" he asks quietly.

"In the shoulder. I think."

"What happened then?"

"She . . . Stella looked shocked. She stopped fighting. She put her hand to her shoulder, and staggered, and the current—it was swift—it was tugging at our legs—it unbalanced her. She went down. Into the water. I . . ." Tears stream down my face. I can't talk.

He pushes a box of tissues toward me. I reach for one, blow my nose.

"Take your time."

I nod. Blow again. "I . . . saw her floating. Facedown. Hair flowing about her head. Blood staining the water around her. The river took her. Fast. Down toward the noise of the rapids. Or waterfall. I think there must have been a waterfall. I was . . . I couldn't think. I kept the gun, and I got out of the river on the other side. I kept running. It was thick with fog. I . . . I didn't even see there was a cliff. I was running, bashing through bushes, and the next moment, the ground was gone from beneath my feet."

He watches me in silence for what feels like forever. A whining noise starts inside my head.

Leaning forward, he says very quietly, "Why did Stella lure you, Deborah? What did *you* have to apologize for?"

This is it. This the moment.

"I witnessed the hit-and-run that killed her child."

He holds my gaze.

"I never came forward," I say softly. The whining noise grows louder in my head. "I was scared to talk to the police. I was a sex trade worker, and my pimp was putting me on street corners to sell sex. I was under-age. He said if we—me or the other girls—ever, ever went to the cops, spoke to them about anything, he would kill us. We believed him. One of the girls had just been found dead when he said that. She'd spoken to the police about something."

"So you were the missing witness who saw the accident, who took her son's backpack?"

I say nothing. I am shaking so hard now.

"Did you take the backpack, Deborah? The one Stella, or Estelle, told the police she'd seen a woman taking?"

I nod.

"Why?"

"I needed money all the time. I thought there might be something valuable in it. Like an iPad."

"Was there?"

It strikes me that maybe iPads were not around fourteen years ago. Terror licks through my gut. *Careful. Careful.*

"No. Just a teddy bear and a storybook."

He hasn't asked about the license plate, so I don't mention it. Having taken the plate makes me seem even more evil, like I could really have come forward with something that would have solved the crime.

"We're going to need you to give statements about that day, Deborah. Are you okay with that? You'll need to talk to the police in Vancouver."

"Will I be punished?"

"The best you can do now, Deborah, is tell the whole truth. Things will go easier for you if you do."

I inhale shakily and rub my arm. He still doesn't ask about the car license plate. So I'm guessing that the cops never did learn that it came off the BMW and was removed from the scene, so I remain mum.

"What about Jackie Blunt, Dan Whitlock, Katie Colbourne, Bart Kundera—why did Stella lure them? Did she say?"

"Yes. Dan Whitlock was the PI that Steven's lawyer used to find me. Dan Whitlock, in turn, hired Jackie Blunt to pay me off and threaten me. Jackie Blunt made me leave town. Katie Colbourne was the one who covered the story, and who dug up Stella's secret mental history.

Stella blamed Katie for the fact she lost her husband, her job, and the fact the whole world turned against her and judged her as a bad mother and blamed her for 'killing' her own son." I sit in silence for a moment. "She lost everything. Absolutely everything."

"Do you feel sorry for her?"

Tears fill my eyes again. I nod.

"Even though she tried to kill you."

"I . . . I don't know what I would do if someone tried to hurt my baby, my child. If they blamed me . . ." I fall silent.

"How did Stella find you all?"

"I don't know—only that she hired private investigators herself, who worked for years."

"Who paid those investigators?"

"I don't know. She didn't say. Please, Sergeant Deniaud, you don't have to tell my fiancé that I worked in the sex trade, do you? *Please*. I . . . Our baby. We're going to get married and have this baby, and I want to start fresh. I got away from that old life. I made good, Sergeant. I worked as hard as hell, and I had to work twice as hard as everyone else because of it. And I built my own company, and hired my own people, because . . ." I stop.

Focus.

"Please," I say simply.

He clicks the back of his pen again. *Click click click click.*

"Is that why you changed your name?"

Fear slams me. I try to swallow.

"Yes."

"Katarina Vasiliev," he says quietly.

I go ice-cold inside. All the dark shit starts rising up like black ink poured into a vessel of water, into the vessel of my body, and it's swirling up in leaky tendrils, filling me up all the way, spidering into my brain.

"I wanted a fresh start," I whisper.

He turns the page of his notebook. He reads from a bulleted list. "You're originally from Alberta. Three older brothers. Police records show your middle brother was found murdered along a rural trail not far from your family farm boundary. Homicide investigation was initiated, never closed."

I swallow and say nothing. My hatred for this man suddenly knows no bounds. The bitter taste in my mouth is foul.

"Records also show that eight months prior to your brother's murder, you had accused him of rape. You made a statement to the investigating officer that your own father plus another brother also sexually abused you. That it had started after your mother died, when you were fourteen."

I say nothing. The Monster in me is rising. Big and black. With fangs. It has fangs. Terrible fangs.

"Your father and brothers raised you—"

"They did not!" I slam my palm on the table. "I fucking raised myself!"

He watches.

Calm down. Fucking stupid bitch, calm the fuck down.

"They abused you, Katarina. Didn't they? At least two of your brothers, and your father. A quiet, nervous girl at school. No real friends, because you came from a weird family. They made fun of you at school."

My innards are shaking.

"Sergeant Gord Fielding, the lead investigator on the Forest Lodge case, spoke to the retired detective who handled your brother's homicide investigation all those years ago. He said it was a really sad case. It had bothered him for years. No one helped you. You lived on a remote farm with your dad and those three older brothers. Brutal cold winters. Isolated. Poor. Hand-to-mouth existence. Alcoholic father. Just you and those men. Your mother gone, no one to shield you."

I glower at him.

Don't talk. Don't talk. Say nothing.

He checks his notes. "Boris Vasiliev. That was your brother's name. Twenty-three years old when he was found with a hatchet sunk into the back of his neck, right where his neck joins his skull. Found along a trail ten days after he didn't come home one night." He pauses. "It was never solved, was it?"

"No."

"Do you know who might have done it?"

"He had a lot of enemies."

"You didn't like him."

"He raped me."

He nods pensively. "You were a pretty ace hatchet thrower, I hear. That's kind of like throwing a meat cleaver?"

My mouth goes dry.

"I . . . I don't know."

"You could hunt like a pro, too. Shoot. Field-dress game. Knew your guns. You were the one who was made to slaughter the farm pigs."

He waits.

Calm. Calm. Stay calm. You are Deborah. You have a right to a good life. You had a right to change your name. You do not have to be defined by your past anymore.

"Sergeant, I had a hard, hard childhood. Yes. I did what I had to in order to survive."

"That's what the retired officer said. You left home after the murder. At age fifteen."

"I went to Vancouver. I was almost immediately befriended by a guy I thought was good. He gave me a place to stay, food, he said he loved me. He said he'd help me, and he brought me to a pimp. They knocked me about and sexually abused me, and kept me confined in a room for days. During that time I was hooked onto drugs. And I got hooked bad. I needed fixes all the time. I got into a bad life. But I changed my name, legally. I've made good. I . . . I have a right to be forgiven for selling my body like that. I built a business. I found a man. A good, good man. Please . . . *please* don't tell him."

He weighs me, watching my eyes.

"I was threatened," I say again quietly. I'm sinking, spiraling. "They said they would kill me—that's the reason I never came forward about the little boy who was killed. Stella's little boy."

His jaw tightens, and I see a muscle at the side of his eye begin to twitch. He closes his notebook. And I wonder suddenly if he had a little boy, too.

"Do you have to tell him?" I ask.

"I'll leave that to you, Deborah." He pushes back his chair and comes to his feet.

"Can I go?"

"For now. We might have some more questions before you leave town."

I stand fast. My jacket is still on. I plunge my hands into my pockets and feel the sugar packets and toast crust there.

"Like what other questions?"

He opens the door and holds it wide for me to exit.

"Maybe something will come up after we've spoken to Stella Daguerre."

Shock whams me. "Stella?"

He nods, still holding the door open, waiting for me to exit.

I can't move. "Did you *find* her? Is . . . is she alive?"

"Yes. She was brought in yesterday. A hunter called in that he'd found her in a makeshift shelter he uses. Not far from the bottom of the rapids where you say she fell into the river. She appears to have made it out of the water. She made it there, to the shelter."

"Where is she? Can she talk? How . . . how is she?"

"Being stabilized and awaiting transport to a bigger medical facility. We're hoping she pulls through."

Hubb is still standing there in the corridor outside the door. She regards me with a strange intensity, then glances at Sergeant Deniaud. Something passes between them. I swallow, unnerved. They're up to something.

Hubb says, "I'll walk you back to the motel."

"No," I say. "I . . . I need to be alone."

I hurry out of the room and make for the building exit. The words of the horrible rhyme dog me with rabid breath.

> Two Little Liars went on the run.
> One shot a gun, and then there was one.
>
> One Little Liar thinks he has won.
>
> For in the end, there can only be one.
> But maybe . . .
>   there shall be none.

NOW

DEBORAH

Sunday, November 8.

With my hands sunk deep into my pockets, I walk back along the windblown street in this desolate town.

Where sheer exhilaration fueled my steps earlier this morning, where my heart was full of the thrill of being alive, of having food, shelter, health, the knowledge that our baby was still growing safely in my belly, I am now fearful. Chilled to my core.

My thoughts turn to Ewan.

They've brought him back from his tour on compassionate grounds. He's due to land in Kluhane Bay this evening.

I pass a little bakery. The creaky sign swings in the wind. I go by the gas station, which has a coffee shop. If I had to imagine small-town Alaska, I would picture this place, but with corporate America logos and signs. I see the fire station. The bay door is open, and two men are washing the engine. Water runs down the paving, freezing into a solid sheen.

I round the corner. The wind hits harder off the lake. I stop and dig my hands yet deeper in my pockets. I put my face up into the teeth of the raw wind, as if it might somehow scrub the horribleness away. Maybe I can't scrub it. Maybe my past will always, always hound me.

Maybe Ewan will be so disgusted . . . but I can still swing it. I *believe* I can swing it—my fresh start. I reckon they haven't found out about my prison term, the conviction. Surely Sergeant Deniaud would have mentioned it if they had? Especially given that the cops know about *Katarina*. The rape accusations. My brother's homicide.

My pardon application was approved almost three months ago. Which means my criminal record should be well sealed by now, and unless I'm arrested and charged with a new crime, and fingerprinted again, my criminal record will not be found in the Canadian Criminal Real Time Identification Services database, CCRTIS. I have researched this. I *know* this. I've been working on getting things right for so long now . . .

I see it as I round the next corner. The red emergency sign. The health care center where I was taken and treated after that SAR woman helped get me off the cliff. I stop and stare. It's a clapboard building, not unlike the Kluhane RCMP station. Just bigger. It has stairs and a wooden accessibility ramp leading up to the glass doors. I see the windows where the hospital ward is—the beds where they kept me.

As if pulled by an invisible cord, I put one boot in front of the other and find myself in front of the stairs.

"She was brought in yesterday. A hunter called in that he'd found her in a makeshift shelter he uses. Not far from the bottom of the rapids where you say she fell into the river. She made it there . . . Being stabilized and awaiting transport to a bigger medical facility. We're hoping she pulls through."

I climb the stairs, push open the door. It's an average, small health care facility. Inside I see an admitting desk behind a glass screen. A waiting area. A corridor that leads to the back of the hospital, where the beds are.

The admitting person is busy with a hunched old man who seems deaf and is giving the clerk trouble. Two people sit in chairs in the waiting area. One with eyes closed, another engrossed in a magazine.

I go down the corridor, my boots squeaking slightly on the polished linoleum that smells like all hospitals do.

I come to the first ward. Look in. Four beds. She's not here.

I pass a nurse's station, which is really just a desk. The nurse is typing into a computer. She barely looks up. I keep going, like I belong. Like I have nothing to hide.

I look into another room. There are two beds in here, one empty. A drawn curtain hides the other. I hear machines wheezing and beeping softly.

I move the edge of the curtain aside and peer in. My heart spasms. *Stella.*

A bandage is wound around her head. A drip feeds into her arm. A tube goes into her mouth and is strapped in place. She has bandages over her shoulder. I wonder if they took out the bullet I shot her with, or if the bullet perhaps just grazed her. Or maybe it's still in there. A memory flashes through me. The others lying dead. Monica trying to crawl away, crying and blubbering. It had been my last chance. Monica had cracked, and it had all come out, and honestly, there'd been no way back for any of us from that point. No way.

But Stella is still alive.

She can still talk, and tell the truth. Which is different from my truth.

Soft cuffs restrain Stella's hands. Her face resembles porcelain. White and almost translucent. There's a chair beneath the window, facing the bed. The machines hiss and squeeze, helping her breathe.

"Can I help you?"

My heart skitters. I spin around. It's the nurse from the station. She's come after me.

"I . . . I'm looking for—I was one of the lost party. I wanted to see how Stella was doing."

"Oh, my dear. I heard all about it—the clinic staff told me you'd been in here, too. I'm so sorry. Thank heavens you are all right, and a baby on the way, I hear?"

I feel a little spurt of warmth, a sense of safety. I nod, smile.

"Congratulations."

"Is . . . Stella . . . is she going to be okay?"

"I'll leave that discussion to the doctor. She's unconscious, but hanging in."

"Can I see her, just sit with her alone for a while?"

The nurse hesitates. "All right. But not long."

She goes.

I wait to be certain she's not lurking behind the curtain. When I am, I step right inside the curtained alcove and draw the fabric shut behind me. I go up to Stella.

"Stella?" I whisper near her ear.

Her lids flutter a bit, and I feel scared. Like she might jump up and grab my throat.

I steel my muscles, which helps firm my nerves. I lean closer. "Stella, can you hear me?"

A flutter, a twitch of her fingers. She moves her head.

At the noise of shoes on linoleum, I tense, glance over my shoulder. The nurse is back. She draws the curtain aside, smiles at me, checks a chart, takes some more readings from the machines, and hangs the chart back at the end of Stella's bed.

"You okay, hon?" she asks me.

I nod. "I'll just sit here awhile."

She hesitates again, noting the time on her watch. "I'll be down the hall."

I don't know how long it is that I sit and watch Stella, and the machines, the clear fluid dripping from the bag hung beside her bed into the tubes that feed into her veins. Reality sort of leaves me again.

Dark, inky thoughts fill my head. I begin to suspect the nurse has forgotten I am still here.

I look at the machines again. Stella's chest seems to rise and fall ever so slightly in concert with the noisy hiss and wheeze of the ventilating machine. I come to my feet, move to her bed. I hesitate, then I think of Ewan. And him arriving tonight. To take me home. I think of the look on his face when I tell him about our baby, how happy he'll be. And it will all be over. Almost all over . . . almost . . . I glance over my shoulder. Listen.

Just the noise of the machines.

I lean close, study the tubing to see where it might be easiest to disconnect—or to stop the air going into her. I reach for the tube that feeds down into her throat. I freeze as I hear a slight noise. It seems to have come from behind the curtain on the other side of the bed. I think I see a shadow move.

My pulse races. I watch and listen carefully, very carefully, every muscle in my body primed to flee.

But nothing happens. It's my imagination.

I put my mouth very close to her ear.

"I can't let you take it all away now, Stella," I whisper against her face. "I can't. I'm sorry."

A small moan comes from her chest. I think she can hear me. Or did I imagine that, too?

It's okay. Stella will understand. She knows she would do the same for her own child—she is remorseful. She should never have left Ezekiel on the dark sidewalk alone with a dog in the rain, and gone into the store without him. For wine. She killed her boy. She would not do it again if she had a second chance. I know this now. She will understand . . .

I pull on the tube.

NOW

MASON

Mason reentered the incident room where Sergeant Gord Fielding and Constable Elise Jayne—a detective with a psychological-profiling background—had been watching his interview with Deborah Strong. Fielding had brought Elise Jayne with him from the RCMP North District headquarters in Prince George to help assess Strong.

"What do you think?" Mason asked as he set his notebook on the desk. His mind raced. He checked his watch, feeling on edge. He hoped he'd made the right call with the witness.

"She's off," said Fielding. "She's definitely hiding something."

"Agree," said Jayne. "Deborah Strong might be a victim, but she's also complicit, or lying for some other reason."

"Was there any change in the status of Stella Daguerre while I was in there?" Mason asked.

"Negative," said Fielding. "She's still unconscious. Still awaiting transport."

Tension torqued tighter in Mason. He checked that his sat phone was still secured to his belt. He had his radio, too. "Okay," he said, going up to his crime scene board. "Let's dial this all back a bit and run through what we know about Franz Gottman."

He tapped the photo of Franz Gottman now up on his board. "From our counterparts in the Lower Mainland and Vancouver Island Districts, we've learned that Franz Gottman, who owns the lodge property, befriended Stella Daguerre on Galiano Island, where Stella had moved and from where she ran her West Air floatplane charter business flying clients up and down the islands. She also flew for Franz Gottman in his later years. Using her own aircraft—his had been decommissioned."

"Correct," Fielding said, folding his arms across his chest as he regarded the crime board. "According to TSB crash investigators, the manufacturer's serial number on the engine of the unregistered, downed de Havilland Beaver Mk 1 matches the serial number on record for Gottman's aircraft, which he applied to decommission years ago. Stella Daguerre was flying Franz Gottman's unregistered plane on the trip to Forest Shadow Lodge."

"She wanted to fly under the radar. Undetected. It was supposed to be a secret mission," said Jayne, opening a file of information she'd just received from the island detectives. "And according to Gottman's housekeeper," she said, "Stella Daguerre was a regular visitor to the Gottman estate on Galiano. The housekeeper and others on the island maintain that Gottman and Daguerre were extremely close. One observer described theirs as a father-daughter-type relationship. Gottman was paternal, a mentor, a counselor to Daguerre. This is consistent with what Daguerre's ex-husband said. He claimed that while Daguerre always remained an expert pilot, and was highly organized, she was also extremely fragile emotionally. Which is why she'd sought private treatment twice prior to the hit-and-run death of her son. Once for depression, and once for some other as-yet-unspecified form of mental breakdown. She kept it secret so her employer and insurers would not find out."

"Which is what CRTV reporter Katie Colbourne dug up," said Mason. "And splashed all over the news."

Jayne nodded. "It cast additional aspersions on her parenting ability. Her state of mind in general. Her character. It turned public sentiment against her. And it fueled another breakdown. In the end, it all cost Estelle Marshall her career with Pacific Air."

"Along with her marriage," said Fielding.

"Stella's ex-husband confirmed he'd always blamed his wife for causing their son's death," said Jayne. "He blamed her for leaving six-year-old Ezekiel outside the liquor store that day. In dark and rainy conditions, with a lively young puppy in his control. The media coverage intensified her husband's feelings, made it all worse. Gottman apparently empathized with Stella. Believed it was cruel she'd lost everything. According to the ex-husband, who knew of Stella's relationship with Gottman, the eccentric billionaire believed Stella should have been offered counseling, treatment, empathy, instead of dismissal. She was a good pilot, had been loyal."

"Gottman was probably right," Mason said.

"Life ain't fair," said Fielding.

Mason glanced at the lead detective. Personally, he felt for Stella—he knew exactly how losing a young son could crush a soul. He, too, had been thirsty for revenge. He'd wanted to kill the punk who'd murdered Luke and Jenny—rip him apart with his bare hands, even though it had been an accident born of inexperience. "Yeah," he said. "Sometimes good people are dealt crap cards."

And then they run afoul of the law.

"And Gottman was a game player," said Jayne. "Judging by the contents of his house. Chessboards, computer games. Puzzles. Scripts for more reality shows that never went into production. His bookshelves show that he had a particular interest in tribal and group psychology and old mysteries, true crime."

"So you think this was all *his* idea?" Mason asked. "This plan to come up with a design—an elaborate and open-ended script—offering something that would hold appeal to each participant in Ezekiel Marshall's death, lure them to a remote location, cut them off from civilization, and kill them one by one?"

"It would be consistent with what we know so far of Gottman," Jayne said. "And Daguerre bought into his scheme and followed through with the script, the idea, despite Gottman's death from cancer a few months ago."

"This is consistent with the props found in the lodge," said Fielding. "The Agatha Christie book positioned next to the checkerboard. The rhyme inside. The carvings on the checkerboard that were beheaded one by one. The painting of Katie Colbourne's daughter in the room upstairs."

"It's all vintage Gottman," said Jayne. "Particularly if you look at the reality shows he scripted. He was an eccentric, an old Hollywood crazy with billions at his disposal. His last partner described Franz Gottman as a creative genius, a man with a tenuous—'interesting' was the word he used—relationship with reality. A man who believed he could mastermind and reshape the truth of the world around him. And Stella Daguerre was fragile, in that she needed his understanding, the sense of kinship that came from plotting revenge. She needed someone to absolve her of her feelings of guilt." She paused. "Stella Daguerre needed love. A very basic human craving, and a powerful psychological driver. My take is that this codependency sustained their relationship. Perhaps Stella Daguerre never intended to go through with it in the beginning. And she humored Gottman. But the terminal illness diagnosis, then death, of her only close friend and paternal figure could have been the trigger that galvanized her to follow through with it. In Gottman's memory. She'd lost her last good friend, or perhaps only friend, and might have felt she had nothing else to lose. And this became a life endgame of sorts."

Jayne walked up to the crime scene board and worried her lip with her teeth. "What's inconsistent, however, in my opinion, is this." She tapped the morgue photo of Katie Colbourne's body with the protruding tongue. "And that." She tapped the photo of Bart Kundera's body. She turned to face them.

"The meat cleaver in the back of this man's skull? Looking into the mother of a young child's eyes, and hanging her? Plunging a knife into Jackie Blunt's neck, not once, but twice?" She shook her head. "It's too raw. Too bloody. Too personal. Too violent. Close range. It doesn't feel like Stella Daguerre's MO based on my psychological assessment of her."

"Despite Deborah Strong's statements?" Mason said.

Jayne pursed her lips, and her brow furrowed in thought. "Stella Daguerre poisoning Dan Whitlock with shellfish, I understand. And we now have the Thunderbird hotel security camera footage that shows Stella Daguerre doctoring a plate of food outside Whitlock's hotel room before knocking on the door and delivering it to him."

"And we have the timing from the CCTV footage that shows Daguerre delivered the tainted food shortly before meeting the rest of the tour group at the floatplane dock," said Fielding.

"Plus, the pathologist determined Whitlock's cause of death was anaphylactic shock due to shellfish allergens. While the Thunderbird staff claim there was no seafood of any kind in the omelet they made for Whitlock's breakfast order," added Mason.

Jayne nodded. "So, given that Stella Daguerre likely poisoned Dan Whitlock, poisoning Dr. Steven Bodine with toxic fungus would be consistent with her MO. Poisonings are more consistent with female MOs in general. The violence is more removed."

Deborah Strong's words echoed in Mason's head.

"She shot him right in the face. Again in the chest. Nathan tried to scramble backward, away from her. He was sitting near the fire. She shot him, too. Through the neck. Monica fled into the trees . . . Stella fired. Into her back. She went down and Monica McNeill crawled, crying, into the forest."

"So you believe Deborah Strong is lying about Stella's role in the other murders, then?" he asked the profiler.

"What Deborah Strong stated would not be consistent with my profile of Stella Daguerre," she said carefully. "Killing people face-to-face is actually a lot harder than people think. As a species we mostly fight each other for dominance in order to maintain a hierarchy. That means when someone cries uncle, the fight's over. It's a similar pattern across most species. We resolve our ranking disputes with violence, but without resorting to actually killing each other, because it helps the overall survival of the species. Even soldiers needed to be trained—conditioned to kill other humans. It's not natural behavior for most of us, and though it can be conditioned, it takes a heavy psychological toll." She regarded the crime scene images of the bodies in silence for a moment.

"Killing with knives," she said quietly, "is particularly challenging psychologically. It takes effort. Unless one is enraged, and passion is overriding the logic function of the brain. It's messy."

Mason studied the photo of Deborah Strong on the board. Quietly, he said, "So if Stella Daguerre didn't shoot and kill Nathan McNeill, Steven Bodine, and Monica McNeill in that clearing, and if Stella Daguerre did not murder Jackie Blunt, Bart Kundera, and Katie Colbourne, and presuming no one outside of their group was stalking and killing them—" He turned to face his colleagues.

"That leaves Deborah Strong."

"Who is very desperate to hide the truth of her past," Jayne said. "Strong is also someone who might have killed before—her brother. She was accustomed to routinely slaughtering pigs. She has a reported childhood proficiency with hatchet throwing, which would make it more natural for her to pick up and throw a meat cleaver into the back of someone's head. She has a drug abuse history. A violent sex trade background. Deborah Strong is someone who has done hard things to survive. She *needed* to survive, and still does. I don't see Stella needing to survive with that kind of passion." She paused. Her gaze met Fielding's, then Mason's. "And as the rhyme said, there could only be one. Deborah

Strong could have cottoned on to the 'game,' realized what was going on, and turned the tables. She did what she could to outwit, outplay . . . outkill the others. Until there was one."

A chill rose in Mason's gut as he recalled the way Deborah Strong had looked directly into his eyes as she'd informed him that Stella had killed the others.

Or maybe there shall be none. The tension in his body went up another notch. He checked his watch.

Fielding said, "The retired Alberta detective I spoke with about the Boris Vasiliev homicide investigation figured that Deborah—Katarina Vasiliev—was good for her brother's murder," said Fielding. "They never proved it. And the detective never pressed harder. He said in retrospect he'd felt it could have been a form of self-defense on Katarina's part. Payback for all the sexual abuse. That her brother got what was coming to him."

"Self-preservation." Jayne nodded. "Deborah Strong is a survivor. Someone who might do anything to live, to thrive, someone who could feel she has everything to lose now that she's completely overhauled her life at huge personal expense."

"But proof," Mason said. "Unless Deborah Strong talks, or slips up, we need evidence that can connect her. Where are we with the DNA from the Schrade knife handle, and the latent partials from the meat cleaver?"

Fielding consulted his watch. "I was told we'd have those results today. We should have them in by now."

Mason's satellite phone rang. His energy quickened. He stepped aside and connected the call.

"Mason, it's Callie."

A sense of warmth washed through him at the sound of her voice. "Go ahead, Callie."

"We found it. The K9 team has located Katie Colbourne's camcorder. It was in the water, hung up in rocks along the riverbank."

Adrenaline coursed into his blood. This could be it—what they needed to break the case. "What's the condition?"

"It's pretty bashed up, but it looks like it might still be functional. It's one of those hardcore adventure cameras designed to take everything from knocks to underwater immersion."

His pulse raced, and he smiled inside. "Good work, SAR one. Damn good work. Thank you."

Callie laughed. "Over and out, Sergeant."

Mason signed off. Fielding and Jayne were regarding him intently.

"They found it. Katie Colbourne's camera. In the river where Stella Daguerre went down."

As he spoke, his radio crackled. "Sergeant Deniaud. Sergeant!"

Hubb.

Quickly he keyed his radio. "Go ahead, Hubb."

"We have a situation. Hospital."

NOW

STELLA

I'm in a dark, murky place, but it feels warm. Soft. Like a lukewarm ocean, and I'm floating—rising, falling on gentle swells, the sun shining red through veins in my closed eyelids. My body lifts on a surge, higher, higher, then I feel a gentle plunge into the valley between swells. Suddenly I go under the water. Down, down, down. Spiraling, head-first, deeper into the ocean, hair floating out around my head. It gets darker down here, colder. Underwater pressure squeezes my ears and chest. Panic licks. I start to thrash. *No air.*

Help!

Deeper I go, faster. I flail at the water, trying to fight back up. But something is tugging my ankles from the bottom, something strong dragging me down to the dark, deep bottom of the sea.

Suddenly a shape appears. I can't see properly through the water. But I can hear a voice. It comes from inside me, but it's not my voice.

No, no, don't fight. It will be all right, Stella.

I still.

Franz? Is that you, Franz?

Relax. It'll be okay. Give in to it.

Franz? Is that you?

I'm calm now, blinking, trying to see into this strange space.

Am I dead, Franz?

I hear him laugh—that wicked, guttural chuckle I love so much, coming from a dark corner in his grand and fantastical old study in his mansion on Galiano. I can almost scent the fine whiskey in his glass, and the aromatic smoke from his Cuban cigar. Almost hear the soft crackle of flames in his hearth. I smile. Or it feels like I'm smiling. My body lifts in lightness a little at the sound of him. *I'm dead. I must be. Because Franz is dead. So I must be if I am here with him. Where is here?*

I try to turn my head, turn around to see the rest of this place. But my movement spins me into a kaleidoscopic vortex of swirling water. Other noises creep in. Snatches of words. Machines. A smell of antiseptic. A woman's voice. A hard slice of cold light shocks through me and seems to intrude from somewhere very far above.

I'm going up again. Up. Up.

I hear yelling. An alarm.

I frown. Suddenly I stop again, and sink slowly back down to where Franz is.

A memory curls through me—how I felt when I saw my plane was gone from the dock, the severed rope ends in my hands.

I never meant to kill anyone, Franz. I don't even know if I killed Dan Whitlock—I don't know if he died in the end . . .

I left before I could see if he suffered, or how sick he might have gotten . . . You were right about one thing, Franz—trap a bunch of people with secrets together, cut them off, make them scared, and you cannot imagine how they will spin out. But as you said, they always do. They always collapse under the weight of their own monsters.

And then they turn on each other.

Tears fill my eyes. I see my boy's little body again. Broken on the paving. Rain falling upon his innocent face, into his open, sightless eye. I reach out my hand in this strange, dark limbo of a place, blindly feeling the space.

Mommy.

A quickening, heart-stopping moment.

Zeke? Ezekiel?

Mom.

Are you here, baby?

I have wanted to be dead for so long. I was so prepared for this to be my exit. I was going to hang myself in the woods, or just let the wilderness claim me. After they'd all looked into my eyes and said they were sorry for what they'd done to my boy.

Ezekiel, baby . . . where are you?

Suddenly he's there. In front of Franz in the shadows. He's on a stool, eating his Tooty-Pops, watching a cartoon. Swinging his feet under the stool. It's a perennial Saturday morning with lemon-yellow sunshine coming through the leafy trees of our house in Kitsilano. I'm on a layover between flights.

Honey?

He looks up and smiles that smile with the dimple I love so much. I hurry over and kiss my boy on the head. His hair smells like hay, and kittens, and soft puppies. My heart sings. I put on the coffee, make toast.

The kitchen fills with the smell of coffee and the fresh, toasting bread. Fruity Tooty-Pops in milk. I can smell the sweetness of it all. My sweet baby boy. The pure sweetness of life.

A noise. Cold. Black. That beeping again. An alarm! Smell of antiseptic. Sliver of white light so bright it hurts. Voices—a man and a woman—arguing, fighting? Then it all fades. Confusion twists around my head. It's tugging me away from Zeke, away from Franz . . . yanking, ripping me away.

No . . . no! I reach for Zeke's hand. He's holding it out.

Mommy! Don't leave me! Mom!

Zeke! His hand . . . Suddenly it's lying motionless on the cold dark street. Blood leaks from his mouth, and the rain falls into puddles around his face. I start to sob.

Zeke.

I hear the voices. I'm breathing again, no longer beneath water. I hear a man with a deep voice say clearly, "Deborah Strong, step away from that bed. Now . . . You're under arrest . . . You have the right to retain and instruct counsel of your choice . . ."

Panic flutters in my heart.

Police? Here? . . . In hospital room. Need to talk . . .

But I can't break through. I can't move. I try to talk, but no noise comes.

No, Stella, no panic. No need to panic. You can choose. Simple. Just make a choice.

Franz, is that you talking?

Mommy.

I go still at the sound of my son's voice. I turn my head away from the hospital noises, from the police, from the sense that Deborah is in the ward. I turn toward Zeke and Franz.

I feel myself going down, down, down. And it's no longer cold at the bottom. It's soft. Warm. Like a baby must feel in a womb.

I go down farther this time, spiraling, deliciously, gently, and it's all so beautiful.

Zeke is there. He smiles. I crouch down, open my arms so wide.

He barrels at me on his little legs with skinned knees. Crashes into me, and I fall back into green grass with yellow dandelions.

I laugh and stroke his hair.

You came home, Mommy.

I can't speak. Emotion is too thick. Tears are running down my cheeks. I nod, stroke his hair. My voice comes back.

I'm never going to let you go again, Zeke.

Franz is suddenly standing there. His strange little half-secret smile curving his mouth. Smoke trailing from a cigar in his hand.

I did it, Franz. I take my son's shoulders in my hands and look him directly in eyes that are the same color as mine. *I did it, Zeke.*

They suffered. I *made* them suffer. They all knew why they were there in the end, and was it worth it? Was that justice? Did the punishment make me feel better? I didn't like hurting them. They were just people trying to survive. Even Steven.

Most of all, I'm free now, because I no longer need anything from them. What I needed was to let them go.

So I forgave them.

Forgiveness is really about freeing yourself from the hate and self-pity, which eats like a cancer into your brain day and night, year after year. That's all we can want, isn't it? To let it go, to stop allowing it to drive us, and to finally be free?

Zeke flings his arms around my neck.

And I drown in his love, his touch. I'm home. I've come home. Finally. After so long. After so much pain.

But I'm home now. I'm with my son.

And then there was one.

NOW

MASON

Mason pulled up outside the health care center in his RCMP truck, bar lights flashing. Hubb was pacing agitatedly in front of the accessibility ramp, her exhalations condensing in white puffs around her pink face.

She ran toward the truck as Mason swung open his door.

"Podgorsky stopped her, sir!" Excitement glittered fierce in her eyes. "Like you said, we just watched her, hands off. Podgorsky was in place, waiting behind the curtain. I followed her—she came right here after leaving the station. Like you thought she might. She swallowed the bait—hook, line, sinker. I radioed Podgorsky that she was entering the facility. He kept out of sight, but kept her in his line of vision from behind the curtain, in case she did something to the victim. She attempted to extubate the victim, Sarge. Deborah Strong tried to kill Stella Daguerre."

"Where is she? Where's Podgorsky?"

"He's holding Deborah Strong inside. He's placed her under arrest and cuffed her." She hesitated. "Sir?"

Mason stopped at the tone in the officer's voice.

"What is it, Hubb?"

"She's dead, sir."

"Strong?"

"Stella Daguerre. She's been pronounced dead by the doctors."

"You said Strong *attempted* to—"

"Yes—Podgorsky stopped her from disconnecting the ventilator. But Daguerre passed anyway."

Mason stared at Hubb, his brain racing. This could be on him. This could be on Podgorsky. He brushed past Hubb, strode up the stairs, taking two at a time, and pushed through the doors of the health care facility.

"It's that way, Sarge." Hubb hurried ahead of him.

She waddled fast down the corridor, her duty belt hampering her short arms, and opened a door into a small utility room. Podgorsky stood beside Deborah Strong, who sat on a plastic chair, her hands cuffed, her eyes wild.

Podgorsky's features were tight. Mason's gaze locked on to his officer's.

"I've explained her charter rights, sir," Podgorsky said crisply, making an uncharacteristic attempt at sounding formal. "She's requested legal counsel of her choice."

Mason looked into Deborah Strong's eyes, and she held his gaze, unflinching.

"I didn't do anything wrong. I didn't kill her. She was a murderer. *She* did this."

"Take her to the station," he ordered Podgorsky. "Hubble, go with. Both of you, stay with her at all times."

He called Gord Fielding on his sat phone. "My officers are bringing Deborah Strong in. Stella Daguerre has passed. I'm going to speak with her doctor."

Mason hung up and found the physician still with Stella Daguerre's body. There was blood on the sheets and her pillow. His pulse kicked.

The doc glanced up as Mason entered. The man's features were drawn.

"I'm sorry, Sergeant. She's gone."

"What happened?" Mason's gaze shot to the ventilator, the tubes.

"Hemorrhagic stroke—massive bleeding in the brain, possibly caused by her head trauma. It happened fast. Nothing we could do."

Mason drew in a deep and uneven breath. He stepped closer to Stella Daguerre's body, and he looked into her face. She had blood on the side of her mouth, and under her nose. It stained the pillow under her head. But something about her features told Mason she was finally at peace.

He swallowed, feeling a strange surge of empathy braided with hot frustration. They'd just lost a key witness.

"Did the suspect do this—did Deborah Strong cause this?" Mason asked the doc.

"Like I said, it was probably a result of head trauma sustained before you brought her in."

"So it would have happened irrespective of what just transpired in this ward between my officer and the suspect?"

"That would be my theory." The doctor reached for a sheet. "An autopsy will confirm."

So not Podgorsky's fault. Not a law enforcement miscalculation on his part. Mason breathed out a chestful of air he hadn't realized he'd been holding. He watched as the doctor drew the sheet up over Stella Daguerre's face.

Deborah Strong was unlikely to cooperate from this point. Retrieving the footage from Katie Colbourne's damaged camera was now essential.

Mason left the small hospital and stepped into the bracing wind. He stood still for a moment. In his mind he saw Luke running down the frozen street toward him, the wind ruffling his hair, his little school backpack bobbing on his back. He heard Jenny laugh. He felt them both here. He sucked in a deep breath of the cool mountain air. Yes, they'd followed him up here to this remote town in the faraway wilderness. But for some reason, Mason was no longer trying to outrun them. He was comfortable just having them near. His ghosts.

He pulled his jacket zipper up higher around his neck and made for his truck.

NOW

MASON

Friday, November 13.

Five days after the death of Stella Daguerre and the arrest of Deborah Strong, Mason sat with Fielding, Jayne, and Hubb in the incident room, watching footage that had been retrieved from Katie Colbourne's camera.

Fielding and Jayne had remained in town to oversee additional interrogations with Deborah Strong. But Strong had lawyered up and remained mute during interviews, refusing to cooperate in any way. The sheriffs had picked up Strong for transfer by plane earlier this morning. Fielding and Jayne were due to fly out later, but the techs had sent some of the retrieved footage for them to see before they departed.

They all watched in thick, tense silence as Stella spoke directly and softly into the camera, lit by a small circle of light in the blackness of the forest—an eerily glowing vignette that reminded Mason of illustrations in dark fairy-tale books.

"I don't think we will last much longer. Steven is worsening. Faster than I thought he would. *I . . . I'm not even sure this is recording properly . . .*" She leaned forward, her face whitening and growing large as she came toward the light. The camera jiggled. Stella returned to sit on a log. She faced the camera again.

"I'm recording this because I want to document what happened. I'm not sure if the camera or our remains will ever be found, or if anyone will ever know what occurred. I didn't know how this was going to play out. It was Franz's idea. My brilliant Franz—" Emotion hitched her voice. She wiped her nose and cleared her throat.

Mason felt a reciprocal tightness of compassion in his chest. It came with a quickening of his pulse. He and the other cops exchanged glances. He could see that Fielding, Jayne, and Hubb were as tense as he was. As excited to learn what had happened out there in the woods.

Stella continued, her voice going hoarse. "He said I should follow through with it, even though he knew he was going to die. He came up with the idea, inspired by Agatha Christie's mystery of the ten little soldier boys. The judge character in that book died, too. He left a message in a bottle for someone to find, explaining what happened. This is my message in a bottle."

She paused, sniffed, and wiped her nose against the cold again.

"Ever since Zeke was killed, I have wanted justice. For my son. For me. For our family. I wanted the driver caught, to stand public trial. To be punished. I wanted them all to pay for what they did. But justice never came. No one helped. A conspiracy of silence hid the truth."

Stella pulled her woolen hat down tighter over her ears.

"I don't know anymore what it means to get justice. I thought I did. I thought I knew what I wanted. I wanted them to pay. To suffer, and to *know* why they were suffering. To be sorry. But what I have done will not bring Zeke back. Maybe truth is a noble goal unto itself—I don't know. But in the interest of truth, yes, I did what Franz suggested. I followed through with the plan he'd set in motion. Today is Tuesday, November third, and this is what I did . . ."

THE LODGE PARTY

DEBORAH

Tuesday, November 3.

Deborah sat sharply upright, fully awake. It was dark. Quiet. Cold. The fire was still glowing. Fear sparked through her—she hadn't intended on falling fully asleep, not with the wolves so close. They'd seen one last night, in the twilight. A big black one with yellow eyes. It had been watching them from between the trees. Nathan had thrown a rock, and it had disappeared. But they knew the pack was still out there.

Waiting.

What had woken her? She peered, shivering, into the black shadows. Fog lay thick over the darkness. Trees dripped. She couldn't see anything. She turned to the sleeping shapes around the fire.

Stella was gone.

Deborah's heart began to pound. She listened carefully to the ambient sounds of the forest. She heard the soft hoot of an owl. No wolves. Water dripping. It was raining softly above the canopy. She stilled. She could hear something. A voice? Talking?

Quietly Deborah got up. She reached for a headlamp and the loaded rifle propped against a log. The others did not wake. Steven was near death. Nathan, too—feverish, alternately shivering and sweating from the infection caused by the broken bone sticking out of his leg. Delirious at times. Monica had mentally cracked. And now Stella was gone, and Deborah could hear murmuring coming from somewhere deeper in the forest.

She crept to the edge of the grove, panned the small beam of the headlamp into the darkness. Again she listened. Afraid. There were animals out there. She fingered the trigger on the rifle, told herself she knew how to use it. It had been a while, but she knew.

Slowly she crept forward on the soft forest floor, spongy with needles and loam and moss. She went deeper. Listened again. The voice was louder. She followed it.

Suddenly she saw a light ahead. Faint. Glowing in the mist, then gone as fog crawled thickly across it. She clicked off her headlamp and pressed closer. The voice grew louder. Stella's voice. Talking to someone.

Deborah came around a large tree and saw her. Her pulse quickened.

Stella sat on a log. She'd placed a headlamp on a stump in front of her. The beam of the light illuminated her from the front. Next to the headlamp was a camera—the red light flashing. It was recording.

Katie Colbourne's camera. Stella had taken it. She was recording— filming herself.

Deborah's mouth went dry. Holding the rifle ready, she crept a little closer and shifted into the shadow of a tree. She watched. And listened.

"I don't think we will last much longer," Stella said softly to the camera. "Steven is worsening. Faster than I thought he would . . ."

A voyeuristic, sick, cold feeling sank through Deborah. She was unable to move, bewitched by this glowing little vignette in the black heart of the endless forest. Transfixed, tense, she watched, her hand on the trigger of the gun.

"I followed through with the plan he'd set in motion. I followed his script. I lured in our victims. I brought in all the props, including the toxic mushrooms, and the wooden figurines which Franz had commissioned, which had been prechopped and fixed back together in such a way that I could easily twist off their heads. I kept manipulating the props, decapitating a carving each time someone died, or disappeared, even though I had not had a hand in their deaths. Because I did not kill anyone. Not directly."

Deborah's heart leaped into her throat. Tension torqued through her chest. She leaned a little closer, her mouth open as she breathed faster.

"I put the bowl of mushrooms in the kitchen," Stella confessed to the camera. "To tighten the mental screws. To mess with Nathan, the mycologist. To mess with everyone who knew he knew mushrooms. I sabotaged the avionics. I brought in the painting Franz had commissioned. I did that a few weeks earlier, when I brought in the bag of groceries and the book, and the checkerboard and figurines, and the bullets and the rifle. I brought in gas for the generators, which I put in the shed. Food in tins to sustain us for a while, for however long it all took. I inserted into the book the rhyme Franz had written. I scoped out the trail I eventually led everyone on, knowing it would never go anywhere, never lead us to Kluhane Bay. Not in time, anyway. Not before the snows came. Not before help came. Because I took the note we'd written to rescuers who might come."

Deborah leaned even closer, a hot rage blooming in her heart. Her finger twitched against the rifle trigger. She'd held on all this time, pretending she was innocent, waiting for the others to die until she was the last one left standing. And then help would come. She'd been certain of it. Because they'd left the note.

"But here's what I did not do. I did not cut free my plane. I don't know what happened to Jackie Blunt. I did not kill Bart Kundera. I did not put the mushrooms into Steven's bowl of food. I did not hang Katie Colbourne. But I know who did. And if you watch the footage preceding this recording, you will hear it yourself. You will hear Deborah Strong forcing Katie Colbourne up onto that chair at knifepoint. You will hear Deborah threatening Katie's daughter, and then you will hear her kick out the chair out from under Katie, because Katie had figured out who she was. And Deborah Strong did not want the truth to come out. You will hear Katie Colbourne dying."

Fuck! Fuckfuckfuck! She can't do this. If anyone hears . . . it will all be over.

Deborah stepped out of the shadows. "Stop, Stella! Stop it right now."

Stella swung around, mouth open in shock.

Deborah aimed the gun at Stella's head and clicked on her own headlamp. "Get away from that camera. Now. Do it."

Stella lurched up to her feet, face ghost white.

"You're sick," Deborah barked at her. She was shaking now. Violently. "Do you know that? You're a sick, sick fuck!"

Stella slowly put her hands out in front of her, took a small step backward. "Deborah, put that gun down."

"Why? Because someone will die?" She issued a wild laugh. "Only one person is going to live. There *will* only be one, Stella. Like the rhyme says. And that one will be me."

"Deborah. Please, set it down."

A noise of a breaking twig came from behind her, followed immediately by a male voice.

"What's going on?"

Deborah swung around.

Steven. Bent over and propping himself up with one hand pressing against a tree trunk.

"Do as Stella says, Deborah," Steven croaked in a weak voice. "Just . . . put the gun down. We . . . need the bullets . . . for when the wolves come." He took a faltering step toward her.

Deborah tightened her finger around the trigger, hatred blackening her heart.

"Stop. Right. There."

He took another step closer.

"Stop, Steven, or I *will* shoot. Because you know what? I'd *like* to kill you. If you hadn't hit and killed Stella's kid, we wouldn't all be here, trapped in this fucking nightmare."

A small noise of pain came from Stella. But Deborah kept her gaze fixed only on Steven, her finger tense around the trigger. Blood boomed in her ears.

Swaying, physically gutted from his illness, Steven stumbled forward another step.

Deborah lifted the gun, fired.

Steven stopped dead in his tracks. She held her breath. He looked into the light of her headlamp, right into her eyes. A dark stain bloomed across his chest. His knees sagged. He lifted a hand toward her, as if reaching for help.

And he sank to the ground with a soft thump.

THE LODGE PARTY

STELLA

Stella flinched as Deborah swung the gun back on her. Her pulse jack-hammered, and her gaze shot to Steven, to the dark stain of blood spreading across his chest.

"Put that camera off," Deborah yelled. "Now!"

Stella swallowed and moved cautiously toward the camera, her eyes on Deborah, on the gun. She switched off the camcorder. The flickering red light stopped.

Steven groaned and lifted his head from the soil. Stella's breath caught in her throat. Instinctively she started toward Steven.

"Stop!" Deborah barked. "Stay away from him. Go back to the fire. To the others."

Stella faced Deborah. "I'm going to Steven."

"I'll kill you. I will," Deborah barked.

But Stella continued toward Steven, sweat pooling under her arms, her mouth dry, her brain racing. She dropped to her haunches.

"Steven?" she said quietly.

His eyes met hers in the darkness. Her heart crunched at the pain she saw there. Her mind boomeranged back to the day she'd knelt down on the wet road and looked into her son's eyes. This man had killed her baby. And then he'd fled.

"Stella," he whispered as a bubble of dark blood formed at the corner of his mouth, "I . . . I killed him. I killed your boy. And . . . I'm sorry." He coughed and wheezed in air. "I am so, so sorry."

Tears flooded into Stella's eyes. They washed down her cheeks. She began to shake. All her hatred . . . every hot, red, sharp bit of it suddenly shattered. It had come to this. She looked up at the forest canopy as the tears continued to pour down her face, up at the roof of ancient branches that had been growing for thousands of years. She heard a wolf howl, and she felt the eternity of the woods and the universe around them.

She felt Zeke near.

Suddenly nothing mattered. And she began to sob, her shoulders shuddering as everything inside her released.

Steven reached for her hand. His fingertips felt like ice as they touched her skin. "I was . . . scared, Stella." He coughed, wheezed, as he tried to breathe in. "I . . . am selfish. And I was . . . terrified." He tried to take another breath. Frothy blood foamed out of his mouth. "I . . . deserve what you did. I . . . deserve to . . . die. Please . . . please forgive . . . me." Steven fell silent, watching her.

Blood that looked black in the darkness began to leak from the side of his mouth.

Stella glanced at Deborah. The woman seemed frozen, her face blanched white beneath the headlamp in the center of her forehead, like a Cyclops eye.

Stella suddenly wanted to flee. She'd gotten from Steven what she'd come for. And now, confronted by hunger and exhaustion and pain and distance and endless, endless forests and mountains, things looked different. She wanted nothing further to do with this awful nightmare she'd set into motion with Franz.

Yet another part of her couldn't flee. *She'd* created this. This was *her* responsibility. And she had nowhere else to go—she could never return home. And if she was going to die out here, she was going to do it on her terms, not Deborah's. Not Steven's. Not anyone's. She would die a human being who was still capable of compassion.

"I'm going to take him back to the fire, okay?" she said to Deborah.

Her words seemed to kick Deborah back into action.

"You stay right there." Still pointing the rifle at Stella, Deborah walked backward and reached for the camera. She picked up the device and slid it into her pocket.

Stella ignored Deborah's order. She slid her hands under Steven's armpits, heaved, and dragged him a few inches. He groaned in pain. Blood poured faster from his mouth. Stella felt the hotness of the blood from his chest wound on her wrist.

Tears filled her eyes. She sucked in a deep breath, pulled harder. Steven moved a few more inches, the heels of his boots dragging tracks through the loam.

Steven screamed in pain.

Stella, weak from lack of food, dropped exhausted to her knees, breathing hard, desperation chasing through her.

"Leave him, goddammit," Deborah said as she stomped toward them. "Just leave him."

Tears sheened down Steven's mud-streaked cheeks. His breathing gurgled. Revulsion for Deborah exploded through Stella.

She tried again to drag Steven. She made it a few more feet. Her boots slipped in the mud, and she fell into the dirt, panting.

Franz's words filled her brain.

"The veneer of civilization is very, very thin, Stella. Like the delicate shell of a bird's egg. The tiniest force will crack it. And the cracks are not where light gets in. They're where the evil oozes out. That's where the Monsters live, in that ooze. My games, my scripts . . . They just help make

the cracks. It's the players who show us the rest. They show us what we all really are, deep down at the core. Beasts."

Stella froze. She eyed this Cyclops beast with the gun. She cleared her throat.

"I'm going to do it, Deborah. I'm going to take him back to the fire with me. I'm taking him back to Monica and Nathan."

"He's dying anyway. He'd have been dead by tomorrow. All of you will be. With or without my assistance."

"Just . . . let me die," Steven muttered. "Let me . . . die." He coughed up a dark gout of blood and began to gasp.

Stella bent her head closer to his, and she moved damp and bloody hair gently back off his face. "I'm taking you back to the fire. To the others. It's warmer."

"Why . . . why, Stella? Why . . . are you being . . . kind?"

"Because I can't not be. I can't leave you out here for the wolves to eat you alive, Steven."

"I killed your son."

Stella stopped breathing for a moment. She blinked, forcing focus back. "I . . . I know," she said softly. "And I can't leave you dying here, like you left him dying in the road." She choked on emotion. "Because . . . I'm better than that, Steven. I'm better than you. I—"

A noise came from the shadows.

Stella fell silent.

Deborah tensed, swung the gun toward the sound.

Monica appeared from the mist and shadows.

"What in the . . . ?" Her gaze shot from Steven to Stella to Deborah. "What happened? What is this?" Her gaze ticked back to Steven. An inhuman sound came from her throat as she dropped to her knees in the loam beside them.

"Did you do this?" Monica shouted at Deborah. "Did *you* shoot him? You bloody asshole, you—"

"Shut the fuck up," Deborah snapped. She aimed the gun at Monica. "And don't you go getting all high and mighty with me, you rich, old bitch. You, who killed the kid. With him." She jerked her chin toward Steven on the ground. "You, whose husband put mushrooms in his food."

Monica's face went white. "What?"

"Get up. Go back to the fire."

Monica glanced at Stella. "Is that true? Was it Nathan?"

"Help me, Monica," Stella said. "Help me drag him back to the camp."

Monica stared, mute, mouth open—a madwoman with matted hair sticking out of her hat.

"Monica," Stella said.

"Is it true?"

"Ask him yourself. He's your husband. Just please . . . help me with Steven. We can't leave him here. The wolves will come. They'll smell the blood."

They got him to the fire. In their hungry, thirsty, weakened state, the effort felt Herculean. She and Monica propped Steven against a mossy log. He looked alien, with his yellow skin and yellow eyes, and the black blood coming out of his mouth.

"Hold your gloved fist against the wound," Stella said. She couldn't think of anything else to use. They were wearing everything they'd brought.

"What's going on?" Nathan asked, sitting up, shivering by the dying fire. He looked feverish in the flame light. Sweaty.

Monica lowered herself beside Nathan.

Deborah stood on the other side of the small fire circled by stones. She held the gun on them. Stella remained standing. Her mind raced as she watched them all, thinking of a way out of this.

"Deborah shot Steven," Monica told her husband quietly.

"Why?"

"Nathan, did you poison him—was it you?" Monica asked.

He met his wife's gaze. He said nothing.

Her hand went slowly to her mouth. She looked at Steven. Tears glittered in her eyes.

"I hate him," Nathan said between chattering teeth. "I hate him and I want him dead."

"Hate you, too, Nathan," Steven whispered. "No . . . balls. No . . . fucking balls."

"And look who's dying now—*you're* dying, Steven."

"Oh, shut up," Deborah barked. "You all shut up. Sit down, Stella."

Stella lunged for the rifle.

Deborah saw her coming and whipped up the butt as she sidestepped. Stella went flailing forward. Deborah brought the butt of the rifle down hard on her head. The cracking sound was loud. Stella felt the blow shudder through her skull. She felt bone crack. The impact resonated through her jaw, making her bite her tongue. She tried to catch her balance but kept staggering forward.

She fell into the dirt. The woods spun around and around in a dizzying kaleidoscope. A feeling of nausea rose from her belly. The forest darkened. Time seemed to stretch. The sounds of the others faded far away, as if into another dimension. She slumped flat onto her stomach. With her face turned to the side, her cheek resting on sharp pine needles, she watched the others through half-closed lids as if observing some distant movie, unable to move.

Deborah turned in what seemed like slow motion. She put the rifle stock to her shoulder and aimed at Steven sitting helpless against his log.

"You're a killer. Say goodbye, Steven."

She pulled the trigger. Her shoulder jerked back slightly with the recoil as the crack of the rifle echoed up into the forest. A bird woke with a start and fluttered and flapped through the branches. A black hole appeared between Steven's eyes. His hands fell limp at his sides. His yellow eyes just stared, suddenly sightless. His mouth hung open.

Monica shrieked like a banshee.

Calmly Deborah turned the gun on Nathan. She fired. The bullet went into his neck. His body juddered. Monica surged up from beside him and ran screaming into the misty darkness of the forest.

Stella's head stopped spinning a little. She could move her limbs. She struggled onto her hands and knees and then up onto her feet. As she wobbled, stumbled, then ran in the opposite direction from Monica, she heard another crack of the rifle.

Stella reached the cover of thicker trees, turned. Monica was crawling, mewling, blubbering. She'd been shot in the back.

Deborah swung around, saw Stella.

Stella gasped and ducked into the trees.

THE LODGE PARTY

STELLA

Wednesday, November 4.

Stella hid. In the base of an old-growth hemlock, under its heavy boughs, silent and shivering, blood seeping from the wound on her head. She listened to the distant cries of an eagle and the howls of the wolves intensifying. She tried to shut her mind to the horror that had to be unfolding, bloody and awful, in the grove.

She had no idea how long she'd hunkered under the protective arms of the old tree. She'd crashed blindly through the woods and scrub for miles. Deborah had not come. Had she lost her? Was she waiting for Stella to move again and reveal herself?

The pale gray light of a new day bled into the forest. Visibility was still almost nonexistent as the clouds tumbled low and dense over the mountains, and soft flakes of snow materialized from the mist.

Stella crept out from under the branches and listened. She couldn't hear Deborah. Perhaps she really had lost the woman. Stella figured she must be facing west. The direction of the lake. She began to move through the trees and scrub, aiming what she believed must be north. She hoped she'd find the game trail again. Then she could track her way back. Part of her was unsure why she was even trying to escape.

Another part of her was driven by sheer obstinacy in not wanting to allow Deborah to win now. Deborah, who'd denied Stella a proper ending to the "game." Deborah, who would never say sorry for her role in allowing Steven and Monica to get away with manslaughter.

She gritted her teeth against the bone-chattering cold and damp, the pounding pain in her head, and she realized there was an even deeper need fueling her—a need to simply live. Primal. Base. Programmed into the very cells and fiber of her being. Stella realized suddenly that she was not actually cut out to end her own life.

Someone would have to do it for her.

Just not Deborah. Never Deborah. She refused to give Deborah that power.

She hiked and pushed through alder stalks and berry scrub, and she moved through dense stands of conifers, memories of what happened in the grove stalking her like rabid creatures. Steven's voice.

"I killed your son . . . I . . . deserve to . . . die. Please . . . please forgive . . . me."

Deborah pulling the trigger. The crack of the rifle. The look in Steven's eyes. Nathan's feverish croak.

"I hate him . . . I hate him and I want him dead."

"Hate you, too, Nathan. No . . . balls. No . . . fucking balls."

"And look who's dying now—you're dying, Steven."

She pushed harder, trying to outrun their voices. Her muscles burned. She went even faster. Cold air turned ragged and sharp in her throat. It rasped inside her chest. She began to cry. She broke into a run, branches slapping back into her face.

The river was suddenly there.

Stella stopped. Breathing hard, she stared at the water.

It flowed fast and silent at her feet, as clear as glass over smooth, round rocks. But from her left came a thundering of white water. Hidden somewhere behind the dense fog was falling water.

Stella hesitated. She looked back. She could go another way.

But suddenly a noise of breaking branches sounded behind her. She spun around. Out of the mist, like an apparition with a rifle, came Deborah. Running straight for her.

Stella's heart leaped into her throat.

She whirled around and went into the water. The icy coldness stole her breath. She waded in deeper. Water filled her shoes. The current tugged at her legs. The deeper she went, the more forcibly the water pulled. She neared the center of the river. Water came to her thighs. She leaned against the force of the current.

Hurry. Hurry.

Behind her she heard a splash. A gurgle of water.

Stella shot a glance over her shoulder.

Deborah was coming, wading faster. Holding the gun up high out of the water. Silent.

And her silence was terrifying. She was an obstinate, mute, incessant Monster.

Stella pushed herself to wade faster, but the overextension of her leg against the swift current made her stumble. She fell in. The shock of the cold stalled her heart. She flailed and splashed at the water as she was swept down. She hit a rock, grabbed it with numbing hands, held. She caught her breath and managed to stand again.

She looked up.

Deborah stood in the middle of the river. She raised the rifle, snugged the stock into her shoulder, put her eye to the sight, curled her finger into the trigger guard. She squeezed.

Stella felt the hit almost simultaneously with the sound of the rifle crack—as if she'd been slammed in the shoulder by a mallet.

Shock froze her dead.

Slowly, time stretching, she turned her head. She looked down at her shoulder. Ripped fabric. Ragged flesh. She put her hand over the wound. Blood welled warm through her icy, pink fingers. She stared at Deborah.

Deborah stared back, gun in her hand at her side.

She's out of bullets. She has no more bullets . . .

But Stella couldn't move against the force of the water. She had no strength left. Blood flowed fresh again from her head. She saw Deborah take the camera out of her pocket and bash it repeatedly against a rock. *Smash, smash, smash.* But she couldn't hear the sound it made as it hit rock. It was drowned by the roaring of the rapids hidden by the clouds behind her.

Deborah raised the battered camera up high, waved it at Stella, then threw it into the river.

Stella tried to push off from the rock she was pinned against. She took a step, tried to wade away. Almost instantly the currents snatched her feet out from under her, and she went down. The water swept and swirled her toward the rumbling rapids. Her head hit a rock, hard. Pain speared through her. She felt consciousness slipping again. And her vision went black as she was carried, facedown, toward the watery thunder.

NOW

MASON

Friday, November 13.

Mason recoiled at the crack of the rifle as Deborah fired at Steven in the camcorder footage. They saw Steven Bodine fall. Mason's mouth went dry. He shot a glance at the others.

Fielding, Jayne, and Hubb sat in tight silence, riveted by the raw, shocking footage, their faces tight, their complexions pale. Save for Hubb, who had two red hot spots riding high on her cheeks.

Hubb met his gaze. "We got her," she said, her voice rough, quiet, strange. "We've got Deborah. On film. Killing Steven. We've got Stella's confession."

He swallowed, gave a small nod, and returned his attention to the screen.

"Put that camera off," Deborah yelled. "Now!"

Stella moved toward the camera. The screen went black.

Fielding wound the footage back. Suddenly they were seeing inside a room in the lodge. The camera was on a bed—a sheet obscuring most of the view. But they could hear the horror unfolding.

Transfixed, they listened to Deborah's voice as she threatened Katie Colbourne with a knife, promising to kill Katie's daughter if she didn't cooperate. She made Katie put her neck into a noose, and then they heard the chair being kicked out from under her.

Mason felt ill as they heard Katie's gasps and gurgles and kicks as she struggled to live.

They wound the footage back even farther, and saw the group arriving at the lodge in the pouring rain, Deborah being pulled out of the water and reeds after she'd fallen into the lake. Then, before that, everyone gathering and smiling in front of the yellow floatplane on a bluebird day in the mountains at the Thunderbird resort.

Fielding leaned forward and stopped the show. He rubbed his face hard.

"Shit," whispered Hubb, sitting back. "Stella didn't kill them. She never even really planned to. Not directly. I wonder if she felt in the end that she got some justice."

"What is justice?" said Jayne. "What is retribution? You could argue she got those in the end. She made everyone suffer. And they knew *why* they were suffering."

"Feel like I need a shower," said Hubb, getting up and stretching.

Mason came to his feet. "Hubb's right. We've got what we need to put Deborah away for a long, long time. It's all yours, guys," he said to Fielding and Jayne. And if he was honest with himself, he was glad it was over. He wasn't sure who exactly got justice, either.

"Want to join us for lunch before we fly out?" Jayne asked as she began to gather up her papers and Fielding collected the rest of their equipment.

Mason checked his watch, shook his head. "I'm good. I have a date. With Hubb and some eight-year-olds."

"Crap," said Hubb. "I almost forgot. Look at the time. Podgorsky should be back with the haul by now." She hurriedly shook Fielding's and Jayne's hands. "A privilege to work with you both, Detectives," she said.

"Hope we meet again, Hubble," said Fielding. "We've got some officers transferring next year. We're going to be looking to boost our investigative team down the line."

She flushed and grinned broadly. "Thank you, sir. Yes, sir." She hurried out the door.

Jayne held Mason's gaze for a moment as he shook her hand.

"You doing okay out here?" she asked. "Settling in all right?"

He thought of Callie. And of Benny, and the other kids awaiting him. He smiled. And he felt it in his heart. "Better than anywhere else in the world right now."

NOW

CALLIE

Callie grinned as Benny and his classmates raced, laughing, toward the table for their lunch, supplied courtesy of the Kluhane Bay RCMP and being served in one of the station garages. Hubb helped herd the students into a neat line.

Mason had done good. He'd invited Ben's class, Grade 2–3—a combined group of only nine students because it was a small school—for a visit to the police station.

"They look pleased," Mason said as he helped Callie hand out paper plates to the kids, who in turn piled the plates high with fried chicken, fries, and minimal helpings of coleslaw.

Callie winced as she watched them dig in. "What is it about vegetables and kids that don't mix?"

"Hey, I never liked the green stuff." Mason paused, which made her glance at him. "Neither did Luke." He held a plate out to her. "What about you? Fried chicken?"

She regarded him for a moment, thinking about his loss, and how seeing Ben and the other kids must drive it home. Then she made a face. "You serious? Do you know how many years you can shorten your life expectancy with just one helping of that stuff?"

"Colonel Sanders lived to ninety." He smiled. It made a light dance in his eyes.

Callie stilled, struck by how his smile changed his face, altered his whole persona. She hadn't actually seen him smile until now. At least not like this. He held her gaze, and a tension crackled softly between them. She took the plate from his hand, looked away, hesitated, then helped herself to a hot piece of fried chicken, just to break the strange feeling that had passed between them.

She found a seat at one of the picnic tables the cops had brought inside for the occasion. Hubb was sitting with a group of kids where Benny was holding court, and Hubb was laughing at him. It made Callie's heart sing to see her son like this. Being himself. Being happy. Confident. With his friends.

Mason seated himself opposite her. He bit into a french fry, and his gaze followed Callie's to the table of children.

"How'd you guess the chicken would be such a hit?" Callie asked as she bit into hers.

"Ben told me."

Her gaze snapped back to his. "When did you ask him?" she asked around her mouthful.

"When I went to the school to invite the kids. He came over to say hi, and we chatted. He told me his favorite food was the fried chicken from the place next door to the hospital."

"You went all the way to Silvercreek to get fried chicken?"

"Nope." He bit into a piece and chewed. "I sent Podgorsky. Told him to buy something insulated to keep the food warm on the return trip."

Silvercreek. Hospital. Peter. Callie's mind shifted back to the day they'd searched for the floatplane, and how badly Ben had wanted that chicken when they'd gone to visit Peter once they'd located the Beaver and the dead pilot. Her mood changed. She lost her appetite. Missing

Peter was rough. And being with Mason wasn't making things easier, because she'd be lying if she said she wasn't attracted to him.

"You okay, Callie?"

She inhaled deeply. "Yeah, I'm always okay." She managed a smile. "You know. Life." She gave a shrug.

"Peter?"

She nodded.

"If you want to talk, I—"

"I don't."

His hands, holding the chicken, stilled. "Okay," he said quietly.

"Mason . . . . I love him. I love my husband." Heat burned into her cheeks as she said it.

"I know."

She cursed softly and set her chicken back onto her plate. "I'm sorry. I . . . I have no idea where that came from. God, I feel like a fool." She started to get up.

But he placed his hand over hers. "Callie, stop. I understand."

She swallowed, emotion suddenly thick in her throat.

"I get it, Callie. Just . . . know that I'm here if you ever need someone to talk to. You helped me. Just by listening. You saved my ass in the Taheese Narrows after I fell. You helped me cross that logjam over the gorge." He wavered. Lowered his voice. "You've helped more than you can know. It's a small town, and it would be good to have some friends here. I'd like to be that—just be your friend. And Ben's." He smiled. It was a soft smile. A beautiful smile. It tugged at her insides in ways it really shouldn't. She fingered her wedding ring as she held his gaze.

"Besides, we make a good team."

"I guess we do."

Ben came over, his cheeks pink. "We saw the police guns, Mom!" He glanced at Mason. "No touch, look only." He grinned. "And the snowmobiles, and the offices, and the jail and shower and survey cameras."

"Surveillance cameras," she corrected.

Ben nodded. "And a police K9, even. Officer Gregson said he was visiting from headquarters with his dog, Trudy."

A friend of Ben's called for him, and he ran back to the table.

"Gregson's still in town?" Callie asked.

"He had a few days off, decided to hang around."

"In *Kluhane Bay*? At this time of year?"

Mason's gaze flickered toward Hubb, who was joking with the kids at the other table. "Guess a local attraction held his interest."

"Hubb? You're kidding."

"Appears so."

Callie watched Birken Hubble for a moment. It gladdened her heart to think of Hubb dating. Her last boyfriend had dumped her out of the blue, and Hubb had been broken up about it. She'd been leery of guys for a while since. Callie would miss Hubb when she eventually had to transfer, as was routine for RCMP officers.

"She's been on cloud nine since she helped arrest Deborah Strong," Mason said. "She's a good cop. She'll go places."

Callie hesitated. "Speaking of Deborah, what'll happen to her now? Will she be charged with the murders?"

"That's Crown Counsel and Fielding's baby now. They're handling it from Prince George. But yeah, she'll be charged in some capacity for most of the deaths. We saw her shoot Dr. Steven Bodine on video. We heard her hang Katie Colbourne. She was caught red-handed trying to murder Stella Daguerre in the hospital."

"Or finish the job."

He nodded. "Likely. And the DNA on the Schrade knife has come back a match to Deborah, a.k.a. Katarina Vasiliev. Plus, partial fingerprints from the meat cleaver are also a match. This links her to both Bart Kundera's and Jackie Blunt's deaths. And when they ran her prints after her arrest, it was revealed that Deborah-Katarina had a recently sealed criminal record. She was convicted thirteen years ago for assaulting another street worker in Victoria who tried to muscle in on her turf. She cut the woman with a knife. Pretty badly. Woman almost died. Deborah did nine months in prison for assault, and for drug possession. She's no stranger to violence."

Callie raised her brows. "So she's an ex-con?"

He nodded and picked up another french fry. "She got clean in prison, was released, went through a training program, stayed clean, waited the requisite amount of time, then applied to the parole board for a pardon and was granted one. However, these things stay sealed only as long as you're not charged with another crime."

"And she didn't tell you about her prison sentence when you interviewed her?"

"She's a good liar."

"What about the other murders—Nathan and Monica McNeill?"

"Unless Deborah confesses to shooting Nathan and Monica, those could be a challenge to prove in court. At least the way evidence stands right now. But the forensic team is still busy with trace evidence from the grove. And from the lodge. They're also combing through the camcorder footage. The prosecutors are feeling pretty confident all round. There's no doubt Deborah Strong is going back to prison. This time, for a very long time."

"Why do you think she strapped Jackie Blunt into the pilot's seat before cutting free the plane?"

He shook his head. "Perhaps she'll tell us in the end. The theory is she believed the aircraft would blow down the lake and sink somewhere in that storm eventually, and she wanted Blunt's body to go with it, rather than have Blunt's body float up somewhere."

"The proverbial cement shoes."

He gave a wry smile. "Perhaps she figured the aircraft might never be found. Or if it was discovered decades later, it would look like Blunt was a pilot who went down with her plane."

"She'll have her baby in there—in prison," Callie said.

He inhaled, nodded.

She looked away. "It breaks my heart, really. For the baby. Deborah tried to make good and almost did. She could have had a clean run."

"Until her past caught up with her, in the shape of Stella Daguerre."

"Sounds like she had a really rough start in life. Seems like once your path intersects with bad people, it's almost impossible to escape the subsequent tangles. And now there's a guy out there—an innocent father—whose baby will be born in prison. He'll be forever tied via his child to Deborah Strong. A criminal. The kid will grow up knowing his, or her, mother is a killer."

"Bad stuff happens to good people all the time. Babies are seldom born bad. Kindergartners seldom write *criminal* or *convict* on their lists of what they want to be when they grow up."

Callie met his eyes. She heard Mason's words on two levels. He, too, could have killed the young man whose stupidity had forced his wife and son into a cliff face and to their deaths. She had no idea what she herself might be capable of if someone threatened Benny. Or Peter.

"Sometimes, Callie, the only thing that comes between a good choice and a bad one is a good friend."

Like the friends who'd stopped Mason when he went to that young driver's house with rage boiling in his blood.

"But then there are friends like Franz Gottman, who ended up pushing Stella Daguerre right over the edge," Callie countered.

He snorted softly. "Yeah. Gottman was . . . special."

"How did Franz and Stella find everyone involved in Zeke Marshall's death anyway?" Callie asked. "How did their PIs manage to do it when the police investigation at the time came up empty-handed?"

Mason pushed his plate aside, wiped his mouth with a napkin. "Stella Daguerre left the PI's report for us to read. In a safe. Time helped. Any cold-case cop will tell you this—time changes things. Alliances shift. People die. Old threats, old fears, suddenly no longer matter. People who kept silent will suddenly talk for any number of reasons. Bottom line, they found the witness of the hit-and-run pretty much the same way Dan Whitlock did. A female investigator did most of the legwork. She spoke to old owners of the stores along the road where Zeke Marshall was hit, and she interviewed homeowners who'd lived there, or still did. They all confirmed that women habitually sold sex on that corner fourteen years ago—"

"But if Whitlock did this, and this PI did it, the cops must have been able to do the same back then?" countered Callie.

"Yeah, but when the VPD detectives located the pimp who controlled the sex trade in that area, no one would speak to the cops. No one would say which girl had been there that night. That pimp is now behind bars, doing time for a homicide and human trafficking, and he's going to be away for a very long time. The PI visited him. He had nothing to lose, and everything to gain by appearing helpful, so he told her a young woman named Katarina Vasiliev saw the accident. He also informed the PI that Dan Whitlock had paid him to give Katarina Vasiliev up, and Whitlock in turn paid an ex-cop with alcohol issues to go threaten Katarina and force her to leave town."

"Jackie Blunt," Callie said.

Mason nodded. "The pimp said he was aware Katarina had taken a car registration plate and a backpack from the scene of the hit-and-run. He told the PI it was a vanity plate. And he said Katarina's old roommate had seen both the plate and Jackie Blunt. The PI hunted down the old roommate, found her in an old boardinghouse in East Van. She's on oxygen and pretty much on her own kind of death row. She said she remembered the vanity plate. It was MONEAL."

"She *remembered*? After all this time?"

He reached for a cup of juice, sipped, and winced at the taste.

Callie gave a wry smile. "I know. It's awful. Requires special kid taste buds."

"No kidding." He set the cup down. "And yeah, she remembered. She said Katarina was terrified and showed the plate to her. The woman, who'd also been a drug-addicted and underage hooker at the time, had been so hungry and short of cash that the letters MONEAL made her think *money for a meal*. And the phrase stuck with her because Katarina was ultimately paid a big bunch of money to hand that plate over to Jackie Blunt."

"Katarina got money for her next meals."

"Exactly. Except Katarina ran into trouble again in Victoria. Was then arrested. Convicted. Did her time. And turned around. The PI did a name search and turned up the legal name-change application."

"Revealing Deborah Strong."

"Bingo."

"And then a vehicle registration search turned up MONEAL as a vanity plate once belonging to Monica McNeill. Moneal?" Callie said.

"Correct. Additional records searches revealed a BMW was sold from BC into Alberta by a guy already on police radar for organized crime links via his brother, and for doing chop shop work for a biker gang."

"Bart Kundera."

"The PI actually tracked down the BMW—it's still in use, different color, but she matched the manufacturer's serial numbers to the BMW Monica had bought new out of the box. Repair work to the front of the BMW was consistent with it having been damaged in the hit-and-run."

"This PI firm is good."

"Run by a bunch of ex-cops. Extensive resources on both sides of the US-Canadian border. Plus, they had time and a whole bunch of Franz Gottman's money on their side."

"What about Nathan and Steven—how were they found by this firm?"

"From the file in the safe, it seems the PI firm did not manage to link Nathan McNeill, but Franz Gottman and Stella Daguerre began to believe he *had* to be linked. Monica likely would not have been able to hide it herself, and she'd have needed help to get rid of the car. Nathan worked not far from Bart Kundera's chop shop. He also worked with a colleague who'd used Bart Kundera's services before, and who could have recommended Bart to Nathan, or at least mentioned him in the past. Nathan was invited on the Forest Lodge junket either way, as Monica's plus-one."

"Franz probably figured it would add nice tension between Steven and Monica," said Callie.

Mason nodded. "And Nathan likely tipped his own hand in the pressure cooker of the lodge."

"He fed Steven the mushrooms?"

"We're not sure yet. But according to Stella's statement on that last bit of camcorder footage, she didn't do it," said Mason.

"So once Franz's PI found Whitlock, from there she chased the money?" Callie asked.

"Yeah. Because someone had to have paid Whitlock a bunch to retrieve the BMW vanity plate and silence the witness. The PI discovered Whitlock used to handle dirty jobs for a top Vancouver lawyer. Who in turn was known about town as a 'fixer' for high-end clients. Hush money payments, that kind of thing. The lawyer was Richard Ormond, from Bates, Ormond, Rhys, and Associates. The law firm also contracted at the time with a legit private investigative agency— BCI Limited—which terminated its contract with the firm because of Ormond's shady connections with Whitlock. They in no way wanted their PIs to be associated with Whitlock's work."

"Dan Whitlock was known to the police?"

"For crossing lines, yes. He liked to work around the edges of the law. Franz's PI located one of the old BCI Limited investigators, who shared the names of some of Ormond's key 'dirty work' clients."

"Was that ethical—to share those names?" Callie asked.

"He apparently told Franz's PI he had no qualms. In his opinion the work was dirty anyway. And one of the names that came up was Dr. Steven Bodine of the Oak Street Surgical Clinic. She checked all the names out, but Bodine's was the name that came up in connection with Monica McNeill. Through a children's charity foundation. She dug deeper, learned from a friend of Bodine's ex-wife that Bodine had had several affairs, and one of them was rumored to have been with grocery heiress Monica McNeill. The affair was alleged to have occurred over the period prior to the hit-and-run, and had ended abruptly right after the hit-and-run. And the PI figured she had him—the male driver was Steven Bodine. Estelle Marshall had told the cops she'd glimpsed two occupants in the BMW that night. A male driver and a female passenger."

Callie swore softly. "The man who hit and killed Zeke Marshall was a doctor—he could've perhaps helped Zeke. Maybe even saved the child's life."

"Instead, he fled."

"And Stella didn't notice a vanity plate on the hit-and-run car?"

"She was fixated on her child, and the driver's face as the car sped off."

"But why did the PI assume that Steven was the driver, and not Nathan McNeill, who could have been driving his wife?"

"Because it was Steven Bodine who went to great lengths and expense to retrieve Monica's plate and to silence the witness through his personal fixer."

"Of course. Shit." She dragged her hand over her ponytail. "You can see now why I wouldn't actually make a good cop. Or a good criminal, for that matter."

He laughed.

Her mind turned to Stella. Being a mother. Failing a child, and being persecuted for it. Losing everything. "Do you think Stella got what she wanted in the end?" she asked quietly.

"I think Stella is at peace now."

She nodded slowly. "Kind of makes one feel like holding one's own children tight after all this." She regretted the words as soon as they came out of her mouth. "Oh . . . I'm sorry. I—"

He smiled sadly. "It's okay. Benny's lucky to have you." He paused. "So is Peter."

She felt heat rise in her cheeks. "I . . . We should wrap this up. Get everyone back to the bus." She met his gaze. "Thanks, Mason. For doing this for the kids."

"Takes a village." He got to his feet, hesitated. "Like I said, we make a good team."

"Yeah. We do."

And as she watched him walk over to the table of laughing children, she knew the town had scored big in getting Mason Deniaud. And because of him, a little part of herself had come back to life, too.

No matter what lay ahead, it was good to have a friend. A man like Mason—he'd have her back if she ever needed it. He'd be there for Benny, too.

And whether Stella had felt good about it or not, she'd found justice for little Zeke Marshall. The truth had been told, in her son's name.

ACKNOWLEDGMENTS

It's an author's dream to work with a team like Alison Dasho, Charlotte Herscher, and agent Amy Tannenbaum—I can't thank you all enough for your editorial guidance, publishing expertise, and support. I'm one lucky writer to have crossed paths with you all. Deep thanks also to the rest of the crew at Montlake, and the Jane Rotrosen Agency.

This book was written during a challenging time in my family's life, and I thank my brother, John J. White, for taking time out of his busy schedule to fly from Australia to help keep the home fires burning while I struggled to meet my deadlines between daily trips to hospitals. Melanie White, thank you for sparing him, and for waking up early to free Skittle! Roxy Tamboline and Joanne White—it wouldn't have happened without your support, either. And I can't say enough for the doctors and nurses who helped my husband pull through a life-threatening illness, and who are still there for my mum.

Also, a big, big thanks goes to my youngest daughter, Marlin Beswetherick, for the brainstorming chats during our forest walks. I can't wait for the day you write your own novels, kiddo, because you have a story brain like few I know! And I just wish I could read books even half as fast as you manage to swallow them whole.

ABOUT THE AUTHOR

Loreth Anne White is a bestselling author of thrillers, mysteries, and romantic suspense. A three-time RITA finalist, she is also the recipient of the Overall 2017 Daphne du Maurier Award, the Romantic Times Reviewers' Choice Award, the National Readers' Choice Award, and the Romantic Crown for Best Romantic Suspense and Best Book Overall. In addition, she's a Booksellers' Best finalist and a multiple CataRomance Reviewers' Choice Award winner. A former journalist who has worked in both South Africa and Canada, she now resides in the Pacific Northwest with her family. When Loreth isn't writing, you will find her skiing, biking, or hiking the trails with her dog (a.k.a. the Black Beast) or open-water swimming. She calls this work, because that's when the best ideas come. Visit her at www.lorethannewhite.com.